D1484035

THE DOG
IN THE DARK

THE DOG IN THE DARK

A Novel of the Noble Dead

Barb & J. C. Hendee

A ROC BOOK

ROC
Published by New American Library, a division of
Penguin Group (USA) Inc., 375 Hudson Street,
New York, New York 10014, USA
Penguin Group (Canada), 90 Eglinton Avenue East, Suite 700, Toronto,
Ontario M4P 2Y3, Canada (a division of Pearson Penguin Canada Inc.)
Penguin Books Ltd., 80 Strand, London WC2R 0RL, England
Penguin Ireland, 25 St. Stephen's Green, Dublin 2,
Ireland (a division of Penguin Books Ltd.)
Penguin Group (Australia), 250 Camberwell Road, Camberwell, Victoria 3124,
Australia (a division of Pearson Australia Group Pty. Ltd.)
Penguin Books India Pvt. Ltd., 11 Community Centre, Panchsheel Park,
New Delhi - 110 017, India
Penguin Group (NZ), 67 Apollo Drive, Rosedale, Auckland 0632,
New Zealand (a division of Pearson New Zealand Ltd.)
Penguin Books (South Africa) (Pty.) Ltd., 24 Sturdee Avenue,
Rosebank, Johannesburg 2196, South Africa

Penguin Books Ltd., Registered Offices:
80 Strand, London WC2R 0RL, England

First published by Roc, an imprint of New American Library,
a division of Penguin Group (USA) Inc.

First Printing, January 2013
10 9 8 7 6 5 4 3 2 1

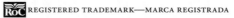 REGISTERED TRADEMARK—MARCA REGISTRADA

LIBRARY OF CONGRESS CATALOGING-IN-PUBLICATION DATA:

Hendee, Barb.
The dog in the dark: a novel of the noble dead/Barb and J. C. Hendee.
p. cm.
ISBN 978-0-451-46493-4
I. Hendee, J. C. II. Title.
PS3608.E525D64 2013
813'.6—dc23   2012021418

Set in Adobe Garamond

Printed in the United States of America

PUBLISHER'S NOTE
This is a work of fiction. Names, characters, places, and incidents either are the product of the author's
imagination or are used fictitiously, and any resemblance to actual persons, living or dead, business
establishments, events, or locales is entirely coincidental.
    The publisher does not have any control over and does not assume any responsibility for author or third-
party Web sites or their content.

ALWAYS LEARNING   PEARSON

THE DOG
IN THE DARK

PROLOGUE

An overly tall, slender woman walked out the southern gates of the city of Calm Seatt. She made her way in a slow, measured pace toward the roadside trees that led out among the open fields and farms. The hood of her forest gray cloak was up and forward, but a sleepless night had left strands of her white-blond hair dangling to waft in the breeze. She pushed those strands back inside her hood, exposing one slightly pointed ear.

Any who might have peered into that hood would have paused at the sight of slanted oversized eyes with large amber irises in a darkly tanned face too narrow to be human. They would have thought her one of the Lhoin'na, the elves of this continent, but her home was half a world away in a place that humans there called the Elven Territories.

Dänvârfij—Fated Music—had forgone the usual forest gray face wrap always worn by her caste. No one here would know her as one of the an'Cróan, an elven people of another continent. She shared leadership of a team of the Anmaglâhk, guardians of her people, though others would call them spies and assassins. They had traveled across the world for nearly a year in relentless pursuit of a purpose given by their caste's own patriarch, Aoishenis-Ahâre—Most Aged Father.

And tonight Dänvârfij had utterly failed at that purpose.

She could not blame her team—only herself—as she knelt before the branch-bare base of a maple tree. Her hand trembled as she reached under her tunic's front and withdrew an oval of smooth tawny wood no bigger than her palm. It was the last and only word-wood left to her team, grown by elven Shapers from Most Aged Father's own tree home half a world away.

Dänvârfij reached out and pressed the word-wood against the maple's trunk as she whispered.

"Father?"

This was what all devoted anmaglâhk called him.

I am here, Daughter.

Most Aged Father's voice filled Dänvârfij's thoughts with an instant of welcomed calm. Even this quickly dissipated under the shame of what she had to tell him.

"Our quarry has escaped," she said. "I have failed."

For so long, no replying voice filled her thoughts. Each time she thought to ask whether he was still there for her, she faltered.

Escaped how?

"By ship," she answered quickly. "They managed to elude us. A human questioned at the port revealed they are bound for a place called the Isle of Wrêdelyd."

Again long silence raked her nerves raw, stirring more shame.

How many remain of your team?

"We are now six, but Rhysís is injured."

Can he travel?

"Soon."

Do not delay. Leave him behind if necessary.

She almost counseled against this but remained silent.

Your purpose is unchanged. Find a ship and follow your quarry. Retrieve the artifact or its known location from the monster . . . Magiere. Torture her, and Léshil, for anything regarding the artifact's purpose. Then kill them and all who are with them. No one else, especially the traitor, must ever learn of this device, whatever it might be.

"Yes, Father."

And regardless of anything else, the traitor must die.

Dänvârfij faltered. The thought of again facing one of the few remaining greimasg'äh—a "shadow-gripper" as one of the most skilled among her caste—was something neither she nor those with her wanted anymore. Half of those who had first set out with her had died by this greimasg'äh's hand in the past year.

Brot'ân'duivé must die. Do you understand?

It was too long before Dänvârfij mustered the calm to answer. "Yes, Father."

CHAPTER ONE

"This is going to be more trouble than I'd hoped," Magiere said as she stepped off the ship's lowered walkway and halted upon the immense dock.

Everywhere about the Isle of Wrêdelyd's great port were ships of every size. Southward, the various riggings of so many vessels marred the skyline like tangled layers of giant rope spiderwebs. Numerous sailors, dockhands, hawkers, teamsters, and warehouse laborers hurried about. Everyday people and merchants crowded the shoreline and piers visible between the hulking vessels. Some of the people were dressed in strange clothes she'd never seen, even during her short stay in Malourné's capital of Calm Seatt on the mainland.

Amid all this, Magiere and her companions needed to quickly find another ship heading far south down the mainland's coast to the Suman Empire. But which, if any, would be making that long journey soon and willing to take passengers on short notice?

"Oh, seven hells!" someone growled behind her. "Why does nothing we try ever turn out to be easy?"

Magiere glanced back as her husband halted at the bottom of the ship's walkway.

Leesil stood staring about the port with their travel chest on one shoulder, over the straps of his pack. There were even more ships anchored offshore.

All Magiere could do was sigh. At least if he could complain so dramatically, his handful of days being seasick on the voyage from Calm Seatt hadn't worn him too much.

"I didn't know it would be this big," Magiere answered. "We need to find a ship leaving soon."

Leesil grumbled something under his breath, and she shot him a scowl over her shoulder. But even after their years together, she still marveled at the sight of him.

With oblong ears less peaked than those of a full-blooded elf, he shared other traits with his mother's people, the an'Cróan of the eastern continent. Beneath a ratty green scarf on his head, strands of silky white-blond hair hung down around his narrow tan face, which still glistened from sick sweats during the passage. Beardless like the full-blooded male elves, he was average height for a human, though short by an'Cróan standards, unlike Magiere, who was nearly as tall as he was.

Leesil's amber-irised eyes, so slightly slanted, looked up and down the broad dock.

"Are we going into the port or not?" he asked as one of his feathery blond eyebrows arched. "I'd like solid ground under my feet for at least a day!"

At that, a rough-featured and bearded hulk stalled in his march up the dock. The big man glanced at Leesil and then at Magiere, as did a few sailors busily coiling ropes. The bearded man was dressed in a hide and fur jerkin, pants, and a fur cape, and was obviously one of the coastal Northlanders. Magiere had learned of them in her time farther north, in her travels toward the icy Wastes.

She turned her attention back to matters at hand.

The late-spring day was overly warm, and her shirt clung uncomfortably beneath her studded leather hauberk. Pushing back dampening locks of black hair, she knew from the stares of those around her that their bloodred tint probably showed under the bright sun. Worse, her overly pale skin stung in the glare.

Leesil also looked too warm in his old scarred-up hauberk of iron rings.

While Magiere wore a hand-and-a-half-long falchion sheathed on her hip and a white metal battle dagger at her back beneath her cloak, a pair of strange-looking winged punching blades hung in their sheaths from Leesil's belt, strapped down against his thighs.

She was concerned about his being so seasick, but as much as she loved him, and with all that they faced ahead, his moaning and griping over the past few days were getting to her. They faced a real urgency in finding passage off this island, for they could still be tracked and followed here. Leesil knew this already. She sighed once more, releasing tension before it got to her. She was about to assure Leesil—again—that they'd soon get ashore, when—

"Léshil? Magiere, wait!"

At a lilting female voice calling out Leesil's an'Cróan name, Magiere looked up the ship's walkway.

A slight young elven female stood at the ramp's top. She wore the old cloak given to her by Wynn Hygeorht, a friend they'd all left behind in Calm Seatt. The hood's folds crumpled across her shoulders, and the cloak's split revealed a dusky maroon pullover. Both of these were obviously bits of human clothing scavenged along the way, like the unmanageable dark green skirt hanging all the way down to the toes of her felt boots.

Leanâlhâm waved frantically; she bore a canvas pack slung over one shoulder. This was the liveliest that Magiere had seen the girl in the three days since they'd snuck out of Calm Seatt.

"We're not going anywhere . . . yet," Magiere called back.

As Leanâlhâm took a first step onto the ramp, a silver-gray wolf, almost bluish in the bright day, stepped to the rail's opening.

Chap was taller than any wolf, for he wasn't truly one. His body was that of the majay-hì, descended from wolves of ancient times inhabited by the Fay during the supposedly mythical war at the end of the world's Forgotten History. The descendants of those first Fay-born became the guardians of the an'Cróan elves, and had barred all but their people from the vast Elven Territories on the world's far side. But Chap was different from even those.

He *was* a Fay spirit, born years ago by his own choice into a majay-hì pup—a new Fay-born in the body of a Fay-descended being. He was Magiere and Leesil's guardian and guide—and also an overbearing know-it-all.

Immediately a third figure loomed at the walkway's top. He was as much taller than a man as Chap was when compared to a wolf. This one's long, coarse white-blond hair had darker streaks, a sign of age among the an'Cróan. He was deeply tan, with lines crinkling the corners of his mouth and of his large, amber-irised eyes. But the feature that stood out most was the four white scars—as if from claws—running at an angle down his forehead, through one high, slanted, feathery eyebrow, to skip over his right eye and reach his cheekbone.

Neither Magiere nor Leesil could pronounce his full an'Cróan name. They'd shortened it to simply Brot'an.

Among the Anmaglâhk, that caste of assassins who viewed themselves as guardians of the an'Cróan, he was one of a handful of "shadow-grippers." These were the masters of the caste's skills and ways. One other had been Leesil's deceased grandmother, Eillean, whom he'd never met. But Brot'an no longer wore his caste's garb of forest gray hooded cloak, vestment, pants, and felt boots. Instead the full hood of his dusky wool traveler's cloak was thrown back over a weatherworn jerkin—more scavenged human garb, like Leanâlhâm's. But there was a reason for his change of attire.

Brot'an was at war with his own caste, but to Magiere he was still an anmaglâhk. That was as permanent as those scars on his face, and she glanced over at Leesil.

Her husband's features hardened at the sight of the anmaglâhk master still in their midst. The hatred on Leesil's face was plain, cold, and focused, for Brot'an had once tricked him into killing a warlord and self-proclaimed monarch. This had ignited a war in Leesil's birthland.

Leanâlhâm started trotting down the ship's ramp in haste, her too-long skirt flapping wildly at each thrust of her narrow feet.

"There's no hurry," Magiere called out. "We're not going anywhere until— Leanâlhâm, slow down!"

Chap huffed sharply in warning and lunged after the girl. Leanâlhâm's next hurried step came down on her skirt's front hem, and she teetered.

"Oh—oh!" she squeaked out.

Chap quickly snagged her skirt from behind and set all four of his paws on the ramp's surface. All that did was throw her more off balance as his claws grated on the ramp's wood. Leanâlhâm's pack swung off her shoulder and forward.

Magiere started for the ramp's base as Brot'an descended behind Chap. Leesil had barely slipped the chest off his shoulder when Leanâlhâm cried out again.

"Oh, no—no, majay-hì!"

Leesil's eyes opened wide—just before Leanâlhâm's flying pack hit him in the gut. Gagging, he dropped the chest, and his arms wrapped around the pack as he buckled. Leanâlhâm's skirt ripped in Chap's teeth, and she careened headlong down the ramp in a tripping stumble. Chap tumbled backward with scraps of her skirt in his jaws, and he scrambled to get his footing. Brot'an grabbed for Chap from behind, but the dog snapped at him. Chap's dislike of the shadow-gripper was twice Leesil's, and Magiere tried to get in front of Leanâlhâm before . . .

The girl shot face-first into the pack clutched against Leesil's stomach.

Leesil's mouth gaped silently as his dark skin visibly paled. Both he and Leanâlhâm toppled backward, and Magiere had to duck a mix of flailing arms and packs. She made a grab for the girl's cloak, but her two tangled companions came to a sudden halt against a great furred hulk.

The large Northlander's big hands under Leesil's arms kept him from dropping onto his rump. Leanâlhâm slid off the pack and fell facedown at Leesil's feet.

Everyone around the dock stopped and stared.

Leanâlhâm rolled over, holding her nose with one hand and whimpering. Whatever she rattled off in Elvish sounded as annoyed as it was pained. Before Magiere could help the girl up, Leesil let out a gurgling groan and clamped a hand over his mouth. At the muffled gags coming through Leesil's hand, the big furred Northlander dropped him.

Leesil's backside hit the dock. He instantly scrambled on all fours around the big man's heavy boots and headed for the dock's far edge. One sailor coiling a rope backed into a barrel and pulled his feet up, and Leesil flopped down, head hanging over the dock's edge.

The problem was that because of his seasickness, he hadn't yet eaten anything this day. The noise of retching dry heaves made Magiere's stomach roll, even with all those eyes upon her and her companions. All five of them had left their homelands and crossed an ocean and then a continent in their separate ways to come halfway across a world—and they needed to get on with their task as quietly as possible.

So much, again, for passing unnoticed.

Magiere was caught between helping Leesil or Leanâlhâm. The girl sat up, eyes watering as she held her nose, and Magiere reached for her first.

"Amaguk!" someone growled in a deep voice, like a shouted warning.

Magiere spotted the fur-clad Northlander reaching for his sword. His startled eyes were on Chap as the dog stepped off the ship's ramp . . . with bits of Leanâlhâm's skirt stuck in his teeth.

"Hold, stop," Magiere called, trying to get the Northlander's attention.

The big man snatched Leanâlhâm's wrist, lifting and dragging the startled girl behind him with one hand. Magiere rushed in, one hand dropping to her falchion's hilt as she raised her other before him, palm outward.

"No!" she barked as she pointed at Chap and then herself. "It is a pet. Mine. Pet."

The big man grew still, eyeing her with a doubtful frown. He thumbed his nose as if it itched, and his dark eyes looked beyond her.

—*It?*— . . . —*Pet?*—

Magiere flinched at those two broken words spoken into her thoughts. They'd come in two different voices, single words stolen from old memories somewhere in her head and shoved forward into her awareness. And she heard the growl behind her.

—*I am*—*no*—*pet*—

There was no hint of warning in those words in her head, but there was plenty in Chap's growl. Before recent days, he'd always communicated with her and Leesil by pulling up any of their memories that he'd seen in them at least once. It was a unique talent of his, as a Fay born into a Fay-descended body. Through bits and pieces of a person's own memories called back up, he made basic notions or commands reasonably clear . . . or manipulated those unaware that he was doing so.

And then Wynn had taught Chap a new trick.

The little sage and her wayward majay-hì guardian, Shade—Chap's daughter—had taught Chap how to isolate spoken words inside memories. In such a manner, he could certainly make his meaning more clear.

However, this new "skill" was annoying because Chap wasn't very good at it yet. More often than not, a whirlwind of flickering, flashing images out of one's past rose up with these memory-words because Chap couldn't always separate just the words.

"Not now!" Magiere ordered as she glanced over her shoulder at him.

Chap flattened his ears. When he bared his teeth at her, most of the fragments of Leanâlhâm's skirt fell from his jaws. Magiere heard the big Northlander shift suddenly.

"Leanâlhâm!" she called sharply.

The girl peeked around the Northlander's thick legs.

"Do you still have the rope?" Magiere asked more quietly.

Leanâlhâm nodded, fumbling for the length of braided hemp around her waist. That brought a snarl from Chap.

Magiere hadn't shared this preparation with him, but after a stupid incident in Calm Seatt when a mob had chased a "loose wolf" through the streets, she wasn't letting it happen again. Unlike in other places they'd been, a wild animal in civilization drew too much attention in these lands.

With the rope in hand, Leanâlhâm hesitated. Chap still snarled, agitating everyone around them, and the girl peered up mournfully at Magiere.

Like Leesil's, Leanâlhâm's appearance was unique. Although she was only a quarter human, her coloring had been far more affected by it than his. In place of her people's white-blond hair, hers was nearly brown.

Leanâlhâm was a beautiful girl. Her eyes had the unearthly largeness and slant of her people. But where the elves' larger irises, even Leesil's, were always amber, hers were like the dark, damp leaves and needles of the an'Cróan forests.

In sunlight, her eyes appeared to fluctuate between shades of topaz and verdant green. Just one more thing to call unwanted attention.

"Go on," Magiere encouraged. "He'll put up with it better from you than us."

Leanâlhâm swallowed hard and started toward Chap on her knees. Chap's growl sharpened, and Magiere whirled on him.

"Chap . . . *sit*!" she commanded, as if he were a common dog.

Chap's crystalline blue eyes widened as he fell deadly silent. Everyone nearby turned quiet as well, but they all still watched, including the suspicious Northlander.

"Forgive me, majay-hì," Leanâlhâm whispered.

She spoke with an Elvish accent, but her grasp of Magiere's native language, Belaskian, and some local Numanese was passable. Her hurt tone said more than the words.

The an'Cróan revered majay-hì, among other natural guardians of their land, as sacred. The indignity of treating one this way was likewise harder for the girl. Aside from Brot'an, Chap was the only nearby connection she had to the world she'd left behind.

Leanâlhâm slowly slipped the rope's loop over Chap's head, but Chap never took his eyes off Magiere.

Magiere suppressed a flinch. This was going to come back to "bite" her sooner or later.

"Are we done here?"

Magiere started at the sound of Brot'an's voice. The anmaglâhk master stood off to the Northlander's far side, though she hadn't seen him slip around Chap and onto the dock.

"Yes," she answered, and started to go after Leesil.

Brot'an stepped in first, but as he reached down toward Leesil, Chap shot out, dragging a fumbling Leanâlhâm across the dock.

Chap snarled once at Brot'an and ducked in close to Leesil, who braced himself on the tall dog and struggled up. Leesil wiped spittle from his chin and nodded once to Magiere. She bent down to pick up their travel chest, balancing it over her right shoulder so that she could hold it with one hand.

"Thank you," she told the Northlander in local Numanese. He grunted, nodded, and turned to go up the dock on his way. But there was still many a curious eye watching a bunch of obvious outlanders with a huge wolf for a "pet."

"Leanâlhâm, come on," Magiere ordered.

Chap passed Magiere with another growl as he pulled the girl along, and Magiere took hold of Leanâlhâm's free hand.

"We're getting you out of that skirt," she added, "and into some pants."

"I like my skirt . . . what is left of it," Leanâlhâm answered quietly. "I can move freely in it."

"Yes, freely, just not on your feet."

Leanâlhâm actually huffed, but that was all, as Magiere headed for the waterfront.

"Brot'ân'duivé was speaking to our ship's crew," Leanâlhâm said, changing the subject. "They told him it will be difficult to locate a captain heading south this same day."

"When did this happen?" Magiere asked, and when no answer came, she glanced down.

Leanâlhâm was anxiously looking about the port, almost as if searching for something she couldn't find.

"Perhaps we will not leave until tomorrow," the girl said wistfully. "Or the day after."

Magiere blinked. Why would Leanâlhâm wish for a delay in such a busy, foreign place? She, too, looked again about the port.

"One of these captains must be willing to take passengers," she said. "If we can find one who'll talk to us, who's heading in the right direction, and leaving today."

No small feat of luck.

Fearless seagulls wheeled in the air above, some diving in almost close enough to touch as they searched for tidbits that might have been dropped on the dock. The humid air smelled of salt and kelp, old wood and oiled rope. Magiere glanced over her unburdened shoulder and looked for her husband.

Leesil's expression darkened, his eyes on Brot'an's back. He hated having the aging shadow-gripper's company forced upon them. Magiere tolerated Brot'an—and openly admitted he could be useful—but Brot'an and Leesil had an ugly history that would never heal.

"Is that the best advice you could find?" Magiere asked Brot'an. "Try for a ship leaving tomorrow or later? We need something today."

Before he could answer, a string of broken words erupted in Magiere's head. This time all of the pieces were in her own voice out of her memories.

—Best—find—large ship—discreet—captain—reasonable price—

Magiere's left eyed narrowed. "Chap, I told you . . . you're to warn me before you do that!"

"Is he jabbering in your head again?" Leesil called out. "What now?"

"More advice," Magiere answered, "and picky as usual." Then she noticed Leanâlhâm.

The girl again peered about the port, looking for something, and her pack hefted on one small shoulder caused her to teeter. They were all weighed down with too much travel gear, and this was no way to traipse up and down the piers, looking for transport. While none of them were fully fluent in the local language, Magiere and Brot'an knew enough Numanese for simple conversation.

"Leesil . . ." she began carefully, not looking back. "If we get stuck here for a day or two, we're going to need a room, someplace safe to sleep and store our gear while—"

—No— Chap cut in, but Magiere went on anyway.

"While Brot'an and I search, maybe you, Chap, and Leanâlhâm can find us an inn."

"No." Leesil echoed Chap's unheard reply.

With anger rising, Magiere turned on both of them. "Neither of you will be a lick of help in talking some captain into taking passengers!"

She was well aware that neither of them trusted Brot'an, but they'd all suffered and sacrificed too much to let themselves be caught here by any pursuit. The thought of losing another day was more than she could face. Her mission was too dire and her final destination so far away.

At present, they were off the west coast of the central continent's Numan Lands. They would travel all the way down that continent, beyond the world's center, to il'Dha'ab Najuum, the westernmost kingdom of the Suman Empire and the seat of its emperor. In that region a vast desert crossed the entire continent, and there Magiere hoped to seek the forgotten resting place of another ancient artifact.

There were five "anchors" or "orbs," one for each of the five elements, created and wielded over a thousand years ago by the Ancient Enemy. Magiere and a few others believed this Enemy would return, and that even now its minions—living and undead—were on the move, searching for the orbs. She had managed to find two, and Wynn Hygeorht had found one. Water, Fire, and Earth were now hidden away, and that left only Air and Spirit.

Wynn had uncovered clues that the orb of Air might lie somewhere in or near the Suman Empire. She'd suggested that Magiere go there and contact an enigmatic domin of metaology named Ghassan il'Sänke. The troublesome little sage believed that if anyone *could* help locate the orb, it would be il'Sänke. Whether he would was another matter. But Wynn herself, intent on using the resources of her branch of the Guild of Sagecraft to search for more clues to the whereabouts of the final orb of Spirit, had chosen to stay behind in Calm Seatt.

Magiere and Wynn had not parted on good terms—which was Wynn's fault—but Magiere still missed her little friend's knowledge, and even Wynn's inability to shut up now and then. Magiere straightened, trying to keep her anger under control, as the others eyed her in silence. So far Brot'an had been particularly quiet, and that was always unnerving.

"Leesil . . ." Magiere began again. "Brot'an and I speak the language best. We can move faster on our own, without all this gear. Take Chap and Leanâl-hâm, and find us a place to hide out. You can meet us later at the end of this pier, midafternoon. If we've found something leaving tonight, we'll board, and if not, at least we'll have quarters."

Leesil's expression remained taut.

Magiere knew he wasn't up to being bullied. Recently both Leesil and Chap had questioned her judgment with good reason, but this time she was right.

Leesil glanced at Leanâlhâm. Shifting his pack farther onto his back, he reached for Brot'an's. The old assassin slipped his pack off and handed it over, and then Leesil took the travel chest from Magiere and balanced it on his shoulder.

"By midday at the pier's end," Leesil said coldly. "No later."

—No—I will—come—

The words rose unbidden in Magiere's head again, and she looked down at Chap.

"Just find us an inn, while I try to find a ship."

Neither Chap nor Leesil looked happy, but they didn't argue further.

"Maybe it is not bad if we do not leave tonight," Leanâlhâm said again.

When Magiere looked into the girl's unusual eyes, Leanâlhâm appeared to realize how odd she sounded, given their situation.

"Maybe it would be good to rest one night on land," she added hurriedly.

Still shifting and hefting too many packs, Leesil raised one white-blond eyebrow in suspicion. Brot'an actually frowned and shook his head once. Magiere fought against sighing yet again as she realized what this was really about.

Leanâlhâm still hoped Osha might catch up.

Osha was the other absent companion, though he should've been here, as he'd been traveling with Leanâlhâm and Brot'an. From what Magiere understood, he'd been sort of a half-trained anmaglâhk. But he, too, no longer dressed as one of the caste, and he was definitely no longer part of the Anmaglâhk. Why was another unknown, and apparently something separate from the war Brot'an had started with his caste.

More than two years ago, the leader of the Anmaglâhk—Most Aged Father—had learned of Magiere's uncovering the first orb. He'd had his caste hunting her ever since. He wanted the orb badly enough to kill without hesitation and even to sacrifice his own underlings.

A team of anmaglâhk had followed her all the way across the world. They'd been lying in wait, watching Wynn's guild branch, until Magiere had returned to the sage not long ago. With the aid of her companions and Wynn's allies, Magiere had managed to slip from her pursuers' reach back in the port city of Calm Seatt.

Most Aged Father's followers wouldn't give up so easily, though she still didn't know why Most Aged Father wanted the orb so badly. How much he even knew about the device was unknown. Brot'an had also come to the Numan Lands and swore he was here to protect her from his caste. And more, for reasons unknown, he'd brought Leanâlhâm and Osha. But as Magiere, Leesil, and Chap had escaped from Calm Seatt, Osha had been instructed to meet them on their ship. He never came, and Magiere knew exactly why he'd remained behind.

They all knew Osha had stayed behind for Wynn.

Those two had a past, a personal attachment, and Osha's failure to join them had left Leanâlhâm wounded. Now the girl seemed to harbor a secret hope that he would catch up.

Magiere didn't know what to say. Was it better to let Leanâlhâm live with the comfort of false hope for a while or force her to face the truth?

"I'd like a good night on land, too," Leesil said, relieving Magiere of the decision, and he turned his eyes from her to the girl. "Come on, let's get to it."

Leanâlhâm nodded sadly, and as Leesil headed toward the waterfront, she followed. Chap rumbled once, but Magiere waved him off.

"Go on. You know I'm right."

Still rumbling, he, too, followed after Leesil, but Magiere watched Leanâlhâm as Leesil led the girl off by the hand.

"And get her some pants!" Magiere called after them, though no one answered. Whether they all left tonight, tomorrow, or half a moon from now, she was certain of one thing.

Osha wouldn't be joining them.

CHAPTER TWO

Not long after, Magiere strode beside Brot'an along the waterfront between the dock and the main city of the isle. She grew even more daunted, never expecting a place quite this big.

Warehouses and shops, most piled three stories high, were a wild mix of weathered log and lumber buildings of all makes and colors mashed together along narrow streets rising up the sharp slope above the open ocean. A forest of smoke trails curled into the sky from chimneys of clay and tile and brick. The air was tainted with tangled smells of fish and oiled wood amid the noise of people, livestock, carts, and wagons tightly milling about.

Brot'an was silent, towering over everyone. More than a few people looked up at him, and Magiere started to feel self-conscious. A young sailor came toward them while whistling a tune. On instinct Magiere held up a hand to stop him.

"Harbormaster?" she said in her broken Numanese. "Tell us where to find?"

He stumbled, and she nearly sighed again—which she'd been doing a lot today. Though her hauberk and sword might have made her intimidating, his gaze fixed on her face and hair.

She knew her appearance affected some men, both attracting and unsettling them, whether she wanted it to or not. She was tall and slender, and her long black hair with its strange bloodred tints swung across her back when she moved. Her skin was too pale and perfect, and her eyes were deep, dark brown . . . when they were normal.

She couldn't help any of this, but on occasion it was useful.

Brot'an stood waiting.

"Harbormaster?" Magiere repeated.

The young sailor blinked, swallowed, and cleared his throat, and Magiere wondered whether she'd used the correct words for what she was after. Brot'an hadn't bothered correcting her, and his Numanese was better than hers. The sailor finally pointed to a faded wooden building nestled between two warehouses down the way he'd come.

"There," he said, and blinked as he glanced over—and up—at Brot'an.

From what little Magiere knew, this continent boasted an elven people called the Lhoin'na. She didn't know whether they looked different from the an'Cróan, and Brot'an was tall even for one of his kind. When his face wasn't covered and his hood wasn't up, his scars drew all the more attention.

"Thanks," Magiere said, and quickly hurried on.

She led the way to the building the sailor had pointed out and found the door wide open. Loud voices carried from inside as she stepped in. Brot'an had to duck slightly to follow. They found themselves in a room with two large desks, a brass telescope of some kind aimed out the front window, and countless maps covering the walls.

Two men—one on either side of a desk—were shouting at each other. A stocky man in a bright blue vest in front of the desk huffed and puffed; his forehead and bloated cheeks were flushing red.

"You can't deny my ship moorage! I want to speak to the harbormaster—now!"

"You'll get the same from him," snapped a spindly man in a yellowed muslin shirt behind the desk. His hair was unkempt, and he pushed his billowing sleeves up, left and then right, as if ready to go at his adversary with his bony fists. Instead he planted those fists on the desktop as he leaned forward. "Your ship's too big!"

"I've docked at smaller piers than these," the stocky one shot back.

"Well, you won't get to here. Unload it by skiff or let your cargo rot!"

"That'll take days, and you know it!"

"Better than your fat hull taking out one of our piers." The slender clerk straightened, dropped into his chair, and began ruffling papers. "Good day, Captain."

The stocky captain's reddened coloring shifted to something like a plum.

"We'll see about this! I'll be back when your *master* is here." He turned and strode out past Magiere and Brot'an without seeming to notice them.

"Won't do you any good," the slender man muttered.

Magiere followed spoken Numanese a little better than she spoke it. Apparently the harbormaster wasn't in, and the muttering young clerk at the desk had ink stains on all of his fingers, as if he normally worked with quill and paper. Arguing with captains was probably not part of his daily duties.

"Can you help us?" she asked.

"With what?" the man answered sharply, not even looking up.

"We need passage on . . . a ship . . . to south," she said, or tried to say, "leaving . . . soon."

"Do I look like a *purser* to you?" he returned.

Magiere didn't catch that one Numanese word, but his tone hit her the wrong way. She took an angry step in toward the desk.

Brot'an instantly shifted in, and when she glanced his way, his narrowed eyes were fixed on her.

She knew her own eyes had probably darkened, as the room had brightened in her sight, burning her eyes. Her irises must have widened, swallowing some of their dark brown into black—as they did when she was on the edge of losing control.

Brot'an slipped in front of her and up to the desk.

"Could you direct us to a ship?" he asked the clerk, who was still hunched over the papers. "Or perhaps the best area of the port to find one heading south . . . and willing to take passengers?"

For the first time, the man looked up at them—up at Brot'an—and he blinked a few times in silence. They both stood out too much, but maybe their appearance was intimidating enough to warrant an answer.

"Forgive me," the clerk returned. "It's been a long . . . What did you need?"

"A ship," Magiere repeated, "heading south, leaving today."

He shook his head. "I'd have no knowledge of captains willing to take on passengers. But most southbounders dock at the south end, so when they leave port they don't cross paths with those headed to Beranklifer Bay, Dhredze Seatt, or up the Northlander coast." He looked back down at his paperwork. "Try down there. Best I can offer."

Feeling anger rise again, Magiere was tempted to grab him and jerk him over the desk.

"Thank you," Brot'an said and turned right into Magiere, murmuring, "That is all we will get from him. We try the southern docks on our own."

Magiere backed away, blinking repeatedly until the room's brightness faded and no longer stung her eyes. She spun out of the harbormaster's office, pausing barely long enough for Brot'an to catch up. Her temper did not improve.

Why was it so hard to control that hunger-driven rage and lock it away anymore?

Then she noted that Brot'an appeared almost worried as he gazed south along the waterfront. This was strange compared to his usual passive expression, and somehow she doubted that it had to do with all the docks they'd have to wander. Then she remembered Leanâlhâm's mention of Brot'an speaking with their last ship's crew.

Magiere was determined to leave this place as quickly as possible to evade any pursuit, and Brot'an had started on that even before they'd reached port. He seemed almost as driven as she was; yet he knew far less than she did about where to go after they reached their destination.

Her anger toward the less-than-helpful clerk shifted to Brot'an, so full of secrets he guarded like treasures. He evaded every question about his real purpose, and she was sick of it.

"What are you thinking?" she asked, trying to be coy.

Lost in his own concerns, Brot'ân'duivé—the Dog in the Dark—had almost forgotten Magiere's unstable state as he moved swiftly along the waterfront.

They needed to get off this isle. The others might be worried about pursuit, but he was certain of it—as he had ensured it. He did not want the anmaglâhk team remaining behind in Calm Seatt. They would plague Wynn Hygeorht in her efforts to locate the final orb. And only he was capable of dealing with members of his own caste.

He wanted them following him.

"What are you thinking?"

The question—too quiet and pointed—caught him off guard. He had slipped into introspection. When he slowed, he found that Magiere had stopped two paces behind and stood there, studying him.

Had he been careless, let his thoughts show on his face? No, she was simply suspicious by nature—and that was useful.

"I was thinking of our pressing need of a ship," he replied.

"More than Leesil or me, you've been rushing," she answered coolly. "Even to questioning the ship's crew before we arrived. What haven't you shared with the rest of us?"

He had underestimated her, but he had no response, so he walked on. She surprised him again, stepping ahead into his path and forcing him to halt.

On the passage here, she had tried to force answers from him: any information concerning what had brought him all this way and why he was protecting her from his own caste. He would eventually have to tell her something, perhaps even part of the truth, but he had been waiting for a moment when they were alone.

They were alone now.

Without a word, Magiere turned away, but not down the waterfront. She

walked into a cutway between two front warehouses that led to an alley behind them. Halting halfway down near a stack of crates, she looked back at
him, waiting. He closed on her, stepping into the shadows between the buildings.

"What is it you wish me to say?" he asked.

Tilting her pale face, she raised one dark eyebrow. "Answer the questions
I've been asking since the night you showed up in Calm Seatt. Why did you
drag Leanâlhâm—let alone Osha—all the way here and into the middle of
this? What made you take the girl from her own home? And why are she and
Osha both so . . . different now?"

Magiere waited, though Brot'ân'duivé remained silent, calculating his op-
tions.

"What have you done?" she demanded.

Brot'ân'duivé looked back out the cutway's mouth at all of the ships in
the bay. Which one might hold a way out of this place? And which one, either
present or coming, held those he wanted close enough to kill?

One more . . . and then another . . . until the last.

Magiere wanted simple answers to seemingly simple questions. Nothing
in all of this was simple.

"For what little I understand of Osha's or Leanâlhâm's transformations,"
he began, "I must go back to your story, to how this all started . . . because
of Wynn Hygeorht."

Magiere studied him for a long moment. "Wynn? It's over two years since
she came to your territory with Leesil, Chap, and me."

Yet the inquisitive young sage had been the unwitting catalyst for everything, just the same. After Magiere, Léshil, Chap, and Wynn had left the
an'Cróan territories, under the guardianship of Osha and the most honorable
anmaglâhk, Sgäilsheilleache, they had managed to procure what Brot'ân'duivé
now knew as the anchor—the orb—of Water. They had found it hidden
away in an icebound castle amid the Pock Peaks, the highest point of that
continent. But the orb's retrieval had not ended that venture.

A select team of anmaglâhk had followed Magiere and her companions even as they fled that forgotten castle for their own homeland. Before they reached home, a direct conflict and one—no, two—tragic deaths had occurred.

Sgäilsheilleache and another anmaglâhk, a greimasg'äh—a shadow-gripper named Hkuan'duv—had killed each other over Magiere and that unknown recovered "artifact."

In the end Magiere, Wynn, Chap, and Léshil had reached the coast in hope of catching a ship to this central continent, likely to take the orb beyond the reach of Aoishenis-Ahâre—Most Aged Father. But before they had left on this new journey, Osha had departed to return to his own people, bearing the ashes of his teacher, Sgäilsheilleache.

At the dawn on which Osha departed, Wynn Hygeorht had followed him. She had given him a journal of her writings to deliver himself to Brot'ân'duivé.

That journal had started everything. After a thousand years of safe seclusion, it had brought war among the an'Cróan.

The weight of the past year and a half's events drove Brot'ân'duivé into weariness. He longed to close his eyes, but Magiere stood watching him. As his thoughts wandered into the past, he carefully kept his expression unreadable. Of course back then he had known nothing of the tragic events surrounding that first orb. While those had played out, he had been unwittingly ignorant within the northern reaches of his people's land.

When had the upturning of his world begun? Did he remember the exact day?

Yes.

As he stood there with Magiere, his thoughts rolled back in time . . . to several moons after Sgäilsheilleache and Osha had left with Magiere and her companions to locate what he now knew as the first orb. He had heard nothing of the orbs then, knew nothing, as he had walked through his people's forest toward the central enclave of the Coilehkrotall clan. . . .

Sunlight broke through the forest canopy in scattered rays as Brot'ân'duivé headed silently toward the home of Sgäilsheilleache, Leanâlhâm, and his old friend Gleannéohkân'thva. It was a moment of rare peace until one subtle rustle of leaves above him did not match those made by the light breeze.

Brot'ân'duivé's soft gait did not falter. He turned in between the branches of a fir tree and became one with its shadows. All conscious thought vanished, his mind as empty and hidden as his flesh, while he slipped one hand up an opposing sleeve for a stiletto.

Most Aged Father's spies moved everywhere in these days. The ancient patriarch's suspicions had grown since the day Brot'ân'duivé had defended Magiere in a trial to the death before the people's council of clan elders. But as he gazed upward, searching the canopy for a single leaf or needle that moved the wrong way against the breeze, he found no sign of his own kind perched above.

There was only a glimpse of white feathers. Something small but much too large to be a mere bird hid between the leaves.

It—*she*—had arms and legs. A leafy branch pushed aside, and she flexed her long, folded wings as she peered down, perhaps looking for where he had vanished from sight.

When unfurled, her wingspan would have been about five times her height, though she could not have been even half as tall as he was. Those wings remained folded behind a narrow, slight-boned torso of subtle curves akin to a young girl's. From pinion feathers to the downy covering on her body and face, she was a mottled gray-white. Instead of hair, larger feathers were combed back as if part of a headdress, matched by the same on her forearms and lower legs.

Brot'ân'duivé returned the stiletto to its sheath and stepped from the shadows.

She flinched, lurching backward into hiding in the tree. Then her head tentatively pushed out through the leaves. She looked down at him, as if perhaps she knew him but was still uncertain.

Her two huge oval eyes were like black river stones at first. When she wriggled farther out of the leaves above, cocking her head like a crow, a streak of sunlight washed her face. Her eyes sparked with red like those of a dove.

The séyilf—one of the "wind-blown"—stared fixedly at Brot'ân'duivé.

Despite the thinness of the branch on which she perched, it barely bent under her weight. Her mouth suddenly opened wide, and something fell from it to the forest floor.

Brot'ân'duivé was seldom startled. He glanced down in reflex and then quickly up again.

The séyilf was gone. When he lowered his eyes to what she had dropped, he saw a round dark stone and crouched to retrieve it.

Smooth like her eyes and still glistening with her spittle, its whole oblong was covered in etchings. He wiped it dry on the pants of his forest gray attire and rolled it in his hand.

These were not the scratches of delicate séyilf talons, such as he had seen on the cave walls of their high mountain aeries. These deeper, short marks were made by harder and smaller claws—made by the fingertips of the Chein'âs, the Burning Ones.

The stone was a summons.

The Chein'âs lived in the lava-heated depths of the mountains that bordered his people's southern territories. By an ancient alliance, they made all Anmaglâhk weapons and equipment requiring the rare white metal only they could find and shape in the earth's hottest depths. Once a young anmaglâhk initiate completed basic training and received approval by a caste elder, word was sent to the Chein'âs, and when the new weapons were completed, they would send a stone—a summons—to the caste. A caste elder would accompany the initiate on a journey to the fiery caves to receive those precious gifts. Upon returning, the initiate had to find a jeóin—"assentor" and mentor—among the caste who agreed to complete final training.

Few had ever seen such a stone with markings. Even fewer ever learned to read them—only greimasg'äh and caste elders. Brot'ân'duivé found one discernable Chein'âs word on the stone. In his own tongue, it meant "a sudden breeze."

All of his people's names, those given at birth and the true ones chosen during name-taking before their ancestors' spirits, had a meaning.

The Chein'âs had summoned Osha—the Sudden Breeze—a second time.

*   *   *

"Are you just going to stand there?"

Brot'ân'duivé rose from the memory without a twitch.

Magiere stood watching him with her arms folded, half sitting upon a stack of crates in the alley between the warehouses.

"Or are you going to tell me what you meant about Wynn?" she added.

Brot'ân'duivé would certainly not tell her of the séyilf, the stone, or what it had done to Osha. That matter had yet to be settled, even after so much time. He did not fully understand what had come of it so far, but Magiere would not be put off much longer.

"It began before I knew anything of Wynn's . . . interference with Osha," he finally answered. "Do you remember an enclave among the Coilehkrotall clan?"

"You mean Gleann and Leanâlhâm's home village?" Magiere frowned, exhaling with impatience. "Of course. We were guests there."

"Yes, you were," Brot'an answered, and he nearly shook his head at her cutting of Gleannéohkân'thva's true name. Humans were so inadequate with any language but their own. He held up a hand as she was about to speak— likely to demand that he get to the point.

"My part began after you left your homeland for this continent," he said. "Osha had already departed to return to his people. Events were in motion from that moment, though I was unaware at the time. Some things only became known to me the day I arrived at Gleannéohkân'thva's home."

And with that he began to tell Magiere a part of his story. . . .

Brot'ân'duivé stepped on through the dense trees toward the central enclave of Coilehkrotall. Wild brush grew higher than his head in places, but there were more oaks and cedars here due to the great width of their trunks. Those trunks bulged in unusual ways and grew more immense along the way.

While foliage remained lush and thick overhead, in the spaces between trees the underbrush gave way to open areas carpeted in lime-colored moss. Someone stepped out and turned away as if emerging like a spirit from the bloated trunk of a cedar.

Brot'ân'duivé did not bother to see who had emerged and barely glanced at thickened ivy hanging from branches overhead. The vines shaped an entryway into the tree's wide opening between the ridges of its earthbound roots—the an'Cróan lived inside massive trees.

He passed more such dwellings with openings and flora-marked entryways, and then a large clay dome of an oven in an open lawn; smoke was rising from its top. Several women and two men stopped, touched their companions, and turned one by one to stare. They nodded to him politely with warm smiles.

Nodding back, Brot'ân'duivé did not pause and continued to the enclave's western outskirts and one large tree almost apart from the others. It was the familiar home of an old friend, a healer among their people, and one of the few in this world whom Brot'ân'duivé trusted. He pushed aside the canvas curtain over the entrance to peer into the main chamber.

"I am here," he said.

Moss from outside flowed inward across the chamber's floor. The tree's interior had grown into a large rounded room with natural ovals for doorways. Curving walls were bark-covered like the tree's outside, though some bare, glistening wood was exposed, not as if the bark had been stripped but rather that the oak had grown this way with purpose. Tawny-grained wood of natural curves shaped the archways to other curtained spaces, as well as the steps rising upward around the left wall to another level through an opening in the low ceiling.

Bare wood ledges at the height of seating places were graced with saffron-colored cushions of floral patterns in light yellow. Brot'ân'duivé saw a smaller chamber through one archway with a curtain tied aside. Stuffed mattresses were laid out upon the moss-carpeted floor, along with soft pillows and green wool blankets. But the three people who occupied the main chamber all turned their heads at his greeting.

"By the ancestors," Gleannéohkân'thva said. "Did your mother teach you no manners?"

"She taught me," Brot'ân'duivé answered, ducking inside. "But I did not listen."

The old healer scoffed, suppressing a smile. He was dressed in a quilted russet shirt, and his unruly hair was shot with gray.

In spite of his poor manners, Brot'ân'duivé nodded to the others present.

Young Leanâlhâm sat on the moss carpet with a needle in hand as she worked upon an embroidered pillow slip. She was dressed much as any other girl who had not yet gone for her name-taking. A plain cotton skirt of amber color spread around her folded legs, and her pullover of soft goat's wool looked a bit too small for her frame.

Leanâlhâm was three years past the time when she should have gone for name-taking. Gleannéohkân'thva and Sgäilsheilleache had their reasons for delaying her . . . because of her mixed blood. She did not speak and dropped her gaze. Brot'ân'duivé's presence always daunted her, but he gave it no thought as he fixed on the third occupant.

"Welcome," she said evenly.

Cuirin'nên'a, mother of Léshil and daughter of great Eillean, stood near the stairs.

She wore a simple tawny gown with a russet wrap around her shoulders. Such plain clothing did nothing to diminish her or what she was. Her hair fell like corn silk all the way to her lower back—she must have cut it recently. Her face was triangular like those of all an'Cróan, though its long angles swept in soft curves down to a narrow jaw and chin. Her caramel skin was flawless, and a long narrow nose of delicate nostrils ended above a small mouth of full lips a shade darker than her skin.

Cuirin'nên'a's almond-shaped eyes were large, even for her people. One could become lost in them, if one was careless.

To Brot'ân'duivé, she sometimes did not seem quite real. Dressed so unlike the anmaglâhk that she was, her seemingly fragile beauty had been—was—a tool she wielded like any other. It made her deadly.

"Greetings," he returned, stepping farther in.

"To what do we owe the honor of your presence?" Gleannéohkân'thva asked wryly.

"Perhaps I missed your company."

Brot'ân'duivé had come to speak to his old friend and to Léshil's mother, though he found it difficult to look at Cuirin'nên'a. It was not her dangerous beauty that affected him, but rather the fact that she was the living reminder of someone else.

Departed Eillean, Léshil's grandmother, was always there in Brot'ân'duivé's thoughts when he faced Cuirin'nên'a. The loss of her had been terrible for his people, as was the loss of any greimasg'äh. Yet his loss of Eillean was one that he had never been able to put aside, though they had never truly bonded.

He did so now, for there was much he needed from the old healer and Léshil's mother.

The three of them had long been involved in the dissident movement among their people.

Brot'ân'duivé had been the newest of them to join that faction. That too had been the doing of Eillean, who had also brought her daughter, Cuirin'nên'a, among them. Most dissidents were not anmaglâhk, but there were a few. All had come to realize that Most Aged Father was no longer fit to lead their caste, and that the old one's view of how to protect their people had in itself become a threat to them.

Gleannéohkân'thva would never speak of such things in front of Leanâl-hâm. She was an innocent, not one of them, and Brot'ân'duivé was in no hurry. They could talk later tonight. As he dropped cross-legged on the moss, something did distract him.

A warmth grew suddenly in one spot inside his tunic, between the outer and inner folds of the fabric on his front left side.

There he had stored one of two word-wood devices used for communication. The other was on his right side. All fully acknowledged anmaglâhk carried one of those, as grown and made by the people's Shapers from Most Aged Father's own tree home. Through this device, any full anmaglâhk could speak with the patriarch through any tree in existence.

But the word-wood on Brot'ân'duivé's left side was far different.

Gleannéohkân'thva as a healer was also a Shaper and had made that one in secret. Only dissidents carried such a word-wood. And one of them had just called out to this tree—and the old healer.

Brot'ân'duivé exchanged a glance with Gleannéohkân'thva, who stiffened slightly with a scowl of his wrinkled owlish face.

"Leanâlhâm," he said gently. "Would you go to the communal ovens and see what is cooking for dinner? If there is no fresh grain bread, perhaps find some from yesterday to steam and soften. I have a craving, little one."

"Of course," the girl answered, setting aside her sewing to rise. "If there is none, I will make you some myself."

"Thank you, dear," Gleannéohkân'thva said with a great grin, watching the girl hurry out through the canvas-covered doorway.

Strictly speaking, he was not her grandfather, but rather the brother of her grandmother. The term for this relationship was much too long for common conversation. But the old healer had raised the girl like his only daughter. She loved him as if he were her own father, in place of the one who had abandoned her. It often appeared she would do anything for him.

That was why the old healer protected her from the truth of his secret activities—and why he now sent her away.

The doorway's tapestry still fluttered from the girl's departure as Gleannéohkân'thva's warm grin vanished. Cuirin'nên'a rose straight from the floor and reached the doorway in one fluid moment. She peered out before looking back and nodding to the old healer.

Gleannéohkân'thva knee-walked to the nearest wall of his home, from which were made all secret word-woods he created. He flattened his hand against that wall, for the tree itself was all he needed to communicate with any word-wood he had grown and shaped from it.

Brot'ân'duivé quickly took out his own wood-word given to him by the healer and pressed it against the wall. Cuirin'nên'a crouched beside him, placing one slender finger between Brot'ân'duivé's and against the smooth oval of wood. And they listened.

"I am here," Gleannéohkân'thva said without identifying himself.

It is Tar'kash. . . . Are you alone?

Hearing the voice of their compatriot inside his thoughts, Brot'ân'duivé answered first. "No. I, Brot'ân'duivé, am here as well, as is Cuirin'nên'a. Speak freely."

Tar'kash was a trusted member of their own dissident cell and currently in Crijheäiche—Origin-Heart—the home of Most Aged Father and the main settlement of the Anmaglâhk. Tar'kash took a dangerous risk in even carrying a non-anmaglâhk word-wood in such a place, much less in using it while there.

Gleannéohkân'thva's tense expression reflected that concern. "What has happened?"

I overheard that Osha was picked up north of the human city of Bela and is being returned home even now. I know that he was off with Sgäilsheilleache, and that the greimasg'äh would wish to know of this. . . .

"What of my son," Cuirin'nên'a interrupted, "or his consort?"

"And Sgäilsheilleache," Brot'ân'duivé added.

None of them were mentioned—only Osha. He returns by ship under the watch of Dänvârfij.

"Dänvârfij . . . Hkuan'duv's last student?" Brot'ân'duivé asked. "What is she doing on that side of the continent? What purpose was she given by Most Aged Father?"

Hkuan'duv—the Blackened Sea—was one of four remaining greimasg'äh, the "shadow-grippers" among the Anmaglâhk. It unsettled Brot'ân'duivé that Most Aged Father would send Hkuan'duv's finest student to retrieve one insignificant young anmaglâhk, who still had not completed final tutelage under his jeóin, Sgäilsheilleache.

Unknown, Tar'kash answered. *She has not been seen in Crijheäiche for moons. But I learned she was already onboard when the ship intercepted Osha on the western coast.*

"And my son?" Cuirin'nên'a demanded sharply. "Something must have been said, for Osha left with him."

Nothing concerning Léshil—my apologies. Tar'kash's voice then grew rushed with urgency. *I must go! I am alone on the forest outskirts, but I cannot risk being seen. Use this information as best you can.*

The word-wood began to cool beneath Brot'ân'duivé's hand. His thoughts were already turning, trying to calculate what was missing. Sgäilsheilleache and Osha had undertaken to protect Magiere and Léshil wherever they wished to go, south along the coast below his people's lands. But why was Dänvârfij aboard one of their ships on the continent's far side? And what was Osha doing there . . . alone?

Cuirin'nên'a pulled her hand from the wall as if that contact were something to be wary of.

"This is not right," she said quietly, almost to herself. "Why does Osha return without the others, especially Sgäilsheilleache? Why would Most Aged Father send a loyalist of our caste to 'intercept' him?"

Brot'ân'duivé could not construct an answer as he pocketed his word-wood. "I will go and learn for myself."

"I am coming," she said flatly.

"No, your presence would cause suspicion," Brot'ân'duivé warned, "or at least undue attention. You have not been that long out of imprisonment for suspected treason. I will send word as soon as I learn anything." He turned to Gleannéohkân'thva. "Send word of this to anyone carrying your word-wood who is near the port. Have them watch for ships . . . and Osha or Dänvârfij."

Gleannéohkân'thva had neither spoken nor taken his hand from the wall. The wrinkles around his eyes deepened. "I do not like this. Osha would never tolerate being separated from Sgäilsheilleache."

Brot'ân'duivé understood the old healer's concern. Whenever Sgäilsheilleache was not away fulfilling a purpose given by Most Aged Father, he returned to this place, his chosen home. He was like a son to Gleannéohkân'thva—and somewhere between a beloved cousin and an uncle to Leanâlhâm, though their blood relations were not that simple.

Such personal concerns had no place here. Their cell, and all dissidents, had much larger issues now. In Most Aged Father's paranoia, he did his best to set the human nations upon each other. He believed that if the enemies of his people, all humans, were constantly at each other's throats, they would never look toward the land of the an'Cróan. They would continue to weaken one another, becoming a lesser threat as a whole . . . or so the patriarch believed.

Most Aged Father did nothing by accident. If he indeed had Osha retrieved and "watched," then something had happened . . . perhaps beyond his control. This was either a new concern or an advantage Brot'ân'duivé could exploit, or both.

He turned to the others. "I will contact you as soon as I—"

Leanâlhâm, looking to Gleannéohkân'thva, ducked through the doorway's hanging.

"New bread in the ovens, Grandfather," she said, her long, loose hair tucked behind her ears. "It will not be long."

"Ah, bless you, my girl," Gleannéohkân'thva answered with an instant grin and a clap of his wrinkled hands.

Leanâlhâm plopped down with a satisfied sigh to return to working on the pillowcase.

Brot'ân'duivé rose, heading for the doorway. "I will speak to you again soon."

He did not look back, though he felt the others, especially Cuirin'nên'a, watching his sudden departure. His thoughts still turning, he was barely into the trees beyond the enclave when he broke into a jog.

If he hurried, he might still intercept Osha before the young one was brought before Most Aged Father.

CHAPTER THREE

A noise, followed by a mix of voices beyond Magiere at the cutway's back end, interrupted Brot'ân'duivé. He spotted four dockworkers come out of the rear alley and stride up the narrow path. Each carried stacked crates, their contents rattling loudly. The lead man could barely peek over his burden's top.

The rhythm of Brot'ân'duivé's story was broken, so he stepped out onto the waterfront. Magiere followed, impatience plain on her pale face, and all four dockworkers ignored them both as they exited and hurried north along the waterfront.

"And then?" Magiere demanded. "What was happening with Osha?"

At Brot'ân'duivé's silence, she stepped around in front of him.

"We didn't even try to keep Osha from heading off on his own to that ship," she said. "Did he walk into some trap?"

Brot'ân'duivé studied Magiere closely and wondered about the motivation for her concern. She had seen Osha three days earlier and knew he had survived any past complications.

"Get on with it," she pressed. "What happened next?"

He debated how much to let her or the others know. Certainly she would share all with Léshil and, so much the worse, with Chap. But Brot'ân'duivé had made a bargain with her, one tale for the other's, and he would not be shorted in the exchange.

He had been careful about what he had told her and had shared nothing of the séyilf, the message stone with Osha's name, or his own true concerns after he had left Gleannéohkân'thva's home.

At some point after completing basic training, Osha had been taken before the Chein'âs by a caste elder to receive his tools—stilettos, garrote, bone knife, and a white metal handle for a collapsible bow: the weapons of an anmaglâhk. The caste elders decided upon initial acceptance and approval for completion of training. Brot'ân'duivé was well aware that Osha had been granted approval by the barest margin.

Before any initiate was allowed to join a mission beyond their people's lands, he or she had to acquire a full-fledged caste member as a jeóin— "assentor"—to act as mentor for final training. Osha had achieved—but not completed—that as well.

It was unheard-of for an anmaglâhk, other than an elder or a greimasg'äh, to ever be called back by the Chein'âs. And Brot'ân'duivé had heard of such a summoning only twice.

As he had trotted through trees after leaving the enclave, he had not stopped pondering this occurrence coming the same day as the news that Osha returned alone and possibly under watch. Osha was quite probably the least capable of any who had been approved for service among the Anmaglâhk. The strange second summons from the Chein'âs had left Brot'ân'duivé deeply disturbed.

"Well?" Magiere said.

He was tired of her demands, tired of speaking of the events and portents that had set him on this path to collide with hers.

"We are wasting time," he said. "We must find a ship."

He stalked off southward along the waterfront, not bothering to see whether Magiere followed.

Magiere's lips were parted in another demand she never got out. She bolted after Brot'an, dodging around to block his way one more time.

"You're not getting out of this," she warned. "What else? Spit it out!"

By the time Osha had set off to catch a ship home, he was returning alone . . . because Sgäile was dead. She'd had no idea that Osha might have been in danger from his own kind, and Brot'an was going to tell her exactly what happened.

"What did they do to him," she demanded, "lock him up because he and Sgäile helped us . . . protected *us*?"

Brot'an lowered his face closer to hers. His slanted amber eyes narrowed, making the scars on his face ripple.

"I recall an implied agreement, one story for another." He paused. "I have no intention of giving away all that I have to be left wanting of anything in return."

Magiere hesitated. This had been the hinted bargain: his story for hers. He stood motionless in waiting and didn't even blink.

"What happened to you up in the Wastes?" he asked. "How did you find the second orb that you hid with the first? Or do you agree here and now that we should look for a ship instead?"

Magiere stared up into his eyes and wondered whether her irises turned dark, expanding amid rising fury and frustration . . . and fear.

Late that afternoon, Chap stood beside Leanâlhâm at the base of the pier, the appointed place, waiting for Magiere and Brot'an.

"Not long now," Leanâlhâm said to him, and he hoped she was right.

She was obviously uncomfortable in an open port among so many humans. She still held the end of that insulting rope looped around his neck.

A moment later Leanâlhâm let out a sharp, aggravated sigh. She reached back to grab the seat of her pants and pulled at her own backside—again. This was something she'd been doing now and again ever since Leesil had forced the girl to change clothes. As a result she was attracting more stares than some oversized wolf on a leash.

The two sights together drew more looks than Chap could count.

Magiere had left Leesil with enough money for a room. As soon as that was settled, he'd slipped out, leaving Chap with Leanâlhâm at the inn. Chap did not want to know where or how Leesil had gotten those pants, obviously cut for a human boy.

Leanâlhâm's face scrunched in frustration as she pulled on the thick canvas fabric.

—*Stop—that*—

She did—and lurched away from him to the length of the rope.

Leanâlhâm stood shaking in fright, her wide green eyes locked on him. Not because of his command but rather because she had heard it at all. She had best get used to the fact that he could use memory-words, plucked from any errant memories he had caught rising in her mind, to speak to her.

Chap had caught only scant fragments in trying to dip into the girl's memories. She was not particularly skilled or disciplined in hiding such—unlike Brot'an. In the moment, her mind was empty of any recollections. At other times it was difficult to catch anything rising into her thoughts—except scant past moments with Osha on their own journey to the Numan Lands.

There had to be a reason the shadow-gripper had brought her. Leanâlhâm did not belong in the middle of all that was happening. It was going to be a long journey ahead, and Chap's patience was worn thin.

Leanâlhâm panted a few times at the scare Chap had given her, but she quickly recovered. She knew he often spoke in this fashion to Leesil and Magiere. This was simply the first time he had tried it with her, considering it had taken a while to catch enough of her memories to do so.

"I do not like these clothes," she whispered pathetically. "I want my skirt."

—*No*—

"These . . . *pants* . . . are not comfortable," she began, and then pleaded, "Please, majay-hì!"

—*You will—call—me—Chap*—

He was also fed up with being treated like some sacred being. It had its uses, but it got in the way. He had little in common with the majay-hì that her people nearly worshipped, and Leanâlhâm was worse than most in that. He wanted nothing to do with any association to his true kin, the Fay, from which the majay-hì descended along with other Fay-born creatures in ancient times. Leanâlhâm needed to abandon some of her people's awe for the majay-hì, as he had more important things with which to deal.

Gazing up and down the waterfront, Chap searched for Magiere, or more likely Brot'an, who would stand out—up—above everyone else. There was no sign of them.

Leanâlhâm stepped closer. "Magiere and Brot'ân'duivé will come soon."

Chap huffed and kept peering every which way. It did not help that he was so much shorter than the flow of passersby.

The decision of who would remain at the inn and who would come to meet Magiere had been made quickly. One of them needed to stay behind to watch over their gear. They could not risk theft in leaving it unattended. The obvious guardian was Leesil, but Chap had run into trouble before while moving about alone in populated areas.

In the end, Leanâlhâm had suggested she go with him, considering that Magiere had already framed him as some sort of "pet." Leesil had agreed reluctantly. So now Chap stood waiting on the waterfront with a quarter-blood girl who was completely out of place and ignorant of all that weighed in the balance.

Two passing young sailors glanced at the girl—then stared a little longer. At least this time she wasn't pulling at her pants. But she ducked behind him, away from the men, and Chap raised his jowls, exposing teeth with a low rumble. Both men hurried on.

"Strong majay-hì," Leanâlhâm whispered.

—*Chap*— . . . —*Use*—*my*—*name*—

Instead she suddenly rose on tiptoes, craning her head. "Look!"

Chap lifted his head as high as possible, trying to see through the crowds.

Magiere's dark hair, pale skin, and hauberk stood out in a break among the merchants, sailors, and dockworkers. Then Brot'an appeared behind her, and Chap rumbled again, his hackles rising instinctively.

There had to be a way to leave behind the old assassin, who never did anything unless it served his own agenda. As Chap's gaze returned to Magiere, he fervently wished she could see this.

He felt an unexpected, unwanted stab of regret for all that she'd been through in the past year—all that she'd put herself through. She'd changed so much, and he sometimes saw a hardened withdrawal in her face that had not always been there.

An unbidden flash of memory hit Chap.

On the sea voyage from the eastern continent to this one, the world had seemed so different. The trip was not unpleasant, except for Leesil's persistent seasickness during the first third of the crossing. Chap, Magiere, Leesil, and Wynn had remained together, eventually arriving on the central continent's eastern shore. They'd then headed west overland with a merchant caravan making the long haul across the entire continent to the Numan Lands and the nation of Malourné, Wynn's homeland.

Magiere, Leesil, and Wynn thought they were taking the first orb—of Water—to the Guild of Sagecraft's founding branch in Calm Seatt. With that, they would be finished with their burden. Leesil had honestly believed that he could then take Magiere home to their Sea Lion tavern in the little coastal town of Miiska.

That haven was so much farther off than half a world away.

Chap had known better—and had suspected Magiere did as well. In the end he'd had to make Leesil, and Magiere, face the truth. They could never leave the orb with the sages, who could not protect it and keep it hidden. The three of them had to hide it somewhere no one would find it.

When they were within sight of Calm Seatt in the distance, they sent a heartbroken Wynn on alone. At the time, they believed she would be safer there, and the three of them had headed north to hide the orb.

Since it had originally been uncovered in a high, cold place, they reasoned that it should be hidden in a similar remote and frozen location. Leesil had groaned for days at the prospect of another slog through an icy land, and he griped endlessly about having to ride a horse, as he hated that mode of travel almost as much as sailing by sea.

They had not even known much about where to go until well into the journey. Only then had they learned from locals about the land of the far north simply called the Wastes. To reach that region, they first had a long journey ahead.

They made for the more northern territories, northwest of Malourné, bypassing the peninsula they would later learn was the realm of dwarves. They avoided sea travel a little longer for Leesil's sake. Later they turned westward for the coast to find sea passage as the faster way to get closer to the icy wastelands at the top of the central continent.

Remembering that deceptively peaceful beginning, Chap wanted to close his eyes. If only he'd known then what had waited at the end of that journey.

"Magiere," Leanâlhâm called, raising a slender hand. "Here."

Even before Magiere and Brot'an reached them, Chap sensed tension between the two. Both appeared stiff, and neither looked at the other. Something had happened, and Chap eyed Brot'an.

Catching memories in the shadow-gripper had proven to be nearly impossible. Chap disliked being in the dark, especially concerning the master assassin. With little other choice, he focused on Magiere.

—Did—you—find—a ship—?

She winced at the memory-words in her mind and shook her head as if to clear it.

"Yes, we found one," she answered, though she did not sound happy or relieved.

"What is wrong?" Leanâlhâm asked.

Magiere finally noticed the girl and looked Leanâlhâm up and down. At the sight of the pants, she grunted with a nod.

"Better," she said, and Leanâlhâm took on a pouting scowl.

"Only one southbound ship was willing to take passengers," Brot'an cut in. "It is a large . . . very large cargo vessel, and by the way it sits in the water, it is heavily loaded. It will be slow and lumbering, likely making many stops along the way."

"It's the best we could do," Magiere added. "Luckily it's going all the way to our destination on the Suman coast, so we won't waste coin seeking additional passage along the way."

"When . . . do we leave?" Leanâlhâm asked hesitantly.

"First light tomorrow," Brot'an answered.

At that, Leanâlhâm looked about the busy port, as if anxiously searching for something . . . or someone. Magiere frowned but said nothing. Perhaps there was nothing more she could say to the girl concerning Osha.

Magiere looked down at Chap. "Did you find us a room?"

—*Yes*— . . . —*Leesil*—*is waiting*—

"Only one room," Leanâlhâm said, "to save money. Leesil is guarding our belongings. Come, we will show you."

As the girl turned toward a steep inland road, she stalled at the sight of people disembarking from a newly arrived ship. Chap stepped ahead, tugging her into motion with the rope leash.

He glanced back as he walked and tried to dip into her rising memories, something he could do only when he had a direct sight line to a person. Chap caught an image rising in Leanâlhâm's mind of another dock at another port, one that he recognized.

Ghoivne Ajhâjhe—Edge of the Deep—was the only port, the only true city, in all of the Elven Territories on the far side of the eastern continent. Inside the memory Chap saw—Leanâlhâm saw—a tall, tan-skinned figure striding toward her down a dock at night. Loose white-blond hair hung past his shoulders.

Osha wasn't wearing the forest gray garb of an anmaglâhk. Over his shoulder was the long and narrow canvas-wrapped bundle, tied to his back by a hemp cord, just as Chap had seen a few days before in Calm Seatt. On that dock, far away in the world, in time, in that memory, Osha stopped before he even reached the shore.

He stared in shock at the sight of Chap . . . or rather Leanâlhâm.

Chap felt himself—felt her—rush out toward Osha.

The memory vanished, sucked into darkness as if Leanâlhâm had forcefully willed it away.

Chap still experienced the strange relief that had hit her in that moment, whenever it had occurred. And now Leanâlhâm still hoped—looked—for

Osha. Chap noticed Brot'an gazing back toward the ships in port as well and eyeing the newly arrived one that Leanâlhâm had watched so eagerly.

Chap stumbled as one of his paws' claws caught in a cracked cobblestone. He righted himself, paying more attention, as they climbed the steep road up another city block.

Whatever Brot'an was looking for, it was not a glimpse of Osha.

Midmorning the next day, the girl whom everyone called Leanâlhâm stood on the deck of a large human merchant vessel and leaned out over the portside rail. She looked as far as she could up and down the closest pier and out across the tangle of all the vessels up and down the shoreline. She could see so few of them clearly.

"Leanâlhâm!"

She heard Léshil's call from the doorway below the aftcastle but pretended that she did not. It was impolite and against her nature, but she could not help it as she searched as far as she could see. All her current companions seemed relieved over a peaceful night spent in the small inn, followed by an uneventful boarding. The ship would set sail shortly, and everyone was relieved but her . . . and perhaps Léshil, but for a different reason.

She leaned out even farther, certain that if they could delay a little longer, Osha would come running down the ramp of some newly arrived ship. She could call out to him, and he would see her, and the captain of this vessel would have to lower the boarding ramp for him.

"Come on," Leesil called. "We need to get below and settle."

Unlike the others, she did not believe that Osha had intentionally remained behind in Calm Seatt. He would not do that, not to her. He was the only one who understood how she felt, cast adrift in this foreign world.

She knew that Brot'ân'duivé believed her sadness was a longing for the home she had left behind. Perceptive as the greimasg'äh might be, he was wrong in this.

Yes, she missed her lost life in that one central enclave. She still mourned her grandfather and uncle—the wise and kind elder Gleannéohkân'thva, and the most honorable Sgäilsheilleache, once hero of their people. Because of her mixed blood, even her own clan had looked at her with polite embarrassment, but those two had loved her and made her a place among the people. She had sometimes suspected the only reason Sgäilsheilleache chose to live with them in between his duties was to show his acceptance of her—and he was adamant about this.

Sgäilsheilleache was—had been—anmaglâhk and admired for his adherence to the people's ways, even above his oath to his caste. His given word was unquestioned, and because of him, if any among the enclave thought she did not belong, they kept silent.

But both her grandfather and uncle had passed on to the ancestors. Only Osha remained, the last one who fully accepted her as she was, even if she did not know who she was anymore.

Brot'ân'duivé was never unkind and always looked out for her welfare. But he was like one of the humans' creations she had come to know—like a portcullis, all cold gears, chains, pulleys, and turning mechanisms.

Osha gave open warmth, even in the secrecy of whatever shame and grief he now bore. He would not abandon her, and as long as he was with her, it did not matter that she no longer had a *place* to call home. For in spite of her grandfather's and uncle's love, in more recent years up to the last season before she had fled her people's land, she had been more and more reminded that she did not belong.

When had she first realized this? Years ago, in her homeland, she had been alone while cutting fruit by the communal ovens.

That warm dawn had promised a bright day. She perspired lightly, though night's shadows had not fully faded among the trees, and wiped her forehead with the back of her small hand. She was happy for one moment, alone without the occasional stares of others. She hummed a tune her grandfather had taught her as a child and—

A disturbing sensation made her skin seem to tighten, and she cringed as if being watched. She tried not to turn, not to acknowledge the watcher. She waited until whomever went about his or her business. Soon enough the whole enclave would awaken, and with much to do, no one would give her much notice.

The sensation only grew more intense.

Leanâlhâm glanced sidelong about the lawn and between the tree homes. There was no one within sight, but the sensation did not pass. It seemed to pull her attention to the trees beyond the enclave. Two sparks appeared in the forest's shadows, and she cringed in retreat, knowing what they were.

The eyes of a majay-hì watched her.

It was barely visible, for its dark coat blended deeply in the shadows of the leaves around it. Its head took shape as she stared into its sparkling crystal-blue eyes.

That color made them appear so cold.

It made no sound and did not move even once. It only kept watching her without blinking.

But she decided that she could not—would not—retreat. She did her best to go back to preparing the food. Not long after, the sensation faded, but when it did, she was shaking too much to hold the chopping blade steady and had to set it down.

In the year that followed, this happened again and again, though rarely the same majay-hì twice. She would feel eyes upon her, find no one present, and turn to look beyond the enclave's bounds.

Sparkling blue eyes always waited in the brush . . . staring at her.

Along with other sacred beings like the clhuassas—the "listeners"—akin to both a deer and an elk but larger, the majay-hì were the guardians of her people's land, an ancient "people" themselves. Her uncle and grandfather's influence would not convince them. And that was how she realized why they came.

The majay-hì defended the land, the people . . . and she did not truly belong among them.

She was of mixed blood.

Those eyes, that judgment, had been the beginning of something far worse to come.

Léshil's footsteps sounded on the deck behind Leanâlhâm, and still she did not acknowledge him. At least here, in this strange world of rough humans, she was an oddity for being an an'Cróan rather than a mixed-blood. Or, even better, they mistook her for one of those other "elves" they called the Lhoin'na. Few here would have ever even heard of the an'Cróan.

And she no longer suffered judgment in the eyes of the majay-hì.

Leaning farther out over the rail, she was desperate for a glimpse of Osha—she knew he would arrive any moment. Then she felt it again, that crawling sensation on her skin.

Here in this faraway place, where being watched by the majay-hì could not happen, her panic came again. She spun about, still gripping the railing fiercely.

Léshil nearly jumped back, eyes widening. "What? What's wrong?"

She peered around him to look for nonexistent trees and brush and the bright eyes that would be watching her. In the dark shadows of the stairwell below the aftcastle, she found them.

The majay-hì whom the others called Chap stood below the deck's edge watching her with unblinking crystalline blue eyes.

Léshil followed her gaze, and his handsome face wrinkled in a scowl.

"What are you doing?" he snapped at the majay-hì. "Get out of her head and stop bothering her!"

Leanâlhâm's fear broke a little at Léshil's offensive tone toward a sacred being.

Léshil stiffened, one eye twitching as his head flinched, but he still glowered at the majay-hì.

"All right, fine, you're not doing anything," he muttered through clenched teeth. "But I didn't come after her to have to chase you down as well. Get your mangy butt below!"

Leanâlhâm's fright wavered under his outrage, but she held her tongue. Léshil was still not well after the last short voyage to this crowded island. His irritation faded to concern as he looked at her.

"Come on," he said quietly.

And it became painfully clear to her that Osha would not come. Perhaps Léshil understood that realization.

There was a time, when she had first met him in her people's land, that she had looked at him with longing—another in the world who, like her, came from two peoples. It had been heart wrenching to learn that Magiere, the pale warrior woman, was the only one he would ever want.

She forgave Léshil's disrespectful ways with the majay-hì—this time—as he led her toward the stairs. For this journey would be so much longer and harder on him . . . and on her.

She was alone, and her last sense of home was taken from her without Osha.

—No—

Leanâlhâm's whole body stiffened, and she scrunched in against Léshil as they reached the stairs. She tried not to look into the majay-hì's eyes but could not turn away. She still did not fully accept the way he spoke to her with words coming in so many different voices and even languages that she knew. But the way he looked at her was too much like the judgment of his kind.

—No— . . . *—Never—from me—*

"Chap," Léshil growled. "I'm warning you. Leave her alone!"

The majay-hì ignored him.

—We—are—all—at least—two—things and—yet not—

He paused.

—Even me—

It was true that he could do—had done—things that no other majay-hì could . . . that she knew of. Though she had touched him, this very act was still something wondrous she thought would never be allowed with his kind.

She saw only a sacred majay-hì.

Hanging his head for an instant, Chap rolled his eyes and closed them. When he turned to go down the stairs, he let out the most unusual sound. It was as if he sighed, and the sound turned into something like an exasperated groan.

Leanâlhâm blinked in confusion as Léshil urged her onward. She could have never imagined such a sound coming from a majay-hì, though she wanted to make one herself.

Feeling a good deal more compassion than she could express, Magiere lightly touched Leanâlhâm's back as the girl passed her in the passage below deck.

"We've only got two cabins," Magiere said, following her. "Brot'an's already in the one you two will share . . . by his arrangement."

She urged Leanâlhâm a short way down the passage. One door on the left was open, but the next one farther down was closed. When Leanâlhâm paused at the open door, Leesil pushed past her into the room and dropped onto a bunk, looking utterly dejected.

"May as well get used to the sight of this room," he grumbled. "It's where I'll be spending most of the trip."

While Magiere pitied his seasickness, she had other things on her mind. Though it shamed her, she wondered whether they couldn't use Leanâlhâm's sorrow over Osha's absence to gain a little information.

"Why don't you help me unpack?" Magiere said as Chap slipped into the cabin.

Magiere's thoughts were still a scramble from everything Brot'an had told her the day before. From the possibility that Osha's people had seized him to the hint that Wynn might have given him an unknown journal before he'd left her in Bela, the information raised more questions than it answered.

It would be just like Wynn to have done something so foolish. And what had she written down?

Magiere hadn't gotten another word out of Brot'an after that. As she hadn't been ready to give him anything in return, they had simply gone in search of this ship to take them south. But perhaps she might have more luck with Leanâlhâm, now that she knew a few questions to ask.

"Yes, I will help," Leanâlhâm said quietly, and started to step into the cabin.

"No."

Magiere looked down the passage to find Brot'an standing in the now-open doorway of the next cabin. He held out his hand and motioned toward Leanâlhâm.

"We will get our own quarters settled," he added.

Without protest, Leanâlhâm turned away to join him, and a flash of anger in Magiere rose to an unreasoned level.

Leesil appeared instantly at her side in the doorway. When she looked at him, he shook his head in warning. Both Brot'an and Leanâlhâm disappeared inside their cabin, and the door closed.

"I wanted to talk to her," Magiere said, turning her ire on Leesil.

"Not now," he answered, and pulled her inside.

Their cabin was small but adequate, with two bunks and a porthole, and Chap sat in the middle of the floor watching Magiere intently. Leesil quickly closed the door and turned to Chap.

"Have you gotten anything yet . . . from *him*?" Leesil whispered.

His voice was so soft, and Magiere became aware of the thin wall separating their quarters from Brot'an's.

Chap huffed twice for no.

Magiere wasn't surprised. For some reason Chap's ability to pick up surfacing memories didn't seem to get anywhere with Brot'an.

Leesil cursed under his breath. "You've got to get into his head!"

Chap growled, wrinkling his jowls.

"Don't expect to," Magiere put in. "It's not likely with a shadow-gripper. If he can come and go within and vanish into shadow, I wouldn't expect him to slip up . . . not while he knows you're present."

Chap blinked up at her, and words rose in her mind.

—*We need—answers*—

At that, Magiere crouched before Chap and looked over as Leesil settled again on a bunk.

"I got something out of him yesterday," she said. "Not much . . . but something."

Chap's ears pricked as Leesil scooted to the bunk's edge.

"What did he tell you?" Leesil asked too loudly.

Magiere placed a finger over her lips.

She wouldn't mention the unspoken bargain she'd made with Brot'an, or that sooner rather than later he expected payment in kind from her. Magiere settled on the floor beside Chap and pulled Leesil down there as well, and she began to speak ever so quietly.

CHAPTER FOUR

Late that afternoon, as the sun settled low, Dänvârfij—Fated Music— stood impatiently at the prow of a small ship as it maneuvered into dock at the Isle of Wrêdelyd. Sailors on deck leisurely threw lines to men on the pier below, and she clenched her jaw in silence, wishing they would finish more quickly.

She had booked passage for her team on the first available vessel leaving Calm Seatt for the isle. But her quarry had more than a full day's head start.

"We will overtake them," Rhysís said softly beside her.

She glanced sidelong at him standing by her at the rail. She was tall enough to look him in the eyes, but she had no response. She knew well the lines of his narrow face. He always wore his long hair loose, and his lips were thin. Of the remaining members of her team, he was the closest thing she had to a companion. In his own way, he was trying to offer comfort.

It did not help.

His right arm was in a sling, as he was still recovering from an arrow wound in that shoulder, but he no longer wore his forest gray cloak. Their entire team—what was left of it—possessed only their anmaglâhk attire. Six of them dressing too much alike would arouse unwanted attention. As things stood, their pants and tunics were all still of the same forest gray. She would have to see to this, and soon.

"They could be gone already," she replied. "Off on another ship."

Rhysís remained silent for a moment. "Or they could still be here . . . with the traitor." His amber eyes narrowed. At times he could not bring himself to speak the traitor's name.

A year and a half earlier, when Most Aged Father had asked Dänvârfij to prepare a team and sail to this foreign continent, she had not hesitated. Their purpose then had been direct and clear. They were to locate the pale-skinned monster, Magiere, her half-blood consort, Léshil, and the tainted majay-hì who ran with the pair. Magiere and Léshil were to be captured, and tortured, if necessary, for information concerning the "artifact" they had carried off. Then they were to be eliminated—along with the majay-hì, if possible.

The last of that had not sat well with her team.

When they had left their homeland, they had been eleven in count. Never before had so many jointly taken up the same purpose. Their task had been of dire importance in the eyes of Most Aged Father, who feared any device of the Ancient Enemy remaining in human hands.

Eleven had left together, but one more had shadowed them across the world.

After the first and second deaths among them, before they knew for certain, Dänvârfij could not believe who that one had to be. Only on the night when she had seen his unmistakable shadow with her own eyes did she acknowledge the truth.

The traitor, Brot'ân'duivé, stole their lives one by one until only six remained.

A greimasg'äh—a master among their caste—was killing his own. Of the remaining six, including Dänvârfij, only five were functional to any degree.

"How soon can we disembark?" a strained female voice asked from behind her.

Dänvârfij looked back.

Leaning heavily on a wooden walking rod as she slid one foot after the other, Fréthfâre—Watcher of the Woods—struggled to make her way across the deck. Though she held the status of shared leader of the team, she was not fit in either body or mind. Perhaps not even in spirit.

Her wheat-gold hair, versus white-blond, hung in waves instead of silky and straight, making her somewhat unique among an'Cróan. In youth she had been viewed as slender and supple. Now approaching middle age, she was unseasonably brittle.

Once Covârleasa—"Trusted Advisor"—to Most Aged Father, as well as a sometimes cunning strategist, Fréthfâre was fanatically loyal to him and the caste.

Dänvârfij had never wanted the crippled ex-Covârleasa on this mission, and her reasons grew more solid with each passing moon.

Fréthfâre was nearly useless in their present situation. Even with his shoulder healing, Rhysís could still run swiftly and silently. He could fight with his feet and one hand. Fréthfâre could barely stand, and at times simply eating was a battle she did not win.

More than two years ago, Magiere had run a sword through Fréthfâre's abdomen. The wound should have killed her, but a great an'Cróan healer had tended her. Even so, she had barely survived, and the damage could not be wholly undone. Now moon after moon of hard travel was weakening her further—though her physical limitations were overwhelmed only by her bitterness and hunger for revenge.

Dänvârfij was ever vigilant in showing respect, both in words and actions, for the ex-Covârleasa, but revenge was no proper motive for fulfilling their purpose.

"Soon," Dänvârfij answered politely. "The crew is tying off. I will gather the rest of us from below."

"Our quarry must not be allowed to escape again," Fréthfâre said. "Begin the search immediately."

The one word, "allowed," carried the weight of blame, as if Dänvârfij had simply stood by and watched Magiere slip away.

Dänvârfij was accustomed to this criticism and paid it no attention. She had other concerns as her gaze ran over Fréthfâre's traditional forest gray cloak of an anmaglâhk. Such attire served them well in silence and in shadow, but not here in the open before so many eyes.

"It would be best," Dänvârfij began, "for one of us to locate an inn where you might be settled. We must track Magiere and the traitor, but we have other needs as well."

Fréthfâre's gaze shifted from Dänvârfij to Rhysís, and she perhaps noted that neither wore their standard cloaks. This was all they could do at present. The team needed other clothing if they were to travel in daylight without the appearance of a uniform.

Fréthfâre's mouth tightened, and Rhysís merely looked away.

This exchange had become too common: Fréthfâre's rash orders, followed by Dänvârfij's careful countering, along with sound suggestions that did not openly question the team's other leader.

"Very well," Fréthfâre agreed, leaning more heavily on her rod. "I will establish a base while you see to our needs."

In poorly hidden relief, Rhysís nodded to Dänvârfij. "I will gather the others. Eywodan was napping when I left. I will wake him and tell him he is getting too old for such a mission."

His attempt at a jest only made Dänvârfij feel tense. Rhysís never joked, so he must be speaking from the strain of pretending that the rift in their command structure was not growing worse.

Dänvârfij nodded once. "We will disperse as soon as the ramp is lowered."

As Rhysís headed off, she watched the busy dock below. All that mattered was that she had neutralized one more thoughtless order from Fréthfâre. Perhaps eventually the ex-Covârleasa would become irrelevant.

Soon enough Dänvârfij, followed by her team, descended the ramp. Once on the dock, she waited as the others disembarked. Rhysís came first, followed by Eywodan, the oldest of their team. Tavithê came next, wearing his forest gray cloak with the hood thrown back.

Dänvârfij almost frowned as she objectively scrutinized the three men.

They were slender and tall—taller than any human male—with tan skin, white-blond hair, and large, slanted amber eyes. Even disguised in human clothes, they would stand out. Something more had to be done. But before she considered what, the last two descended the ramp.

With an audible groan, Fréthfâre managed to remain upright, but her double grip on the rod was not the only thing supporting her. The sixth and final member of their team came with her. Én'nish, the other female among them, held on to Fréthfâre's arm *and* waist.

At least one of them had to go find lodging with Fréthfâre, who had been on her feet too much and would not last much longer. It would be embarrassing beyond words for the ex-Covârleasa to have to be carried. She would never ask this, but it would become necessary soon enough.

For an instant Dänvârfij considered letting that happen. It was an unworthy notion that she quickly pushed aside as Én'nish guided Fréthfâre's hobbling steps onto the dock.

Én'nish was small for an an'Cróan and slight of build. Deceptive, as both could work to her advantage in a fight. But she was young, reckless, and suffered from their kind's mourning madness over the loss of her betrothed—at the hands of Léshil. Her hunger for revenge easily matched the ex-Covârleasa's. Though Dänvârfij had opposed Én'nish's inclusion in their purpose, Fréthfâre had convinced Most Aged Father otherwise.

For now, Dänvârfij wanted off this busy dock. The others followed her at a creeping pace to match Fréthfâre's, as Dänvârfij took in their surroundings.

The port was much larger than expected—and louder and more crowded. Humans moved about everywhere, speaking in loud voices to be heard over others rushing past in all directions. Flocks of seagulls sailed overhead, occasionally smothering all voices with their piercing shrieks. Many locals glanced more than once at the tall, tan-skinned, white-haired elves in matching attire who were heading toward the shore.

Upon reaching the waterfront, Dänvârfij, seeking partial privacy, continued up the nearest steep street. One block up the cobbled slope, where the press of smelly humanity thinned, she stopped to assess her companions again.

This was what was left of her team, and she would do her best with them. She would not fail Most Aged Father again.

All other thoughts cleared as she made a mental list of their every need for success in both locating and capturing their quarry. Mundane daily necessities would be as essential as attaining information. Their monetary funds were limited, and Fréthfàre held most of them. Before the team had arrived in Calm Seatt, they had been living in the wild or stealing from farmlands.

Priorities had changed.

Dänvârfij found the others expectantly watching her, not Fréthfàre. This brought some relief, followed by brief shame at her own reaction.

"There is a slim chance our quarry may still be here," she began quietly in their own tongue. "But more likely they are already gone. If so, we must learn what ship they took and their direction of travel, if not their destination. We need food and lodgings, if we stay more than a day, and diversified clothing to blend in."

The others listened carefully, and Rhysís nodded once.

"If we buy passage on a ship," she continued, "we will need local currency."

"This is what you wish us to acquire first?" Tavithê asked. "Money, clothing, supplies?"

"Yes, but one of us will accompany Fréthfàre to procure lodging." Dänvârfij looked to her crippled partner. "If you think this the wisest way to begin."

Fréthfàre was clearly in great pain. To her credit, she behaved as if Dänvârfij's plan had been her own as she addressed the others. "Én'nish accompanies me. Tavithê, Rhysís, and Eywodan will attend to acquiring local coin first. Fulfilling the other needs will be better served in that."

"No killing," Dänvârfij put in quickly. "We want no undue attention."

She glanced again at Fréthfàre, who did not countermand her.

"I will begin tracking our quarry," Dänvârfij continued, donning her cloak and pulling up her hood. "I will stand out less if I am alone. Én'nish, once you aid Fréthfàre in finding lodging, meet the rest of us in this spot, past dusk, to show us the location."

Without a word, Tavithê, Rhysís, and Eywodan split off in separate directions and vanished into the port city. Dänvârfij had no doubt they would succeed in their tasks. But as she began to turn back toward the waterfront, Fréthfàre spoke again.

"I hope you will not squander this second chance given by Most Aged Father," she said pointedly. "You have not striven hard enough in what is necessary to obtain the artifact."

Dänvârfij neither stopped nor argued.

Fréthfâre could not begin to understand how hard she had striven to obtain the artifact.

This current expedition consisted of the second team, and the second attempt, that Most Aged Father had launched to take the artifact from Magiere. Dänvârfij had been the sole survivor of the first attempt, sent to the icy mountains of the Pock Peaks.

Fréthfâre had no idea what Dänvârfij had done so far at Most Aged Father's bidding in those eternally white-capped mountains. Fréthfâre had no notion of what Dänvârfij herself had lost in that attempt.

Uncertain where to go amid the constant blur of human faces around her, Dänvârfij strode down the waterfront walkway. Blinking repeatedly, perhaps she tried to shut them out. In the flashes of darkness on the backs of her eyelids was a weathered face with sharp features and hair cut so short that it bristled upon his head.

Hkuan'duv—the Blackened Sea—had been her jeóin, her assentor, mentoring her for five years as his last student. She had come to love him as more than a teacher, regardless of the difference in their ages. Only after he had given her his assent, and she had been at labors among their caste, did she understand he loved her in turn.

Neither of them acted upon this, for the Anmaglâhk lived lives of service. They were not forbidden from bonding, but it was rarely done, and even more rarely with another caste member. They were wed to the guardianship of their people—in silence and in shadow.

Dänvârfij never revealed her awareness of Hkuan'duv's true heart or hers to him. In the following years, they occasionally shared purpose in a mission. She found quiet contentment and simple joy in knowing she might again spend such times with him.

It was enough, for it had to be enough.

But two years ago Most Aged Father had given her and Hkuan'duv the initial purpose of tracking the monster, Magiere. The pale one had led them to a six-towered castle in the Pock Peaks. Their orders had been to wait and watch until she acquired what she sought there . . . an artifact left in hiding by the Ancient Enemy. They were to take it from Magiere and her companions by any means.

They soon discovered, to their near disbelief, that one of the most honorable of their caste—Sgäilsheilleache, Willow's Shade—had sworn to protect Magiere and hers. It had all ended in horror beyond Dänvârfij's imagining amid the wetlands of the Everfen.

Hkuan'duv and Sgäilsheilleache had pulled their blades, going at each other. It was an unthinkable act among their caste. They killed each other in the same instant. And a young anmaglâhk named Osha, with Dänvârfij's own horror mirrored in his eyes, had witnessed this event.

Sgäilsheilleache had been Osha's jeóin, his assentor. Osha had watched his teacher die at the hands of a greimasg'äh. Something in their world fractured in that moment for both him and Dänvârfij. Ever since, she had felt the crack widening, threatening a collapse.

In the aftermath, outnumbered and in failure, Dänvârfij had fled in grief. She would never forget stumbling alone through the marshlands of the Everfen, half-aware that she somehow must reach her people. . . .

A seagull's screech overhead jerked Dänvârfij from her pain-filled memories and brought the port of the isle back into focus. She slowed, studying the people coming toward her. An old woman pulling a cart filled with live, wriggling crabs caught her attention. The woman was bent and weary, but her eyes were sharp, strong, and alive. Seemingly content in her labor, she bore a smile, for whatever reasons.

Dänvârfij stepped closer. "Pardon."

Of her team, Eywodan spoke Numanese the best. He picked up spoken languages faster than anyone she had ever known. But she had mastered most of the important words and basic syntax of Numanese.

"Harbormaster?" she asked. "Help me find?"

The old woman squinted up through milky blue eyes. If Dänvârfij's foreign appearance surprised her, she did not show it. Instead she straightened and pointed to a faded wooden building down the way, nestled between two warehouses.

"There ya are, deary," she answered kindly. "Best hurry. He don't stay long after dusk."

Dänvârfij nodded with a feigned smile. "My thanks."

Moving quickly, she tried to forget the old woman, who was only a human. Something about that wrinkled face and cracking voice made Dänvârfij miss her land . . . her people. Even as she neared the small building, weatherworn with peeling paint and smudged windows, she could not stop the nagging memories.

The last time she had longed for home was after Hkuan'duv's death.

She had not been able to bring him or his ashes home to the ancestors. She had simply run through muck and moss-laden trees until she dropped in exhaustion and her knees splashed down in greenish standing water. Unaware of anything but the image of Hkuan'duv's body burned into her mind, she did not notice the tree nearby until a pattern of drops from its wet branches fell upon her hood and shoulders.

Removing the tawny oval of word-wood from her tunic, she pressed it against the tree to contact Most Aged Father . . . to tell him what had happened . . . to cause him great pain with her news. Two of their finest, one of virtue and one of skill, had died by each other's hand.

The long night she'd spent afterward, kneeling in the muck and shivering alone, was the second-worst memory she would carry. When she contacted Most Aged Father again the following dawn, he told her of a coming an'Cróan vessel already slipping silently through human waters.

Run for the coast, he told her.

She fled across land to reach the south shore of the nation of Belaski. In the end she had to fight her emotions as she nearly wept at the sight of a päirvänean, one of the living ships of her people. She would again be among her own kind.

Once aboard she breathed in pure relief as the ship wheeled, heading toward the continent's far northern point, where it would round again toward her homeland.

The ship did not make it that far.

The ship's *hkoeda*—"caregiver" of that living vessel—informed her that they were to anchor just beyond the human city called Bela. He told her that another anmaglâhk would board there, and she wondered who it could be. Few of her caste were out this far, always keeping the human nations turning a suspicious eye on each other . . . directing their curious attentions away from her people.

Later, in privacy, Dänvârfij placed her word-wood against the living ship's hull. The Päirvänean—Wave-Wanderers—were as alive as any tree in the world, even more so. Through the ship, she spoke to Most Aged Father again.

She was left utterly numb when he told her of Osha's coming to the ship.

With the horror of what she and he had both witnessed, she had no wish to be trapped on a ship with him for the entire journey home. Worse, Most Aged Father gave her further orders concerning Osha.

On waterfront of the Isle of Wrêdelyd, Dänvârfij finally closed upon the harbormaster's office. Taking long, labored breaths, she stared at one of its weathered windowpanes without really seeing anyone inside beyond the glass. For, no matter how she tried, she saw only the ghost reflection of Osha as he had stepped aboard the ship on that long-past morning. . . .

Dänvârfij had steeled herself where she stood on the deck of the Päirvänean. The crew around her kept their distance as she watched the small skiff return from the forested shoreline. It had departed the ship with only two aboard. Now there were three, the third sitting in the prow with his back turned.

There was no mistaking Osha. He was the only one in the skiff dressed as an anmaglâhk.

Two of the crew rowed the skiff in near the ship's hull, but Osha did not move.

Dänvârfij looked away, anywhere, at anything besides him. Her gaze drifted about her surroundings, from the sidewall, with its shallow swoop-and-peak edge, to the deck's tawny wood with its complete absence of planks.

The glistening wood was as smooth as the rainwater barrels nestled near the masts. The latter had been fashioned by elven Makers born with an innate gift for shaping inert wood into useful things. The entire hull appeared molded in one solid piece, without a single crack or seam in its smooth surface. For it was one piece, born in a secret place as one living being.

Dänvârfij had always loved sailing on her people's living vessels, but she drew no pleasure from it in this moment. Rolling her head back, she looked up to the bulges of furled sails hanging from pale yellow masts. The fabric was an almost iridescent white, made from shéot'a cloth, as delicate as silk but much stronger.

One of the crew onboard hesitantly stepped past her to drop a rope ladder over the side. She lowered her gaze and steeled herself once more.

Osha came up over the rail wall and landed lightly upon the deck.

He looked thin and worn, and his forest gray cloak was ragged at the edges. Otherwise he appeared no different than he had during that moment of horror in which she had last seen him. His face was long, and his features somewhat flat for an an'Cróan. It gave him the look of one of the great silvery-furred deer, the clhuassas—"listeners"—who guarded their people's land along with the majay-hì.

Osha's eyes were still haunted as they locked on to hers. Then they filled with shock. He had not expected to find her here. Shock turned to something near hate.

"Below, now," she ordered.

His fury faltered. "What do you . . . ? What are you—?"

"Now," she repeated.

Confusion held him until too late. Two an'Cróan soldiers flanked him while remaining beyond his reach. Both were armored in hauberks of hardened leather with ornate bone and horn plates. Each carried a long bow of subtle curves that curled more at the ends. Though both bows were strung, neither soldier had nocked an arrow from the quivers perched over their right shoulders.

There was only one thing that could supersede their own chain of command: an anmaglâhk operating under the direction of Most Aged Father for the sake of the people's safety. Here and now, even Dänvârfij wondered what possible threat Osha posed, as one of the soldiers glanced briefly at her.

She had her orders . . . her purpose.

Osha never looked at either soldier. Shock faded from his eyes. Without a word he simply headed toward the aft and the stairs to below.

She followed him with the soldiers close behind her and directed him to a small cabin, where she finally waved off the escort. The two men exchanged glances of doubt, but they nodded and turned away. Neither of them appeared any more comfortable with what was happening than she felt. But she stepped inside and closed the cabin door.

Alone, all they did at first was stare at each other.

Dänvârfij did not know much about him, only rumors that he was the most inept initiate to ever be granted acceptance by a caste elder. But elders did not make idle decisions, so whichever had accepted Osha must have seen something in him. And, by the grace of the ancestors, this inadequate young man had gained Sgäilsheilleache as his jeóin.

In that, Dänvârfij would not underestimate Osha. There was something more to him than her eyes could discern—there had to be.

"Am I to be imprisoned?" he asked in a cold whisper.

How he must be struggling to control himself. In his view she was second only to Hkuan'duv in blame for the death of his teacher. She fought her own unwanted anger, for she saw him the same way in the loss of Hkuan'duv.

How could any honorable anmaglâhk go against his own caste—even at the behest of his mentor—to protect a human monster and her allies?

The very thought made Dänvârfij's stomach twist.

She did not answer his question and simply continued to watch him. She knew from experience that silence could unsettle those who were already shaken. Anger would eat at him until he might make a slip. She could gain a better idea of what she did not yet know about why he was here . . . why she had been sent to do this to him.

"You go against the wishes of Most Aged Father," he said. "I spoke with him by my word-wood. He told me a ship had come to bring me home."

"I spoke with him as well," she countered.

Osha went still, his breath catching once. "Did you tell him that Hkuan'duv hunted Sgäilsheilleache . . . and killed him when he would not break his sworn guardianship?"

"I told Most Aged Father the truth!" she shot back, losing control. "Sgäilsheilleache turned on his own caste!"

Osha's features twisted again. He looked stricken, as if he, too, could not stop seeing that moment, and Dänvârfij regretted her outburst.

"You mark Sgäilsheilleache as a criminal," Osha whispered. "Am I? Of what am I accused?"

She had no answer. Osha had not taken part in the fight. In full faith of his own sworn guardianship of the humans, he had pinned the small sage, Wynn Hygeorht, up against a shack. He had protected her with his body once weapons were drawn, but he had never raised a hand against his own.

When word of this event spread among her caste, she did not know how others would view or judge the outcome. Sgäilsheilleache had sworn guardianship, a tradition of the people far older than the Anmaglâhk. But that he had done so for humans and, worse, for the monster Magiere left everything in doubt.

What had happened between Hkuan'duv and Sgäilsheilleache was not easy to understand. Hkuan'duv had obeyed the ways of his caste and the word of Most Aged Father. But Sgäilsheilleache had stood fast by the honor and traditions of the people as a whole. What was left in the aftermath became murky . . . difficult to define . . . impossible to count wholly as right or wrong.

Most Aged Father wanted to know what had truly happened, before rumors spread to taint the caste. He was taking no chances—and Dänvârfij supported him. She had been ordered to take Osha into custody, to keep him from speaking to anyone else, and to bring him back for questioning.

"Am I still anmaglâhk?" he asked, catching her off guard.

"Yes, certainly."

"Then why shut me in this room?"

He paused long enough for an answer, but she could not give one.

"I have done nothing to breach any of my oaths," he continued, his tone sounding in warning. "I am still of my people and their ways . . . older than my oath—your oath—as anmaglâhk."

Dänvârfij remembered the exchanged glance between the soldiers. Perhaps they had not been concerned at leaving her alone with Osha. Perhaps they experienced confusion, doubt, even suppressed fear at what they had witnessed here.

In truth, Osha was not wrong.

No one else besides Most Aged Father knew even a little of what had happened in the Everfen, and he had not gained the whole account as yet. Only the two who now stood in this small cabin could give him what he needed.

Osha had not breached any code of their caste, and Dänvârfij wavered. This was the first time she had ever doubted Most Aged Father's wisdom.

Osha strode past her for the door.

On instinct she grabbed the side of his cloak. As he whirled on her, his eyes narrowing, something fell out from beneath his cloak. Before she could look, he slapped her hand away and reached up one sleeve . . . for a stiletto.

Dänvârfij back-stepped, reaching for a blade.

With a weapon in hand, Osha snarled at her, "Do not give me reason to . . ."

His voice failed. His eyes glistened as if tears might come amid anger, though they did not.

"Do not give me a reason," he whispered this time. "Not for more lost blood between us."

There was no doubt who would die if this moment did not pass. It would not be her, though she would be the cause of it. She did not want this.

Dänvârfij slowly pulled her empty hand from her sleeve and held it up in plain sight. Osha slid his blade back up his sleeve, and it was then that Dänvârfij finally glanced down.

A worn book with a faded blue cover, perhaps made from the dyed cotton over paperboard that humans often preferred in bookmaking, lay at Osha's feet. It was open to some middle page of its contents.

The characters written there were those of her people's tongue but written hastily as opposed to the formal work of a scribe. Perhaps it was a journal, but anmaglâhk did not carry such things unless instructed to do so for a purpose.

"What is that?" she asked.

Osha, never taking his eyes off her, snatched up the book and shoved it back inside his cloak.

"It is personal. It has nothing to do with anything here." He started to turn away.

"Wait. Most Aged Father orders . . . requests that we do not speak to *anyone* of what happened until he has seen us first, heard us first. Will you obey?"

When Osha glanced back at her, his eyes were still filled with pain and anger.

"If I am not forced to speak of it," he said slowly, "in exchange for my rightful freedom . . . then I do not wish to speak of it at all! I am leaving this cabin and going up on deck, and you have no cause to stop me. Do not try. When we have returned home, make any claim you wish before the people . . . like an an'Cróan. They will hear *both* of our stories, as is our way."

She kept from wincing at his last reproach, for in this he was right.

Osha ripped the door open and left without a backward glance, as if daring her to stop him.

No matter whether he went up on deck, she was still guarding him. He would go before Most Aged Father to explain the actions of Sgäilsheilleache. Yet, caught between their people's ways and those of her caste, she was at a loss under the weight of his words.

Had this been any part of what drove Sgäilsheilleache in those last moments of his life? Pulling out her word-wood, she pressed it against the ship's hull.

"Father?"

I am here, Daughter. Do you have him in custody?

She faltered, for she did and did not. One other detail pushed forward in her thoughts.

"Father . . . he carries a small text, like a journal. He guards it as something dear to him. I do not know why or what it is."

Most Aged Father was quiet too long before he asked, *A human's journal?*

With her hands braced against the windowsill of the harbormaster's office, Dänvârfij breathed through her mouth to force calm and clarity. She was not wholly successful. Perhaps it would have been better had she never seen that book in Osha's possession.

There was no choice now but to deal with the present.

Turning, she opened the harbormaster's door without knocking and stepped into a large room with two desks, an enormous brass telescope, and a variety of maps covering the walls. Two humans inside were engaged in a conversation.

"I don't think he'll take no for an answer," said a slender man with unkempt hair, a loose shirt, and ink-stained hands. "He's come back twice."

"I'll deal with him," said the other. "His ship's too big to dock at the available piers, and he knows it. Sorry I left you alone so long today. Couldn't be helped."

Both men finally took notice of Dänvârfij's presence, but she focused her attention on the second. He was clearly the one in charge, and she took his measure in a glance.

He was not tall, but his chest and shoulders suggested strength. He wore boots, breeches, and a belted burgundy tunic—with no visible weapons other than a cudgel-like cane leaning nearby against the closer desk. Unlike the slender one's, his fingers were not stained with ink. He left the paperwork to others and focused on more active duties. His hair was dark, almost black, pulled into a tail at the nape of his neck, and his face was clean shaven.

As he boldly took her measure in turn, he assumed the manner of someone accustomed to being obeyed.

"Can we help you?" he asked.

Hkuan'duv had spent years teaching her the art of interrogation. He had been a master, able to keep a captive alive for days to extract every ounce of information. She knew how to use pain and fear and the promise of relief in equal measures.

This was not an interrogation. How could this human be motivated?

Dänvârfij pulled back the hood of her cloak, letting both men stare at her long white-blond hair.

"I need . . . find someone, find name of ship," she said, attempting her best Numanese as she met the harbormaster's steady gaze. "Who left here . . . maybe today or . . ." She could not think of the Numanese word for "yesterday."

The harbormaster took a step closer, frowning in puzzlement, fixating on her strange appearance, her dark skin and amber eyes—as she intended.

"Where were they headed?" he asked.

She realized she had not made herself clear. Ignoring everything else in the room, the slender man with the unkempt hair turned to a stack of paperwork on his desk.

"Do not know," she answered. "Need to know. Where . . . someone take a ship from here?"

The harbormaster's frown deepened. "You're looking for someone, and you don't know which direction they went?"

"Need to find," she answered coldly.

He stood there for a long moment, studying her, and then asked, "Did someone hurt you? Steal something from you? Some man you trusted?"

She blinked, finding him far too blunt but not bothering to correct him. "Need to find," she repeated.

He shook his head in seeming resignation and turned to pull a paper off the other desk. "Here's a list of the ships that set sail today."

She did not even glance at the paper. "How many?"

"Five."

"Where they go?"

Setting the paper back down, he walked to the wall and pointed to a map. "Two headed for Calm Seatt, one headed up north, and two sailed south along the coast."

"What is north?"

At this he shook his head. "You don't know what's north of the isle?"

"What is there?" she insisted, still meeting his eyes.

"Nothing much. A few Northlander villages and one big shipyard just shy of the great cold Wastes."

This did not seem a destination Brot'ân'duivé would choose. He would not take Magiere to an uncivilized land where she could more easily be tracked and taken from him. He must be headed somewhere for a *reason*.

A few villages and a shipyard did not offer possibilities, nor did Calm Seatt. Doubling back was a legitimate tactic, but he had already faced great difficulty in hiding so many companions. No, he would flee in order to plan. And by the map, there were many ports south along the coast of these human nations. Several appeared to be large cities, by their symbols.

"One of the ships heading south was military," the harbormaster added, "so unless the man you're chasing is a soldier, I'd count that one out."

Now he had her full attention. "What of other?"

"A big cargo vessel called the *Cloud Queen,* going all the way to the Suman capital port at il'Dha'ab Najuum. She'd be the only of those two to take on passengers."

She had the name of Brot'ân'duivé's ship and its final destination, though this did not necessarily mean the traitor would go that far. She now had to find a ship traveling that same route.

"I need to follow," she said. "Help me find passage . . . for tonight or to-morrow."

Crossing his arms, he shook his head again. "I don't have anything taking on passengers leaving that soon. Check back the day after next. Nearest that I know of right now is a small Suman vessel setting sail in five days."

As his words sank in, her disappointment was bitter. It would not be pleasant to deliver such news to Fréthfâre.

The harbormaster stepped nearer until she felt his breath on her cheek.

"I'll find you something," he said. "Are you hungry? I was just going for dinner."

She stepped back. As if she would sit and share food with a human.

"No . . . I . . . thank you. I will come back." She turned to leave.

"You do that," he called cheerfully after her.

Nightfall was nearly complete when Dänvârfij stepped out onto the waterfront to breathe in air that had not cooled much from the day's warmth. Although she would have preferred a direct interrogation, her inquiry had not been a complete loss. As she turned up the shore, still filled with a scattering of passersby, she hoped the others had acquired all else that was needed.

They might be stalled here longer than any of them had anticipated.

CHAPTER FIVE

Aday after setting sail, the girl everyone called Leanâlhâm stood on deck near the front of the ship named the *Cloud Queen*. The strong wind that moved the vessel made it hard to quiet her thoughts.

At dawn she had to force herself to rise, to eat, and even to go up on deck, and the morning was now half-gone. This would be the way of things, forcing herself to go on. Each dawn would crawl toward dusk and another long night, until . . .

Léshil hunched over the rail and let out a long groan. "I shouldn't have eaten . . . anything."

Indeed he looked pale, and the others stood a short ways beyond him, but she had little desire to join them.

Léshil and the majay-hì were blatantly obvious in their determination to keep watch over Brot'ân'duivé. As if either of them could without the master anmaglâhk knowing. Léshil was openly hostile to the greimasg'äh, though now he was too seasick to watch over anyone. Meanwhile Magiere continued prodding Brot'ân'duivé with what she seemed to view as subtle queries—though she was as subtle as a thunderstorm.

Of all Leanâlhâm's current companions, Magiere was the one with whom she was most at ease. Magiere could be terrifying when that strange horror beneath her nature surfaced. But she was also fierce, like Sgäilsheilleache, in defense of those she cared for or anyone she simply chose to protect.

Leanâlhâm's mother had been a half-blood, born of rape. She'd fled in grief and madness while Leanâlhâm was still an infant. All assumed that Leanâlhâm's mother had later died, but it was this mother who had given her the birth name that meant "child of sorrow," an unfortunate name.

Magiere did not care about such things. She defied what anyone thought of her or of those who mattered to her, and no one risked saying anything about either to her face more than once.

Leanâlhâm had yet to find that kind of strength within herself.

Then there was the majay-hì, whom everyone—even Brot'ân'duivé—called "Chap." And this was repugnant, to force a name, even one that he wanted her to use, upon a sacred being. His watchful eyes were too often on the greimasg'äh, but unlike Léshil's, the majay-hì's gaze was fixed, cold, as he sat in perfect stillness. It was disturbing—frightening—until he did blink, now and then glancing at her.

Brot'ân'duivé had made it very clear that he expected his young charge to remain silent regarding events that had brought them here. Leanâlhâm had bent to his will in this so far, but she was growing tired of it. This tiredness sharpened every time someone spoke that awful name put upon her.

It was too much to face. Osha was gone, and with him the last piece of a world she had been forced to give up. She ached in isolation and loneliness, and had no one to tell what had really changed for her.

And then she found the majay-hì watching her again.

Part of her felt that he more than anyone might understand what she suffered. But he was so strange, a majay-hì in form but not in his actions and his *words*. That he could speak into her head was unnatural. She had learned of what Wynn called "memory-speak," the way majay-hì, clhuassas, and other sacred ones communicated with their own. But they did so with memories, not words.

Leanâlhâm's gaze shifted again to Brot'ân'duivé, his face as unreadable as always. She certainly could not speak with him about anything that mattered.

Then another movement caught her eye.

The captain's young second-in-command came straight toward her around the forward mast. The day before, she had noticed him watching, staring at her, as she had boarded. He had not tried to speak to her, so she had given him no more thought.

To her horror, he walked right up to her and smiled, showing a row of white teeth as he squinted at her curiously.

"Hope your quarters are comfortable, miss," he said in Numanese. "I meant to check earlier, but things are always a bit busy the first day out of port."

Leanâlhâm shied away. She caught most of his words, though he spoke too quickly and was too close. His toothy smile faded.

"Sorry, miss, I forgot to introduce myself. First Mate Hatchinstall, at your service."

With another grin, he thrust out a hand at her.

Leanâlhâm cringed, backing along the rail.

Chap fixed on Brot'an and waited for any memory to slip into the old assassin's mind. Even so, he couldn't stop dwelling on Leanâlhâm and the meaning of those flickers of memories he'd seen in her the day before.

Various majay-hì had watched her from the forest, perhaps for a few years or more before she'd left her homeland. What did it mean? Her emotional state was a more immediate concern. As much as she functionally accepted life beyond her homeland, she was still an'Cróan. Aside from wanting to know other, more important secrets, Chap did not like being kept in the dark as to why Brot'an had dragged Leanâlhâm—and Osha—across the world.

"Maybe you ought to go below," Magiere told Leesil. "You don't look good."

"I need the fresh air," he groaned.

Then Chap spotted a sudden movement up the rail.

Leanâlhâm cringed in retreat from a man's outthrust hand.

"It's all right," the young man said in a rush. "I didn't mean to—"

A hiss of breath and the slide of steel on leather made Chap flinch and look up.

Magiere was on the move with her long falchion in her hand. He tried to tell her to stop but was too panicked to find the words among her memories. She swerved around Brot'an, and Leesil had barely straightened as she passed him.

"Get away from her!" Magiere snarled, the words rasping in her throat.

In a lunging step off the cargo hatch's edge, she went straight at the young man's back. Leanâlhâm's eyes widened at the sight of her.

"Magiere!" Leesil shouted. "No!"

Seasick or not, he spun off the rail and went after her, as did Brot'an. Both got in Chap's way, and none of them were quick enough. The young man started to look over his shoulder. Leanâlhâm's small mouth opened, but she never got out a warning.

Magiere grabbed the collar of the young man's coat. She wrenched him sideways with one hand, and he tumbled onto the cargo hatch.

Chap had no relief that she'd not cut the young man down, as she turned to go after her target.

Leanâlhâm cried out, threw herself at Magiere, and clung to her hauberk.

Half a breath later, Leesil slammed against Magiere's back. He closed his arms around her and pinned down her arms and the falchion. Leesil's growing fear and worry over Magiere's lack of control over herself—over her dhampir nature—had taught him to act fast and hard. Magiere hissed, but he had a solid hold on her.

Chap closed in, rounding all three of them, and Magiere's eyes had turned utterly black. In the bright daylight, tears ran from that darkness where her irises had expanded to block out the whites.

"No, no!" Leanâlhâm kept shouting, still clinging to Magiere's hauberk.

Brot'an stepped in and pulled the girl off, though she struggled to get out of his grip. Sailors began running toward them from all sides, and the captain nearly jumped from the aftcastle on his way.

Chap circled tightly, trying to gauge the worst threat while hoping Leesil did not lose his hold.

"No, please!" Leanâlhâm pleaded in Belaskian, still fixed on Magiere. "I am all right!"

Captain Bassett pulled up his first mate, looked the young man over once for any harm, and then turned on the passengers. Chap glanced back to find Magiere still in Leesil's hold, though she had averted her face.

"What's happening here?" the captain demanded.

Bassett was a wiry man with gray stubble on his jaw, and he was dressed in worn boots, a battered brown hat, and a treated hide jacket. He had not drawn the cutlass hanging from his left hip.

"A mistake," Brot'an returned, pushing Leanâlhâm behind himself. "The girl knows too little of human ways and mistook the young man's gesture."

It was as good an explanation as Chap could have offered, though he could not voice it.

"Hatchinstall!" the captain barked.

"Sir, I was only checking to—"

"Tell your men to keep their hands off her girl!"

At Magiere's shout in Numanese, Chap wheeled around to get in her way. She was fixed on the captain now, but at least her eyes had almost reverted. Their whites showed but not the brown in her irises. She thrashed once against Leesil's grip, but even at her worst she had never used her full force against him—as yet.

Chap snarled at her in warning.

"Shush," Leesil said. "Leanâlhâm's fine, so stop it."

Keeping his grip on her, he looked to the angered captain. "Sorry," he managed in Numanese. "Maybe . . . wrong knowing."

The young first mate, now behind his captain, rubbed his neck as he scowled in silence.

Chap dipped into his mind for any surfacing memories. He found flashes of Hatchinstall with the crew in ports where they spent nights in revelry. The young man's own exploits were rather tame compared to tales of seafaring men. A simple series of pretty women flickered by, but all interlaced with a vivid first sight of Leanâlhâm coming aboard.

He had intended no harm and was only charmed by the girl's unique, foreign beauty. But Leanâlhâm's fearful response was real enough. She was an'Cróan through and through, and he was a human she didn't know.

Unfortunately Magiere had overreacted to an unnecessary degree.

Brot'an cut in again. "As I said, a mistake, a misunderstanding."

Leesil would have been the better peacemaker, if he were not so inept with spoken languages.

"We see that no threat was intended," Brot'an added, "and apologize for any offense given. The girl is unfamiliar with any people but her own. That is what caused her alarm, not your crewman."

"I didn't mean to frighten her," Hatchinstall said, as if it mattered greatly to him. "I was just . . . I wanted to make sure her . . . their quarters were all right."

The captain listened in silence, but his attention remained on Magiere.

"My other friends are protective," Brot'an added. "Please forgive this disturbance."

Chap bristled at Brot'an calling any of them his friends. The captain relaxed slightly, and the brown had fully returned to Magiere's irises. Leesil began to loosen his hold on her.

"Good enough," Bassett said, "but my men have work to do. Maybe you ought to go below to quarters . . . away from the chance of another misunderstanding."

Magiere scowled openly as Leesil released her. She did not sheath the falchion and held out her free hand to Leanâlhâm.

"Come on," she said.

To Chap's surprise, Leanâlhâm ducked around Brot'an and grasped Magiere's hand. Both headed off and below, and Chap huffed in frustration. Leanâlhâm's presence was becoming both a blessing and a curse where Magiere's growing instability was concerned.

Leesil raised both hands, palms up, and cringed with a shallow smile—a quick apologetic gesture. He then hurried off after Magiere and Leanâlhâm. Brot'an followed in turn with a nod to the captain.

"And get this beast off my deck and back on its leash!"

Chap had been watching Brot'an as the captain barked that command. When he turned his head, he found Bassett glaring down at him.

Brot'an, waiting near the doors to below, was the only one left in sight to whom the captain could be speaking. When Chap didn't move, Brot'an snapped his fingers.

"Come," he ordered.

Chap stiffened all over and choked back a snarl. His teeth ground together as he caught only pieces of the captain's sharp reprimand for his underling.

". . . away from the passengers . . . not your concern . . . If they have needs, they come to me . . . or you to tell me, and that's all!"

Chap locked eyes with Brot'an and could not stop the quiver of his jowls. Trapped in the role of pet that Magiere had forced upon him, he finally stalked toward the stairs to below.

But Brot'an had best never think of using that leash himself.

At least the momentary crisis was over. When Chap neared the bottom of the steep steps, he heard voices in the dim passage.

"It is all right, Magiere," Leanâlhâm was saying.

"No!" came the answer, and Magiere sounded heated again. "They aren't going to blame you for some sailor who can't keep his hands to himself!"

That was not what had happened, but Chap raised no words in Magiere's mind as he turned in to the passage with Brot'an right on his tail. The old butcher suddenly pushed past, forcing Chap to shoulder up against the wall.

"Leanâlhâm," Brot'an called, continuing down the passage and opening the door to their cabin. "I would speak with you now." ·

Before Magiere could stop her, the girl hurried on. She was almost inside the other cabin before Magiere took a few steps and Chap scurried after.

"She's better off with us right now," Magiere blurted out. "Brot'an, stop ordering her around!"

The tall anmaglâhk slipped in after the girl and closed the door. Magiere kept going, reaching for the door's handle.

Chap cut her off with a clack of his jaws. She halted, turning and narrowing her eyes on him, but Leesil caught up quickly.

"Let Brot'an talk to her," he whispered.

Magiere glared at him, but he did not let her get a word out.

"This is going to be a long voyage," he continued. "Brot'an is an'Cróan, like Leanâlhâm, but he's . . . well traveled. I don't trust him as far as I could throw this ship. . . . Seven hells, I'd like to throw him *off* the ship. But right now he's the one to talk to her."

Chap did not agree, but there was nothing to be done about it. He had another concern at the moment—Magiere. Her expression was tense and angry for another breath, and then she leaned forward and put her head against Leesil's shoulder.

"Shhhhhh," he said softly into her ear. "Come on."

He looked a bit pale and sickly again, but he led her into their cabin. Chap followed, and only once they were inside did the concern on Leesil's face begin to show.

"Leanâlhâm isn't the only one who needs a bit more calm," he said, pulling Magiere down next to him on a bunk's edge. "We've been politely confined to quarters, if you didn't notice."

A retort might have formed on Magiere's parting lips, but it disappeared, and she looked at the floor. Leesil pulled his legs up to sit cross-legged beside her. As he stroked the back of her hair, Chap watched the pair in silence, feeling like an outsider.

Then again, weren't they all outsiders now, especially Leanâlhâm?

When he was around her, he could feel her sense of loss, of being lost. He wished he had given more thought to such loss himself when he, Magiere, and Leesil had left their home to follow Wynn . . . to travel to this continent they knew nothing about.

But others along the way had suffered loss as well.

Chap eyed the sword hilt still clutched in Magiere's hand; the blade's point rested heavily on the floor. That it was still in her hand became the focal point of all that had just happened.

—Put it—away—

Bent over where she sat, Magiere raised only her eyes to him.

—Do not—draw it—again—unless—told—

Chap did his best to simultaneously echo these words to Leesil as well, so he understood what was happening. It was even harder to do than speaking to one person. Every being had a different memory of even commonly shared events, let alone words spoken or heard in past moments. Chap was uncertain of success until Leesil reached over with one hand to gently turn Magiere's face.

"Listen to him," Leesil said firmly. "He's right. We don't need—want—anything like the last time . . . up in the Wastes."

Magiere jerked her chin from his hand and looked away.

"I had to. I couldn't stop," she whispered. "I had to save you . . . both of you."

That wasn't good enough for Chap after what had *almost* happened on deck.

—The sword— . . . *—Now—*

Magiere flinched at his command, though she would not look at him or Leesil. Finally she unbuckled her belt, stripped off the sheath, shoved the falchion into it, and held it out to Leesil with her eyes still averted.

He took the weapon, leaned it up against the bunk's far end, and then he grabbed her and pulled her into his lap. She collapsed there, closing her eyes in visible exhaustion as he stroked her head but looked to Chap.

Whether he was seasick or not, Leesil's amber eyes mirrored Chap's concerns about Magiere. There was nothing more to be done except to watch her always. But Leesil's mention of the Wastes set Chap's mind to wandering.

The one last terrifying event Leesil hinted at had not come until near the end of that journey. So much had happened before that, from the very beginning. After they left Wynn and sent the sage into Calm Seatt with the overland merchant caravan, the three of them had headed off in search of a place to hide the orb of Water.

The beginning had not been bad, perhaps even interesting at times. Back then they'd still trusted each other in all things, though Chap had not yet learned how to speak to them with memory-words. Still, free of conflicts, they enjoyed some closeness like the older days while exploring a strange land, finding a new path, encountering new people and races never before seen by them.

Yes, the beginning was always the better part in memory. . . .

Chap had ducked through the brush, sniffing about and staying ahead of the horses as he led the way northwest to find a route to the central continent's western shore.

"My butt is killing me," Leesil whined.

Or, rather, Chap tried to stay out of earshot of Leesil's endless complaints.

"It hurts all the way up my spine!" Leesil kept on. "Why are we risking our necks riding these half-mad bags of bones with four sticks for legs?"

It was Chap's turn to whine, not that anyone would hear him, as he halted to look back.

"Will you stop?" Magiere said, pulling her horse up next to Leesil's. "We've got nowhere to be, nobody chasing us, and no one we have to catch. Why can't you enjoy a little peace for once . . . or at least give us some peace!"

Chap huffed once in agreement. He'd listened to this exchange over and over for almost a moon.

Leesil hated sea travel, but he hated horses more. If he wasn't on his own two feet, he wasn't happy. And neither was anyone who had to be around him.

But Chap had agreed completely when Magiere stopped at a village and bartered for two horses and a mule. She and Leesil couldn't make this leg of the journey on foot. The distance was too great, and they had too much to carry—especially with that cursed orb inside a second chest strapped to the mule's back. Chap, of course, remained comfortably on foot.

His long legs had no trouble carrying him for leagues in a single day. It was a relief to lope freely out in front, seeing everything his two charges would be walking into—before either one of them did so. At first he had sympathized with Leesil's desire to do the same.

No longer.

"I wanna walk!" Leesil grumbled.

"Well, you're going to ride," Magiere shot back. "Now keep that horse moving before Chap gets fed up with *you* and leaves *both* of us behind."

She should not have put such a notion in Chap's head, though it had occurred to him already. Of course, he would never do so . . . never.

Wynn had told him a great deal about this region, including Dhredze Seatt, the stronghold of the dwarves that filled the mountain on the peninsula beyond her homeland. Chap was greatly concerned with keeping the orb away from civilization whenever possible. He had led Magiere and Leesil northwest to bypass the dwarves' region; he was determined to keep the orb unknown to anyone before they reached the barren northern regions. There he might find someplace to hide it where minions of the Ancient Enemy of many names—or anyone else—would never find it.

A few days past, he had judged it was time to turn more westward, directly toward the coast. Dusk was coming quickly now, and they'd soon need to make camp.

"Cheer up," Magiere said dryly. "We can't be far from the coast. We'll sell the horses and buy passage on a ship."

Chap groaned out in front. Why would she say that?

Leesil uttered a series of scarcely intelligible foulmouthed retorts over seafaring again.

Chap barely heard this, as something else made him pause. His ears rose as he listened carefully until it came again.

An angry, deep-throated shout ended with a loud thud. Snarling growls followed, carrying through the trees.

"What was that?" Magiere asked, pulling her horse up beside him.

Chap's instinct was to order her back until he learned the answer. Before he could think of a way to do so with just her memories, she kicked her mount, and it lunged past him.

"Magiere!" Leesil called sharply, all traces of whining gone.

Chap bolted after her as she pressed her horse on. Grunting, thudding, and snarling grew louder ahead beneath the pounding of hooves from Magiere's horse and the sound of Leesil catching up from behind.

A screeching, grating yowl rolled through the trees and pierced Chap's ears.

It shook him deep inside, as if he should know its sound.

Magiere reined her horse in behind a stand of trees at a clearing's edge. She was out of the saddle, standing on the ground, before Chap caught up. The sight awaiting them was almost too much to take in all at once.

In the clearing, a battle was beginning between one and many—and the one held the many at bay for the moment. He could only have been tall enough to reach Magiere's chin, at best. But he was almost twice as wide as a human. His skin was both rough and slightly flecked, as if his heavy bones and thick sinews were covered by flesh-colored granite.

Steel-streaked ruddy hair whipped around his head as he spun about at the clearing's center. A curly cropped beard of a slightly darker hue covered his broad jaw. He wore a shirt of linked chain over a quilted leather hauberk, and heavy steel pauldrons and couters protected his shoulders and elbows.

Two war daggers were sheathed at his hips, but in one hand he held a double-bladed war axe with a long, stout haft. He swung it as if it weighed nothing to him, though it made the air hum in its passing. And when he turned in a circle and eyed all of his opponents, Chap saw something more that he recognized.

Around the dwarf's neck was something like what Magiere wore about hers.

Wynn had once described Magiere's orb handle or key as a *thôrhk*—a dwarven word, the only word that the sage knew to describe such a device. Magiere's had ends with facing knobs for pulling an orb's central spike.

The dwarf's *thôrhk* was fashioned like braids of metal, but in place of the knobs on Magiere's, his ended in stout, short spikes, akin to the one on the haft's end of his huge axe.

Wynn had taught Chap as much as she could on the journey to her home-land. And Chap knew what, if not who, he looked upon.

This was a thänæ: one of the dwarves' "honored ones," so marked by that neck adornment. But what was he doing out here alone in the wilderness against these . . . *things*?

One of the creatures made a threatening charge and stopped short, half-way to the dwarf. The sight of it pricked an ugly memory in the back of Chap's mind. It had to be another fragment left behind, after his kin, the Fay, had torn out any memories of his time among them when he had chosen to be born into flesh.

The creature facing the dwarf was only a bit shorter than he was, or per-haps its half-crouched stance made it appear so. Wild spotted fur covered its beastlike torso, peeking between the gaps of scavenged armor crudely lashed over its hulking shoulders and bulging chest. It charged again on all fours—no, threes, for with one arm it gripped an old flanged mace with one flange missing. The creature swerved aside at the last instant, spun out of the dwarf's striking reach, and raised the mace to slam it threateningly against the clearing's earth.

The thick fingers of its hand ended in dark claws in place of nails.

Chap counted twelve of the creatures, all snorting, snarling, and screech-ing. They looked like some twisted cross between an oddly colored ape and a dog. Broad but short muzzles wrinkled below their sickly yellow eyes. Every feral noise displayed oversized canine teeth. Longer bristles sprouted above their heads and in tufts from their peaked ears.

They clambered, leaped, and spun on twos and fours as they feinted at the dwarf, forcing him to twist every which way. More disturbing were the pieces of rusted and rent chain, leather, and felt-pad armor over their muscular torsos. Each creature gripped some form of a thick cudgel made from gnarled tree roots or branches . . . except for the one with the damaged mace.

The dwarf shouted a string of guttural words.

Chap did not understand what he heard, but the words seemed like some kind of enraged challenge. And the creature with the mace came at the dwarf.

In the instant it took Chap to take in all of this, Leesil pulled his horse up behind Magiere's. Barely keeping his feet, he tumbled out of the saddle and took in the sight as well.

"He's not going to last long in there!" Leesil declared, but before he'd even finished speaking, Magiere charged into the clearing.

"Give room!" she shouted.

The dwarf never even looked at her as the largest one came at him. The beast nearest to Chap swerved at Magiere's voice. It barely saw her before her falchion struck it.

Magiere's blade careened off its skull in a spray of blood, skin, and fur. Though it shrieked in pain, it barely flinched and twisted its head. The creature's short, broad muzzle widened in a howl, exposing thick fangs, top and bottom.

"Ah, seven hells, she's done it now!"

Chap glanced about at those bitter words, but Leesil was nowhere in sight. When he turned back, that *thing* threw aside its cudgel, dropping to all fours as it went at Magiere. Chap bolted out as another one turned her way from off to the right.

Magiere sidestepped as the wounded one swiped for her leg with a clawed hand and snapped for her gut with its jaws. She brought the falchion in with both hands amid a twist to the side. The heavy blade bit into the back of the creature's neck.

The creature's noise ended instantly under a wet grating of steel on bone.

Sod tore from the earth in the second one's claws and hit Chap full in the face. He briefly lost sight of everything, and he swerved. When his sight cleared, the second one had gotten by him, with a cudgel raised in its three-limbed scamper toward Magiere's back.

Chap panicked, for they were badly outnumbered against opponents they knew nothing about. He charged straight into the second creature's legs and snapped at the back of its knee.

Where was Leesil?

Furred flesh tore in Chap's teeth. He wheeled around his target as the beast stumbled, spinning to slam the cudgel down at his head. He ducked under as the weapon broke the earth and lunged up into its face. His teeth closed on the top of its muzzle and ground through fur and flesh into bone. For an instant he stared into its sickly yellow irises.

The creature screamed, thrashing its head up and back.

Chap's teeth ached sharply as it tore its face out of his jaws. The force slung him aside, and he tumbled and rolled to his feet to go for its throat. It wailed, its own blood spattering across its beastly face and into its eyes, but it had not gone down. It shrieked at him as it groped for its fallen weapon.

A white-blond blur dropped out of the dusky sky from the branches above.

Leesil landed hard atop the creature's shoulders with his knees. It toppled, and its head and shoulders slammed to the earth. With that momentum, Leesil drove one of his winged punching blades point first into the back of its neck.

Another muffled crack of bone filled Chap's ears as he saw a third beast charging in. He spotted Magiere, now at the clearing's center and back-to-back with the dwarf. The two faced the rest of the pack all around.

Chap bolted and leaped into the face of the third one. As it dropped its cudgel, trying to claw him, he bit through and tore one of its peaked ears. Before it could stop screaming and grab him, he pushed off with his rear legs and hit the ground running. Leesil would have to deal with that one, as Chap needed to make sure no more got through.

A strange cry, almost like some foreign word he did not understand, filled the clearing.

Six of the twelve beasts remained on their feet and hands. All suddenly wheeled, loping for the nearest trees around the clearing. They vanished into the growing darkness, and the clearing grew quiet but for the panting of those who remained.

Chap still tasted fur, flesh, and blood in his mouth, but he looked about for his companions.

Magiere stood with her back to the dwarf and watched the tree line for movement. Her breaths came deep and rapid. As for the dwarf, he did the same while facing the other way. Three bodies lay around him, and beneath his heavy right boot he held down the head of one creature, though it didn't move. Leesil passed into Chap's view as he trotted toward Magiere, but Chap's gaze had caught something lying nearby.

He trembled—not from exertion or at the severed head of Magiere's first opponent. It was those lifeless yellow eyes in a beastly face that made him grow frightened.

That thing was familiar to him now.

Years ago, when the three of them had traveled to Magiere's dark homeland, he'd been lost inside a phantasm cast upon him by an undead sorcerer. In that nightmare vision he'd seen a feral version of Magiere dressed in black-scaled armor. It was only a sorcerer's trick that played upon his worst inner fears, but he'd never been able to shake it.

In his vision she'd stood in a night forest with skulking and hulking silhouettes all around her. Among them, at the forefront of those she led, these same kind of creatures appeared. She had led an army of the enemy's minions into the forest of his nightmare . . . and everything living shriveled and died in her wake.

He also knew of these creatures from Wynn's tales on their long journey across the continent to Calm Seatt. They had passed through barren, wild regions devoid of civilization. A part of that route was called the Broken Lands. Wynn had spoken of these creatures, among other monstrosities, said to roam there. But neither Chap nor Magiere nor Leesil ever saw anything while with that large, guarded caravan.

Here they were, what Wynn had called *gôb'elazkin*: the "little gobblers" or goblins, for they ate anything that lived. And they were not so little.

What were they doing so far west, moons away from their territory, in a place where they just happened to encounter Magiere?

She did not appear to see them as anything more than savage animals too humanoid in form. Neither did she recognize them for what they were, as she had never seen them before. But Magiere and the dwarf suddenly took off for the far tree line.

"They're gone!" Leesil shouted at her in Belaskian. "It's over!"

Something in his voice got through to Magiere, and she halted. The dwarf also paused, and they both stared back at Leesil. When Magiere reluctantly turned back, the dwarf growled under his breath, kicked a clot of sod from the earth, and followed. For a moment everyone stood silent except for the sounds of their panting.

The dwarf straightened proudly and slapped one hand against his chest.

"I am Fiáh'our," he announced loudly in Numanese. He appeared to think this should mean something to them.

Magiere blinked uncertainly, still breathing hard, but her spoken Numanese was passable.

"Your name is Fee-yaaah . . . ?"

"Fiáh'our," he repeated, and then laughed at her stumbling over his name. "Most of your kind call me Hammer-Stag . . . of the family of Loam, Meerschaum clan of the Tumbling-Ridge tribe. I thank you for adding your sword to my axe this night." Glancing toward Leesil and Chap, he drew his shoulders back. "Even though it was not necessary, and I would have preferred to kill all the *sluggïn'ân* before they could flee."

Magiere studied him—and then saw the *thôrhk* around his neck.

"Slug-and-ay-en?" Leesil parroted back.

Hammer-Stag chuckled. "*Sluggïn'ân* . . . what you Numans call 'goblins.'"

"I'm Magiere," she put in. "That's Leesil, and this one's called Chap."

Chap wondered how much of this exchange Leesil could follow, considering his spoken Numanese was not as good as Magiere's. He appeared to listen closely as he inched in behind her.

"Well met!" the dwarf barked, and then frowned a little as he eyed Magiere in puzzlement. "Your accent is strange. Not Northlander or Wastelander . . . perhaps Witenon or from somewhere further south?"

"Farther off, to the east," she answered, and, jutting her chin at one of the corpses, she changed the subject. "Why were these things attacking you?"

"Because I am hunting them," he answered.

Everyone paused at that.

"Hunting?" Magiere echoed. "Are they just animals of some kind?"

Hammer-Stag uttered a "tsk-tsk" and shook his head. "From your lips to the Eternals' ears, I wish . . . for they would not be so worrisome if that were true."

With a great, growling sigh—far too dramatic for Chap's taste—the dwarf took on a stern expression.

"They tried to raid the village of Shentángize one night past," he continued. "No one there dared step beyond the stockade at night. I had no choice but to set out, with only my axe for company."

Magiere blinked again and glanced over her shoulder at Leesil.

"You . . . hunt . . . ?" Leesil tried to say. At a loss for the next word, he nodded to a severed head beyond the dwarf.

Hammer-Stag squinted, his eyelids closing around his small black irises like iron pellets.

"Of course! They are cunning, vicious, and eat anything alive." He peered more closely at Leesil's face. "Ah, I should have known it was a Lhoin'na dropping from the trees."

Both Magiere and Leesil fell speechless at the dwarf's blustering words. Neither of them corrected him concerning Leesil's true heritage. Hammer-Stag's gaze dropped, and his eyes widened in wonder.

"By the Eternals!" he breathed softly.

Leesil blinked and looked down. Chap had already followed the dwarf's gaze to the winged punching blades still in Leesil's hands.

Made from shining white metal, their forward ends were shaped like flattened steel spades but with elongated tips and sharpened edges. At the blades' heads were crosswise oval openings, allowing him to grip their backs. Each weapon's outer edge extended in a wing that curved back along his forearm's bottom to protrude beyond his elbow. Arcs of rounded metal came out halfway down the wings and around his forearms to hold the weapons in place.

"You do indeed hail from a *long*—and *deep*—ways off," the dwarf said.

None of them knew what that meant, and Chap was a bit disturbed that

Hammer-Stag recognized either the weapons or something about them. As if avoiding this, Magiere turned the talk in another direction.

"We were about to make camp, as soon as we retrieve our horses. We don't have much food, but you're welcome to—"

"Horses?" Hammer-Stag uttered warily. "Where?"

Chap realized the concern, but it was not the horses or the mule that he feared for most. He glanced at all of the scavenged weapons and attire of these goblins and thought of how they had to have come by those. Everything that he, Magiere, and Leesil had brought with them—especially the orb—had been left with . . .

"Valhachkasej'â!" Leesil spit out, and he took off running.

Chap bolted as well, easily racing ahead. When he reached the trees, he found the horses untouched, but his sudden appearance spooked the mule. It took off into the brush.

Leesil ran after it, cursing as he vanished among the trees. "Stupid, obstinate, flea-bitten bag of bones!"

Chap began to follow, but when Magiere caught up, along with Hammer-Stag, he decided not to leave either of his charges alone with this stranger. With all the noise that Leesil and the mule made, it would be easy enough to know if they ran into trouble.

As Magiere took hold of both horses' reins, the dwarf tsked again.

"I cannot leave all of you out here," he said, "to become a meal yourselves. I will stand you a modest feast at what passes for a greeting house in Shentángize. There we will find you all a dry place for the night. The settlers cannot cook like my people, but anything will do." He then sighed, deeply and forlorn. "Even though human ale is a rather poor draft."

Again Magiere stared at Hammer-Stag as if dumbfounded. Hammer-Stag's loud and confident manner was a bit overwhelming and off-putting.

Chap preferred sleeping outdoors unless they could find a large settlement with lodging on its outskirts. It had been more than a moon since they'd slept inside. The tiny village mentioned would not do at all, with too many eyes easily taking notice of outsiders. He was trying to find a way to warn off Magiere, when . . .

"How many . . . live in this village?" she asked.

Hammer-Stag shrugged, his eyes rolling upward as if he was counting. "A hundred, perhaps more."

Magiere looked down at Chap and whispered. "I think it'll be all right."

At that, it was Hammer-Stag who eyed Chap with puzzlement.

Leesil came cussing and fuming into sight, with the mule resisting him at every step.

Chap lost any chance to warn Magiere off without attracting more attention. Sooner or later they would board a ship with the orb hidden away in a large chest that might have to be placed in cargo rather than in their cabin. In a village, at least, he could keep it in sight, and Magiere was still waiting.

Chap huffed once in agreement.

"What now?" Leesil grouched, looking between Chap and Magiere.

As Hammer-Stag shrugged and strode off, Magiere just cocked her head after the dwarf, and Leesil followed. Chap stepped in behind them.

As much as Hammer-Stag claimed to be hunting these goblins, he was soon making enough noise with his incomprehensible singing to attract stragglers back upon them. There was little chatter between any of them, and at any question about Shentángize, Hammer-Stag most often shrugged off the inquiry with, "You'll see it soon enough," and went back to his bellowing.

Chap had about enough when they finally broke through the trees into a clear area, and they spotted a stockade beyond the fallow fields. It was little more than a long, rounded wall of sharpened poles made from tree trunks driven into the earth and lashed together. A single broad gate framed by two crude watch platforms showed on the stockade's near side.

"Did they build this to keep out those . . . goblins?" Magiere asked as they stepped onward.

That seemed unlikely to Chap, as the dwarf had been fighting perhaps a dozen.

"The number of sighted packs seems to be increasing," Hammer-Stag answered, "though they have rarely been seen this far west in many years. I tracked one pack tonight, but I will go out again . . . and again until certain I have cut down the last of them."

Chap wondered why the dwarf took this duty upon himself, but then they stood before the gate.

"It is me, Fiáh'our!" he shouted. "Open the gate!"

Low voices rose beyond the stockade wall, and the gate swung outward just a little. A few dirty faces peered out by the light of a raised tin lantern. Without waiting, Hammer-Stag pulled the timber gate wide as if it were made of twigs.

"I have guests," he declared, "battle mates to be made welcome! Someone see to their horses."

As two boys scurried out, Magiere held up a hand before Chap could step in the way.

"Let us get our belongings first," she said quickly.

Hammer-Stag raised a bushy eyebrow with a shrug, as if this was not really worth concern. After grabbing their packs, Magiere and Leesil jointly hefted the chest hiding the orb. They carried it between them as Chap stepped ahead to clear the way.

They followed the dwarf over dried, cracked mud into a shabby village of randomly placed dwellings. They had little time to look around, as Hammer-Stag never slowed. He strode straight to the largest building at the center; its smokestack was billowing and light was seeping from its few plank-shuttered windows. He jerked its door open.

"I have returned victorious!" Hammer-Stag called out as he entered.

A few of the occupants left the collection of rough tables and chairs nearest the burning hearth. Villagers crowded in to greet the hulking dwarf with pats and nods.

"How many?" one asked. "How many did you kill?"

"Two dozen over the last few days," he proclaimed. "They were on me like a horde wherever they heard me coming." He then turned and gestured to his three new companions. "But at the last of it, these came to fight at my side. For my sake, give them food and drink and all else that they want."

Chap noticed Magiere's eyes shifting about as her pale face began to show panic.

She hated being the center of attention even when it was not a risk. Leesil, on the other hand, smiled for the first time all day. He kept a tight grip on his end of the chest as he pushed in around Hammer-Stag.

Several villagers had to duck and dodge the bulky chest and packs. Magiere's expression turned stunned and then livid as Leesil dragged her past tables filled with villagers now all abuzz.

". . . Timons, get the stew."

". . . Marta, fetch the ale. . . . Not that, the other stuff!"

"Tea," Leesil put in quickly. "Bring . . . tea?"

He had once spent years drinking himself to sleep and now would not touch ale or wine. He and Magiere rested the chest on the floor near a quickly vacated table as Hammer-Stag joined them. Chap paced in agitation once around the table and chairs before finally sitting close to Leesil . . . with a good view of the whole place.

Hammer-Stag already had a fired clay mug of ale in his hand. He slammed it down on the table as he dropped into his chair, and foam sloshed everywhere.

"A good night indeed," he proclaimed.

Magiere was looking closely at his *thôrhk*. She had hidden away her own, made of Chein'âs metal like Leesil's blades, in the pack at her feet. Instead of mentioning Hammer-Stag's *thôrhk*, she settled her elbows on the table and leaned in.

"We need passage on a ship heading far north," she said. "What's the best route to a port for that?"

"Far north?" Hammer-Stag frowned. "Why? Beyond Northlander coastal towns, villages, and trading posts, there is nothing but savages and icy wastes . . . unless . . ." He shook his head. "Ah, nothing for you up there."

"Do you know a route?" she repeated.

His frown deepened, and he let out a resigned sigh. "Head west by northwest for two days by a horse's stride until you find the coastal trade road.

Follow that straight to the nearest coastal town, which should be Cantos, about five more days off."

Magiere settled back in apparent relief.

"Only seven days?" she asked, and he nodded once. "Thank you."

Then her gaze returned to the *thôrhk* around his broad neck.

So far she'd found only one use for her own—to open the orb of Water. Chap knew what she must be thinking: why would this dwarf wear such a device?

"Where did you . . . What is that?" she asked carefully.

Leesil was silently but intently watching this exchange, even as a smudge-cheeked young maiden in burlap brought him a clay kettle and cup. She was trying not to stare at him—and failing.

All further talk ended as large bowls of lamb stew with potatoes and peas were plopped down before them. Then Hammer-Stag handed a mug of ale to Magiere; she took it with a nod but did not drink. Finally a wooden platter with a fresh loaf of dark forest bread was laid on the table.

The people fussed over Hammer-Stag and asked whether he needed more ale as they set out the meal. He shook his head with a brief smile, as he seemed pleased by Magiere's last question. Once the villagers had no more reason to linger, he tapped one spiked end of his *thôrhk*.

"I am a thänæ among my people, an honored one," he said. "Only those few such as I wear a *thôrhk*. I now further prove my worth in life through my deeds, if in death I hope to stand among the Eternals."

The only part that mattered to Chap was that the dwarf's *thôrhk* had meaning among his people but nothing to do with the purpose of Magiere's similar one. She appeared to realize this as well and turned her attention to the meal.

Leesil leaned down to put a bowl on the floor. Chap lapped the gravy, though he kept his eyes on the room and everyone in it. The stew was savory with chunks of tender lamb. They had been living off jerky and dried fish for a moon, and before he knew it, he was licking the bottom of the bowl.

Amid shoveling mouthfuls, Hammer-Stag appeared about to speak again when Chap heard the common house's door open. He looked up as two more dwarves entered. As they had with Hammer-Stag, the local people welcomed them in and offered food and drink. It was not until they were halfway in among the locals that Chap spotted the *thôrhk* through the split neck of the lead dwarf's leather hauberk.

Hammer-Stag rose abruptly, leaving the remainder of his dinner on the table.

"Forgive me, but two companions just arrived. It is time to swap tales of our exploits. The *telling* is everything as the culmination of great deeds."

Chap doubted Leesil could interpret the Numanese meaning for "culmination," but Magiere seemed to follow the dwarf's meaning. Deeds accomplished were told to others for some purpose among his kind beyond sharing news of events.

Hammer-Stag winked at Magiere. "You have earned your place in this telling always. From my lips to the Eternals' ears!"

In spite of herself, Magiere tried to smile as she nodded to him.

Hammer-Stag grabbed his mug and was off with a final wink to join his companions at a table in the far corner. Chap did notice him wave over the proprietor—a large, scruffy man in a stained apron. They spoke briefly in low voices. Almost immediately the proprietor maneuvered through the tables to Magiere and Leesil.

"Are you finished?" he asked. "Had enough?"

Chap would have liked another bowl—maybe two—but Magiere answered, "Yes, we're fine."

"Then if you're tired, I have a room out back. Not much, but one of my girls laid out mats and blankets. Any friend of the thänæ will always be favored here."

Apparently being a friend of Hammer-Stag meant something in this small, isolated place.

As Magiere rose, Chap looked across the room and saw the dwarf raise his mug to them, as if in a gesture to say good night. Leesil nodded back, hefted his pack, and grabbed one end of the chest as he waited on Magiere. They were then ushered through a door in the room's back and down a narrow passage to a small room.

"Told you it wasn't much," the proprietor said, setting a lantern by the door.

Though shabby, the room was clean, with three mats laid out with a small stack of woolen blankets nearby. The prospect of sleeping indoors on a full stomach finally appealed to Chap.

"It . . . good," Leesil said, and the proprietor nodded once and left them.

Chap trotted over to claim one mat, and as Magiere followed, she did something he had noticed her do more and more often. It had not troubled him at first, but it began to.

She dropped her pack on the outside mat and pulled the chest containing the orb up beside her bed. Leesil was watching her as well and looked to Chap.

Magiere's nighttime ritual had become too common, as if she never wanted the orb far from her reach, even while she slept. During the days, she was also reticent to get too far from it. At first Chap had thought she was merely protective of it, as they all should be.

Leesil's frown suggested otherwise—for both him and Chap. Leesil picked up two wool blankets and tossed one on Chap's chosen mat.

Not noticing their scrutiny, Magiere removed her hauberk and lay down. Even as she closed her eyes, she reached out one hand as if to check again that the chest was there.

Chap paced in a circle, pawing the blanket out into a suitable nest. Leesil turned the lantern down but not out, and then dropped on his mat. But when Chap finally curled up, he made sure he could see the whole room, including Leesil . . . and Magiere.

Perhaps she was simply being cautious until Chap could find a place to hide the orb forever.

A soft creak pulled Chap from his memory as he lay upon the cabin floor aboard the *Cloud Queen*. Magiere and Leesil were resting on a bunk, and Chap raised his head.

He tensed as the cabin door inched open little by little. His jowls drew back, exposing teeth, and a hooded head pushed through the narrow opening.

Leanâlhâm peered hesitantly at him.

"It is only me," she whispered.

Chap relaxed with a sigh. What was she doing here and, more important, where was Brot'an?

Leanâlhâm hesitated upon seeing Leesil on a bunk.

Magiere, apparently asleep, was stretched out beside him with her head on his shoulder, but Leesil was awake, looking sickly again. He likely feared disturbing Magiere, for he only raised his head slightly at the sight of Leanâl-hâm, and then silently waved her in before letting his head drop back against the bunk.

The girl almost retreated outside again.

Chap huffed softly rather than startle her with words called up from her memories. She finally stepped all the way in. Quietly closing the door, she stood there with her back against it. Perhaps she shied a little at meeting Chap's watchful eyes.

The episode up on deck must have been traumatic for her. She looked lost and alone, and somehow bruised inside.

Chap wondered what Brot'an had said to her in private. It seemed clear that she'd slipped away and, with nowhere else to go, had come here. But Chap had suspected for some time that Brot'an was making her hide something, forcing her to keep something to herself. The girl's present tentative expression only added to his certainty.

He sat up, and she looked at him with worry on her face. In the corner of his sight he could also see Leesil.

—Brot'an is—

"Chap, I'm not in the mood," Leesil groaned.

—Brot'an is—too hard—on the—girl—

Leesil slapped a hand against his forehead, and Magiere stirred a little.

"Knock that off!" he whispered sharply, but he did not quite settle back again, and peered over Magiere, first at Leanâlhâm and then at Chap. "Wait . . . what do you mean about Brot'an?"

Leanâlhâm's widening eyes fixed solely on Chap.

She knew that he understood everything said around him—and more that was not spoken aloud. It unsettled her whenever Leesil spoke to a "sacred" majay-hì in a disrespectful manner. Perhaps more so when Chap was not speaking to her, for she could hear only half of the conversation.

Chap ignored Leesil and hopped up onto the cabin's opposite bunk. He pawed the empty space beside him as he looked to Leanâlhâm. Hesitating at first, she finally came to settle on the bunk's edge. When he shoved his nose into her small hand, she jumped a little, and he flipped his muzzle up, making her hand slide down his neck.

All the while she kept staring at him as if he was too bizarre to comprehend.

That was getting annoying. But as she watched him, her memories of the majay-hì returned again—the ones standing in the shadowy brush and watching her.

Chap looked into Leanâlhâm's green eyes.

—I am—not—like them—and—they—are not—what—your people— think—

She sucked a breath, as she often did at the memory-words he called up in her mind. But at the sound she made . . .

"Chap?" Leesil grumbled in warning. "What are you doing?"

Magiere stirred, opened her eyes, and murmured, "What's going on?"

"Nothing," Leesil answered. "Leanâlhâm came in."

Magiere rolled her head and peered sleepily across at the girl sitting with Chap.

"You stay here as long as you like," she said.

Chap felt Leanâlhâm's tension subside a little. Her narrow fingers actually combed into his deep fur and then became still.

—I am—majay-hì—and not— . . . —I am—Chap—

—You are—an'Cróan—and not— . . . —You are—human—and not—

—So—who does—this make—you—now?—

—Being—more than—one thing—is not—being—less than—one thing—

—All—here—with you—are—like you—in—this—

—You—are not—less than—whole—

The sudden alarm on Leanâlhâm's face actually frightened Chap. A rushing past moment flashed through the girl's mind, and he latched on to it.

He—she—stood in a dank, dark forest of curtaining moss and dripping vines among close, cramped trees. He stepped out into a clear area of grass, and in a copse ahead, something glimmered beyond the black silhouettes of gnarled oaks.

He—she—shook so much that it made every breath quiver.

A rustle rose in the grass, and his breath stopped.

At first he saw nothing. He only heard a soft sliding somewhere ahead in the dark . . . coming closer through the grass.

Chap, caught between facing what lay ahead, whatever was coming, or flight, felt that his legs might buckle. And he could not move.

The sounds of a mild struggle in the cabin cut through Chap's focus.

"Magiere, please!" Leesil yelped. "My breakfast is barely staying down as it is."

Chap couldn't help but look. Magiere had pushed herself up on one elbow and was glaring at him from the other bunk.

"Get out of her head—*now!*" she ordered. "She's had enough for one day."

Then he noticed that the small hand upon his neck was gone.

He glanced back to find Leanâlhâm cowering where the bunk's far end met the cabin wall. She sat there with tears streaming down her dark tan face.

"Leanâlhâm?" Magiere whispered, but when the girl did not respond, she turned her vehemence back on Chap. "What did you do?"

Chap snapped his teeth at her, huffing twice for no. He had not caused whatever crippled Leanâlhâm from within. But he'd somehow pushed Leanâlhâm too far in clinging to the memory he had seen within her.

It was gone now. Leanâlhâm's mind was empty of memories, as if she cowered from those as much as from anything in the present.

—Lie down—rest— . . . —You are—safe—here—with me—

She looked at him, but only as if she was uncertain of what she saw.

—Everything—is all right—in here—

The terror on her face began to wane; in its place came a wash of exhaustion. With her large eyelids slowly closing to hide all the brilliant green, she slid along the wall behind the bunk and half curled up behind him.

He could not turn a circle, for there was not enough room anymore. He did his best to struggle about and settle along the bunk's edge to wall Leanâlhâm off from the world. But his thoughts were working upon what he had seen in her.

There was no way to know when in the stream of her past that dark moment had taken place. But the place itself was somehow familiar—not that he had ever been there himself, but perhaps as seen in someone else's memories.

Leesil came to mind, but Chap was uncertain why. His train of thought was interrupted as something slid clumsily up his back.

Leanâlhâm's small hand settled tiredly between his shoulder blades, and her fingers clutched his fur. It was enough for now that one more piece of Leanâlhâm's reticence over a majay-hì might have been broken.

CHAPTER SIX

For Leesil, the days and nights slipped by in sickening sameness as the *Cloud Queen* sailed along the coast. Once, he felt a flicker of hope that he might get off the ship for a night when he learned they were approaching Kêdinern, some port he'd never heard of.

It turned out to be a small town with no piers big enough to dock a large cargo ship. Captain Bassett set anchor offshore, and the crew used skiffs for a bit of light cargo exchange. Bassett went ashore for the night, but no one else set foot on the beach besides a few sailors handling the deliveries.

Leesil, still nauseous and weak, was left staring out at solid ground far beyond reach, and he stumbled back to his bunk. He wasn't keeping much food down, and even drinking water was an effort. Peering out at that shore had only made him feel more trapped on this floating, rocking prison.

After the one-night stop, the ship sailed south again. More empty days and nights passed with him lying on his bunk in misery. Magiere took care of him: wiping his face, sitting with him into the night when he couldn't sleep. Eventually even this made him feel worse, as he was failing in his need to watch over her.

Then one afternoon brought another glimmer of hope.

Magiere came to tell him they were making port and docking this time in a place called Berhtburh, an actual city. As she finished, the ship rocked sharply—along with his guts clenching up—and the vessel seemed to slow and settle. Even Magiere appeared suddenly concerned and headed out the cabin door. Leesil forced himself from his bunk and followed more slowly.

He made the climb up with effort and found almost everyone—including Brot'an—on deck at the port-side rail. Leanâlhâm was the only one missing, likely hiding in her cabin. It was later in the day than he realized, for the sun would soon touch the waters to the west.

Magiere turned from the rail and waved him over.

"Come and look," she said, sounding pleased, or as pleased as she ever sounded. With her hair loose down her back, she'd forgone both her hauberk and cloak in the warm weather. She was dressed only in black breeches and a white shirt that billowed in the breeze.

Fighting dizziness, Leesil staggered in beside her to see a sprawling small city with four long, sturdy piers jutting out from its waterfront. He looked about and spotted Captain Bassett up at the wheel with the young man who'd upset Leanâlhâm. Neither gave the passengers any notice.

"Prepare to make port!" the captain called.

Those words were music to Leesil's ears.

The ship slowed further, almost drifting along as it approached the outside pier. Soon the crew hustled about under the captain's commands. But Leesil mostly watched the waterfront coming closer—and not quickly enough for him—until the ship finally docked.

"A sight for sick eyes," he mumbled, gripping the rail as he gazed down at the pier.

Both Brot'an and Chap looked at him, though neither responded, nor did Chap raise any annoying memory-words in Leesil's head. However, Magiere laid her hand over his on the rail.

"One sailor claimed this place has a few cheap inns," she said. "Do you want to go ashore for the night?"

"Try to stop me."

But when he looked into her face, really looked, a stirring filled his chest.

Had he heard something else beneath her words? Could she be suggesting a night *alone* with him—and without Chap?

He'd spent so much time worrying about keeping her calm, about keeping her dhampir half from taking over. It had been so long that he'd almost forgotten what it was like to be with *her* . . . in their earlier, better life together.

He didn't begrudge anyone else a night ashore, including—especially—Chap, but Leesil and Magiere would get a room of their own.

"I will remain aboard," Brot'an added. "We need nothing onshore, and Leanâlhâm requires seclusion."

Leesil didn't agree. What the girl really needed was more human interaction with proper guardianship from someone besides Brot'an. At the moment, he didn't care enough to argue. Then unbidden words rose in his mind.

—*I—stay—too*— . . . —*I—watch—Brot'an*—

Leesil glanced quickly at Chap. Other than that he did nothing to draw attention to the dog's having said anything to him. Of course Chap wanted to keep an eye on Brot'an; they both did. But as little as Leesil trusted Brot'an, he sometimes worried about Chap's attitude toward the old shadow-gripper. It went beyond distrust.

The captain was in no mood for another altercation. Likely he'd take an even dimmer view of anything *between* the passengers. Chap wasn't above being . . . well, overly vigilant when it came to Brot'an. Perhaps a subtle warning might temper that.

"Chap says he'll stay, too," Leesil announced.

Brot'an didn't acknowledge this, though Magiere's brow wrinkled. Perhaps she, too, had concerns about Chap, but she said nothing. Crouching down, Leesil scratched Chap's neck, pretending to say his good-bye, but he leaned in to whisper, "Watch him. . . . Learn what you can, but do nothing to get us thrown off the ship."

Chap wrinkled his jowls and flicked his tongue up over his nose. Leesil let the rude gesture pass. They'd both made their points, and he hoped that Chap took him seriously.

"Are we going?" Magiere asked.

Nothing was going to stop Leesil from getting off this ship with her for a whole night. Not Brot'an. Not Chap. Not even fear of being thrown off for good should Chap do something rash.

"Try to stop me," Leesil repeated.

Shortly past dusk, Magiere led the way into a small, shabby room at an inn close to the waterfront. To her surprise, she grew suddenly nervous as she dropped her pack at the foot of the bed. For so many moons, she and Leesil had seemed trapped in a standstill, where a thousand words boiled beneath the surface but were never spoken. After what had happened at the journey's end upon leaving the Wastes, he'd watched her carefully at all times, waiting for her to lose control again.

Always there to calm her, to *deal* with her, as if she'd become his sole and constant crisis to face. In turn, she'd both resented and needed him. She didn't want to lose herself—to her other self. He was the one most capable of reaching her when she was pushed too near that edge. But the last quarter moon on the ship had been different.

He'd been so sick that she'd watched over him, and he'd been less watchful while needing her. As annoying as he could be, it was a relief to take care of him . . . and embarrassing to remember that she *wanted* him to need her.

Leesil followed her into the little room and closed the door. Dropping his pack next to hers, he looked about the shabby place: the tiny bed with its worn-thin blanket and the one window, its panes glazed dull by wet coastal winds. There were no table or chairs or even a water basin, but this was what they could afford.

"Not luxurious," he commented, "but I don't care."

The walk here had done him good, and the sickly pallor had faded halfway from his tan features. Unstrapping both sheathed punching blades, he dropped them atop the packs, went to the window, and closed his eyes as if listening.

"Strange how much I hate being at sea," he said, "but I like hearing the waves against the shore. Reminds me of home."

Magiere didn't know what to say. He wanted to go back to their little Sea Lion tavern, to run the faro table while she tended the bar, serving ale and whatever wine had come in from up their own coast. When the nights grew late, and the last of the patrons ambled out the door, it would be just the two of them in their bed upstairs.

He didn't want to be here chasing after ancient devices wielded by an enemy believed to have waged war on the world. But she had no choice. She couldn't stop until all five orbs were recovered and hidden where no one might find them ever again.

Leesil looked so young standing by the window. With his eyes closed and only the port lights glimmering upon his face and white-blond hair, she couldn't quite make out his faded scars.

As if they'd been wiped away forever.

With no warning, a terrible fear gripped Magiere. She sank onto the bed, and the words boiling beneath the surface spilled out before she could stop them.

"Don't leave me. . . . Promise you won't, no matter what happens."

Leesil turned sharply from the window. "Leave you?"

In three fast, hard steps, he was beside her on the bed's edge and grabbed her face. The way he looked at her left her stunned. He stared into her eyes like a man who'd been drowning and then thrown a lifeline.

"Is that what you're . . ." he began. "Magiere, you're stuck with me. Understand? You're not going anywhere without me."

Knowing she shouldn't go on with this, she still couldn't stop. "What if I lose myself and can't . . . don't come back?"

She had finally said it. The possibility was now real.

He couldn't pretend, not to her, that he didn't fear the same thing. This was the wall of smoke that hid them from clear view of each other. Both of them, not just her, were afraid to step through to see the other in the wake of this ugly truth.

Magiere didn't see fear in Leesil's face. His hands never even twitched upon her cheeks.

"Not going to happen," he whispered fiercely. "Not ever. I'll always bring you back."

She stared into his amber eyes, the only place she could lose her doubts and share his certainty. Suddenly his mouth pressed against hers as his fingers combed up into her dark hair.

Magiere stiffened, still afraid to drop her guard because it was *him* so close. But his mouth worked softly against hers until she felt the tip of his tongue touch against her eyeteeth.

Nothing about her, not even those teeth that changed, elongated, whenever she lost herself, revolted him at all. He loved her . . . wanted her . . . entirely.

Grabbing the front of his shirt, she leaned back, pulling him down atop her.

"Magiere," Leesil whispered with his hands still in her hair.

That was the last word either of them said for a long while.

Late that night, Magiere lay on her side watching Leesil and hoping he was sound asleep for once. She feared even moving and waking him after so many restless nights aboard ship. But sleep didn't come for her.

Her head was too full of worries pulling against fragile hopes. And that opened the floodgates of memory. She couldn't stop thinking about, remembering, so many things buried inside her. Like on another night, when they'd shared a rare welcome and a meal by the generosity of Hammer-Stag at the village of Shentángize.

Leesil believed her problems had begun later than that, on the way back out of the Wastes.

Magiere knew better.

It had all started in that tiny back room of the common house, or "greeting house" as the dwarf had called it. She'd lain awake then, as now, watching Leesil sleep. . . .

Magiere lay in between Leesil and the chest containing the orb. Though her eyes were on Leesil and watching him by the lantern's dimmed light, her hand still rested on the chest, as if she feared removing it but didn't know why.

Leesil's rib cage rose and fell almost in sync with Chap's snoring, where the dog had curled up on the mat closest to the door. She would—could—never tell either of them how she felt while touching the chest.

As long as she remained this close to the orb, she kept reliving the moments back in the six-towered castle in the Pock Peaks. She'd used her *thôrhk* gifted by the Chein'âs, the Burning Ones, to hook and pull the orb's spike, releasing its power.

She didn't know why the thought of that moment brought her more satisfaction than food or sleep or sometimes even Leesil's touch. She tried not to think about what this device had been made for, what purpose it had served in the end war of the Forgotten History. But each night she grew eager for the silence and stillness to relive those moments again. Yet every time she did, the urge to know what was within that orb, what held such power, ate at her more and more.

Magiere quietly looked from Leesil to Chap.

Both appeared fast asleep. Slow and silent, she peeled off her wool blanket and turned on her side to sit up. When the straw-stuffed mattress crackled under her shifting weight, she froze and looked over her shoulder.

Chap let out a slight grumble but immediately returned to his short, doggish snores. Leesil didn't even skip a breath.

Shifting closer to the chest, Magiere carefully pulled its latch pin and lifted the lid. Reaching inside, she drew aside a fold of canvas wrapped around the chest's contents.

There it lay . . . the orb.

Slightly larger than a great helm, its central globe was made from a dark material. Not black, but as dark as char, not metal or any stone she'd ever seen, its surface was faintly rough to the touch like smoothly chiseled basalt. Atop it was the large tapered head of a spike that pierced down through the globe's center—and the spike's head was larger than the breadth of her fist. Its roughly pointed tip protruded through the orb's bottom, and both spike and orb looked as if they'd been fashioned from one single piece. There was no mark of separation to hint that the spike could ever be removed.

Magiere knew that it could, because she'd done so.

Knobs at the open ends of her *thôrhk* fit perfectly into two grooves in the protruding spike's head. She suddenly found herself reaching for her pack, where the *thôrhk* was stored, and she pulled it out without even looking.

That circlet, broken by design, was made of metal. Thick and heavy looking, its circumference was larger than a helmet's, and it was covered in strange markings even Wynn hadn't been able to decipher. About a fourth of its circumference was missing, and those protruding knobs at its ends pointed inward across the break, directly at each other.

An impulse took Magiere as she looked down into the chest.

She wouldn't fully open the orb—no, of course not, or not as she had accidentally in the six-towered castle. Just a little, just to peek at what might lie within it, if she could. It would do no harm to pull the spike only far enough to see it separate from the orb. That was all she would do.

With one last glance to check on Leesil and Chap, she lowered the *thôrhk*'s open ends around the spike's head. Fearful of any grating sound, she took what seemed like forever to slip the *thôrhk*'s knobs along the grooves . . . until they settled fully into the spike's wide head.

The *thôrhk* fit perfectly, like a handle made for this. An almost sleepy contentment stole over her with a soft buzzing inside her head, but she didn't retreat. Her eyes widened as she wondered . . .

Were those words in that sound?

A painful urge flooded Magiere; it was a hunger unlike the kind she felt

amid rage whenever her other half overwhelmed her. It was far more sorrowful than that.

There were no words within that buzzing in her head. Only the urge, the
need to do . . . to go . . .

North . . . and farther north . . . and farther . . .

Magiere tugged steadily upon the spike.

A hum rose around her, seeming to fill the dim little room until it was all
she could hear. She felt moisture on her face—from nowhere. A sudden mist
formed around the orb before her eyes, like hanging vapor over a dawn field
after a cold night. Droplets condensed on the back of her hand holding the
thôrhk. She saw moisture begin to appear and cling to the orb's dark surface.

A fierce hunger grew inside her . . . and still she didn't stop.

Under her pull, a crack appeared between the orb and its spike.

Light washed up over Magiere, blinding her for an instant. Rainbow hues
spread through the orb's sphere, bleeding into each other until its whole form
burned her eyes with pure teal.

Any and all traces of hunger vanished inside Magiere. Her flesh felt fully
sated, with no need to eat or drink, as if she would never again have to face
the world as that monster that lay within her.

But the sorrow kept growing with the hum.

A droplet fell away from her face without her knowing how it had gotten
there. It arced in toward the crack between orb and spike and was sucked
away.

"Magiere!"

That shout was followed by a rolling snarl on the edge of her awareness.
She ached inside, and in place of that vanished hunger in her flesh, a more
sorrowful hunger in her spirit wanted to go . . .

Amid the orb's brilliance, the ghost shape of two hands slammed down
on top of hers.

The *thôrhk* wrenched from her grip as its knobs slipped out of the spike's
grooves. She heard it clank off the orb's side to clatter into the chest's bottom
as the spike dropped back into the orb.

All of its light winked out.

"No!" Magiere cried in the sudden dimness.

She lunged in, clawing to find the *thôrhk*.

Strong hands pulled her away. As she toppled, snarls erupted into growls and the snap of jaws. Hunger rushed back, and all she could think of was her lost *thôrhk*. Anger grew from that unknown sorrow, and it fed the hunger rising to burn in her throat.

Magiere thrashed to get free, and then the trunk's lid slammed shut.

Chap stood upon the chest with his jowls pulled back and his ears flattened as he growled at her.

Magiere froze, feeling Leesil's arms tighten around her from behind. Someone began pounding on the door.

"What's going on in there?" a voice called from the outer passage.

"Nothing," Leesil answered in broken Numanese. "Trip . . . when get up . . . to go . . . Sorry."

Footsteps faded down the outer passage amid unintelligible grumbling, but Magiere hadn't taken her eyes off Chap.

Jowls quivering over exposed teeth, he glared at her in open anger, and her hunger withered. She finally stopped resisting and became still.

"Leesil?" she asked in confusion, for it had to be him behind her.

Chap fell quiet but remained fixed upon her, and Magiere shriveled inside at the thought of what she'd almost done. Leesil released her, hurried to the door, and looked outside. He closed it quietly and then picked up the lantern to flick its shutter open as he returned.

Chap's crystal-blue eyes appeared to grow brighter the closer Leesil brought the lantern.

Magiere remembered the night in the deep cavern below the six-towered castle, when she'd unintentionally opened the orb fully. The cavern walls, wet with moisture from the frozen land above and the deep fiery depths below, had begun to bleed water. Globules had rained inward all around the cavern and hit anything in their paths as they were sucked into and eaten by the orb's full light.

This memory wasn't one she called up herself.

Magiere cringed under Chap's admonishment, called up from her own memories.

"What do you think you're doing?" Leesil whispered. "And why are you crying?"

At the second question, Magiere quickly put a hand to her face. It was so damp from the mist that had formed around the orb that she wasn't certain why Leesil had asked that. She looked to the chest beneath Chap's paws. Horror replaced the unexplained sorrow and the fury that had come when she'd lost sight of the orb.

"I don't know," she whispered.

In the little room in the port of Berhtburh, Magiere shoved away the memory of that first terrible moment—the first of many that had followed. When Leesil murmured next to her and rolled onto his side, she froze, not wanting him to wake, not yet. Now that she'd let herself remember, let herself see the past for what it was, she didn't want to stop. Rising quietly from the bed, she grabbed her shirt and pulled it on as she went to the window.

The faint rush of waves and the glimmer of moonlight on the ocean beyond the port pulled her back to . . .

After saying farewell to Hammer-Stag and his comrades, Carrow and Tale-Pole, Magiere left Shentángize with Chap and Leesil. They followed the dwarf's instructions and two days later found the road to the coast. Five days more and they reached a town where they were lucky enough to catch a Numan trading ship heading north up the coast.

To Magiere's relief, Leesil had apparently decided that the event in the back room at the village had been an accident of curiosity. He didn't mention it again, though soon enough he was seasick and wasn't mentioning much of anything.

Chap was not so forgetful . . . or forgiving.

Several times in their small cabin on the vessel, she'd reached for the orb's chest to make certain it was still there. When she had settled back, she always found him watching her . . . until she pulled her hand away and curled up, ignoring him. Worse were the times during that voyage north when she'd found herself alone with him.

Unbidden memories rose in her head about that night beneath the six-towered castle. She had opened the orb fully then, and remembering it brought her no sense of satisfaction.

Chap was not going to let her forget.

Amid the chaos of water bleeding from the cavern walls and raining inward to be swallowed in the orb's light, each of them had experienced something different. When they later shared this, none of it matched.

Chap related through Wynn that he'd sensed the presence of a Fay. He could not determine how or why one of his kin, whom he'd disowned, had manifested at the orb's opening.

Leesil said he'd seen the head of a huge scaled serpent or reptile, opening its jaws and bearing down above Magiere to swallow her whole. From what he'd described of that form composed of black shadow, Wynn had given it a name: a wêurm, or some immense form of dragon out of her people's folklore.

And Magiere . . . she had sensed the clear, almost overwhelming presence of an undead.

What did it mean—Fay, dragon, and undead? She didn't want to think about it and soon avoided being alone with Chap.

Their small trading ship sailed north for more than a moon, and as it cut through the frigid water under cold winds, Magiere watched the landscape slowly change. Fewer and fewer trees dotted the shoreline, making way for barren rocky land. Snow soon crusted the squat bluffs, though it was only late summer. Days grew longer, and the nights shortened too much.

Before long all the land in sight appeared frozen.

On a bright afternoon so chill that it stung, Magiere stood alone on the deck at the prow when she saw what had to be a coastal settlement along the frosted shore.

"Last landfall before we turn south again."

She glanced back to find the captain looking out beyond her. He was a big man, and though Numan, he wore a bearskin coat, open and flapping in the wind as if he didn't feel the cold.

"We won't go farther north than this," he added.

"No farther?" she echoed, for she'd hoped to put off trekking overland a bit longer. "Why?"

"The season will soon change. The water here can freeze solid for leagues out from shore. Only Northlander longboats travel where the ice shifts and flows like water . . . and can crush a larger vessel's hull. Even some of their vessels get stuck. No farther for us—we head back after trading in White Hut."

He pointed ahead.

Though disappointed, Magiere understood and watched the rapidly approaching settlement. It appeared small and primitive. She'd asked the captain to take them as far as possible, so he knew their journey was not over.

"It's only a trading station," he went on. "But you might find a guide with a sled and dog team for hire. Check with the local Northlanders, most of whom speak passable Numanese. They know the ways of working with the Wastelanders."

"Wastelanders?"

"The Ongläk'kúlk, the natives who live out on the fringe of the white wastes."

Magiere blinked, taking in his words. The course of the day was shifting rapidly.

She hurried below to get Leesil and Chap, and by the time they were packed and up on deck, several longboats approached from the shore. As the crew prepared to offload cargo, the captain put Magiere, Leesil, and Chap on the first boat heading back.

It might not have been a ship, but calling it a boat didn't measure up. With two square sails furled to single cross poles on stout masts, it was narrow compared to a Numan ship but easily more than half the length of the vessel they had left.

When the longboat beached, and they climbed out around its tall and curling bowsprit, Leesil heaved an overly dramatic sigh of relief. Magiere took their packs, handed off by large Northlander rowers. Leesil finally paid attention and helped unload the chest. Magiere was at a loss when they plopped the chest at her feet and the Northlanders busily unloaded supplies acquired from the ship.

She and Leesil had dressed in heavy sheepskin coats with fur on the inside, and hoods and gloves as well, but she felt the bitter cold on her face. If it got any colder, it might be a problem for Chap, especially at night.

Magiere looked to the cluster of weatherworn, shabby buildings. The few people in sight were dressed in clothes made of thickly furred animal hides.

"What now?" Leesil asked, still appearing queasy. "Tell me this is the end of the line by sea."

Magiere shook her head. "I don't know. I'd thought we might hire a Northlander vessel wherever we ended up. But the captain said the coastal waters will soon freeze, and even these longboats have trouble with that."

"No more boats, ships, or even a raft!" Leesil insisted. "And certainly no horses here, thank the dead gods."

Chap snorted as Magiere frowned, waiting for Leesil to hit the hard realization—and then he looked about again.

"We'll not make it far on foot with all this gear," he said quietly, "and we'll need even more if we're heading inland."

Uncertain what to do, Magiere sighed this time. The largest structure in White Hut had a painted plank over the door, but she couldn't read it. Black smoke rose from its haphazard chimney. The building was a dome of sod, as if dug into, or made into, a large hillock.

"That's the biggest one," she said. "We'll try there."

Hauling and dragging their belongings, they walked into the trading post settlement. When they passed under the unreadable plank of that largest structure, they entered a smoky room filled with rough tables and stools spread around the dirt floor. Maybe a dozen people, mostly men all dressed in furs or thick hides, were seated or standing about. More than half sucked on pipes or sipped something steaming in clay and wooden bowls or cups.

Many wore their hair long, most looked somewhat greasy, and all had darkly tanned skin.

Following some slightly rancid odor beneath the smoky haze, Magiere spotted a large iron pot. It hung on a hook over a fire in the makeshift hearth at the room's rear. She could feel everyone's eyes on her.

These weren't villagers who stared openly. They took brief or indirect glances with no expression at what they saw. It was like being studied by a predator feigning disinterest while it tried to figure out whether what it saw was another predator . . . or prey.

Leesil was far too silent. Magiere almost felt him turn instantly on guard as he glanced around, as detached as those in the dim room.

A long, faded counter made of battered planks on crates and barrels stretched across the left of the room. Crude shelves behind it were loaded with canvas bags, tins, folded furs and wool cloth, rope, and other sundry supplies and equipment, some of which Magiere didn't recognize. Beneath those burdened shelves, a row of barrels stretched down the floor behind the counter.

There was no one tending the counter, so whoever ran this place must have been among those about the room. This had to be the heart of the so-called trading post, and Magiere had her first hint of how bad things could get.

She'd never been inside a place quite like this, but she recognized the feel of it, what it suggested about the land. Only the strong survived, if not thrived, here. This was a land where the weak died easily, suddenly, through ignorance or arrogance—or both. It showed in every face in the dim room.

Magiere hadn't told Leesil or Chap about the captain's mention of a sled and dogs. That was likely their only option now. It didn't matter how much they'd been through in their years together. They were in a land they knew nothing about.

They were the weak in these Wastes.

"We're looking for a guide," she said in Numanese and hoped someone understood. "To take us north and inland."

No one spoke until a large man in what appeared to be a wolf-skin cloak took the stem of a clay pipe out of his mouth and looked right at her.

"Why do you want to go into the white?" he asked in clear Numanese.

It took Magiere a breath to catch his meaning; he was likely referring to the deeper region of the Wastes. That was exactly where she, Chap, and Leesil had decided to go. Someplace so far from the civilized world that no one would ever find what they'd hide there.

The man frowned at her silence and returned to biting his pipe stem. He wasn't wearing gloves. His hands, as well as a patch below his right cheekbone, were marred with small black spots. Magiere approached his table but didn't sit on any of its empty stools.

"That's my business," she finally answered. "If this is your place, we need a sled, dogs, a guide, and supplies. Where do we find such?"

Leesil closed on her right and Chap on her left. She had no time for their arguments and didn't look at either of them. They still had coins left from when Leesil had sold a valuable necklace belonging to a vampire that they'd killed back in their homeland. That money had gone a long way, but they had to make it last longer. And would foreign coins be any good here?

"Depends," the man said, "on how far you're going."

Fewer eyes turned her way, as most in the room went back to their own thoughts, cups, and pipes. Magiere sat down, and Leesil joined her, though Chap kept shifting nervously about nearby.

"We're not sure how far," she said. "A moon, maybe more."

The man didn't even blink; he simply nodded. His nose was almost flat, and his pupils looked black in the dim room. At a guess, he wasn't Numanese, and certainly not a Northlander, from what she'd seen of those people. Perhaps he had a mixed heritage of some kind.

"I am Ti'kwäg," he said. "This is not my place, but I have dogs and a sound sled. I know the white . . . the part of the Wastes that you seek."

And after Magiere made her own introductions, the bartering began.

In the end she was relieved that he wanted to be paid in coins, though it left her puzzled. She didn't see how money, especially foreign, had much use up here except in this place called White Hut. Maybe it was a way for him to deal directly with Northlanders and Numan ships bringing in goods rather than buy such through the trading post. Either way, she didn't care. Precious metal wouldn't be much use where they were going.

Ti'kwäg finally nodded and told her to stock up on small and light luxuries such as tobacco, tea, herbs, and especially sugar. He said these could be used to trade with his mother's people for fresh meat and oil made from animal fat. This advice alone assured her that it was worth having met him, and confirmed he was half-blooded. His mother had to be one of the . . . whatever the captain had called them, other than Wastelanders.

Before she verbally agreed to hire Ti'kwäg, she spotted Chap staring hard at the man. Had Chap caught something in the guide's surfacing memories? She waited for him to call up any of her own memories and indicate either concern or agreement that she should proceed.

Chap finally looked up at her and huffed once for yes. Either he trusted what he'd seen in Ti'kwäg or at least thought the man competent.

Magiere, Leesil, and Chap spent the evening preparing for a long journey. They managed to pay for lodging, though here that amounted to a tent on the outskirts. They got little sleep their first night in this frigid land without a ship's wooden walls to shield them, and Magiere spent the night full of uncertainties regarding what was to come.

Could they find a safe place to hide the orb? And if not . . . what then?

At dawn Ti'kwäg met them in front of the same shabby main building, with a long sled pulled by a team of eight muscular, overfurred dogs. He packed and lashed their gear himself, and frowned when Magiere insisted that he fasten the heavy travel chest onto the sled as well. He did so, and the next stretch of their journey began as they headed northeast and inland.

Long days and short nights blurred from one into the next.

Magiere found it easier than expected to keep up with the dog team, for they traveled mostly on frozen ground, which slowed down the sled. She'd expected to hit snow and ice sooner, and when she asked about it, Ti'kwäg scoffed. They would soon see all the snow and ice they could ever want, but he didn't appear bothered by this.

She assumed he'd spent most of his life beyond the hardened earth, with only snow and ice under his feet and the rails of his sled. Occasionally she wondered about his past but never asked. He knew what he was doing, and that was all that mattered.

Leesil, as usual, recovered quickly from seasickness. He, too, had no trouble keeping up with the sled. Once in a while one of them rested by riding on the sled's base. Much of the time Ti'kwäg ran beside his dogs to help tug the sled over patches of rougher ground and shout at his team in some strange guttural tongue. The dogs appeared to know exactly what he wanted from them.

Slowly the nights began growing a bit longer. Even so, they often stopped while it was still daylight, though the temperature dropped faster than the sun. Ti'kwäg had brought a thick tent made from some kind of treated animal hide. He'd packed plenty of oil that stank when burned, but the tiny flame out of a whalebone lamp kept the temperature inside the tent above freezing . . . barely.

They lived on water from melted snow, smoked fish, biscuits, and a paltry amount of dried fruit that had cost more than anything else. Ti'kwäg's only vice was his pipe.

He asked no questions about their destination and seemed content with his duties and what he'd been paid so far. All in all the arrangement worked out better than Magiere had imagined when she'd envisioned herself, Chap, and Leesil traveling over this barren land.

Only two things bothered her.

First, she felt more and more smothered by Chap's relentless watchfulness. He never stopped eyeing her every move. And second, her longing to touch the *thôrhk* to the orb again kept nagging her.

Magiere couldn't stop thinking of how it had felt to pull the spike just a little, how all of her hunger had vanished as if it had never been. She wanted to know from where that strange pull to go north she'd felt and still felt had come. It was so unlike the oppressive presence that had entered her dreams—her nightmares—to lead her to the Pock Peaks and the orb's long-lost resting place.

The one thing that Magiere didn't want to feel again was the sorrow.

It had been so heavy inside her when she had opened the orb the last time.

That feeling hadn't struck her when she'd opened it fully in the cavern beneath the six-towered castle. And so she didn't speak to either Leesil or Chap of this new awareness.

She understood it less than she did anything else. It would be another reason for Chap to get in her way.

One night, after an especially long day, Chap finished his supper of dried fish first. The cold was getting to him more than it did the rest of them, for he wasn't conditioned to it like Ti'kwäg's dogs were. He curled up on top of a fur near the tent's flap and closed his eyes, and soon his breathing deepened. When Leesil dragged the fur away from the tent flap, which was Chap's preferred sentry post, the dog barely stirred. Not long after, both Leesil and Ti'kwäg bedded down, and Magiere stretched out beside Leesil.

She didn't sleep and watched Chap. He was dead tired and fully out for once, but she waited longer until Leesil and Ti'kwäg both breathed just as deeply. Then she slipped from under the blanket, crawled off the fur she shared with Leesil, and headed silently for the tent flap.

Though the shelter's hide was thick, it provided barely enough space for all four of them to stretch out prone. They'd always left the chest on the sled at night. Ti'kwäg had assured her that the dogs would raise an alarm should anything come near.

She hadn't cared for this at first, but now it served her needs. A few days after leaving White Hut, she had again taken to wearing her *thôrhk* around her neck over the collar of her wool pullover and beneath her armor and heavy coat. As she emerged from the tent, the sun was barely below the horizon. In the dying dusk, several dogs raised their heads, but none made a sound. They knew her by now, and the sight of her going to the sled was commonplace . . . though not at night.

Magiere tugged the *thôrhk* out from beneath her coat and hauberk. It took longer to loosen enough of the lashings to open the chest's lid. She pulled aside the cloth's top fold, stiff from the cold, and she exhaled vapor into the air.

Seeing the orb and just being this close to it brought her a strange contentment. This time she set the *thôrhk*'s knobs fully into the spike's grooves

and waited. Without even pulling on the spike, almost instantly, she felt . . .
something.

It was more pronounced this time.

Beneath a tinge of that strange sorrow, she felt the pull—*north and to the*
east.

Amid those disturbing dreams that had driven her onward to initially
find the orb, she'd been terrified as much as obsessed. This was different—
there was no desperation or fear. Only the clear but gentle pull and . . .

And the sorrow.

Slowly she pulled on the spike, but less than she had that night in the back
of the common house, only enough until . . .

The air began to hum. Tiny flakes of ice and snow on her glove began to
grow as the wind blew wetly in her face. Sorrow welled inside her, and a growl
from behind her broke through the hum.

She ignored both. It didn't matter as for once she felt nothing of the monster inside her, as if it had died.

"Magiere!"

She barely turned her head to see Chap charging her and Leesil coming
right behind.

Magiere released her tension on the *thôrhk*, and the orb's hum instantly
silenced. She'd barely removed the *thôrhk*'s knobs from the spike's grooves
when Leesil grabbed her, pinning her arms and dropping his weight into the
snow. She fell, held tightly in his lap.

"What are you doing?" he shouted.

He was angry, but she didn't answer. Chap arced in between her and the
chest on the sled and actually snapped before her face.

Magiere didn't even flinch.

Her mind was racing. This new pull was nothing like what had led her to
the Pock Peaks. It was not a demand, not constant prodding, but more
like . . . a plea from something lost, trapped, and begging to be found. And
then she remembered Leesil's strained expression in the Pock Peaks every
time she'd known to change directions slightly, to lead them right to the

castle . . . and the orb. He'd hated that she'd become some unwilling, driven hound sniffing out a trail even she couldn't see or understand.

But he'd followed her. He always followed her.

"Let go of me," she said quietly.

It took a moment before he did, though Chap didn't back off. She stood up, looking at the still-open chest, though she couldn't see the orb without having to get around Chap. And in the moment it wasn't worth fighting him for that.

When she turned slowly to face Leesil, Ti'kwäg was standing outside the mouth of the tent, watching all of this with suspicion. Magiere turned her eyes on Leesil.

"We have to go northeast this time," she whispered. "We need to head further east."

It was fully dark, but Magiere was certain Leesil turned pale.

Magiere turned from the window of the small inn in Berhtburh when Leesil murmured in his sleep. She suddenly wanted to push down all of those memories, at least for a little while longer.

She returned to the narrow bed to watch his tan face. Now she saw the faded scars like claw marks on one side of his jaw and a single thicker scar down his cheek on the other side. And there, down on his exposed wrist, were the oldest ones . . . from her teeth. There were newer scars along his other forearm.

He'd gained them all in his determination to stay with her.

Magiere slipped in beside Leesil, pulling the blanket up over both of them and feeling him nestle closer to her in his sleep.

She couldn't stop until this was all over and done—until all five orbs were hidden away and forgotten once more. But now that she'd let herself remember again, she kept wondering.

Tonight she'd begged him not to leave her.

Was that even fair to him?

CHAPTER SEVEN

That same evening, a small, two-masted Suman merchant vessel reached the port of Kêdinern and docked at a narrow pier. Dänvâr-fij was below deck in a cabin with Fréthfâre and Eywodan, deciding on their best course of action.

They had been forced to wait five days at the Isle of Wrêdelyd before finding passage on this Suman ship called the *Bashair*. One dark-skinned human sailor told her the name meant "good omen."

Being so far behind their quarry had pushed Dänvârfij's frustration to the limit, and she related her need for haste to the captain, a slender, dusky-skinned Suman named Samara. Though she was not fluent in Numanese, he was and spoke it with a strange musical accent more appealing than the guttural tone of the Numans. He said they would make frequent stops, but his ship was lighter and swifter than the larger cargo vessels.

Remembering that the harbormaster at the isle had described the *Cloud Queen* as such a vessel, she had gained a little relief from that. She and hers might yet overtake their quarry, but on this night, halted in another port, her impatience regained its edge.

The cabin was small but comfortable, with refined wool blankets, linen casings for the mattresses, and pillows of a soft and strangely shiny material. The latter were not as fine as her people's shéot'a cloth, but similar. She cared little for such things but had been surprised by this trace of luxury on a Suman vessel, as she knew little of this human people.

Her team had not even touched their own food stores, as Captain Samara had made sure they were well fed. The ship's cook often served savory dishes from the captain's homeland made with rice and vegetables. Occasionally the strange spices did not sit well in her stomach, but at least tea was served instead of the ale and beer gulped by most other human sailors she had encountered.

The only problem with the cabins was their size, suitable for only three occupants at the same time. Her team could have all gathered on deck and spoken only in their own tongue, but Dänvârfij preferred to keep discussions private. Here and now she could only converse with Eywodan . . . and Fréthfâre.

"How long will the ship linger in this port?" Fréthfâre asked.

Sitting on the edge of one narrow wall bunk, gripping her walking stick, she looked different in her new disguise. Dänvârfij had not quite adjusted to the sight.

Back on the isle, Rhysís had "acquired" their new clothing. None of them knew how the so-called Lhoin'na—those other elves—truly dressed, so they had simply done their best with human clothing. This was not easy, considering that some of them were well above average human height.

Fréthfâre was laced up in a long red dress, fortunately designed with cuffless sleeves that ended above the wrist. Her hair was pinned up and covered with a small matching hat. If not for her eyes and skin, she might have passed for a human female of high standing.

If not for her eyes and skin . . . and her stooped, hobbling stride, which drew attention.

The others needed loose clothing in order to fight if necessary. Dänvârfij wore the breeches, white shirt, and black vest of an adult human male. The items were all a close fit in length, though she had to pull in the waist of the pants excessively. It all felt strange and uncomfortable compared to the soft forest gray clothing of an anmaglâhk. At least she could move freely, and she had tied back her hair under a black scarf.

"How long?" Fréthfâre repeated.

The annoyance in her voice grated upon Dänvârfij.

"Until tomorrow," she answered. "They are resupplying some stores. Their cook seems to use much fresh water."

"We need to learn if our quarry landed here, and if so, when they left," Fréthfâre went on. "A larger vessel may be slower but might not stop at smaller ports. Knowing if it stopped here, and how long ago, will let us calculate how much—or not—we have gained on our quarry."

Dänvârfij did not need to be told this. She nodded curtly and looked to Eywodan. "You and I will go," she said. "If this can be learned, two will be enough in this small settlement."

He also looked strange, dressed in brown breeches and a light quilted jacket—both slightly short for his height. His hair was pulled back into a long, thick braid, and among all of them he had kept his forest gray cloak and hood.

Eywodan nodded in agreement, as both she and he spoke passable Numanese.

Dänvârfij turned to the ex-Covârleasa. "Should I send Én'nish to attend you?"

"No," Fréthfâre answered curtly. "Just bring back some useful information."

Fréthfâre could not answer the simplest question without an implied accusation of probable failure.

Dänvârfij headed for the cabin door, and Eywodan followed her out and off the ship. The port was indeed small, barely large enough to qualify as a town. She thought it unlikely to have a harbormaster, let alone an establishment for such.

A familiar rush of water reached her ears.

Not the sound of ocean waves, and she glanced to the right. A small river flowing into the sea divided one side of the town from the other. From where she stood, she saw several people boarding a barge to be pulled against the current by a harnessed mule on each side of the waterway. The sight jolted her and brought unwanted thoughts of the last time she had herded someone onto a barge.

Eywodan stepped in next to her and peered about. When he then looked behind, she turned.

A stocky young woman herding two small boys came down the pier after them.

"Hurry, ducks," she said to them. "We visited Papa too long, and your supper is late."

"Why can't he come home?" one boy asked petulantly.

"He's very busy. Now on with you two."

Dänvârfij guessed the woman might be bonded with a mate who was a captain or lower officer. Perhaps she had taken their children to visit him while his ship was in harbor.

Eywodan stepped in front of the woman. "Pardon."

She looked up—and up—at him, and a flash of fear passed over her round face. He smiled slightly, bowing his head once, which was more than Dänvârfij would have thought to do.

"We have only arrived," he said. "Can you help us find the master of this port?"

She appeared to settle a little, though she still eyed his height nervously.

"Harbormaster . . . here?" she said. "We're a bit of a small place for that huffy nonsense. Most of the inbound stop off at the Kettle and Drum while they're docked."

She pointed off along the shore, and at first Dänvârfij could not make out the destination. There were two buildings large enough—though smaller than those of the isle—to qualify as what humans called a warehouse. Along the dimly lit waterfront, there was one two-level building that leaked light from its shutters.

"Ask Master Liunt, the owner," the woman added. "He hears of all who come and go."

"My thanks," Eywodan said, and the woman pushed the boys along with one more watchful glance over her shoulder.

Dänvârfij was relieved that Eywodan had found them an option so quickly. Again she glanced toward the barge some fifty or more paces beyond the river's mouth. The crack of a reed switch and the bray of a mule carried through the night. The dim shape of a man aboard the barge poled the vessel away from the shore.

When she turned back, Eywodan was watching her, not the barge. She silently admonished herself for becoming distracted.

"I can go alone," he said. "One of us among the humans would be less remembered. I will ask about the *Cloud Queen* on the pretense of trying to catch companions I failed to meet up with on the isle."

A half-truth was the easiest lie to make believable. He was trying to be courteous about noticing her wandering focus. He was also right. One overly tall, tan-skinned elf with amber eyes would attract enough attention.

"I will wait in the shadows," she said, "by the river."

His brow wrinkled slightly. She grew wary that he was on the verge of asking her what was wrong. Instead he turned away to head along the waterfront. Once Eywodan was halfway to the house, inn, tavern—whatever the Kettle and Drum might be—Dänvârfij walked off the pier, heading the other, shorter way to the narrow river.

She ignored the stone-and-timber bridge over its mouth and stepped downslope, listening to the river gurgle softly into the ocean. Upstream, the barge was the only thing she could make out in the dark, as if the mules were not there and the vessel powered itself against the current. . . .

Like the river vessels of her people.

Raised from living wood, they could propel themselves against the current or anywhere upon water that they and their small crews wished to go. But this had not made her last barge ride easy, let alone a comfortable homecoming.

Not with Osha there as well.

She could not keep her mind from slipping back. . . .

Dänvârfij had kept watch on Osha's every movement during the voyage home. The an'Cróan soldiers were always near, awaiting orders, though Osha gave her no reason to call upon them. Neither had he given her anything else, not a word more than he cared to for any attempt to question him. Even those were not true answers, always laden with grief that she felt as well and always within a finger's breadth short of a threat.

Or worse than that, if, thinking she could force more out of him, she stepped in his way.

She made that mistake only once when Osha was on deck, and she had tried to get more from him concerning the journal. He had turned on her that time, and foolishly she had not backed away. Two nearby soldiers tensed, and one tentatively reached over his shoulder for an arrow.

Osha's eyes shifted to that soldier. "Do so, if you wish," he whispered.

The soldier hesitated, looking to Dänvârfij in that moment of uncertainty.

"Do it!" Osha barked.

Silence took the whole deck. The only thing Dänvârfij heard was the wind in the sails and the rushing water around the hull.

"But be certain in your heart," Osha went on to the soldier, though he turned his gaze back to Dänvârfij. "Certain of whatever she told you about me. If so, then act!"

All of the crew froze in place. Not a creak of the deck or a rope broke the sounds of wind and wave. They were all watching now, watching as one of the Anmaglâhk faced down another, with two soldiers ready to strike that one by the other's command.

Dänvârfij heard the sharp, quick breaths of the second soldier. That one reached out slowly and pulled down the first one's hand reaching for the arrow. Osha never took his eyes off her.

"Move," he said flatly.

She did so, and he walked off, heading below.

Dänvârfij frequently communicated with Most Aged Father, and he admonished her to never let Osha out of her sight. At her questions concerning what to do after that moment on deck, he said nothing at first. It was as if "Father" was as uncertain as she was.

Then he cautioned her not to create an altercation . . . *in front of the people.*

When they reached their home port of Ghoivne Ajhâjhe—Edge of the Deep—nothing had changed, though there was no altercation with Osha over boarding the waiting river barge. A nearly silent eight-day journey followed as the living vessel propelled them up the Hâjh—the "Spine"—River, which ran through the territory. Only the unintelligible whispers of the three barge attendants and the sound of the rippling water spoke to Dänvârfij.

Osha never said a word, even whenever the young barge master brought meals to where he sat alone at the vessel's front.

When they neared Crijheäiche—Origin-Heart—the large enclave that served as the center of all Anmaglâhk activity, in spite of everything Dänvârfij could not hold back her relief. Her first hint that they drew near was when curtained doorways began appearing in some trees. Soon every other oak, cedar, and fir was larger than the last, and the spaces in between broadened. As Crijheäiche came into view, she stood up on the back of the barge, but she did not approach Osha.

Five long docks with other barges and small boats moored along them appeared on the shore ahead. It had been so long since she had been home—not since she had left this place with Hkuan'duv.

Where the docks met land, no trees blocked her view, and the scents and sights of Crijheäiche filled her awareness. Curtained doorways in trees were unusually large here, and trunks bulged to what some would have thought an impossible size at their bases. Market stalls of planked wood, shaped flora, and colored fabrics lined the way into the enclave settlement. Inside these, occupants were busy with all forms of endeavor. Fishermen nearer the docks provided fresh catches, and as the barge slowly pulled into a stop, a wild tangle of aromas filled her head. Beneath the scent of baked and roasted foods were rich spices and herbs.

For all the industry here, everything was still woven into the natural world. Yet Dänvârfij's relief at returning home waned when she saw what else awaited her.

As Osha rose upon the barge's forward end, four anmaglâhk stood on the riverbank entrance into Crijheäiche. Their long hair of sandy to white blond blew free in the breeze. None had their cloaks tied up, but even here, Dän-vârfij knew they all wore weapons carefully hidden from sight: stilettos up their sleeves . . . garrote wires inside their tunics.

One stepped toward Osha.

Dänvârfij quickly raised a hand and shook her head to warn that one off. She hurried out, even stepping once into the water's edge with a splash to get ahead. With a glance back at Osha, who did not even look at her, she led the way slowly while waiting to hear his footfalls. Even when she did, it was difficult not to rush, to have done with all of this.

The strange sight of her, of Osha, and of four other anmaglâhk escorting them turned too many eyes their way. The market's buzz dulled in their passing, and Dänvârfij second-guessed how all of this was being handled.

Father had said to hurry, but perhaps it would have been better to have arrived at night, with far fewer present to watch. Even in Osha's defiant but willing compliance, he looked like a prisoner before the eyes of the people.

But Father had given the orders, and he knew best. Perhaps he wished to cast doubts upon Osha before any of the story leaked out concerning what had happened.

As Dänvârfij strode through Crijheäiche's inland outskirts toward Most Aged Father's dwelling place of countless years, she fixed on nothing but that massive oak itself.

Sitting amid a wide mossy clearing, it was ringed by other domicile oaks beyond a stone's throw away. Those places, reserved for anmaglâhk and other temporary visitors to the enclave, would have been considered huge by common standards. They were minuscule compared to the one at the clearing's center.

Its roots made the earth rise in ridges spreading out from its base. Its breadth would have matched six men laid end to end. Even in the an'Cróan forest, it seemed improbable for such a tree to exist—yet it did. Three more anmaglâhk stood sentry before the opening in its base.

She would have found this unusual enough, as Father did not need to employ guards in Crijheäiche. It was as if they waited for something.

Were they waiting for her and Osha?

One sentry stepped into her path. She paused, expecting him to move aside.

"I have orders to bring Osha directly to Most Aged Father."

The sentry did not move, and then the sound of light but shuffling steps rose from inside the tree. The curtain covering the opening pulled back, inward, and Dänvârfij stared in confusion at the woman who appeared.

Tosân'leag, elder of the Avân'nûnsheach—the Ash River clan—was dressed in a deep maroon robe. Immediately following her appeared Sheadmarên, a female elder of the Coilehkrotall—the Lichen Woods clan—the clan of Sgäilsheilleache. Last came a thin, diminutive male.

He was barely two-thirds the height of an'Cróan but as dark and amber-eyed. He wore only loose breeches of roughly woven material torn off at the knees. Blue-black symbols decorated his arms, torso, and his neck up to his cheeks, and twisted cords of grass bound parts of his wild hair.

Rujh, chief of the Äruin'nas.

It was said that his people had lived here for ages before the ancestors of the an'Cróan came seeking a new homeland. The Äruin'nas were now part of the people, though they lived separately, and Rujh sat for them on the council of elders like any of the an'Cróan clans.

All three elders wore dour, troubled expressions, though Rujh's was tainted with an edge of spite, as always. Tosân'leag was an elder of a clan of scholars; she and Rujh barely tolerated each other, and yet they appeared together.

To Dänvârfij's knowledge, none of the elders ever entered Most Aged Father's dwelling tree, nor did he appear before them unless summoned or some event required his presence. Only the Anmaglâhk went inside the great oak—and only those called to do so. That non-anmaglâhk had stepped into Most Aged Father's sacred home left Dänvârfij's mind blank.

"What is happening?" she asked aloud before thinking better of it.

Tosân'leag looked at her with eyes both hard and dread filled.

"Tread carefully, young one," she said. "I see churning waters ahead for your caste . . . that may drown us all."

Rujh would have usually made some guttural rebuke at such prophesying, but he made not a sound and burned Dänvârfij with a glare. Sheadmarên simply stared at the ground, though once she made a quick glance beyond, perhaps toward Osha.

Dänvârfij feared something of what had happened between Sgäilsheilleache and Hkuan'duv might have already spread. All three elders turned away, and the sentinel anmaglâhk stepped aside.

It took another instant before Dänvârfij realized she was to enter. Tosân'leag's obtuse warning kept her feet rooted in place, though Most Aged Father was waiting.

"Are we going in or not?" Osha asked dully from behind her.

Of all strange reactions she could not explain, she looked back at him and asked, "Will you come?"

He did not look at her but stepped past to the doorway and vanished through the hanging. Dänvârfij followed, keeping up with Osha, and descended the steps inside.

They emerged into a large earthen chamber, a hollow space beneath the massive oak. Thick roots arched down all its sides to support walls of packed dirt lined with embedded stones for strength. Glass lanterns hung from above and filled the space with yellowed twilight. In the chamber's middle was the tree's vast center root.

As large as a normal oak, the heart-root reached from ceiling to floor and into the earth's depths.

A thin voice carried from that center root and filled the earthen chamber. "Come to me."

Dänvârfij stepped closer, rounding to the heart-root's front. The oval opening in its earth-stained wood was hard to spot from the side. It was as natural as the steps that grew out of the inner walls and the roots that supported the tree's great bulk over her head. She heard Osha step closer, behind her. He did not move again until she entered.

The interior of the heart-root's smaller chamber was more dimly lit than the outside. Its inner walls appeared alive even in stillness. Hundreds of tinier root tendrils ran through its curved surfaces like taupe-colored veins in dark flesh. Those walls curved smoothly into a floor of the same make, where soft teal cushions rested before and to the sides of a pedestal that flowed out of the floor's living wood. The back wall's midpoint bulged inward as well to support the pedestal.

Wall and floor protrusions melded into a bower, and among the copious dried moss therein, two eyes stared out from a decrepit form. Once he would have been tall, but he was now curled fetal, with his head twisted toward his visitors.

Dänvârfij stood in awe of the founder of her caste—Aoishenis-Ahâre, Most Aged Father.

Thinned and dry white hair trailed from his paled scalp around a neck and shoulders of bare shriveled skin draped over frail bones. His triangular elven face was little more than jutting angles of bone beneath skin grayed by want of daylight. Deep cracks covered features around eyes sunk deeply into their large slanted sockets, and his amber irises had lost nearly all color. All that remained was a milky yellow tint surrounded by whites with thread-thin red blood vessels. Cracked and yellowed fingernails jutted from the shriveled and receding skin of his skeletal fingers. His once-peaked ears were reduced to wilted remnants.

But to her, he was "Father." Who but he could survive so long . . . lead for so long?

The heart-root of the oak had been carefully nurtured from the living wood since the tree's first day sprouting from the earth. Some said he had planted this tree with his own hands to sustain him for the sake of fulfilling the people's future needs.

Although Dänvârfij longed to ask him why the elders had come, it was unthinkable for her to speak first in the presence of Father. Then she noticed someone else standing in the shadows of the near right wall.

Juan'yâre—Ode of the Hare—had become Most Aged Father's new Covârleasa after the half-undead monster, Magiere, had tried to kill Fréth-fâre. Dänvârfij did not know Juan'yâre well but instinctively did not trust him. Too much about him struck her as sly and deceptive, even his physical appearance. His small-boned stature and boyish features made him appear youthful, though he'd been assented by his jeóin thirty years ago to take his place among the caste. At least he was unfailingly loyal to Father, and in the end that was what mattered.

Father turned his head upon the moss with great effort and looked to Juan'yâre.

"Leave us. Wait in the outer chamber."

Without a word Juan'yâre slipped out, and Father turned his milky eyes on Osha.

"My son," he said coldly, "have you betrayed your caste?"

Osha's tight expression melted into sorrow and pain, but his answer was firm. "Never . . . Father."

The patriarch's tone instantly softened. "I did not think so, but it had to be asked." He motioned with two fingers of a limp hand that did not lift from the moss. "Come tell me what happened."

Osha stepped nearer, his stiff anger fading, and his voice sounded almost numb. "I can tell you no more than what I have through my word-wood . . . before reaching our ship. Sgäilsheilleache had sworn our people's oath of guardianship, which cannot be broken. He upheld it while Magiere, Léshil, the sage, and the majay-hì recovered the artifact they sought. And even beyond to see them safely home, as he should have. But Hkuan'duv . . . and . . ." Osha's anger returned. "Hkuan'duv—and Dänvârfij—they tracked us into what the humans call the Everfen. The greimasg'äh ordered Sgäilsheilleache to turn over what had been recovered. Sgäilsheilleache refused, as was right by his guardianship. And they . . ."

Osha's eyes wandered. "It happened so quickly . . . mere breaths . . . and they were both dead."

Dänvârfij fought an urge to interrupt, wanting to go at Osha for loyalty to his jeóin's oath over their caste. She waited in silence.

Father knew most of their separate stories of a combat that had taken a great greimasg'äh and one of the most honored of their caste. But he wanted more concerning what that pale-skinned monster, her half-blood mate, and the deviant majay-hì had found. Father needed to know about the unknown artifact that none among them but Osha had seen.

And Osha must have seen it.

When Dänvârfij had followed Hkuan'duv in trailing their quarry into the Pock Peaks, he had told her all that Most Aged Father knew was that Magiere sought an unknown artifact. It was reasoned by Father to be something once wielded by the Ancient Enemy in the ancient forgotten war that was said to have covered the world. Such a device could never remain in human hands.

Then there was Osha's secretly carried journal. Father expected many answers, and Dänvârfij waited for the questioning to begin.

It did not.

Father was quiet for so long, simply regarding Osha. He shuddered as his gaze suddenly wandered. Those old eyes, which had watched over their people from their beginning in this land, began to slowly close. Of all the things Dänvârfij had ever seen, what she witnessed almost broke her.

Tears rolled from the patriarch's old eyes and would not stop. They trailed in streams down his withered face.

Dänvârfij breathed slowly so as not to shed a tear herself. She knew how much Father cherished Sgäilsheilleache, though he held all of his caste close to his heart.

Osha dropped, his knees sinking into a cushion. He slumped until his hood hid his face from view. Dänvârfij would not let emotion take her likewise.

"All because of that woman," Father whispered. "Because of that half-living *thing*!"

It was clear he spoke of the monster, Magiere.

With great effort, he raised one frail hand from his mossy bed and reached out toward Osha—and Osha looked up at him.

"Leave us, Daughter," Father whispered. "Stay near until I call for you."

Dänvârfij started slightly in confusion.

It had been her understanding that *she* was bringing Osha for questioning, that *her* testimony would be compared to his. Aside from what needed to be learned concerning what had been taken from the six-towered castle . . .

If she left, Osha could say anything for Sgäilsheilleache, and not a word would be spoken for Hkuan'duv.

"We will speak later," Father whispered. "Go now."

And he still held out a hand to only Osha.

It was unthinkable to question a request from Father. Confused, hurt, and shunned, Dänvârfij left the heart-root chamber, passing Juan'yâre without a word as she rushed up the stairs.

She was breathing too hard, her head spinning, as she slapped aside the entryway cloth and stepped out of the great tree. She did not acknowledge the startled glances and tension of the anmaglâhk sentries as she rushed past them.

As yet no one else knew that Hkuan'duv and Sgäilsheilleache were dead, but the sentries must know something of great importance had happened. She would not be the one to tell them more. Even if she would have been, her throat burned too much from her racing breaths.

A shift of shadow near one of the oaks ringing the clearing made her breath stop altogether.

Out of the shadow came Brot'ân'duivé.

"A greimasg'äh . . . here?" she whispered to herself.

Never glancing her way, one of the remaining few shadow-grippers like Hkuan'duv strode toward the great oak. Brot'ân'duivé was the tallest man she had ever seen, but he looked travel worn. His forest gray cloak was dusty and marred, with tree needles clinging here and there.

Dänvârfij was only a dozen paces beyond the oak's entrance. As the greimasg'äh neared Father's oak, she saw those well-known scars that skipped over his right eye. But his dark face glistened with sweat that caught in the fine creases around his eyes and mouth. Wherever he had come from, it had been a long, hard, and fast journey.

Brot'ân'duivé might still be the greatest among their caste, but he was old for an anmaglâhk. Most of them were counted fortunate to see more than seventy years. He was beyond that, though she did not know his true age.

His expression appeared fixed, cold, and purposeful. She had seen him only a few times in her life but had never spoken to him. It was well-known that the relationship between this greimasg'äh and Father was deeply strained, and Brot'ân'duivé was rarely seen in Crijheäiche anymore.

Dänvârfij turned back as he approached the three sentries. Two of them closed together, blocking the entrance, and the greimasg'äh halted, not blinking as he faced them.

"Move aside," he ordered.

"Forgive us, Greimasg'äh," said the left one with a quick bow of his head. "Father is counseling a recently returned caste member, and no one may interrupt."

Brot'ân'duivé answered in a half whisper, "I know full well who he is . . . *counseling*."

The right sentry visibly stiffened.

Even among the caste, not all was known about the Greimasg'äh—the Shadow-Grippers. They had skills that could be learned but never taught. Some claimed that shadow and silence became their very armor and weapons. And if their chosen target ever lost sight of them—if such ever saw a greimasg'äh coming in the first place—that one was quickly dead.

Dänvârfij had more than once asked Hkuan'duv about this. She received only a sad smile and shake of his head for an answer.

"I told you to move," Brot'ân'duivé said again.

"Please, Greimasg'äh," said the sentry on the left. "We cannot allow—"

"It is the right and responsibility of a caste elder to look in on those who return without their team. I will not instruct you a third time."

Dänvârfij did not approve of Brot'ân'duivé's using his authority in this manner, but he had earned his place among them long ago. All present knew his great deeds for the sake of the people.

The left sentinel stepped aside with a quick nod of respect, but the one on the right did not. In a snapping motion, his left hand darted toward his other sleeve. It never landed.

The path to the door was suddenly clear before the left sentinel back-stepped into a ready position. The other one lay on the ground, gasping for air as he clutched his throat.

Dänvârfij had not even seen the greimasg'äh's strike. But no one moved into Brot'ân'duivé's way as he swept through the curtained opening and vanished into the great oak. She stood there helpless, knowing she could not follow without Father summoning her.

An anmaglâhk had tried to draw a weapon upon a revered elder of their caste. And Tosân'leag's words reverberated in Dänvârfij's head.

I see churning waters ahead for your caste . . . that may drown us all.

"Dänvârfij?"

Eywodan's voice cut through her memories, and she found herself staring at the river running into the ocean. She turned to see him walking toward her, still looking somewhat unfamiliar in his human clothing.

If only she had known back then all that she knew now. With those sentries, she or one of them might have lived long enough to kill the traitor at Father's entrance.

She waited quietly until Eywodan closed the distance between them.

"The tavern's keeper said the *Cloud Queen* left three days before," he related, "bound for the port of Berhtburh. No passengers remained behind, and I cannot see our quarry having ventured farther into this small settlement. It should be safe to assume they are all still on the ship. Since we left the isle five days behind them, we are closing the distance."

At least they had a proper gauge of time and distance and the relative speed of both ships. Should Captain Samara not linger long here or in any port along the way, they might overtake the other vessel before it reached its next port.

And the traitor would die first.

CHAPTER EIGHT

B ack on the deck of the *Cloud Queen*, Chap had watched Magiere and
Leesil head into Berhtburh for the night. He didn't begrudge Leesil
a night ashore or Magiere time alone with her husband. The suggestion on her part had actually been a relief, for she'd sounded like the Magiere
of earlier days.

Brot'an was there as well, watching the pair depart.

"I am going below," he said in Elvish, a statement that dared Chap to
challenge him.

Chap didn't even growl; someone needed to remain aboard to keep watch
on the old assassin. By way of answer, he headed for the aftcastle door in
indifference, as if he, too, wanted nothing more than a nap in his own cabin.

Brot'an followed him to the bottom of the steep steps, and as Chap padded to the cabin he shared with Leesil and Magiere, he heard Brot'an move
on toward the one he shared with Leanâlhâm.

Chap did not actually enter his cabin. Instead he remained outside the
door. Rising briefly on his haunches, he pawed down the cabin door's handle
as if attempting to open it.

The door cracked open with a rattle from the handle. When Chap heard
the other cabin door close, he waited for two breaths. Certainly Brot'an was
listening for another door to close.

Chap rose on his haunches, gripped the door's handle in his jaws, pushed on the frame with one paw to jerk the door shut. It closed loudly as if shoved from the inside. He waited until muffled voices rose in the other cabin, and then he slinked back to the stairs. Climbing those steep steps without a scrape of claws on wood was tedious.

The Numan sailors on deck had grown accustomed to the sight of him, enough so that none called to the captain or mate when he appeared. Only a few glanced his way as he crept to the aftcastle's right side, away from the boarding ramp, and searched for a place to hide.

He wriggled into a small space between and behind two large water barrels until his rear end bumped the ship's rail wall. With a clear view of the ship's ramp, he settled to wait.

Evening fell into full darkness, but if need be, he would lie there all night. Now and then he peeked out. More sailors drifted off below deck until only two remained on watch, playing cards near the forecastle. Apparently the captain considered Berhtburh a safe port.

The full moon was large in the sky, and after a while Chap's eyelids drooped. They snapped open again when the aftcastle doorway creaked open. He quickly narrowed them so that any stray light catching his crystal-blue irises would not betray him. Holding his breath, he peeked around one barrel.

A tall form walked quietly toward the ramp down to the pier.

Brot'an was up and about in the night.

Chap never believed for an instant that Brot'an would remain aboard only to keep watch over Leanâlhâm in their cabin. Both sailors at the forecastle looked up from their cards, but they knew the passengers and likely assumed the tall elf, like Magiere and Leesil, was headed into town.

Chap held his breath until Brot'an was down the ramp. Then he scurried across the deck and watched the shadow-gripper head up the pier. A rumble rose in his throat as he hesitated in following.

Leanâlhâm was still so wary of human strangers. What if she left her cabin during the night to find herself with no one but the sailors aboard? It seemed unlikely, and Chap trusted that Captain Bassett and the first mate could handle any problems that might arise. And he had to find out what Brot'an was doing.

As Brot'an stepped off the pier's base, Chap slunk down the ramp. He stayed in the ship's shadow until the anmaglâhk master turned north along the waterfront. Fortunately few people were about at night, and he had little trouble avoiding being seen. Three dockworkers were too drunk in their merriment to even notice him rush by along the warehouses. He hurried to catch up as Brot'an continued straight out of town and disappeared into the trees along the rocky shore.

Chap slowed at the fringe of the woods, listening and sniffing until he picked his quarry's scent. Curiosity grew even before he tracked the old one to a clearing no larger than a wagon.

What could Brot'an possibly want out here?

The shadow-gripper stopped before a spruce tree, tilted in its growth by years of coastal winds. He dropped to one knee on the damp ground near its trunk and reached inside his tunic to grope for something.

Chap crept as close as he dared, until he stood poised behind trees leaning opposite ways and peered through the wedge of space between them. He tried to see what was in Brot'an's hand, but the shadow-gripper pressed the object against the spruce's trunk and held it only with two fingers.

Through the darkness, Chap made out part of a tawny oval shape trapped against the bark by Brot'an's hand. It appeared to be a smoothly polished piece of wood.

Then Brot'an began to speak. "Are you there? Answer me. I do not have much time."

Chap tensed at the query, thinking he had been spotted, but Brot'an remained on one knee with his head down; he looked at nothing. Chap glanced about, seeing no one else among the trees. To whom was the old assassin speaking?

Brot'an spoke again, and this time clear relief replaced his normally guarded tone.

"I am glad to hear you and that you are well, but much has happened—"

He stopped, as if interrupted, and then . . .

"Cuirin'nên'a, let me finish! Your son is safe, and I watch over him, but Léshil and his purpose are not our only concern. We are still followed by the team Most Aged Father sent, and I do not know how far behind they are. Do not risk exposing yourself, but if you hear word through our underground—anything passed from Most Aged Father to his loyalists—learn more if you can. Tell me whatever you uncover when I contact you again."

Chap's eyes were locked wide and unblinking at what he heard. Brot'an had placed a small oval of wood against a tree and appeared to converse with Leesil's mother . . . a continent away. But Chap could hear only Brot'an.

How was this possible?

He remembered what Magiere had told him of the story Brot'an had shared with her, of how Brot'an had received a message, though the old assassin had been inside Gleann's tree dwelling and no messenger had come. And now there was that small bit of polished wood.

Was it the key? Did it have something to do with this particular tree? Did the type of tree matter?

However Brot'an accomplished this feat, he could communicate over great distances. This was difficult to imagine, but Chap had seen stranger things among the an'Cróan, such as their living ships, the Päirvänean.

"There is more," Brot'an added and then paused. "Yes, Leanâlhâm is with me, but Osha has separated from us . . . by his choice. I believe he stayed in Calm Seatt with the young sage Wynn Hygeorht."

He paused even longer, perhaps listening to a reply. When he spoke again, his tone was somewhat harsher.

"No, you are wrong! He is not an *unknown variable,* though we do not know his true place in what will unfold. But Osha can be trusted, even on his own. He will never give us away."

Brot'an paused again, and his voice softened. "I am right in this. Now you must stay safe. If possible, use our inside agents to learn what you can of this team that follows me. I have eliminated half of them and know some that remain, but until the rest are delivered to our ancestors, you must try to gain any hints of what they relate to Most Aged Father. You will hear from me again when I can get away from the others."

Brot'an's eyes closed briefly, and he slumped as if wincing in pain or some deep sorrow.

It all left Chap wondering what Leesil's mother had said.

"Yes, still . . . always," Brot'an whispered, perhaps confirming something, and he finished with, "In silence and in shadow."

Chap swallowed back a growl at that litany. No matter how Brot'an dressed, no matter whom among his own caste he murdered, he was—and always would be—anmaglâhk.

Brot'an's hand slid tiredly off the spruce. He tucked the oval of tawny wood back into his tunic before he rose.

Chap belly-crawled in against the base of a tree as Brot'an passed right by where he hid.

Returning toward the waterfront of Berhtburh, Brot'ân'duivé walked purposefully through the rocky shore's woods. He could not stop thinking of all that he had left back home, all he had left Cuirin'nên'a and the other dissidents to face without him.

His adamant response to her questioning of Osha's trustworthiness had surprised him. Even he did not truly know what lay ahead for the young man. Pausing, he put his hand against a tree to give himself a moment to just breathe.

Osha was not a dissident, Anmaglâhk or otherwise. He was also not one of Most Aged Father's inner circle of loyalists. Osha appeared to fit nowhere in the scheme of things that could be clearly perceived.

Brot'ân'duivé did not like unknown factors or being left in the dark. Perhaps it was best that Osha had disobeyed and remained behind with Wynn Hygeorht. Perhaps this was somehow intended.

Brot'ân'duivé no longer regretted having been forced to take Osha from his people. Not after it was clear that Most Aged Father would turn loyalists against other anmaglâhk in pursuit of his goals. Osha would have been caught in the middle.

Closing his eyes and feeling his age bearing down on him, Brot'ân'duivé leaned harder against the tree. The weight of it was as heavy as his fatigue on that night he had stepped into the heart-root of the ancient oak where Osha was alone and "counseled" by Most Aged Father. . . .

Brot'ân'duivé never glanced back to see whether any sentries still standing followed him. He rapidly descended the steps into the earth, but he questioned the wisdom of a recent decision.

Upon arriving in Crijheäiche a full day ago, he had considered pressing on via the Hâjh River to Ghoivne Ajhâjhe on the coast. If he had, he might have intercepted Osha before the young one reached Most Aged Father. But he had not known whether Osha would be brought by barge or on foot at a run through the forest. So he had waited, and it had not been as long as he had expected.

By the time one of Brot'ân'duivé's dissident anmaglâhk came to him out in the trees beyond Crijheäiche, Osha was already approaching the settlement by barge. Brot'ân'duivé had not been quick enough to intercept the barge before it landed, and though exhausted, he now descended into Most Aged Father's domain in full haste.

Osha had no idea what had happened in his absence, that the caste was divided in more ways. Even among the Anmaglâhk there had been a handful of active dissidents for many years before Brot'ân'duivé had joined them after Léshil's birth. Now there were others—the loyalists, as he called them—who swung the other way in secret as well.

These fanatics had become more than a counterfaction to the dissidents.

The dissidents among the people—anmaglâhk and not—disapproved of Most Aged Father's using the caste to start civil wars and seed political discord among the human nations. More than a thousand years ago, it was said—mostly by Most Aged Father—that the Ancient Enemy had used and harnessed humans and then turned them against the allied forces.

142 · BARB & J. C. HENDEE

Most Aged Father believed that enemy would return—was returning.

Directing the human nations' suspicions upon each other was no longer about turning their curious eyes away from the people's territories. It had become something more.

Most Aged Father sought to decrease the humans' numbers before that enemy rose again.

Brot'ân'duivé harbored no love for humans. Neither did he believe in some subtle attempt at genocide. What would happen should any powerful faction among the humans learn of the new goal of the Anmaglâhk, the loyalists?

Retribution.

Most Aged Father's paranoia endangered his own people, but the loyalists among the Anmaglâhk followed him in this, even unto turning upon their own caste. Among the few clan elders who sympathized with the dissidents enough to be warned by them, none were yet alarmed enough to openly pull down Most Aged Father.

Yet more of the people at large were beginning to silently, secretly take sides.

Brot'ân'duivé did not know where all of this would lead. He knew only that Most Aged Father was mad and must be removed. But more than this, if the Ancient Enemy did return, it would only drive the people to fear. And they would turn to Most Aged Father for protection.

Then there would be no end, no limit, to what they would let him do.

The answer was not a matter of killing one or the other. Both the Enemy and Most Aged Father had to die . . . at the right moment. And if the Enemy died by the hand or intent of a half-blood, an outsider, neither human nor an'Cróan could claim that victory in turning their remaining ire on the other.

As to Most Aged Father . . .

Brot'ân'duivé emerged into the large earthen chamber of the great oak. Hearing an angry, reedy voice, he headed straight for the opening into the heart-root chamber.

"You must have learned more, my son," Most Aged Father pleaded. "You were there when she found the artifact!"

"No, Father, I was not there when Magiere found . . . what she called an 'orb,'" Osha answered in a strained, exhausted voice. "I did not even see the place from where she took it. I was injured and lay unconscious in an ancient library, while Wynn tended—"

"But after—later—you must have seen it! What did it look like? What is its purpose?"

Brot'ân'duivé stepped into the heart-root, and Most Aged Father's milky eyes fixed instantly upon him.

Any feigned sympathy beneath the ancient one's fervent questioning vanished as his eyes widened slightly. Shock was then replaced by a glint of hatred.

Osha looked up in equal surprise from where he knelt upon a cushion.

"Greimasg'äh?" he breathed.

Brot'ân'duivé saw the strain on Osha's face. Had the young one even been given rest or food after the long journey here?

"My elder *son*," Most Aged Father cut in, eyeing Brot'an. "You have not been called. I am receiving a report. Leave us until we are finished."

An order, not a request, but Brot'ân'duivé was far past pretending to follow either.

Juan'yâre suddenly appeared at the heart-root's opening; alarm twisted his bland features.

"Father, should I have him removed?"

Brot'ân'duivé contemptuously ignored the new Covârleasa. "By all means," he told Most Aged Father, "call a few of our brethren down and have them try to remove me."

Most Aged Father hesitated at that taunt. The prospect of attempting to physically remove a shadow-gripper would end only in humiliation—if not death—for those who tried. Word of it would spread too quickly to be contained.

Brot'ân'duivé saw all of this reflected in the old one's eyes.

"No, my Covârleasa," Most Aged Father said. "Your concern is admirable but misplaced. Leave us."

With clear reluctance, Juan'yâre backed out of sight.

Brot'ân'duivé immediately gestured for Osha to rise.

"Where is Sgäilsheilleache?" he asked.

The question's suddenness had its intended effect, and Osha's strained expression twisted into pain.

"Dead," he answered weakly. "I burned his body and performed the rites."

"Osha!" Most Aged Father cried in alarm. "You were not to speak of this yet."

Brot'ân'duivé merely stood there as Osha's words fell on him like a sudden chill. Sgäilsheilleache represented that which could not be replaced: an anmaglâhk, neither dissident nor loyalist, who put the people and their ways before all else. He defended both in action and in self—in all ways and at any cost.

This is what it meant—should have meant—to be Anmaglâhk. To take back the way of life of his people from any who would steal it from them.

"How?" Brot'ân'duivé asked.

"A greimasg'äh . . . Hkuan'duv . . . came after us," Osha answered, and anger began leaking into his voice. "He demanded Sgäilsheilleache take the orb from Magiere and surrender it. Sgäilsheilleache refused to break his oath of guardianship. They fought and killed each other in the same instant."

Brot'ân'duivé stood there in silence. One of their highest, a shadow-gripper, had gone after one of the caste. Of all the things he feared hearing here, this had not been among his speculations. This could have only happened because . . .

He looked long and hard at Most Aged Father, but the old one met his gaze without a twitch or blink.

Sgäilsheilleache had killed a greimasg'äh in single combat, in defending one of the oldest of the people's ways. How much more could he have become? How much had they lost in his death?

For an instant Brot'ân'duivé succumbed to a silent rage. If Hkuan'duv had survived, it would not have been for long.

"Brot'ân'duivé!" Most Aged Father snapped. "This information is not to be spread, even among our caste. Not until they have been prepared for such tragedy." His voice turned coldly polite. "And of course your wish is always to serve the needs of your caste as well as the people."

Brot'ân'duivé studied him. "Is Osha under arrest?"

"Arrest?" Most Aged Father echoed, feigning surprise. "Of course not. He is simply giving me his report."

"Then let us both hear anything further. As a caste elder, who should be informed when a member returns without his team, I would be most interested."

Brot'ân'duivé played a dangerous game and knew it. Most Aged Father had not finished his interrogation but would certainly have no desire to continue it with a witness who could not be dismissed. It was a long moment before the old one answered.

"I think we are finished here, for now."

Brot'ân'duivé half turned, gesturing Osha toward the exit.

"How far will you take him?" Most Aged Father asked, and Osha halted in the opening, looking back.

"He is hungry and tired from his journey," Brot'ân'duivé answered. "He is in pain from having lost his jeóin. I will take him wherever he needs to go, for without proper rest, grief might drive him to purge it, and its cause, with the wrong people."

This veiled threat made the obvious clear. If Most Aged Father interfered further with Osha, Brot'ân'duivé would make the truth of these events known to all.

"Very well," Most Aged Father said slowly.

Brot'ân'duivé gripped Osha's arm and turned to usher the young one out of the heart-root.

"Osha, my son," Most Aged Father called out, "I meant to ask about a book which Dänvârfij saw in your possession . . . written in our tongue with a human scrawl. Can you tell me what it is?"

Brot'ân'duivé felt the muscles in Osha's arm clench. The insinuation in Most Aged Father's voice was like a stench in the chamber. Brot'ân'duivé did not look back, but he watched as Osha turned his head.

"It is . . . it is nothing, Father," the young one stuttered out. "A gift, a token given to me by a human woman."

Most Aged Father tutted like an amused parent. "A gift? I hope you have not taken to consorting with this *woman*. May I see the token?"

Brot'ân'duivé felt the sinews in Osha's arm tighten harder, but the young one's voice turned lighter this time when he replied.

"It is personal to me, Father. May I go now?"

In that instant Brot'ân'duivé knew that since the last time he had seen this most inept of anmaglâhk, Osha had somehow learned to lie. It might have saddened those who knew his unique innocence in all things, including service.

It only sharpened Brot'ân'duivé's curiosity about this book.

"Of course, my son," Most Aged Father answered. "Go and rest and heal your wounds."

Taking the lead, Brot'ân'duivé pushed Osha out and led the way toward the stairs. He did not see Juan'yâre along the way. Halfway up the steps, he whispered back to Osha.

"We are leaving Crijheäiche *now*. Are you able to travel?"

"As far as you can get me from here," came the answer, and then, as they neared the top, "Greimasg'äh?"

"Yes?"

"Thank you."

Brot'ân'duivé raised his eyes in the woods north of Berhtburh's waterfront and wondered what had pulled him from this memory. Something, a living presence in the night.

He felt it like a shift of air not quite a breeze. Carefully maintaining his fatigued demeanor, he looked out to the ocean, and then turned all the way around, as if at a loss for where he would go next.

In that turn his eyes never focused on any one thing.

He took in everything that passed through his field of sight. He saw nothing, but he knew he was not wrong. Something was out there watching him.

He strode away toward the waterfront. No one could follow him for long if he chose not to allow it. But he did nothing to lose whatever, whoever, was there. Not until he neared the first warehouse before the piers.

Turning into the broad cutway at the warehouse's far end, he emptied his mind completely and let shadow swallow him even as he broke into a jog. Amid the total inner silence, he heard nearly mute steps following him.

At the cutway's rear, he turned right into the adjoining alley, rushing one block south behind the warehouses to the next side street before turning back to the waterfront. He stood there at the corner, watching along the warehouses by the light of dim lanterns.

Something darted out of the previous cutway, as if having lost track in following him. It looked both ways and finally froze, peering straight at Brot'ân'duivé.

Chap stood glaring at him; lantern's light shimmered on the majay-hì's fur as his hackles rose. What light sparked in Chap's crystal-blue eyes soon caught on his near-white teeth as he snarled.

Had the majay-hì overheard anything out in the woods?

Brot'ân'duivé was too tired to care and did not have the energy for any more of Léshil's and Chap's insistence upon treating him like an enemy. He simply walked away, casually heading out along the pier to the *Cloud Queen*.

The following dawn, Chap stood waiting on deck for the first sign of Leesil and Magiere's return. He had little to tell them, and it seemed the war to extract any truth from Brot'an was to be fought in feints and skirmishes rather than in outright battles. But there was one thing, one name spoken in the night, that Leesil would want to hear.

Cuirin'nên'a—Nein'a—his mother.

Worse, Chap instinctively knew that when Brot'an had paused in the woods to lean against the tree, he had been pondering something weighty. Try as Chap had, again he could not dip into the old shadow-gripper's memories. It was becoming infuriating. Upon returning to the ship last night, Brot'an had simply gone to his cabin and not come out again.

Amid the people milling on the waterfront and piers, Chap spotted a head with pitch-black hair bobbing through a cluster of hawkers. He did not see sparks of red in those tresses until . . .

Magiere pushed through, with Leesil behind her. She actually smiled for an instant before looking back to make sure she had not lost him. They looked happy.

Chap hesitated at ruining that. But it was not to be, as they climbed the ramp with Leesil now grimacing at boarding the ship again.

"How was *your* night?" Leesil asked. "All quiet?"

—*No*—

Chap watched tension flood Leesil's tan features. Magiere stepped in at Leesil's side and caught his expression. That one moment of relief, maybe happiness, that Chap had seen in her from afar instantly vanished.

"What happened?" she demanded. "Is Leanâlhâm all right?"

—*Leanâlhâm—is fine*— . . . —*Brot'an—left—the ship—last night*— . . . —*Come*—

Magiere winced at the rush of words but nodded. Chap repeated for Leesil as quickly as he could find the memory-words to match. Leesil was the first to head below.

Chap followed with Magiere, and once inside their cabin, Leesil dropped on a bunk's edge as Magiere closed the door and then joined him.

"What happened?" she asked.

Chap hesitated. Calling up the right memory-words would be laborious. He chose to raise the words for Magiere and let her tell Leesil. That especially might be best when it came to the mention of Cuirin'nên'a.

—*Brot'an—left—the ship—and—headed—into the woods*—

At a soft knock on the door, Chap's snort gave way to a growl. The door cracked open before anyone called out, and Leanâlhâm peeked in.

"You are all back," she said, appearing relieved.

Had she thought Chap was off the ship as well? He took one look at her face, and his exasperation vanished. She had been in her cabin all night with no one but Brot'an for company.

"May I come in?" she asked shyly.

"Of course," Magiere answered, though she frowned with a quick glance to Chap. "Next time we make port, you should come with us. You need to get off the ship whenever possible."

At that, Leanâlhâm looked less relieved.

Chap knew it would not be wise or kind to shoo the girl out in order to relate what little he had learned. He needed only three words easily found in both Leesil's and Magiere's memories.

—*Later—but—soon—*

CHAPTER NINE

Two days out of Kêdinern, Dänvârfij's ship docked in late afternoon at the port of Berhtburh. She immediately disembarked, though this time she took Rhysís with her. He never complained, but she could see he felt confined aboard the vessel.

Since the night in Kêdinern by the river's mouth, Eywodan had been too watchful, too silently concerned over her state of mind. Rhysís was more than able for any purpose, and he would never give note of her demeanor or ask her about her thoughts.

Still, she needed to stop dwelling upon the past. Some things could not—or need not—be changed.

There was more to Rhysís than met the eye in some ways. Dänvârfij preferred Anmaglâhk garb, even for everyday life, and felt out of place in these human clothes. She suspected Rhysís rather enjoyed their new disguises.

He had chosen his attire carefully and was now dressed in fine breeches and a deep blue tunic. Before, he had always worn his long hair loose, but now it was tied back with a matching but darker blue scarf that covered his head. To her, he looked ridiculous; the contrast of color with his eyes made them stand out too much. He had also discarded his sling and was trying to restrengthen the shoulder of his bow arm.

Berhtburh was larger and busier than Kêdinern and might almost qualify as a city. Here, among an apparent diversity of peoples and manners of attire, she and Rhysís would not stand out so much. Some men along the waterfront were nearly as tall as Rhysís; maybe one or two were as tall. But in their hide-and-fur clothing, and their long, coarse hair and shaggy beards, they looked more like animals than any other type of human she had ever encountered. Their weaponry, from axes and maces to war picks and hammers, betrayed a penchant for reckless carnage.

Two an'Cróan, or "elves" to these humans, passed with little notice along the bustling shoreline as they searched for a harbormaster's office.

"There," Rhysís said.

He pointed to a building no wider than a broad cutway, for it looked as if it had been built into the mouth of one, squeezed between one huge warehouse and a fishery. In the late afternoon heat, the stench from the fishery made Dänvârfij cover her mouth and nose.

When they reached the narrow building, Dänvârfij hesitated at bringing Rhysís inside. He spoke less Numanese than most of the team, but she changed her mind. At Kêdinern, the harbormaster would remember only a late middle-aged elf. Here, anyone present would remember a younger couple. It was best to mix any notice of their presence.

She ushered Rhysís in and followed him.

Inside was a typical harbormaster's office. Desks, maps, a telescope, cabinets full of drawers, and other things lay about in some organization she could not fathom, though the place was long and cramped compared to the wide one on the isle. Four clerks worked in the distance along the interior, for it was barely wide enough for both a desk and room to walk. All the clerks were dealing with either captains or sailors in a buzz of words she could not follow.

Then she noticed Captain Samara of the *Bashair*.

He was speaking to a wizened elderly man with thinning silver hair that curled around his ears. The stooped little human wore a leather vest that hung too loosely on him, but he gripped a finely crafted cudgel with a brass head shaped like a creature Dänvârfij had never seen.

This had to be the harbormaster, judging by a similar possession of the one on the isle.

Captain Samara spoke too low to hear, but his manner was overly polite, almost subservient. She studied the little harbormaster, and there was a nearly imperceptible hatred in his eyes.

"Until tomorrow, then," he almost shouted, his voice venomous. "Just be gone by midmorning."

Samara was the only dark-skinned Suman in the place. Perhaps the harbormaster did not care for him or his kind. The captain nodded once, quick and curt, as if wanting to be gone. When he turned to leave, he spotted Dänvârfij with Rhysís near the door.

"Do you require assistance?" he asked. "May I help with anything?"

"No," Dänvârfij said, "thank you."

Samara hesitated but then nodded and left. Rhysís glanced after the captain, but Dänvârfij found the harbormaster watching her the same way he had looked at Samara. She approached him cautiously.

"Pardon," she said and decided to use Eywodan's story. "We were . . . to catch . . . *Cloud Queen* . . . at Wrêdelyd. Our way from Calm Seatt . . . was delayed. Can you tell if ship . . . came here . . . and when left?"

The man's left cheek twitched at her broken Numanese, and he turned away. "This is a business office for captains and merchants. We don't cater to those who can't keep their own schedules."

He hobbled off, clutching his cudgel, and handed a paper to a clerk at the next desk down the narrow space.

Dänvârfij stared after him. Rhysís took a step to follow the harbormaster, but she barred his way with her arm.

She did not care for the little man's demeanor and might have favored extracting the information. That was not a wise choice in a busy port, even when dealing with one who appeared to hate other types of humans as much as he did her kind. She pressed her arm back a little to make Rhysís stay and went after the harbormaster.

"We have family on *Cloud Queen* . . . and need catch up," she said as an embellishment. "Please . . . can you say . . . when left here?"

"I don't give out information about ships leaving my harbor!" he barked. "Now get out."

A few others along the office, both patrons and staff, looked over.

Dänvârfij backed away and turned, finding Rhysís watching this exchange. A subtle scowl spread over his face. With a quick lift of her chin, she motioned him toward the door, and once they were outside, his features were tightly set.

"We wait until after nightfall," he said, quiet and calm. "I will get you an answer from him."

It was tempting and possibly their only option. She was about to agree when a young clerk slipped out the door. A shock of dark blond hair hung in his eyes, and his fingers were stained with blue ink.

"Pardon, miss," he said, offering a slight smile. "Don't mind the old badger. He treats almost everyone that way."

He held a large open book, covered in lines of writing, in his hands. Dänvârfij was wary and uncertain how to respond. She did not need to, as the young clerk looked up from scanning a page in the book.

"The *Cloud Queen* left harbor two days ago," he said, "heading for a cargo exchange at Chathburh. That's a big port, and I'd guess she'll be there several days. If you're sailing on the *Bashair*, Captain Samara won't stay here long. It's a small, fast ship, and you should catch your family, if fair weather holds."

After facing the harbormaster, Dänvârfij was slightly stunned by this human's polite helpfulness, to the point of following her out to offer assistance.

"Thank you," she said, and then chose to press for more while she could. "Can you say . . . *Cloud Queen*'s captain . . . if he say . . . passengers stay here? We are afraid to miss family . . . if they stay this place to wait on us."

She had learned from Samara that any captain dropping off passengers needed to at least report the number of people. Or so it seemed in major ports. The clerk glanced at the book and shook his head.

154 · BARB & J. C. HENDEE

"No, he didn't leave anyone . . . or none that he reported."

"Thank you," she said again, and he grinned once with a nod and went back inside.

Humans always confused Dänvârfij. They were savages who lived short and cruel lives in their limited awareness. That some could be generous only left her more disconcerted.

"We have the information, tenuous as it is," she told Rhysís. "We should return and inform Fréthfâre."

He looked up at the sun, still hanging in the sky. "We could go into this city first. In Calm Seatt, Én'nish mentioned a fondness for almonds covered in the humans' . . . chocolate. I thought to purchase some."

If he had announced that the Ancient Enemy stood right behind her, Dänvârfij would have been less surprised.

Rhysís had a reputation for near total silence, even when he had lost Wy'lanvi, his young friend, to Brot'ân'duivé's blade. Now he wished to buy sweets for Én'nish? Perhaps it was his need to have someone to watch over.

"She spends much time caring for Fréthfâre," he went on, "and little time caring for herself. A small comfort might be welcome."

Dänvârfij had already decided to indulge him. There was something more to his attentiveness, but she was not about to pry into his personal matters. And Én'nish did spend nearly all her time caring for the crippled ex-Covârleasa.

"We will find a sweet shop," she said.

Anmaglâhk lived lives of service requiring no such comforts. Whatever additional motivation Rhysís had for this act, Dänvârfij wondered whether perhaps they had all been among the humans too long.

By early evening, Dänvârfij was back aboard the *Bashair* and alone with Fréthfâre.

"Two days?" Fréthfâre said bitterly, shaking her head. "We are not closing the distance fast enough. We have gained half a day at best since our last stop."

After Rhysís had purchased his chocolate-coated almonds, Dänvârfij had returned feeling more confident about their chances to overtake Magiere's ship. Within moments of being trapped in this cabin and reminded by Fréth-fâre of her failures, she felt smothered by dark doubts once more.

"We cannot make this ship go faster," Dänvârfij replied, knowing she was being baited.

"Oh, but we can," Fréthfâre countered. "We take the ship for ourselves."

This had occurred to Dänvârfij as well. She would do so, if necessary, but such an action risked exposing her team. The young clerk at the harbormaster's office seemed to know Captain Samara—enough to speak well of him. Others in the office had seen her speaking to Samara. With so few in the office, someone could remember two tall elves with amber eyes.

She stepped to the cabin's one small porthole and gazed out at other ships docked along the next pier.

"That might bring undue attention," she returned, "should the event become known. The human clerk seemed certain we could catch our quarry at Chathburh. By the way the harbormaster rules his office—and all ships docking here—it is unlikely the captain of the *Cloud Queen* would have failed to report passengers disembarking permanently. It would be wiser to disembark at Chathburh and set a trap for them there."

She looked back to Fréthfâre, bent over on her bunk.

"Unless you would like me to consult Father first," Dänvârfij added.

That suggestion nearly always brought an end to Fréthfâre's manipulations. Most Aged Father would counsel them to wait, not risk commandeering a ship they could not sail themselves without keeping and controlling some of the crew.

"We will do as you suggest," Fréthfâre said tiredly. "And hope that Father's faith in you is no further undermined."

Dänvârfij said nothing more. Pricks and jabs from the vengeance-driven ex-Covârleasa were now too commonplace for her to feel them. But the small, stuffy cabin reminded her of being inside Father's heart-root chamber. She struggled again to push away the past—and the past pushed back.

She could not stop thinking of the day Brot'ân'duivé had forced his way into the great oak while Most Aged Father was questioning Osha. The greimasg'äh had not been down there long.

She had waited above, watching for him to reemerge. To her shock, Osha had come out with him. Not one of the sentries tried to stall them, and the one still rubbing his throat had backed away. Her instinct was to stop them and ask what had happened, but she had no authority.

Neither looked her way as they strode past. Clearly Most Aged Father had turned Osha over to Brot'ân'duivé.

Juan'yâre came out on their heels but only watched them with panic on his face. Then he spotted her.

"Come," he said, gesturing to Father's home.

She had nearly run forward, following him into the oak and down into the heart-root, only to find Father dark and pensive. All sign of tears had vanished from his dry, bony cheeks as he raised milky eyes to her and Juan'yâre.

With two fingers of a hand that did not lift from the moss, he urged Juan'yâre closer. Father whispered something to his new Covârleasa, and Juan'yâre's eyes widened slightly before he nodded.

"Yes, Father." And he rushed out.

Dänvârfij heard Juan'yâre's footfalls racing up the outer steps as Father turned his attention to her.

"Tell me more of this book, this journal, that you saw in Osha's possession."

She longed to tell him, but she had already given him everything she knew. This left her feeling she had disappointed him. But when she could tell him nothing more, he was only kind.

"Daughter," he said finally, "go above and tell two of your brethren to join us . . . but leave one sentry on the door."

She did so, but when she returned with the two, Most Aged Father waved her off.

"Go eat and rest, Daughter. You have served me and your people well."

Dänvârfij bowed her head and turned away, though she paused at the heart-root's entrance. The two young anmaglâhk leaned close to Father as he whispered quietly to them. And then she left.

Once outside, she breathed deeply to hold down grief and anger spawned not long ago. She was hungry, and so very tired inside, but still she looked about.

Brot'ân'duivé and Osha were nowhere to be seen. One anmaglâhk remained as a sentry—the same one Brot'ân'duivé had struck down—with his throat darkening in a bruise. He suddenly looked right past her without blinking.

"Greimasg'äh!" he said hoarsely and bowed his head.

At a loss, expecting to see Brot'ân'duivé, Dänvârfij turned to follow his gaze. It was not so, and her confusion doubled.

An elder anmaglâhk came striding purposefully behind Juan'yâre and toward her. This one was short and stocky by an'Cróan standards. Beardless like all male elves, his skin was rough and slightly pockmarked. Her lips parted in silence as he drew near.

It was Urhkarasiférin, another greimasg'äh like Brot'ân'duivé.

She stared as Urhkarasiférin, never looking her way, passed her. She could not bring herself to leave even after Juan'yâre pulled back the curtain and Urhkarasiférin entered without losing a stride. The new Covârleasa cast her one troubled glance before he quickly followed.

And still Dänvârfij stood there.

Only three of the Greimasg'äh remained among the people and the caste. None, and Brot'ân'duivé least of all, frequented Crijheäiche except for duties to the caste. Yet two had come here within less than a day.

What did it mean?

At a knock on the ship's cabin door, Dänvârfij straightened in sudden awareness.

"Covârleasa, may I enter?" Én'nish called.

She insisted on calling Fréthfâre by that title, though it was no longer accurate.

"Yes," Fréthfâre answered.

It took Dänvârfij a moment to ground herself as she turned from the porthole. Én'nish entered with a tray of steaming food and tea.

"Dinner was prepared early—herbed rice with salmon," she said to Fréthfâre. "You hardly ate lunch, and I thought you might be hungry."

The young anmaglâhk looked different, less angry, and perhaps even content. Dänvârfij wondered why, and then remembered the almonds. Rhysís must have given those to Én'nish by now.

Dänvârfij turned back to the porthole. For such a small thing like chocolate-covered almonds to produce such a change hinted that they had indeed been too long among humans.

CHAPTER TEN

Chap stood on deck near the port rail as the *Cloud Queen* sailed on toward Chathburh. Under the breeze that drove the ship, the distant shoreline slipped by at a leisurely pace beneath a cloud-coated sky. No further incidents had occurred with either Magiere or Leanâlhâm, so Captain Bassett had relented, letting the passengers spend more time on deck. They could not be expected to pass the whole voyage in their cabins.

Magiere had settled to half sit on a tall barrel, midship near the cargo hatch, and appeared content in watching ahead. Leanâlhâm stood nearby with her back to Chap, but when the girl turned her head, he saw unhappiness in her profile. She tensed if a sailor passed too close in rushing about his duties. Leesil clutched the rail tighter every time the ship crested a swell. Still pale, at least he had begun to get his "sea legs," as one sailor had jibed. He'd been coming up on deck more frequently and kept his food down more often. But Chap didn't think too long on his companions.

Instead, he pondered Brot'an's excursion into the woods north of Berhtburh. The old assassin stood a dozen paces beyond Leesil, nearer the forecastle, and with arms folded and face expressionless, he stared blankly toward the distant passing shore.

Chap had told Magiere and Leesil of trailing Brot'an. Most of what he'd overheard that night was still unclear, even when combined with what

Magiere had learned. Chap was determined to gain more until he'd stripped Brot'an of every secret.

Wynn had given Osha a special journal. At the same time, Leesil's mother and Brot'an, as well as the aging healer, Gleann, had already been part of the dissidents working to undermine Most Aged Father. Upon Osha's return to his people, he had been detained. Last and most disturbing, Brot'an could communicate with Cuirin'nên'a and other dissidents on the world's far side.

And there was that strange bit of polished wood in Brot'an's possession.

From fragments in Wynn's memories during their journey to her homeland, Chap knew something of her errant journal. The rest of these recently gained bits of information were revelations, though as yet none of it connected to why Brot'an had brought Osha and Leanâlhâm to this continent.

Perhaps here and now the best choice was for Leesil to take on Brot'an next, under Chap's supervision and without Magiere.

Chap glanced around, wondering how to get her out of the way. Another sailor rushed by, hauling a bucket that slopped seawater onto the deck. Leanâlhâm backed up, almost tripping over the cargo hatch's edge.

"I think I . . . I will go below," she said nervously.

Magiere frowned. "It does no good to hide all the time."

There was Chap's chance. He called up memory-words in Leanâlhâm's mind.

—*Say—you—are—cold—and need to—get out of—the wind—*

The girl stiffened, blinking as she spun toward Chap.

"What did I tell you about that?" Magiere growled at him.

Chap wanted to groan in annoyance. The girl had about as much guile as a half-witted toddler!

"It is nothing," Leanâlhâm replied, still eyeing Chap, and then she hesitantly looked to Magiere. "I am . . . I am getting cold. That is all."

At least she made a show of pulling her cloak tighter, and perhaps she was cold.

Magiere's brow wrinkled. She looked suspiciously at Chap, and then with a huffing sigh she pushed off the barrel and took Leanâlhâm's hand.

"Come on. We'll see if we can get some hot tea in you."

The two headed off for the aftcastle door and below.

"That was about as subtle as a rock to the head."

At Leesil's half-voiced snipe, Chap looked up.

"You're lucky Magiere wouldn't think Leanâlhâm was in on it," Leesil added.

As if knowing what this was truly about, Leesil turned toward Brot'an. An echo of Chap's own malice washed over Leesil's tan but paled features.

Brot'an never looked their way, as if he didn't know what was coming. Chap knew better, and that this would not be easy.

"Let's get on with it," Leesil whispered.

Three sailors sat within hearing, busily repairing a spare sail. The captain was on the aftcastle with his first mate, and the pilot was at the wheel. It was time to make a few things clear to Brot'an, but before Chap and Leesil even got close . . .

"Is there something you two want?" Brot'an asked in fluent Belaskian.

—Go—at him—with—what—we know— . . . *—Force him—off guard— for me—*

To Leesil's credit, he didn't flinch or betray that Chap had said anything with memory-words. Chap did not even need to guide him in the first assault. Leesil fired back in Belaskian, so that no one nearby would understand.

"Tell me how—and why—you were talking to my mother. What in seven hells have you gotten her into now?"

Brot'an would first see only a son who'd suffered a long life of guilt and a long journey, years back, to find and free his mother. Nein'a—Cuirin'nên'a—in being suspected as a dissident had been imprisoned for more than a decade in a remote glade. Brot'an, amid defending Magiere during her trial before the an'Cróan's council of elders, had a hand in freeing her. But Leesil—and Chap—never forgot one more fact.

Brot'an did nothing unless it served his own ends.

It wasn't easy to surprise him. Perhaps one of his amber eyes—the one between those four scars—twitched once at Leesil's first assault. Leesil didn't let up.

"Magiere told us Most Aged Father sent a ship after Osha . . . to bring him in like some criminal, and that you went to Origin-Heart to find out why. What did they do to Osha? What was in that journal Wynn gave him, and what does it have to do with anything?"

Brot'an, still silent, glanced down at Chap—this also was no surprise. Brot'an was no fool. He knew well that Chap could feed Leesil questions to ask aloud. Brot'an knew which of the two he now faced was the greater danger.

Still, Chap was frustrated that he couldn't penetrate the shadow-gripper's mind, let alone speak to him directly.

The old assassin could have reacted any number of ways to Leesil's interrogation. He could have turned the tables and demanded more of what had happened in the Wastes before offering anything in exchange. Leesil would have given him nothing for that. Brot'an could have tried to walk away, though Chap would have cut him off.

Instead Brot'an turned his back to the sea, leaned leisurely against the rail, and closed his eyes.

It was so submissive that Chap became wary, though Leesil grew visibly angry.

"You've started killing your own kind," Leesil said. "What have you pulled my mother into with all this bloodshed between you and your caste?"

Chap would have cursed aloud, if he could have.

—No— . . . *—Press—him—about—Osha—* . . . *—Stay focused—on— what leads to—the journal—*

Brot'an opened his eyes and regarded Leesil tiredly. "Léshil," he sighed.

Chap knew they had faltered. Leesil put himself at a disadvantage in focusing on his mother; that was not the way to put Brot'an in a corner.

—Osha—not—Nein'a—is—the way—to make—him—slip—

Leesil took a hissing breath through clenched teeth, and Chap almost shouted into his head again.

"What happened to Osha when he got back?" Leesil asked.

The question came out with much reluctance, and Brot'an would not miss this.

"I freed him," Brot'an answered flatly, "and took him from Most Aged Father and out of Crijheäiche. But I did not know how determined the patriarch would be to gain the journal."

"What was in the journal?"

Brot'an glanced away and down, shaking his head.

Brot'ân'duivé hesitated. Léshil likely viewed his questions as easy to answer—and they were not. Cuirin'nên'a's mother, the great Eillean and Brot'ân'duivé's secret love, was one founder of the dissident movement. Cuirin'nên'a had followed in her mother's ways and sacrificed much to bring her half-blooded son into this world and train him beyond the caste's reach.

It was necessary that Léshil remain outside the influence of any one people, culture, or division, so that none could cast blame or claim success in the face of any other faction. It would also be easier to keep him free for what would come, and to direct—control—him amid his feelings of being cast adrift in the world.

At least all of this could have been, if Léshil had not fled his parents and run into Magiere. And the one who orchestrated that meeting was obvious.

Brot'ân'duivé did not look at Chap in this moment. No one could have known back then what hid within a majay-hì puppy that a grandmother delivered secretly through a mother to a lonely half-blooded boy.

Only after Eillean's watchful suspicions were satisfied had Brot'ân'duivé even been allowed contact with other dissidents. But he believed that Léshil should now be privy to some of the truth. The mixed-race grandson of the one Brot'ân'duivé loved—and had lost—had a pivotal role in their plans, should the worst come and the Ancient Enemy of many names return. If nothing else, giving Léshil some information might be one step to pulling him back on course until a destination could be found for him.

But Léshil was not the only one listening—nor truly the one asking these questions.

Brot'ân'duivé feared sharing anything with the deviant majay-hì.

"So, you got Osha out of Origin-Heart?" Léshil pressed again. "Was he all right?"

"No," Brot'ân'duivé answered. "But nothing adverse happened in his meeting with Most Aged Father."

Perhaps this was the place to start, on a course that could divert Chap to something superficially satisfying. And it might put this pair in his debt. A debt he could collect from Magiere.

"Osha was exhausted," he continued, "from many days of travel . . . and the loss of his jeóin, Sgäilsheilleache."

The aggression on Léshil's face faded slightly. "I know he was."

Brot'ân'duivé knew that he had underestimated how heartsick Osha had been. At times he wondered whether he felt things to the same degree as others. Perhaps a life of discipline automatically disallowed this. When it came to even those who mattered to him, this had more than once caused him to be shortsighted where they were concerned.

He recounted to himself the details of that day when he had led the weary, emotionally damaged young anmaglâhk through the forest on a long journey to the main enclave of the Coilehkrotall clan. Simply knowing that they headed to the home of Gleannéohkân'thva appeared to give the young one strength. Osha might recover among people who cared for him—the family of his jeóin, who shared his loss just as deeply.

"I led him through our land, making certain we were not followed," Brot'ân'duivé began. "He told me in detail of what happened between Hkuan'duv and Sgäilsheilleache. I do not need to repeat this . . . as you were there."

Léshil's gaze hardened. Perhaps he, as well, had suffered the loss of Sgäilsheilleache.

From sheer exhaustion, Osha had fallen silent for the remainder of that day until they made camp. Sitting by the fire, he finally began to speak, telling Brot'ân'duivé more that would shake the foundation of their caste. Hkuan'duv and Sgäilsheilleache were not the first to die in an effort to steal the artifact from Magiere. Most Aged Father had sent a team of four after her. Along the way, two skilled senior anmaglâhk—A'harhk'nis and Kurhkâge—had been lost in the Pock Peaks.

Brot'ân'duivé could barely account for the ramifications: four of their finest dead because of Most Aged Father's paranoia. No one outside the patriarch's closest circle had learned of this until Osha's return. Even then less than a handful knew the truth.

Such information was more evidence to wrest control of the caste from that too-long-lived madman—and Most Aged Father had known this. But sitting by the fire that night with Osha, Brot'ân'duivé kept all of this to himself, as well as the message stone from the Chein'âs delivered by a séyilf.

Osha had been too raw, broken, and unprepared for another purpose.

"Spit it out!" Léshil barked. "What was in that journal?"

"Little of use," he answered. "But Most Aged Father did not know that."

Late that night in camp, once Osha had rested, he had suddenly grown wary and glanced about the forest.

"There is no one here but us," Brot'ân'duivé had assured him.

Still hesitant, Osha had pulled a small book from inside his tunic, held it out, and explained how he came by it.

Brot'ân'duivé looked directly at Léshil and ignored Chap.

"The irony was that Wynn intended the journal for only me," he said, "and Osha would have rather died than fail her. She wanted me to know the basics of what happened in the Pock Peaks."

"Wynn did this?" Léshil asked in mixed surprise and anger.

"Not everyone doubts me as you do," he answered dryly. "She is as aware as any of you—perhaps more—that Most Aged Father is mad with fear."

No, Wynn's sending him information had not surprised him. What had was Osha's reluctance to speak of the sage at all, as if any mention of her caused him pain. The young one had simply delivered the journal as he had sworn to do.

"Wynn intended to place information in my hands, should I need it," Brot'ân'duivé added. "And as it was so intended, it is at my discretion to tell you anything within it . . . or not."

Léshil's expression turned livid. Chap began to rumble, his hackles rising as his ears flattened.

Brot'ân'duivé softened his voice as he looked Léshil in the eyes and remembered the first of many times he had paged through Wynn's delivered journal.

"It was difficult to read, between her hurried scrawl and the strange dialect she used, but it became easier with effort. The account was not long and simply covered the basic events of your journey . . . from the beginning."

Skimming toward the end, he had carefully read a brief account of what happened inside a six-towered castle in the Pock Peaks, and how the artifact had been carried out. When he reached the passages describing the Everfen, he had stopped and tucked the journal inside his shirt for later study. He had gained the basics, and for the remainder of that night he had focused on tending Osha.

"Wynn gave away no deep secrets," he said. "Again, she only gave me the basics of what happened, perhaps in case Most Aged Father attempted to twist the truth . . . which he will . . . which he has. Who beside me could stand against him in that? Certainly not her . . . or you."

"You told Magiere the journal was at the heart of whatever changed Osha and Leanâlhâm from the people we knew."

"It was, for them and others," Brot'ân'duivé answered. "Most Aged Father believed the journal held information pertaining to the artifact—the first orb. I did not realize until too late how far he would go."

Léshil frowned and glanced down at Chap, perhaps to formulate his next question . . . or for Chap to give him one. The majay-hì never looked at Léshil. Chap's gaze remained fixed on Brot'ân'duivé, but it would do him no good.

How could the majay-hì hope to snatch a memory from a shadow-gripper?

For one who could use his will to sink in silence and in shadow, in both thought and flesh, memory could be as willfully hidden. As long as Chap was watching, Brot'ân'duivé would always be hiding, even—especially—in plain sight of this majay-hì. He would bury Chap in darkness if he had to.

The ship lurched up another swell and this time fell sharply.

Brot'ân'duivé looked up. The overcast sky had darkened and so had the sea. The waves were mounting higher.

"All passengers below," Captain Bassett shouted from the aftcastle. "Might be some rough weather ahead."

Suddenly weary, Brot'ân'duivé left the rail and headed for the stairs below the aftcastle.

"What next?" Léshil called after him. "Did you get Osha back to the enclave?"

"Yes," Brot'ân'duivé answered without halting. "And that is enough for now."

He could have told Léshil more, but that did not serve his need. Simplified truths were always the most undetectable of lies.

Leesil watched Brot'an walk away as Chap snarled and took a step after the master anmaglâhk. He quickly reached down to grab the dog by the scruff.

"No," Leesil whispered. "Let him go . . . for now."

Unless Brot'an felt like talking, they wouldn't get anything more out of him. Since he had the excuse of the rising storm, chasing him down would get them nowhere, especially after he locked himself away in his cabin. Better to try again later, but soon, when they could catch him off guard.

Even when Brot'an did talk, he gave away so little, and Leesil had more than once wanted to turn the talk back to his mother. But Chap had kept at him about Osha as the way to learn more of what happened due to Wynn's journal.

Leesil wanted to kick Wynn in the seat of her pants for that stupid book.

The whole time he'd been trying to get at Brot'an, he'd had a lingering feeling—no, a certainty—that the shadow-gripper said less than he knew. Sighing, Leesil took his hand from Chap's fur.

"Too bad you can't get inside his head."

Chap's rumble sharpened into a sudden snarl—and the ship bucked again.

Leesil's lunch threatened to come up. He grew miserable, thinking the storm might put him back in his bunk.

"Come on," he choked out. "Let's see how Magiere and Leanâlhâm are doing."

Leesil pulled himself along the rail to within reach of the aftcastle's forward wall. Chap crept along ahead of him and more than once lost his footing as the deck dampened with sea spray. They ducked into the steep steps leading below, and Leesil jerked the deck door closed. When he stepped down into the lower passage behind Chap, Magiere slipped out of Leanâlhâm's cabin as Brot'an was about to enter.

"She's resting," Magiere told Brot'an quietly. "I don't think she slept well last night. If she wakes and this weather scares her, tell her she can come to our cabin."

"She will be fine with me," Brot'an returned, and before Magiere could argue, he slipped into the cabin and shut the door.

"What's wrong with him?" she asked, spotting Leesil down the passage.

"Tell you later. Let's get back to our room . . . before I re-enjoy my lunch."

As he came toward her with one hand against the wall, she grew visibly concerned and reached for him. Chap was not beside him, and he looked about.

There was Chap, sitting on his rump and glaring at Brot'an's cabin door.

"Are you coming in?" Leesil asked.

—No—

The ship rocked sharply and didn't right itself quickly enough.

Chap slid backward, and his butt hit the passage's wall. Leesil slid, too, struggling to stay on his feet. He was getting too sick to care about Chap's foul temper in *trying* to sit vigil at Brot'an's door.

Magiere grabbed Leesil's wrist and pulled him into the cabin. Once inside, Leesil left the door open in case Chap changed his mind. The door kept swinging on its own with every roll of the ship.

"What's going on?" Magiere asked, as Leesil stumbled onto a bunk.

Her hair was in a single braid, but long strands had escaped to hang and float around her pale face. Groaning, he tried to answer in between the roiling in his stomach. He managed to relate what little Brot'an had said.

"Is that why that obstinate mutt is sliding around in the passage?" Magiere asked. "Because Brot'an didn't tell you enough? What were you two thinking?"

Leesil was almost too sick to fight back. "What do you expect? That we'd just sit on our hands . . . paws . . . until Brot'an blackmails more out of you than he'll give?"

"He's not going to give up anything while Chap's in plain sight."

"We know that!" Leesil shot back. "But what else can we try while we're stuck on this bucket, waiting for it to sink?"

"Oh, stop it," Magiere told him, and another bang of the cabin door against the wall pulled her attention. "At least Chap's watching someone beside *me* this time."

"That you know of," Leesil grumbled, "and only because you don't have the orb to . . ."

Leesil bit his lip as Magiere whirled on him. They'd barely regained part of the distance between them since leaving the Wastes. He had no wish to endanger that by treading on dangerous ground.

The ship rocked sharply.

Just before the door slammed completely shut, they both heard scrambling of claws on wood. Magiere suddenly toppled to the bunk's end as the whole cabin tilted. A loud thump carried from out in the passage and was instantly followed by a sharp yelp and a snarl. Leesil moaned, digging his fingers into the mattress to keep from falling into Magiere.

"Go get him," he told her, "before he ends up knocked out cold . . . or slides all the way into the cargo hold!"

The cabin leveled but then began tilting the other way. Magiere grabbed the bunk's end and made her way up to snatch the cabin door's handle and pull it. The door swung sharply inward, and she grabbed the door's outer handle as well and half dangled there for a moment.

Another thump echoed loudly out in the passage and was followed by another irritated snarl.

"Chap, damn you, get in here . . . now!" Magiere shouted, clawing her way up the door.

On the next tilt of the cabin, Leesil flopped onto the mattress and clung to it. He lay there in misery, unable to stop the memories, all from that one bitter slip he'd almost made with Magiere.

And only because you don't have the orb to . . .

His thoughts slipped back to the Wastes. . . .

Leesil ran beside the sled for days until he was numb inside as well as out. He and Chap had given up trying to keep Magiere from slipping her *thôrhk*'s knobs into the orb spike's grooves every few nights. It was her way to readjust their direction.

To Leesil's best awareness—and he was certain Chap kept vigil at night— she did this only in their presence and never tried to pull the spike by even half an inch. She didn't need to, or so she claimed, but the look on her face, and her occasional tears, made every muscle in Leesil's body tighten until she took her *thôrhk* off that cursed orb.

And in the mornings she redirected Ti'kwäg if necessary.

Magiere never said anything about where they were going. Either she didn't know or she wasn't sure or she wasn't telling them.

Leesil was sick inside at the thought of what this could mean. How could the orb be directing her—and why? He kept thinking back to the voice that had whispered in her dreams . . . directing her to the orb's original hiding place. She swore this time was different.

He didn't believe her.

At this journey's start, he'd believed they suffered these hardships, so very far from their home and their tavern, to hide the orb someplace where Most Aged Father or the Enemy's minions would never find it. Now Magiere had succumbed to some other unnatural drive.

Between Leesil and Chap, they watched her day and night as they pressed onward, farther north and east. Even Chap knew they had no choice. They had to keep going until they found a safe place to hide the orb. They seemed to agree that they'd know the right place when they saw it, and in that they let Magiere have her way for now. But the farther north they went, the more barren and bleak the land became, until calling it "land" wasn't even funny as a joke.

Endless white around them hurt their eyes. More than half of their supplies were gone. Foraging was pointless, and the temperature was below freezing at all times.

Ti'kwäg began rationing the oil burned in the bone lamp. Its tiny flame barely kept their shelter a hair above the freezing temperature outside. In spite of the strange nature of this journey, their guide never questioned Magiere about where she was leading them. He kept to his duties, though at times it was clear he had concerns about their dwindling oil and rations.

Leesil began wondering how they could make it back to the coast, even if they succeeded in their task. One day when they'd pushed beyond the time they would usually stop, Ti'kwäg pointed ahead.

The guide had the lower half of his face covered with a rabbit fur that he always tied around the back of his head before fastening his hood. Leesil couldn't see the man's expression, but Ti'kwäg's gaze was steadily fixed on something ahead.

Leesil squinted, trying to make out what it was. At first all he noticed was wind-driven snow strangely piled as if built up on something left on the frigid plain. Then he saw a smoke trail above a dome.

"What is it?" Magiere called from where she jogged behind the sled.

"A settlement," Ti'kwäg called back. "A good thing for us."

It wasn't long before the sled slipped between a number of ice domes caked in snow. Leesil staggered to a halt and bent to brace his hands on his knees. Looking down, he saw that he'd almost stepped into a hole in the ice, and he shuffled back from it.

"For fishing," Ti'kwäg called as he began checking his dog team.

Chap was looking all ways with obvious worry. The flap of the fur that Leesil had prepped and tied around the dog kept getting into Chap's face.

Ti'kwäg was a careful sort who always appeared to know what he was doing. He'd not likely have led them somewhere dangerous. Before Leesil could ask about this place, small people covered in furs came crawling out of hide-curtained holes in the domes. Ti'kwäg pulled down his rabbit fur and smiled as he began babbling in a language Leesil had never heard.

Brown skinned, all bulked up in their fur clothing, the people smiled back, all of them chattering at the same time as they closed around the guide and his sled. A young woman broke from the pack and came toward Leesil. She held a small bowl that steamed heavily in the cold. When she neared, he saw the bowl was nearly filled with a rich brown fluid.

Shiny black hair escaped from under the top of her furred hood and down her round forehead. Her skin was darker than his. She peered at him and blinked her thin eyes, each barely a slit in her face, until an expression of wonder took over.

Leesil started to get a little uncomfortable, and then she broke into a great grin and shoved the steaming bowl toward his hands.

"Apkalawok!" she chattered at him.

"Thank you," he said, taking the bowl and not knowing what else to do. She lifted her hands, cupped together, and pantomimed a motion of drinking.

Whatever was in the bowl smelled something like a broth. He tasted it carefully and found it wasn't quite as hot as it looked. He gulped half of it down, though it left a greasy film in his mouth. Then he pointed to Chap, who was off behind the sled and watching a couple of bulky-bundled children eyeing the dog in turn.

"Some for him?" he asked, pointing to Chap and then the bowl. But when he looked down, he was startled. Now three young women instead of one stared at him.

One of the new girls giggled and touched a fur-covered hand to her cheek, just below her right eye. The other new girl squeaked something back that began with, "Ooooooooh."

Leesil needed no translation. They were discussing his amber-colored eyes, and he swallowed hard at the way the second girl leaned in a little in peering at him.

At that, the first one whispered something to the others, placed one of her wrists on top of the second girl's wrist, and mimed tying something invisible around them. This made them burst into a fresh fit of giggling; one of them was blushing so much he could see it, even through her dark skin.

They were all grinning at him.

"Ah, not this, not now," Leesil moaned. The last thing he needed was more girls looking at him like a catch for handfasting, or marriage, or . . . something else. He looked about for help.

Magiere still hung back beyond Chap. Four men among the group had separated to one side and were talking in low voices. One glanced away toward Magiere.

"Come on," Leesil called, frantically waving her over and trying to ignore his admirers. "It's broth, and it won't stay warm long."

Magiere took a few steps to round Chap and the sled.

One of the young women turned, looking to where Leesil called. She froze, and then grabbed one of her companions' arms. All three went silent, though Leesil couldn't see their faces anymore.

More of the short natives spotted Magiere. Their chattering faded, as did their smiles. One among the cluster of four men said something to Ti'kwäg. The guide glanced at Magiere, shook his head at the four, and uttered something short and sharp in their tongue. At a guess, it sounded to Leesil like a caustic rebuke.

"What's wrong?" he called.

"Nothing," Ti'kwäg answered. "She is . . . very tall for a woman, and her skin is very white."

This simple but strained reply left Leesil wondering if that was all there was to it.

Ti'kwäg intercepted Magiere. "We sleep indoors and eat hot food tonight. Tomorrow we will trade here and then move on."

She nodded, but she, too, noticed the others watching her as she circled around them to join Leesil. Everyone except perhaps those four men appeared to accept Ti'kwäg's assurances. The trio of girls hurried off amid whispers.

"You think you could avoid the local girls just once?" Magiere growled.

"That's not . . . I never . . . wouldn't even think . . ." Leesil bumbled out.

Magiere glanced sidelong at him from the corner of her eye. Her teasing him wasn't much relief after that strange, tense moment.

Leesil soon found himself crawling along a narrow snow tunnel into one of the ice-dome dwellings. Emerging into an area beneath the dome, he was surprised at the warmth inside. Oil burning in large bowls heated the entire room and yet the ice did not melt. The floor was lined with furs, and as he began stripping off his heavy coat, he smiled when Magiere crawled out in the open.

"I didn't think I'd ever feel warm again," he said.

She tried to smile back.

Chap squirmed out of the tunnel with Ti'kwäg on his tail. There was more chatter, followed by a few stern looks in Chap's direction as several of the people came in as well.

"Their dogs sleep outside," Ti'kwäg explained. "I had to convince them that he always stays with you."

Chap rumbled softly, possibly offended, but he looked around with a sigh of satisfaction at all the furs on the floor. Then Magiere took off her gloves and pulled down her hood, and even before she'd stripped off her coat, gasps and more low chatter filled the space.

She froze with her coat barely off her shoulders.

The small native people stared from her face to her hands. Too many talked at once in hushed voices, though Leesil heard one sharp word repeated several times—*"Kalaallisut!"*

Ti'kwäg barked something at them and shook his head adamantly.

"What's wrong?" Magiere asked.

This time Leesil was more than worried. They were in too small a space should this turn ugly. Ti'kwäg held up one palm toward Magiere.

"It is nothing," he answered again, and then continued some argument with several of the others. A few finally nodded, but with another glance at Magiere, they turned one by one to crawl back out of the tunnel.

"They will bring food," Ti'kwäg said, settling on the furs near Magiere. "But for better or worse, no one will share this communal space with us. They are a generous but superstitious people. Your skin . . . and your hair . . ."

At that he stopped and began removing his coat. Magiere finished stripping off her own.

"What about my skin and hair?" she asked.

Leesil scooted in on Magiere's side, and Chap circled, finally settling off to Ti'kwäg's left and nearer the entrance. Leesil still wasn't accustomed to not being cold, but he was more interested in what the guide hadn't finished saying.

"Stories . . . legends are real to them," Ti'kwäg went on, "such as tales of pale creatures who live out in the heart of the ice beyond where these people will go." He shook his head. "Some speak of shapes or shadows in the blizzards that they call 'the others,' or the *Kalaallisut*. There is not a word for it in your language. It means something like a thing of ice or white that moves, but the word is not for a living being."

Leesil saw Chap listening with rapt attention, and too often the dog glanced at Magiere. Not because of any suggested link to her, but rather because, at Leesil's guess, he and Chap were both wondering what was out there, where she was leading them . . . and why and how.

"Too many stories," Ti'kwäg said with a shrug, "that always end with searchers who find no trace of those who went too far into the deep white. Stories for an ignorant people with ancestors who were lost, starved, or frozen out there . . . or who fell through ice or were dragged off by the great bears."

Leesil shifted in discomfort at the natives' having viewed Magiere as something "white" and not alive.

"Do not concern yourself," Ti'kwäg said. "They are just stories."

Leesil knew he should be grateful that their guide had dismissed all this so readily, but he wasn't. He was relieved when food was brought and the whole topic came to an end.

There were more bowls of the same greasy broth, along with fatty meats so tender they came apart at his touch. None of it looked appetizing at first, but then he thought he'd never tasted anything so good in his life. He had to force himself to stop after three helpings—and to almost physically pull an emptied bowl out of Chap's jaws.

There were also bowls of clean, warm water, intended for washing by the way Ti'kwäg took one and sank his hands into it.

Magiere seemed slightly more at ease after Ti'kwäg's assurances, but she ate only one serving. After washing up, and her long struggle getting grease off Chap's muzzle and whiskers, she curled up beneath a pile of furs with Leesil. They slept soundly for once.

At dawn, trading commenced. Leesil handled this with Ti'kwäg's assistance, as bartering didn't always require a shared language. All he needed to do was indicate goods and supplies offered and raise fingers as counts of exchange for what he sought. Tobacco, herbs, and sugar proved especially popular.

Unfortunately, though the people traded dried meat and fish readily enough, they were reluctant to part with much oil. Ti'kwäg said they were storing up for a long winter.

"They are nomadic in this season," he told Leesil as he repacked the sled. "We may come across more settlements on the move."

By midmorning they were running beside the sled again, heading northeast across the frozen plain. Magiere appeared relieved, but as countless days passed, the temperature continued to drop. Days grew shorter and nights grew longer.

Soon Leesil forgot what it had felt like to sleep without his coat in that warm little dome of ice. He remembered only being cold and chewing dried fish that had frozen to other pieces inside its bag. Ti'kwäg often broke their supper apart with a heavy hunting knife and seared it over the whalebone lamp's small flame. He began rationing their oil even more.

One night, as Ti'kwäg and Magiere began binding and bending the wooden rods to support the hide shelter, Leesil noticed Chap, exhausted and shaking visibly, standing near the sled. The sight made him angry. He longed to do something to help his oldest friend, but, aside from the tiny amount of heating oil Ti'kwäg allowed them to burn, they had nothing else to fuel a true fire.

Leesil dropped to his knees in the snow. In frustration he began rummaging through his pack. There had to be something to burn, anything to put a little extra heat into the shelter. He found a few pieces of spare clothing, a thin rope, a grappling hook . . . and then his hand closed over something slender and solid at the pack's bottom.

Pulling it out, Leesil studied the strange object in his hand. He'd almost forgotten it was there among his meager belongings.

The narrow wooden tube, barely wider than his thumb, had no seams at all, as if it had been fashioned from a single piece of wood. It was rounded at its bottom end, and its open top was sealed with an unadorned pewter cap. The whole of it was barely as long as his forearm, and what it held inside . . .

Back in the Elven Territories of the an'Cróan, Magiere had been placed on trial before the council of the clan elders. Most Aged Father had denounced her as an undead. To speak on her behalf, Leesil had to prove he was an an'Cróan and accepted by their ancestors regardless of his mixed blood. He'd allowed Sgäile to lead him to their ancestral burial grounds for his name-taking, a custom observed by all an'Cróan in their early years before adulthood. From whatever the young elves experienced in that place, they took a new name, though they never shared the true experience with anyone. Well, most didn't. Amid the burial ground's clearing stood a tree like no other Leesil had ever heard of, let alone seen.

Roise Chârmune, as they called it, was barkless though alive. It glowed tawny all over, shimmering in the dark. The ancestors not only accepted Leesil, they had *given* him a name . . . put it on him . . . before he even understood what it meant. He'd tried never to think of it since he'd left that land.

Leshiârelaohk—Sorrow-Tear's Champion.

Among the ghosts—the an'Cróan's first ancestors—in that place had been one woman, an elder among those who had first journeyed across the world to that land. And her name was, had been, Leshiâra—Sorrow-Tear.

All those ghosts had tried to put some fate, like a curse, upon Leesil. He neither wanted nor accepted it. They believed he would play a destined role as her champion, whatever that meant. Leesil had no intention of championing anyone but Magiere. But that wasn't all they'd done to him—given him.

He gripped the tube's cap, and his fur-covered hand slipped twice before he could get the stopper out. He dropped the cap and tilted the tube until its narrow contents slipped out into his hand. This item was the proof he'd needed when he returned to Magiere's trial. He'd been accepted by the ancestors and had the right to testify before the council of clan elders. He had taken this thing from the very hand of a translucent ghost, one warrior among those ancestors. The branch had been tawny and barkless, glistening and glowing, and as alive as the central tree from which it had come.

Leesil turned even colder in the near dark of the Wastes as he looked upon it.

The branch had turned to gray, dried, dead wood.

After Magiere was released, at last acquitted of Most Aged Father's charges against her, Leesil had forgotten all about the branch. He'd wanted nothing to do with it until Sgäile had returned it to him in this new case on their journey to seek the orb in the Pock Peaks.

Leesil hadn't wanted it back as a reminder of what those ghosts tried to do to him with a name. Sgäile had appeared offended, hurt, so Leesil had simply shoved the branch and its case into his pack. He'd never even looked at it again until now.

All the branch offered now was a slim chance to give Chap a moment of warmth. If Leesil could use a little oil to ignite it, perhaps along with the tube, they might trap a little extra heat in the tent. He looked up, about to call to Chap, but his grip faltered.

The branch slipped from his mitten and he tried to grab it but dropped the tube as well. His hand was so numb that he was too late. The grayed, dead branch toppled into the snow. Cursing to himself, he reached down for it.

Snow around the branch appeared to melt a little, or at least its moisture somehow spread over the gray wood. As he blinked, the branch began to change, and he drew his hand back.

Gray receded under the spread of a tint. Soon it appeared to swell a little. The last mark of death vanished from the branch, as did any stain of moisture. It became the glistening, tawny, living thing that he had first gripped in the an'Cróan burial ground of their first ancestors.

How could it have changed back to what it had been? And only upon touching the snow—frozen water.

"Chap?"

Leesil barely heard Magiere's call, and then it came more loudly in panic.

"Chap!"

Leesil looked over his shoulder. Chap lay limp on the crusted snow; the flap of fur from the hide tied around his torso hid his head.

Leaving the branch behind, Leesil scrambled up into a run. He crashed down on his knees beside Chap's limp form before Magiere even got there, and ripped back the flap of fur covering Chap's head. The dog's eyes were closed, and worst of all, he was no longer shivering.

"What's wrong?" Magiere half shouted behind Leesil.

Leesil shoved his arms under Chap and heaved the dog up. When he tried to stand, he almost fell under Chap's sagging weight. Magiere braced him from behind and tried to help grip Chap.

"No!" Leesil ordered. "Get the bedding out . . . now!"

He made a stumbling run for the shelter before she could say another word. All he could think of was something he'd seen in his youth, in the Warlands. On occasion, in deep winter, some fool or unfortunate child had fallen into the lake that surrounded his master's keep. The victim's body temperature needed to be raised as quickly as possible.

Leesil hit his knees again at the shelter's mouth and didn't wait for a startled Ti'kwäg to move. He struggled to shove Chap into the shelter and was already stripping off his outer clothing by the time Magiere crawled in with an armload of skins and furs.

"Lay some of those out," he said. "Use most to shield him from the snow beneath."

When she had two furs spread, Leesil stripped the fur off Chap and flopped the dog atop the bedding. He snatched the knife Magiere had used to gouge holes for the shelter's poles, and he slashed the straps of his hauberk. After removing his hauberk, he took off his wool pullover and even his shirt.

Magiere watched in confusion, but the instant Leesil grabbed three more furs at once and crawled over Chap, she began pulling off her own coat and armor. Neither of them even noticed Ti'kwäg watching her, looking her up and down as more pale skin was exposed.

Leesil pulled Chap in against himself, and the dog's paws were almost as painfully cold as the snow outside. Chap didn't move at all.

Ti'kwäg stared in astonishment at what Leesil was doing . . . for a dog. Magiere dropped to her knees, half-naked, and burrowed in on Chap's other side. Leesil pulled the remaining furs over all of them.

"Get some heat in here!" he snarled at Ti'kwäg.

Leesil stuck his face against Chap's muzzle and gained the barest relief when he felt the dog's weak breaths.

"Do it now," Leesil told the guide, and Ti'kwäg turned to digging out the oil.

All Leesil could do was press his face against Chap's.

"Wake up, you mangy mutt," he whispered. "Don't you die on me, you pain in the ass!"

Chap didn't respond, but Magiere whispered with her face buried in the back of Chap's neck, "Come back."

It was one of the longest nights of their lives, and Leesil didn't sleep as he hung on to his oldest friend. He never thought about the branch left in the snow until he heard a grumbling groan. The late sun's light wasn't even strong enough to notice through the crack of the shelter opening's flap.

Magiere rose on one elbow, and her breath stopped as she looked down at Chap.

Chap twitched, and his forepaw poked Leesil in the stomach.

Leesil had never been so grateful for a face full of foul-smelling dog's breath.

They had a very late start that day. It took more arguing with Ti'kwäg to get Chap bundled up and tied down in the sled's rear. Chap didn't make another sound and lay there quietly as Leesil pulled a fur over the dog's head. He was exhausted from a sleepless night full of fear. Only then did he remember something left behind.

Off to the side, where the shelter had been raised, was a bulge in the new snowfall. He went to scrape the crust off his fallen pack, but what he'd seen right before Chap had collapsed kept nagging at him. Any instant Magiere, wanting to know what took him so long, would shout at him. But her shout didn't come.

Leesil dug about in the hardening crust of last night's thin snowfall—and there it was.

Whatever snow clung to the branch came off more easily than expected. He searched for the wooden tube and pewter cap until he found both. Quickly encasing the branch and trying not to think about it, he shoved the tube into his pack. When he stood up, he saw why Magiere hadn't nagged him to hurry up.

She stood out beyond the dog team already tethered to the sled, and stared into the distance. Ti'kwäg watched her and more than once cast an anxious glance back at Leesil. When Leesil finally trudged toward Magiere and dropped his pack on the sled's end, she didn't turn to him. She continued staring ahead.

"What is it?" he asked as an uncomfortable feeling crawled up his neck.

Magiere pointed ahead.

Leesil saw nothing out there but a white, frozen wasteland.

That entire half day became a dim memory, with a strange mist floating low over the snow-crusted ice. Magiere was always out ahead as Leesil jogged beside the sled to keep an eye on Chap. After a while he gave up watching Magiere at all. It was nearly dark when Ti'kwäg barked something to his dogs, and the sled came to a stop. Leesil halted, looking for Magiere.

She was way out ahead of them and standing still, as if waiting for them to move on. Finally she returned as far as the team's lead dog and then spun around to stare off into the distance.

Leesil checked on Chap—who merely grunted—and then stumbled out toward Magiere. He followed her gaze through the deepening dusk and at first saw nothing. The longer he looked, the more he noticed that the eastward horizon was too dark compared to the stars already appearing above it.

A black silhouette along that edge of the world blocked out any lower stars. Perhaps it was a range of ice higher than the plain. Maybe the ice met and piled up against solid ground, for they had been headed inland for too many days to count.

"Mountains," Magiere whispered.

Leesil didn't want to know how she knew this, and instead asked, "Is that where we're supposed to go?"

"It's where I have to go."

"Not tonight," he countered. "They're farther off than they look on an open plain like this."

She finally looked at him. "I want to go now."

Had they at last reached their destination? Were those mountains nothing more than a safe place to hide the orb? He hoped so but wasn't certain anymore. Whatever drove Magiere was different from the last time, when she'd been after the orb. This time it was something to do with the orb itself.

Leesil wanted to hack a hole in the ice, no matter how deep he had to go, and drop that cursed thing into the depths forever.

Magiere turned back for the sled without his insistence, and they spent another near-restless night. Chap fell asleep as soon as the shelter was up, and had to be awakened to eat. It was another three days before Leesil could clearly make out those mountains ahead.

Another four days passed with Magiere pressing them onward too long and too late. Their destination was always in sight and growing upon the horizon. At least the extra time let Chap fully recover. Another dawn came, and Ti'kwäg began having trouble with the dogs.

The sled too often stalled as some of the team yelped, snarled, barked, or even tried to break off or turn around. This didn't sit well with the guide, though he always forced them onward. Leesil asked Chap whether he knew what was wrong. Chap huffed twice for no but appeared equally troubled by their behavior.

Two more days out, with Chap finally on his feet, and they were close enough that Leesil knew they should be into those mountains by the next day. The subtly rolling plain was so white that he was half-blinded and only stumbled along in following the sled like a beacon. Later he realized he hadn't paid enough attention to Magiere out front. Too often Chap was out there on her heels and pushing himself more than he should have.

Magiere came to a sudden stop.

Leesil almost stumbled into Ti'kwäg's back as the guide halted the sled, and Leesil tried to clear his sight.

Out beyond Magiere was a massive wall of jagged white rising into the sky. He couldn't tell whether it was truly a range of iced-locked mountains, a fracture in the plain forced upward over centuries, or maybe the edge of a land mass coated by the frigid conditions.

But Magiere had stopped, and he didn't believe it was simply that they couldn't go on.

They were *here* . . . wherever she'd been taking them. The more he tried to make out the massive wall of white barring their way, the more something on it caught his attention.

There were dark spots, not quite black, amid its craggy surface.

Leesil cupped his gaze with both hands, trying to block the plain's glare. Those spots weren't pocks and fractures. Some were too round, too smooth to have happened on their own—they were like half circles, like . . . openings into tunnels.

Magiere still stood beyond the sled team with her back turned, and Chap began circling her in agitation with steamy air jetting in sharp pulses from his nose.

Leesil jogged out toward the pair. He heard Chap's low, broken rumble before he closed half the distance, and he slowed. As he approached Magiere's back, he couldn't help looking closely at Chap.

Turning his head, and always keeping Magiere in his sight, Chap wove back and forth at Magiere's left side. When he finally looked to Leesil . . .

A sharp image rose instantly in Leesil's head, and there was no mistaking Chap's meaning.

Leesil saw the amulet, the one Magiere had carried herself in their early days and then given to him long ago. It had been more than a year since he'd even looked at it, for there'd been no need. Pulling off one fur mitten and feeling the cold bite his hand, he fumbled to open his coat's neck. He jerked on the leather cord around his neck until the amulet came out to dangle before his eyes.

That plain bit of topaz set in pewter was glowing enough to see even in daylight.

It did that only when an undead was nearby.

He hadn't felt its warmth through all the layers of clothing and armor he wore. How long had it been doing this out of his sight? He looked out to those unnatural dark spots on the ice wall and stepped closer behind Magiere in an attempt to get her attention.

"How long do you suppose those have been—?"

Leesil stopped short as Chap stepped in, rumbling low at him. Most times, before Leesil even felt the amulet begin to warm, he had heard Chap's eerie hunting cry. Now the dog was almost silent but for the sound of heavy panting.

Leesil went numb all the way to his bones. He grabbed Magiere's arm and jerked her around.

Her squinting eyes were flooded completely black, the irises having expanded to block the whites, and tears were already freezing on her face. The glare of the plain must be burning her eyes like nothing before. Her teeth had fully changed, fangs elongated behind her shuddering, half-parted lips.

Leesil looked to the massive white ridge. "What is this place?" he whispered. "What have you done?"

Nothing changed, though she blinked slowly. She turned her head to peer toward the great ridge, and her features twisted into something feral.

Leesil shouted, "Where have you brought us?"

As Leesil lay on his bunk aboard the *Cloud Queen*, that memory kept repeating over and over, and he couldn't stop it.

CHAPTER ELEVEN

After Magiere ordered Chap into their cabin, he lay in misery upon the floor until the storm began to abate. Leesil appeared in very poor shape again and had remained lying on the bunk with his eyes closed. Staring at the ceiling and equally quiet, Magiere rested on the other bunk, though he could not tell whether she was seasick as well.

When the *Cloud Queen* began riding more smoothly, Chap rose a bit wobbly legged. The very thought of food made his stomach roll. Just the same, he pawed open the cabin door. Neither Leesil nor Magiere said anything as he peered down the passage toward Brot'an's door.

His nauseous misery was forgotten as that other door cracked open. Brot'an stuck his head out and glanced both ways before noticing Chap.

"Standing guard?" the aging elf asked dryly, and then he raised his eyes once to the passage's ceiling before looking back into his cabin. "The weather has turned again. I am going up for a while."

The last of that had to have been for Leanâlhâm, and Chap wondered what effect the storm had on the girl. Brot'an stepped out, closed the door, and walked right by Chap to vanish up the far steep steps to the deck.

Chap waited until he heard the hatch door open and then he followed.

Outside, the sky was still dark gray, but the wind had faded to a bluster and the ship no longer rocked as it had in that sudden squall. Brot'an stood off at the port rail and gripped it with one hand to steady himself. None of the sailors shouted any orders for Brot'an to return below, so Chap stepped farther out into the open.

Without a companion to advise or manipulate, he had little chance of prodding secrets from Brot'an. Obviously the old assassin knew this too well.

Staring lazily toward the distant shore, Brot'an leaned upon the rail. "I am going to enjoy the fresh air while I can," he said. "You are welcome to *enjoy* my company while I do so."

Chap knew better than to be baited but could not suppress a snarl. Changing his mind, he headed below, knowing that was what Brot'an likely wanted, but he went to Brot'an's cabin instead of his own. Pausing there, he hesitated at scratching.

Likely Leanâlhâm was not up to being disturbed, let alone being used to get Brot'an talking. Perhaps he should rouse Magiere, if not Leesil. On second thought, Magiere was not a good choice, as pitting her against Brot'an was what the aging assassin would want. And Leesil had little to offer in coaxing Brot'an further.

It was frustrating not being able to go at Brot'an directly. Chap was determined to find out what Brot'an was after—and it certainly was not some selfless intention to protect Magiere. Brot'an was *not* Sgäile by any measure.

Chap returned to his own cabin and pushed his nose through the cracked door. It creaked open enough for him to stick his head inside.

Leesil was still on the left bunk, but now his eyes were half-open in his sickly pale face. The way he stared at the ceiling made Chap wonder whether there was something wrong other than seasickness. On impulse Chap reached out to dip any memory that fixated his longtime companion.

He nearly pulled out at what filled his head.

Chap—Leesil—saw Magiere's black irises fully expanded to swallow the whites of her eyes. Tears from the glare of the white plain rolled down to half crystallize on her cheeks. He saw fangs between her lips, driven apart by the change of her teeth.

Chap—Leesil—looked upon his wife, and horror-driven anger made him shout, "Where have you brought us?"

The memory vanished as Leesil sat up too quickly—and glared at Chap. His angry expression vanished, and he glanced away.

The shock of that memory caught Chap off guard, though he'd been there in that past moment. It was something else to experience how vivid it had been for Leesil.

As Leesil lay back down, Magiere elbowed up on her bunk. She looked first to Chap and then her husband.

"What?" she asked sharply. "What's wrong?"

Before Chap could call up memory-words, Leesil answered tiredly, "It's nothing."

It seemed only moments had passed since Magiere had heard Leesil's sharp retort just as the storm had hit the ship. His words still hung in her mind.

That you know of . . . and only because you don't have the orb to . . .

She wondered whether in that moment he had been thinking back to . . .

Magiere cringed under Chap's steady gaze, and Leesil wouldn't look at her. The guilt she felt, the weary resignation in her husband, and the dog's continued fearful wariness made her want to hide.

Since their night in Berhtburh, when she'd regained a little closeness with Leesil, she'd hoped he might put some of the past behind them. She was trying so hard to control herself, trying not to let what had changed within her gain any more hold upon her.

Now Leesil wouldn't look at her, and Chap wouldn't stop watching her. She knew what they were thinking—what they feared—and she clambered off the bunk.

"Where are you going?" Leesil asked.

"I need some air."

"I'll come with you."

"No," she answered, more harshly than intended, and there was Chap in the doorway. "Just . . . just let me get some air," she told him.

Chap backed out of the half-open door.

Magiere fled the cabin and rushed along the passage to the stairs and up on deck. A snap of wind tossed her hair across her eyes, and she had to push it back. The crew was busy expanding more sails, though judging by the ship's rocking, the sea hadn't settled completely. Then she spotted Brot'an at the portside rail.

It took three breaths before he looked her way.

His hair appeared even more age-streaked today, or maybe it was just the dark gray sky that made it look so, but the fine lines around his eyes looked deeper. Perhaps he'd just noticed her, or maybe not. One could never tell how much Brot'an was aware of even when he wasn't looking.

Unable to find a way to escape him without returning below to the others, she went to join him.

"How is Leanâlhâm?" she asked.

"Still resting," Brot'an answered. "I assume the same for your companions, though before the storm they were intensely inquisitive."

"I know."

He raised his right eyebrow, stretching those scars that skipped over it. "I told them as much as I wished to . . . less than they wanted . . . yet more than *you* have told me, which is nothing."

At his accusation, Magiere's misplaced anger at Leesil and Chap faded. In fairness, back on the isle, Brot'an had told her something of what made the rift between him and Most Aged Father widen to an extreme. She hadn't offered anything in turn, but it wasn't as simple as just telling him.

How could she? She'd only recently been able to look back on any of it. There were some parts she could remember barely, if at all.

"What do you want to know," she asked Brot'an, "to really know? And don't just ask me what happened up in the Wastes. There was too much."

He appeared thoughtful, as if considering what specific information he wanted most.

"You found the first orb in a castle," he began, "and in the journal Wynn sent to me, she alluded to an ancient guardian. What of the second orb, where you found it? Was it guarded as well? If we face the same possibility in seeking another orb, I need to know."

Magiere wavered. He hadn't asked about the hardest part she'd have to tell. It wasn't the worst for her, Leesil, and Chap, but that part she wouldn't ever share.

At her hesitation, Brot'an pressed further. "I have tried to answer your questions. I have come here to protect you from my caste. When you found the second orb in the north, was there a guardian?"

Damn Wynn for her relentless scribbling! That was the only way Brot'an could know or guess this much. Magiere looked out over the rail at the water smashing against the ship's hull only to roll away in broken foam, all white.

"Yes," she whispered. "There was a guardian."

Quietly she began to speak. . . .

Magiere didn't even remember pulling her falchion as she led the way across the last stretch of the white plain.

Her jaws ached under the change in her teeth, and her eyes burned worse than ever before in the glare. All she saw was a low, dark opening in the brilliant white crags ahead of her. It was all she needed to find her way. When she stepped into the mouth of darkness, the tunnel beyond was as bright as a normal day to her—a relief compared to the blinding glare outside.

Only then did she hear the soft echo of feet and paws following behind her. Only then did she become half-aware of Leesil and Chap still with her.

Fierce hunger burned up her throat and into the back of her mouth with the urge to hunt. She couldn't stop—didn't want to—as she stalked onward, watching for any movement, listening for any new sound . . . sniffing the air for something not quite alive.

Down the broad ice passage, a shimmer of light played upon the glistening walls around her and out ahead. She slowed, peering about, until her eyes fixed on Leesil's amulet, which was exposed atop his coat.

Its amber glow burned her sight as though she'd looked too long into a lantern, and she flinched away from it. He stepped past her down the tunnel, and she made to follow him as the shimmering light upon the walls caught on dimmer spots.

There was something locked in the ice of the walls.

Magiere stared through misted ice at the twisted face of a Wastelander native. Only his head, mouth still gaping and eyes stretched open in the moment of his death, was frozen inside the wall.

A shuddering, keening whine echoed in the tunnel.

Magiere spun, her grip tightening on the falchion's hilt before she spotted Chap behind her. He was looking beyond her, up the passage, and she turned the other way.

Leesil stood farther ahead, close to the tunnel's left wall and staring at it. He held his amulet closer to the ice and curled his other hand to catch his coat's cuff and wipe a patch of wall with his sleeve.

The light from Leesil's amulet revealed a shadow in the ice before his face.

Magiere took only two steps before she made out another head . . . and then another. There were more, frozen inside the walls along the passage. Open, dead eyes stared out at her. Much later she would wonder how long they had been there, and about Ti'kwäg's stories.

Natives of the Wastes had gone in search of their lost ones, and shadows had moved within the blizzards upon the white plains.

"Seven hells," Leesil whispered, and he turned up the tunnel, as if not wanting to meet those eyes staring out of the walls.

The heads should have horrified Magiere as well, but they didn't. They sparked only a dull awareness, some faraway memory.

These frozen heads meant even less to her now than when she'd seen human and inhuman skeletons curled in hollows all along the tunnel down into the great cavern below the six-towered castle. With their skulls down, foreheads pressed to the floor in submission, they spent eternity cowering in death before the emissary of their god.

There was a name for that thing: Li'kän.

That naked, near-white, and deceptively frail woman had been left alone there for a thousand years to watch over the first orb. She was one of the first that the world had ever known among the Noble Dead. The ones the world forgot.

And there was another like her somewhere in here. Magiere felt it. She should've felt the anger-driven fear in Leesil's eyes, heard it in Chap's noise, but there was only hunger now burrowed into her bones, until . . .

She wanted something to tear apart.

Between that drive and the pain of Leesil's blinding amulet, Magiere was vaguely aware that they could be reliving something similar to what they'd encountered in the Pock Peaks. Leesil stood ahead, his back to her, and it was all she could do not to rush past him. Finally he stepped onward, and, hearing Chap's claws coming nearer, she closed on Leesil from behind.

Leesil stepped into an intersection before she caught up.

Instinct—a warning—surged through Magiere.

He stopped amid the openings on all four sides of him. He was too far out of reach to grab, and she shouted at him. All that came out was an echoing screech that smothered Chap's sharp, sudden snarl.

Leesil spun at Magiere's shout, and a dark blur dropped out of—from—the ice ceiling above him.

Magiere charged, her boots slipping on the frozen tunnel floor. Leesil didn't even look up and . . . he ducked and rolled aside.

Before the shadow landed in the intersection, Magiere saw it as a man dressed in fur garb. Leesil pulled both of his winged blades as Magiere rushed the figure from behind and raised her falchion with one hand.

Another—and one more again—came out of the side tunnels.

Leesil came off one knee to swing at their nearest attacker rushing in from the left. The one in the intersection went straight at him. Magiere lost sight of all else as Chap's howl echoed loudly, as if from everywhere, and the one going at Leesil stalled and turned.

The assailant's face caught in the swinging light of Leesil's amulet.

This time instinct made Magiere falter; a sliver of reason slipped in.

He was shorter than she was, and had the black hair and rounded features and slit-like eyes of the nomadic Wastelanders. But his skin looked bleached compared to their dark tones, as if half his color had been bled away. Dressed in only pants and a makeshift cloak, both of fur, his torso was as pallid as his face, but he didn't shiver in the frigid air. No vapor escaped his mouth with his breath, and his lips opened slightly, exposing elongated fangs.

There was no madness of hunger to match her own in his eyes—not as she'd seen in the feral vampires she'd faced in the Pock Peaks before Li'kän had appeared.

He carried no weapon at all.

When Magiere's blade came down, he twisted his head aside and slapped the steel away. Her balance faltered as the falchion's tip cracked the icy floor. All she could do was claw for his throat with her free hand. When her grip closed on his neck, she tried to grind her hardened fingernails through skin and muscle.

One of his hands latched on to her wrist.

Reason held beneath Magiere's hunger. She tried to jerk the falchion up, and her prey wrapped his other hand over hers on the blade's hilt. She caught only fleeting glimpses of what was happening all around her.

Chap rolled along the floor; the fur strapped around his body made him slide away as the one at whom he'd leaped slammed down on his back. A crack echoed off the walls as Chap's head hit the floor, and he barely righted himself as his opponent flopped over and scrambled up. Chap rushed again, leaping to strike the creature's chest and head with all of his snarling mass.

Leesil swung hard as he dropped low, barely clipping the thigh of the one who'd entered from the left. He had to roll and slide away as his opponent stumbled but quickly righted to come at him again.

The one to whom Magiere clung lurched forward. His bare feet didn't slip like her boots. She heard a thump nearby, like bodies striking something hard, and then Leesil's grunting exhale. Chap's growl sharpened to a yelping bark, deafening in her ears, and Magiere felt her back hit a wall.

Her prey's strength matched her own, and a flash of fear rose inside her.

Hunger and rage swallowed fear—and reason.

She shoved hard with her grip on her opponent's neck and jerked back on his hold upon her sword hand. That twist of two forces turned him halfway, and she slammed his head into the icy tunnel wall. She didn't wait for him to go down as she spun.

Leesil was on his back near the left passage's mouth. The undead he fought was on all fours and trying to get a grip on one of his legs as he kicked the attacker repeatedly in the face. And then that undead got a hold on him.

Leesil arched up, slashing a winged blade at the undead's face.

Chap yelped again, and Magiere had to choose.

She rushed the one clawing up Leesil's body, and swung. Her falchion's tip clipped the assailant's collarbone. He shrieked as if burned and lurched back onto his knees. Leesil rolled away to his feet as the high-pitched noise pierced Magiere's ears. Her fury broke for an instant.

The undead—another male like the one she'd faced—spun away with a spasm of pain. Somewhere within, she remembered that her sword caused the undead pain—left scars on them—like no other weapon could. A guttural mumble behind her made her turn.

Her first prey was up again and charging her.

Off to the intersection's other side, Magiere glimpsed Chap's attacker, a woman dressed like the other two. All looked like Wastelanders paled by death and unbearable cold, except their eyes weren't black but crystalline and colorless.

Magiere drew her falchion back as the first one came at her again.

Leesil rushed into its path and shouted at her, "Chap—now!"

Magiere instantly turned away. Chap was bleeding from one shoulder. The female closed on him too quickly as Magiere went for her.

Chap wouldn't retreat and, trying to leap at the woman, dashed straight into his prey.

Her hand slammed down on his head as he launched. Hardened nails raked him, and as he dropped hard, his right forepaw struck her thigh. His claws tore through her fur legging.

These were not normal undead—not even like the ferals that they'd faced in the six-towered castle. No matter how skilled Leesil and Chap might be, they were all in danger here.

Magiere let hunger flood her to the bones, and she roared as she lunged at the female.

The pallid woman's head whipped, hair flying, as she looked straight at Magiere with colorless eyes.

"Näm'ajhuhk! Yihk!"

The woman halted and looked away at that deep shout ringing off the walls.

Magiere faltered as well, looking about for any new threat. She followed the sudden glance.

All three fur-clad undead had gone still. Even Chap backed away, still rumbling. Leesil retreated to the mouth of the tunnel they'd first followed and passed out of Magiere's sight line, though she heard him panting.

All three small undead dropped onto their knees, leaned down, and pressed their foreheads to the frozen floor, as . . .

A tall man strode toward Magiere from the tunnel that led straight ahead, deeper into the mountain.

At first she wasn't certain whether he was like the other three, though he was too tall, apparent even in the darkness up that passage. As he neared, her eyes made him out before the light of Leesil's amulet truly revealed him.

He was no Wastelander—never had been. His hair was dark brown, near-black, but wavy, almost tightly curling, and his features, longer and narrower, were different from those of the other three. His eyebrows were dark colored as well but thick and shiny like his locks. He was bare chested, and his shoulders were wide. He wore pants made of treated hide and a cloak sewn from dozens of strips of varied furs.

He ignored all the others and stared only at Magiere with an emotionless expression.

She had seen the like of his slender features, prominent cheekbones, and full lips before. Aside from his pallor, he was much like the few Sumans whom she'd spotted in the ports of her homeland. And he was so pallid as to be nearly white like the one Magiere had faced upon finding the first orb . . . like Li'kän.

Magiere looked to his long neck, his throat, before realizing why. He wasn't wearing a *thôrhk*, an orb handle, like Li'kän had. He slowed his approach and studied her face, maybe her eyes, perhaps her mouth in the slow drop of his gaze.

Magiere half raised the falchion, but her other hand came up toward her throat. She felt for where her coat had broken open at the neck, and then her fingertips touched one knobbed end of her *thôrhk*.

His eyes widened slightly.

He stepped into the intersection's space, and Magiere tensed to rush him. Chap's sharp snarl halted her. The dog looked between her and the pallid Suman in quick glances. Blood matted the fur of his right foreleg below the shredded part of his fur wrap.

"Don't do anything . . . yet!" Leesil whispered from behind.

As Magiere fought to remain still, an image—a memory—sharpened in her head.

She envisioned Li'kän at the time the ancient undead first appeared in the six-towered castle. That frail-looking undead's eyes had been as crystalline as those of the man before her. Li'kän was utterly savage, tearing apart anything, even another undead, that got in her way or crossed her sight. She cast them aside, broken, without thought or notice. And she'd never said a word.

This one—this pale, tall Suman—had spoken.

Reason sharpened in Magiere as she realized what Chap was trying to tell her by that memory. They faced another who was like but unlike Li'kän. This one hadn't gone mad after a thousand years alone in silence.

With his eyes still on Magiere, the man raised one hand. He barked a single unrecognizable word like a command, and the three undead, heads still bowed with eyes down, rose to their feet. They backed only a few steps into the shadows and went still.

"Magiere?" Leesil asked, his voice tense with warning.

She tried to force her mind to work harder, to gain back her wits. The orb had led her here for a reason, but had it been a deceit? Was it trying a different way to use her, as had that thing in her dreams that led her to the six-towered castle?

This man had made himself servants, and Li'kän had not.

Perhaps that was only because such might be found here, even in this vast barren region. Li'kän had been trapped in the highest peaks of Magiere's continent where no one had any reason to go until Magiere herself had gone after the orb.

This undead did not stare at her in hatred, as if she were an invader to be dispatched. He appeared . . . relieved . . . even pleased by the sight of her.

The barest hint of a smile spread across his mouth, and she instantly wanted to take his head. He took another step, and Leesil appeared on her right as Chap sidled in on her left. The tall, white ancient halted. He raised both empty hands outward, and then slowly pulled them in, gesturing to himself.

"Iàng qahhar'ur," he said.

Magiere shook her head. He frowned, and then . . .

"Man'äm qahhar-ís . . . e ra'fi?"

At the last of this, he gestured to her. These words sounded different, almost musical in tone. Maybe some other language, though there was one word that seemed similar.

"I . . . do not . . . understand," she struggled to get out in Numanese.

The tall undead tilted his head to one side and then straightened. He never even glanced at Chap or Leesil, and again he touched a hand to his chest.

"I . . . am . . . Qahhar," he said, faltering over the words. "Well met . . . lost . . . grandchild."

That cold place was deathly quiet for a long moment.

"We back out now," Leesil whispered. "If we reach the tunnel's mouth, we can keep them—"

Qahhar turned his eyes on Leesil, and all the pleading hope and the hint of a smile vanished from his face.

Magiere fought to keep her dhampir nature under control, though she wanted to let go, let instinct take her for the way this undead looked at her husband. Something inside her wouldn't respond to that desire. Something held it down even as Leesil carefully swung out one forearm with its wing blade to block her way.

Qahhar looked at her again. A mournful sorrow flooded his features, as if he had begun to weep, though no tears rolled from his colorless eyes.

"My lost grandchild," he said, taking another small, hesitant step. "Beloved . . . guided you to me. I waited so long to be forgiven for my sin . . . for my desire to stand alone."

Magiere stiffened. What did he mean by his "beloved"?

Though, unlike Li'kän, he spoke and understood words, and he knew more than one language, what he said made no sense. Something hard and urgent flickered across his features.

"Alone," he whispered. "I begged forgiveness for my pride . . . for thinking only I was worthy."

At a soft pressure on Magiere's leg, she looked down to find Chap close against her. Another memory swelled in her thoughts when he glanced up once at her.

She saw the orb, the one they had brought, where it had sat upon a stone pedestal in the great cavern below the six-towered castle. What was he trying to tell her now?

"You are beautiful to my eyes," Qahhar said. "And I have . . . mourned my sins. In my regret, I thought to keep from being alone."

He gestured weakly toward one of the three undead still standing in the shadows with their heads bowed, though he did not look at them.

"These did no good, and only now . . . Beloved has forgiven me for thinking that only I am a fit guardian . . . for destroying the others of the Children who were sent with me."

Magiere stared at him. From what Wynn had learned about Li'kän, that undead had journeyed a long way to the Pock Peaks a thousand years ago with a horde of servants and two companions named Volyno and Häs'saun.

Over the following centuries, somehow those other two had either perished or vanished, leaving Li'kän all alone in her endless silence.

Or had she destroyed them, as Qahhar just claimed he had done?

Had he then tried to make himself companions from Wastelanders who had wandered too near his prison, only to find later that these creations did not fill his need? Li'kän hadn't tried that—either by choice or because no one was near enough by the time loneliness would have driven her to such an act. But, like her, Qahhar had survived in a place where there couldn't have been enough life to sustain him.

And what had he meant by "fit guardian"? Magiere didn't even want to guess.

The memory of the orb on its pedestal flashed again in her mind. This time she understood what Chap meant . . . what had sustained Qahhar for all these centuries.

"Show me what you guard," she ordered.

"No!" Leesil hissed.

Qahhar's cold eyes appeared to brighten with relief. Without a word, he turned smoothly and headed back the way he'd come. All three servants remained where they were, with their heads bowed. Magiere desperately wished she had an instant to speak with Leesil and Chap alone.

"We have to follow," she said. "I have to see."

Leesil's features twisted into panicked anger, but Chap stepped onward after Qahhar. Magiere could only look away from Leesil and follow as well.

How many times would she do this to him and grow fearfully sick inside until she heard his footsteps come after her? How many times before she didn't hear those footfalls?

Walking near Chap's right haunch, Magiere kept back from Qahhar as he led them up the far icy tunnel. It was a while before she noticed how the tunnel darkened even more, lit only by the glow of Leesil's amulet as he came behind her. Then she felt more than saw the steadily increasing slant of the floor.

They were going upward rather than into the depths. She kept her eyes on the back of Qahhar's fur cloak as she followed. By his words and what Chap had shown her, she had no doubt of what she'd find at the end of this tunnel. She could hardly let herself believe it was possible, and she didn't want to believe.

Magiere saw faint shimmers along the walls ahead of Qahhar that couldn't be coming from Leesil's amulet. However, their group couldn't be approaching the top of the mountain ridge; by the size of the peaks that she'd seen outside, they hadn't gone far or high enough. But they must be somewhere near the surface if light now seeped in through the ice. Or shouldn't there be layers of rock to block it out?

Soon she made out more heads frozen inside the walls. Their dead eyes were turned toward the passage—toward Qahhar as he passed them without a returned glance.

Leesil hadn't said a word along the way.

The passage leveled off, and Magiere spotted stronger light ahead. Qahhar stepped out of the tunnel into a vast cavern, and Magiere followed. It was so wide that she couldn't have thrown a stone to its far side. Looking all around, she found other features familiar and unsettling.

They stood upon a broad ice shelf that circled the entire cavern. Four narrow walkways stretched from the shelf in the form of a cross, joining at a middle platform over the center of a chasm. But unlike the stone cavern below Li'kän's castle, everything here was made of ice.

Qahhar blocked Magiere's view of the center platform as he stepped to where the ledge met the nearest walkway bridge. The path he trod was no wider than twice his shoulder width. When she went to follow, she paused and peered over the shelf's lip.

The chasm was too deep to see the bottom. She looked into an endless fall from the light permeating the cavern into a pitch black far below. Along that descent was nothing but craggy walls of ice. She shut her eyes as vertigo made her dizzy.

When Magiere opened her eyes again to step onward, Chap had cut in front of her with a snarl as he stepped onto the bridge.

Qahhar stopped, turned about, and for the first time looked upon the dog.

Chap froze in place but didn't retreat as Qahhar's expression turned as blank and emotionless as his colorless eyes. The undead's gaze lifted, and at the sight of Magiere, his mournful and grateful expression returned, and he moved on.

Magiere urged Chap onward, as there was no way to get around the dog on the narrow bridge. When Qahhar stepped onto the central platform and off to one side, Magiere was able to see what waited there, though she'd already imagined it.

Instead of stone like the last time, a four-legged stand of ice like a tall and narrow table rose from out of the platform's frost-glazed surface. A perfectly round hole had been carved or had formed in the stand's top.

A dark globe slightly larger than a great helm rested inside the opening. A spike, its broad tapered top larger than her fist, pierced down through the globe's center. The spike's pointed tip protruded through the globe's bottom, showing between the stand's legs. Both spike and globe appeared formed from a single piece.

As before, when she was near the first orb, Magiere's hunger faded. That relief came like a curse, for hunger fueled her fury—and fury was her strength.

Another long-forgotten guardian kept another orb . . . in another cavern, this time in the heights instead of the depths. The orb they already possessed had led her, and it was the last thing she'd expected and would have ever hoped for.

Magiere wanted to flee this place but couldn't bring herself to do so.

Qahhar turned his gaze from the pedestal to her—to the *thôrhk* around her neck.

"Mine is here," he said. "Always safe. The others did not know how to guard the anchor."

His last word made no sense, though at a guess he meant the orb. He headed to the walkway across from the one they'd used. At her footsteps, he looked back and smiled.

"Wait here," he said.

Chap snarled and tried to rush forward. Magiere grabbed him with her free hand. Qahhar looked upon the dog, still snarling at him, and Magiere raised her falchion. The undead appeared confused at her action and shook his head.

"I will remain in your sight . . . and return quickly."

With that, he stepped off along the far bridge.

Magiere watched him carefully. She had to tighten her grip on Chap's scruff as he tried to assault her with memories of every undead that ever attacked or betrayed them.

"We're leaving now . . . before that thing does something!"

Leesil's harsh whisper startled Magiere after his long silence. She didn't obey, and Chap finally settled to an endless rumble of breaths as she watched the guardian.

Qahhar reached the opposite side of the cavern's ringed ledge and turned to a sidewall near the far tunnel opening. For a moment he appeared to close his eyes, and his lips moved, though Magiere didn't hear anything.

When he reached toward—*into*—the wall's ice, she sucked in a breath and held it. He withdrew his hand, and even from a distance she could tell what he held.

Another *thôrhk* . . . or orb handle.

How he'd hidden it there or why she couldn't guess, other than the fact that it would be hard for anyone else to find, let alone reach, it. This also meant that Qahhar had skills to be wary of. More than once, Magiere, with Leesil and Chap, had faced an undead that knew magic. It never turned out well.

Returning to the platform, Qahhar held up his *thôrhk*, identical to the one Li'kän had possessed. He hung it around his neck, and his voice filled with relief.

"In sending you, Beloved has forgiven me."

Magiere didn't want to hear that again, but something inside her held on to a suspicion. What she'd done—what she'd felt—to find this place didn't match the horror in her dreams that had guided her to the first orb.

"I will let no harm come to you," Qahhar went on, "or those you choose to keep. I will guard you, as precious to me as you are to Beloved. You will stand with me, and neither of us shall ever be alone again . . . until Beloved calls for the anchors."

With that, he reached out as if to touch her face.

Magiere back-stepped, pulling Chap before he lunged, but Leesil dodged around her and stopped barely out of the guardian's reach.

Confusion spread across Qahhar's pale face, but Magiere saw the malice on Leesil's.

She instantly released Chap to grab Leesil's coat and jerk him back. Chap shifted to her right as she reached behind and under her own coat with her free hand. Magiere felt for the hilt of her Chein'âs dagger at the small of her back.

"Illimasuktok e kisarpok!"

A shout coming from somewhere outside the cavern echoed off the walls. Qahhar's widening eyes looked toward where they'd all first entered.

"What's happening?" Leesil asked.

Magiere didn't know. Qahhar looked at her as if she were suddenly a puzzle. Chap's snarl rose to a pealing half yowl as a memory erupted in Magiere's head.

She saw the sled outside with the chest holding the orb they'd brought, and Ti'kwäg standing beside it.

Magiere realized that shout had come from one of Qahhar's servants. They must have gone outside and spotted the sled. She fought the urge to run for the passage. Leesil sucked a loud breath, and she knew Chap had raised a similar memory for him.

Magiere began to panic again as Leesil backed off to her left.

"Tell him you've been sent to guard *it* . . . this orb," he whispered in Belaskian.

Magiere hoped that wasn't a language that Qahhar knew.

"Tell him that you're its guardian now," Leesil added.

Leesil could bluff his way through a tangle better than anyone she knew, and she guessed at what he was up to. If those servants had gone to the sled, Qahhar might now know they'd arrived with an orb. Would he accept that she was somehow taking both?

Lying wasn't one of Magiere's skills, not like it was Leesil's. She said either nothing or something, and if truth bothered those who heard it, that was their problem. This was different.

She looked Qahhar in the eyes and spoke clearly. "Beloved has forgiven you . . . and I have been sent to gather the orbs. There is no more waiting needed."

Qahhar's brow slowly wrinkled. "No, my grandchild, you have misunderstood. You are not of the Children."

Magiere was lost again—children of what?

"Beloved would never accept one such as you as sole guardian," Qahhar finished.

A memory rose in Magiere of Li'kän in the library of the Pock Peaks. The scribbled writing of her "story" covered all the walls. Chap was feeding Magiere notions, and she guessed at what he wanted her to say.

"Li'kän, Volyno, and Häs'saun gave me their orb," she said. "Hand over yours, as Beloved wishes."

She hoped Qahhar had no way to know that Volyno and Häs'saun were long gone, and that Li'kän had been forever locked away in the cavern beneath her castle. Qahhar became very quiet, still watching, and then slowly shook his head.

"If Beloved had you take the anchor of Water from Häs'saun, it was only to bring it to me, to show me that Beloved has forgiven me . . . and sent you to me, Grandchild. You will stay, as you are *for* me."

"No, she isn't," Leesil rasped.

Qahhar fixed on Leesil, and his face drained of all emotion. In a blink, he rushed and struck with his hand for Leesil's throat. Leesil jerked one arm up almost as quickly as Qahhar could strike. The punching blade barely got in the way. It shielded his throat, but not the arm that held the blade up.

Qahhar's hardened nails raked across Leesil's forearm and screeched off the wing of his blade.

Droplets of red spattered away from Leesil's arm and the undead's fingers.

Magiere threw herself at Qahhar. . . .

* * *

—Enough!—

Chap stood in the *Cloud Queen's* aftcastle doorway, having trailed Magiere up to the deck. At that one memory-word raised in her head, she stiffened upright and looked about until she spotted him.

He had expected to find her with Brot'an and had even hoped to use her to extract more information, but he'd not anticipated finding her telling Brot'an this part of their journey.

—What—are you—doing?—

Magiere winced, still looking at Chap.

Chap's concern was not about Magiere reliving the second ugliest moment of their journey into the Wastes. Or the third ugliest for him. In truth, from what he had seen in her rising memories compared to what he had heard her say, she had not been detailed in her account. But she shared things that Brot'an should not know, such as the orbs' influences upon her, other details of their appearance . . . and of *thôrhks* or "handles."

What Brot'an might piece together from such scattered bits was one of Chap's greatest concerns.

Brot'an looked only at Magiere, as if Chap's sudden presence was nothing but a pause.

"Continue," he told her flatly.

Magiere didn't utter a word, but as Chap saw the cascade of memories in her mind, he could not stop his own from returning. . . .

Magiere's shrieking roar echoed in the ice cavern and assaulted Chap's ears as, pulling her falchion, she rushed at Qahhar. Leesil spun clear as droplets of his blood spattered the platform from out of his shredded coat sleeve. Magiere's other hand whipped out from behind her back with the silver-white dagger as her falchion swept for Qahhar's neck.

The ancient undead dodged aside, reaching for Leesil more quickly than

Chap could follow. Chap launched to snap at Qahhar's hand, but his jaws closed on empty air. Something smashed against the side of his head.

Everything turned white and then instantly black before Chap's eyes.

Clarity did not return until he hit the platform hard and started sliding. He writhed blindly to right himself before slipping over the platform's edge. His claws bit into the ice, but he still kept sliding. He felt his tail drop over the edge when he finally stopped.

Chap saw Leesil trying to reach him, but Leesil was limping badly.

Leesil had been behind him or out of direct sight since they'd followed Qahhar up the final passage. Leesil must have been injured during the clash with the three minions. More blood dripped between his fingers clutching his wounded arm.

Chap scrambled up; the cavern was still blurred and shifting under the ringing in his head. As he stumbled forward to get between Leesil and the ancient undead . . .

Magiere swung the falchion backhanded, low and across as Qahhar came at her. He tilted easily away from the heavy blade's arc, as if the ice beneath his bare feet were as sure as rough stone.

The falchion swung clear, and Qahhar lunged in. Magiere followed, slashing downward with the Chein'âs dagger.

Chap had only an instant to hear the sizzle in the cold air. Any hard motion of that white metal blade made its black and hair-thin center seam ignite with orange-red light.

Qahhar gave the white blade no notice, hooked his fingers, and went for Magiere's throat.

The blade's lead edge and tip sliced his collarbone and down across his ribs.

His scream was drowned by the sizzling crackle of his flesh. Smoke rose into his face and eyes along the blade's charred path as Magiere jerked the dagger back up. But she didn't strike again.

Chap got around Leesil as Qahhar took a wobbling step back, and Magiere kicked out with one foot. Her boot struck Qahhar's seared chest, and with a cry of pain, he stumbled away, teetering toward the platform's edge.

Magiere didn't follow her prey, and before she shouted, "Run!" Chap knew what they had to do.

They already had one orb to get away from this place; they had to forgo seizing the second. Magiere grabbed the back of Leesil's coat, and Chap swerved, bolting along the narrow walkway they'd traversed on their way in.

If Qahhar's minions were closing, he could not let them catch Magiere and Leesil on the narrow bridge. After reaching the ledge, he slowed partway to the passage's entrance and remained watching until his companions caught up. Once they did, he rushed on, glancing back often.

Leesil had sheathed both winged blades, or Magiere had done it for him. He tried to squeeze his coat sleeve against his arm but stumbled and limped as Magiere pulled him along. In the light of his still-glowing amulet, a thin trail of blood on the ice followed his every step.

Leesil was losing too much blood. Soon the cold would get to him even before blood loss dropped him and killed him. But even in panic Chap could not stop now.

When he reached the intersection of the passages, no one was there. Instead of turning to relief, his panic increased. Where were Qahhar's followers?

Chap looked all ways, and then peered down the tunnel that led outside. An echoing howl of rage flowed into the intersection from the way they had come, and Chap spun about.

Qahhar had not fallen into the chasm.

"Go!" Magiere ordered, shoving Leesil onward.

Leesil released his wounded arm and reached for a winged blade with his blood-soaked hand. Magiere slapped his hand away.

"No!" he choked out. "I'm not leaving!"

Through her elongated teeth, all she got out as she pushed him again was a garbled snarl.

Chap hated the thought of leaving her to guard their retreat, but he had no idea what had become of their own orb. Snatching the back of Leesil's coat in his teeth, he called up Leesil's memory of the orb upon the sled.

Leesil struggled, almost toppling backward, and Chap ducked out of the way. As Leesil righted himself, Chap saw Qahhar coming at them out of the passage behind them.

Magiere turned, lunging into the mouth of that tunnel.

Chap barked once at Leesil before turning to race off the other way. All the way to the outside world, Chap heard Leesil struggling to catch up, but at least he'd listened and followed. It wasn't until Chap was down the snow-crusted slope that he was certain of what he saw.

Out on the endless white plain, what had been the speck of the sled was now a patch of dark red, almost black in the cold dusk. Racing across the snow, he spotted the first corpse.

The dogs were dead, slaughtered with their bodies scattered in pieces. He did not see Ti'kwäg anywhere, but one of Qahhar's servants—the female—was lifting the orb's chest off the sled. The two others rose from beyond the sled's back, and Chap knew their guide had been lost like the dog team.

All three undead were smeared in blood, already crystallizing on their faces, hands, and torsos. All three turned their heads and spotted him.

A screeching shout carried over the plain from behind Chap.

Either Magiere or Qahhar had escaped the mountain, and by Magiere's sound, the other had followed. Both still survived.

Chap couldn't look back, not even for Leesil, and fixed upon the undead woman as he charged. She simply dropped the chest and crouched to face him.

He had one chance, only one way to take at least two of these things with him. He'd once done something desperate when they'd been overwhelmed by feral undead in the six-towered castle.

He would give these three something to feed upon.

As Chap charged, he called upon Air from the wind, Water within the ice, the Earth beneath the crusted plain, and Fire from the heat of his own body. He mingled these with his own Spirit, bonded to the elements of Existence that his kin, the Fay, had created so they would not wander in a timeless void.

Only Wynn, with her mantic sight, would have seen the trails of phos-phorescent blue-white vapor flickering over his body like ghostly flames. Chap swallowed the sorrowful thought that he might never see her again and threw himself into the female undead.

She only stumbled instead of toppling. Clawing and snapping at any part of her that he could reach, Chap finally latched his jaws onto her shoulder. He ground his fangs deep to the bone, and she screamed.

Magiere's weapons were the only other things that could cause the undead as much pain as his teeth and claws. He held on with his jaws as the woman's acrid, oily black fluids leaked into his mouth. She tried to tear him off, but he wouldn't let go.

Her screeching snarls deafened his ears as she thrashed and tore at the fur wrap around his torso. The sharp stench of her fear thickened until it drove her to her last resort.

Teeth—fangs—sank sharply through Chap's fur and skin at the back of his neck.

Pain turned the world to a blur before his eyes. In barely two breaths after his lunge, he was falling. A jarring impact flattened him against the woman, and her teeth were gone from his neck. She shuddered in spasms beneath him, and, still only half-aware, he broke away from her. One of the other two vampires was near—and charging.

Chap stumbled as he saw the thing rushing at him.

Leesil flashed by, ramming straight into Chap's attacker. Both rolled and flopped across the snow-crusted ice.

Chap had to turn away as the third undead rushed from behind the sled's back and spotted him. The undead's gaze quickly shifted as he looked to the woman. Chap already knew what the male saw.

Spidering lines would already be spreading over her skin, splitting and rupturing into cracks that bled black fluids. Her eyes and ears would begin to leak the same to stain the snow like oily ink. Chap heard her last scream, and the sound of thrashing upon the snow ceased.

No undead so far could survive feeding upon a Fay born into the flesh.

He was more life than they could consume—but it cost him. In his weakness, the cold was eating into his body.

The third undead turned his eyes on Chap—and then shuddered and stiffened. He was not looking at Chap . . . but beyond him. That one's eyes widened, along with his blood-crusted mouth, and he retreated one step.

Chap risked one look back as he charged at Leesil's opponent.

Magiere and Qahhar were barely beyond the pieces of the dogs. She'd dropped her falchion somewhere along the way, and they went at each other with bare hands, screaming and clawing.

Chap didn't know whether Magiere could stand against something as ancient and powerful as Qahhar. They were both a mess, he covered in smears of black and she in bloodred.

Chap grew frantic as his thoughts raced.

There were still two more Wastelander undead, Leesil was wounded, and Chap felt his strength waning. They were all going to die out here, and that would leave not one but *two* of the Ancient Enemy's devices in the hands of these minions.

Qahhar was more dangerous than Li'kän, for he wasn't mad, or at least had retained his reason, unlike her. But Chap could not turn to help Magiere.

He charged past the one staring at her and went straight at the one atop Leesil.

Leesil had managed to pull out a winged blade with his good hand. But the undead attacking him had that hand pinned down and had wrapped his other hand around Leesil's throat.

Chap landed on the attacker's back, and they both collapsed on Leesil. Chap sank his teeth into the back of the creature's neck. The undead arched with a howl, and something, perhaps an elbow, rammed back into Chap's side.

He felt something crack.

Breath shot out of him in a whimper between his clenched teeth. He held on to the male's neck as the undead thrashed, rolled away, and pinned him against the cold, crusted plain. The thing screamed and stiffened atop him for an instant before it tore free of his jaws and scrambled away.

Its quick escape tumbled Chap over, and the first thing he saw through pain-blurred eyes was a trail of black spatters in the snow. Then he saw the undead scrambling off, out onto the plain, as the falling snow began slanting in the rising wind.

Chap struggled onto his belly and tried to rise as he looked about. He saw no sign of the third undead who had been behind the sled. Instead there was only a still body lying awkwardly in a broad red stain upon the snow. Chap looked away from Ti'kwäg's remains and struggled around to find Leesil on his side, looking at him.

Leesil's eyes were barely open as his quick, shallow breaths puffed out vapor quickly torn apart by the wind. Next to his outstretched arm with that one winged blade was a pale-skinned severed hand upon the snow. Its owner had run off, but where was that third undead?

And why was everything so silent now, but for Leesil's weak breaths and the rising, biting wind?

Chap squirmed around a little farther but could not get to his feet.

Out beyond the blurred stain of dog corpses, something moved through the curtain of slanting snowfall, coming closer, only one figure, not two. Its shape was still indistinct as it stepped through the dark stretch where the dogs had been torn apart.

Chap looked all about in fright, at a loss for why the two male undead had run off, and fearful that one of them now returned. And what of Qahhar?

Amid the snowfall, Magiere took shape in Chap's blurred sight. And relief was short-lived as, looking for Qahhar, he tried to see beyond her. Something was wrong with Magiere's face . . . something more than her change in facing the ancient undead. She clutched something round in one hand.

The bottom half of her face was smeared in wet black liquid, dripping from her chin, though the rest of her features appeared marred here and there with her own blood. Her pure black eyes shone with madness above her stained mouth . . . lips . . . parted.

More black fluid flowed down her chin, turning into a stream that dribbled down her coat and spattered the icy ground in the wind.

Chap was too weak to turn away and he looked again to the thing in her hand.

Magiere's fingers were curled like claws in the snarled hair of Qahhar's head. His eyes were open and slack like his gaping mouth. The stump of his neck was raggedly torn off, flesh clinging to dangling vertebrae as it still dripped . . . like Magiere's mouth.

What had she done?

Chap panicked, cowering from the answer, and struggled up to all fours. When he hobbled toward Magiere, she just stood there, staring at him. He snapped his jaws in a sharp bark, and pain filled his whole chest and took his breath, but she flinched.

Magiere's irises began to recede a little.

With that, she started shuddering in the freezing wind as she looked about in confusion at the bodies of the dogs, at what was left of Ti'kwäg, and then back to Chap. Horrified fear spread over her face when she realized what she gripped in her hand.

She half dropped, half threw the head aside and nearly stumbled back over the sled. Heaving in one strong breath, she started gagging and choking, and then collapsed on her knees.

Chap sickened inside as Magiere dropped forward on all fours, arched her back, and vomited black fluid. In spite of this horror—what it might mean—Chap tried to fill her head with memories of Leesil. Chap barked and snapped, spasming in pain each time.

Magiere flopped back on her knees against the sled, and Chap kept barking as he wheeled to stumble toward Leesil. She finally scrambled after him without even rising to her feet.

They found Leesil with his eyes closed.

Magiere grabbed hold of his coat's left shoulder as Chap took the other in his jaws, and they dragged him to the sled. By the time Magiere finished ripping open the shelter hide and canvas strapped over their gear, Chap was shaking from the bitter cold. She hauled Leesil onto the sled into the space she had made, and then turned to heave the orb's chest back up onto the sled's front end.

Chap watched without interfering as she did all these things. He had no idea what else they could do. Even the passages within the ice crags might not be safe, as they did not know where Qahhar's remaining followers had gone.

Weary and spent, half of her face still covered in black, Magiere leaned on the chest.

The only thing Chap could do was try to climb up. Magiere grabbed his haunches to help, and he burrowed in next to Leesil to share body heat . . . what little they had.

To Chap's shock, Magiere turned away.

She stumbled off, first back to the place she'd fought Qahhar, and she picked up something from the ground. Then she kept on instead of turning back.

Chap sat up, barking at her, until the pain and coughing were too much to bear. He tried to raise memories in her of home, or forests, or anywhere but here. She didn't stop, and soon vanished amid the falling snow. He huddled next to Leesil and listened to his oldest friend's shallow breaths, and he tried to lick Leesil's face, anything to rouse him. In the end all Chap could do was grab the shelter's hide with his teeth and try to pull it up over both their heads.

He lay there, knowing where Magiere had gone. It seemed too long until the sled rocked under a sudden weight dropped on its front end.

Chap wriggled his head out from under the tarp.

There was Magiere, lashing down the second orb along with Qahhar's *thôrhk*. Her falchion was back in its sheath; as to the Chein'âs dagger always carried at her back, he did not know. She dug under the tarp and into one of their packs, and took out her spare shirt to shred it in her teeth. As she wrapped it tightly around Leesil's torn forearm, Chap made out her face.

Her irises were pure black again.

Even the bandages ended up stained with black smears from her hands. She had been cut as well: there were smears of blood on her hands and upper face. As she worked on Leesil, Chap's fears only grew worse.

Close to her now, he could not see an open wound anywhere on her, even where the bloodstains were thickest.

When she finished, she stood there, no longer shuddering in the cold, though he could still see sickness and revulsion in her face. She reached out to gently push his head down and pull the cover over him and Leesil . . . without looking at either of them.

Chap lay wondering what Magiere could be doing now. And then the sled lurched, turning and turning, until it began to slide along its rails. He took one last look.

Magiere was out beyond the sled and pulling it by the remains of the rigging. Chap wondered from where she'd found the strength—and then he did not want to know.

"Port of Chathburh ahead!" called a sailor from the crow's nest.

Chap stood with Magiere watching him as if this time it was *she* who caught *his* memories.

"So, there was another guardian," Brot'an reiterated. "You have said you acquired the second orb, but did you kill this guardian?"

Magiere dropped her eyes and swallowed.

"Yes," she answered flatly.

If only that had been the end, had been the worst of it for her . . . for all of them.

"Nothing's going to prepare you, Brot'an," Magiere half whispered, "nothing, if we have to face something like that . . . thing again."

Chap wanted her to stop, for if he had his way, Brot'an would not be there if and when they found a fourth orb. But he raised no memory-words in her mind.

"And Chap later hid both orbs?" Brot'an asked. "How and where?"

—*No—more—* . . . —*You've given—him—enough*—

Magiere didn't look at Chap. Neither did she confirm Brot'an's assumptions or give him anything else. The truth was, she didn't know *where*. Instead she closed her eyes briefly.

"We'll reach port soon," she said. "I'm going to tell Leesil and Leanâl-hâm."

Abruptly Magiere pushed off the rail. Brot'an said nothing more nor tried to stop her.

As she passed, Chap waited for any acknowledgment from her, but it never came as she descended below. And when he turned back, Brot'an was watching him.

Magiere had given the old assassin all he would get. With a twitch of his jowls, Chap headed below.

Brot'an would never learn where those orbs were hidden, not ever. Chap would see him dead first.

CHAPTER TWELVE

Brot'ân'duivé was standing on deck when a short while later Léshil and Magiere appeared out of the nearest aftcastle door. Léshil was overburdened with baggage.

"We don't need both packs," Magiere admonished. "We're staying three nights at most."

"It could be longer," Léshil countered with hope in his voice.

Leanâlhâm cautiously crept behind them out of the aftcastle door. She hung back upon spotting human sailors rushing about to moor the ship. Several waited around the cargo hatch as another above rigged the boom and tackle for whatever goods would be exchanged in port.

In spite of all the hectic activity, Brot'ân'duivé still dwelled upon what little Magiere had told him. Obviously she had kept back something burdensome that Chap knew as well. Some of what she had said, from the guardian with minions, both potent enough to trouble Magiere and Chap, to the initial resting place of another orb amid a cavern of ice, hung in Brot'ân'duivé's mind. That device they all knew now was the orb or anchor of Fire. Yet Brot'ân'duivé was no closer to anything more useful.

Forewarned, perhaps, about what dangers might wait with the next orb, he still had gained nothing about the function of these devices or how they were once used in service to the Ancient Enemy. And what danger did they pose, should Most Aged Father claim even one of them?

There was little relief in the fact that the patriarch knew of only the first orb and had even less knowledge of it than Brot'ân'duivé did. Why had the Enemy scattered the five orbs so far and placed such guardians upon them a thousand years ago? Why were those guardians the most potent of the humans' undead?

Brot'ân'duivé needed to know more, including what had happened for Magiere to change in not-so-subtle ways since she had left his homeland. He could hardly force the issue if he wished for her—if not Léshil or Chap—to believe he was here to protect her. Asking outright about the orbs' ultimate purpose, if she even knew, would only put her on guard. Besides, in truth, if any of them did know, it was most likely the majay-hì.

Chap was a source of information far beyond Brot'ân'duivé's reach.

The sailors finished mooring the vessel, and he watched a team of four prepare to lower the ramp as his traveling companions drew near. Leanâlhâm, her breaths quickening, stared at the city beyond the waterfront.

"Are we going into . . . into that?" she whispered.

The port of Chathburh was large, perhaps as much as Calm Seatt. While its waterfront was more spread out than the one on the Isle of Wrêdelyd, it was as busy, if not more.

Crowded piers did not appeal to Brot'ân'duivé, either, but the sight of Leanâlhâm's nervous eyes left him surprisingly worried over her state of mind—and her future. For better or worse, she had become his responsibility.

She could not be in true mourning over Osha, as he was not her mate. That sadness would pass, but she was failing to adjust here. She had no wish to return to her people and, considering her association with him, there was possible danger if she did. Soon he would be embroiled in a desperate and uncertain purpose in trailing Magiere to another orb. Judging by what little he had learned so far, Leanâlhâm should not be there if—when—that happened.

Magiere stepped onto the ramp's head, tugging along a reluctant Leanâl-hâm.

"Hold on!" Léshil called, dropping all three packs and crouching to dig through one. "We're at Chathburh, right? I think I remember Wynn giving me something to help us here."

At mention of the young sage, Leanâlhâm hurried back to hover over Léshil.

Magiere raised an eyebrow. "From Wynn? Such as what?"

"Hang on. . . . Here it is." Léshil drew out a folded paper and shook it open.

"It's a list of places to stay along the way, cheap or free," he muttered, scanning the sheet and squinting as if it was hard to read. "Here it is—Chathburh. She says there's an 'annex' for the guild . . . three streets inland from the northernmost pier, then one street north beyond the waterfront." With a frown, Léshil looked up to Magiere. "What's an annex?" She shrugged, and he turned back to Wynn's notes. "She says to 'tell the sages there that Premin Hawes sent you.'" Léshil paused at that. "It seems they'll give us free rooms and meals, but . . ."

He scowled as he read on. "' . . . But whatever you do, don't mention my name.'"

"What did she do now?" Magiere asked sharply.

"I don't know!" he snapped back.

"So, we lie about knowing a guild authority . . . who helped throw us out." Magiere's voice turned more heated with every word. "But not mention Wynn, who, it seems, is actually known here?"

Leanâlhâm glanced back and forth between them with worried eyes.

"Oh, stop being a pain," Léshil grumbled at Magiere.

Brot'ân'duivé slowly shook his head. Three nights—and, he hoped, more—in some more secluded room would be a welcome respite from all of this.

Magiere leaned in on Léshil. "I'll say it again: *you* are—were—a bad influence on her."

Léshil rose to his feet in indignation, but before he could counter, he flinched and spun about. There stood Chap, though no one had seen him come up. Léshil leaned down into the majay-hì's face.

"Nobody asked you!"

Chap eyed Léshil with as much disapproval as Magiere did, but Leanâl-hâm tugged on Magiere's sleeve.

"We will stay with sages like Wynn?" she asked. "We will meet other sages like her?"

Léshil blinked at the girl's sudden change. "I guess. If it's a guild place, it'll probably be crawling with them."

Leanâlhâm drew back at his words. "Crawling . . . with them?"

"No, no," Léshil quickly corrected, "just a figure of speech . . . Probably a lot fewer of them than in Calm Seatt."

Brot'ân'duivé wanted to sigh but did not. Even in the girl's wish to learn more of the sages, she still feared being among too many humans. But why did Leanâlhâm take an interest in sages like Wynn Hygeorht? He hoped it was not an adolescent need to attract Osha's attention.

Before Magiere could go at Léshil again, Chap growled softly and stalked past her onto the ramp. Leanâlhâm hurried after but paused at the ramp's top at the sight of the busy piers.

For the moment Magiere appeared to be more herself, merely irritable at any opportunity. She, as well, paused behind Leanâlhâm to look over the city awaiting them. Then she urged the girl ahead, and the two followed Chap.

Brot'ân'duivé knew better than to offer Léshil assistance with the packs. He waited until the half-blood disembarked, and then followed. Even Brot'ân'duivé could not help wondering at the prospect of spending a few days among sages.

"This can't be it," Magiere said.

Chap stopped, looking the place over, and agreed with a single huff. After working their way through the streets, as Wynn had instructed, this was not what he'd expected.

The building hardly appeared a fit haven for scholars. Nondescript and only two stories high, it had been hastily stained years ago without the boards being properly stripped or cleaned.

"Why not?" Leesil asked, shrugging as he looked over the paper again. "The sages back in Bela set up in an old decommissioned barracks. Wynn says the place used to be an inn for rich patrons. When the owner died, no one bought it, so it became city property, left for years. The guild purchased it for almost nothing."

Chap felt like grumbling this time. Wynn even rambled on paper, with more information than anyone needed to know.

The walk from the harbor had been quick, but amid dodging passersby and wagons and hawkers' carts, Leanâlhâm had kept ducking around everyone and alternately clinging to either Magiere or Brot'an. Once, when she could not reach either, she had panicked and grabbed Chap's tail. She quickly let go, turning red faced despite her fright and averting her eyes.

Chap considered reassuring her that they were in no danger. But talking to the girl with memory-words would startle her even more, and possibly bring on another motherly retort from Magiere or even Leesil.

"Who's doing the talking?" Leesil asked.

Not him, as far as Chap was concerned. They did not need another bit of bumbling from Leesil's poor language skills.

"I will," Magiere answered, stepping up to the door and knocking before anyone agreed.

A moment later the door opened. A short, middle-aged woman in a teal robe looked out with a pleasant expression on her round face. Hesitation and surprise set in as her gaze flitted from one strange visitor to the next on the porch.

Chap couldn't blame her.

Leesil and Magiere both looked like mercenaries out of the wild, and as to Brot'an, the less said about his appearance, the better. Then there was a frightened green-eyed elven girl half hiding behind Magiere. Not to mention an oversized wolf just visible behind everyone.

The poor sage blinked twice and frowned. In her place Chap would have hesitated as well.

"Can I . . ." the sage began. "How may I . . . ?"

Magiere tried to smile. "We're carrying a message south for Premin Hawes of the Calm Seatt branch. She . . . We were told we might stay here, if you have room?"

Relief flooded the woman's features.

"For Premin Hawes? Of course!" she replied, moving aside to usher them in. "I'm Domin Tamira. We have few visitors at present, but the annex is rarely even half full. You can have your pick of rooms on the top floor. Have you had supper?"

At this warm welcome, all five travelers stepped in while Domin Tamira chattered so much that Chap lost interest. They passed through a wide foyer, which must have been the reception area in past times, for there was still a worn counter off to the left. A comfortable sitting room to the right was filled with old, overpatched armchairs and small couches. Bookcases stuffed with volumes, some as old and worn as the building, filled nearly all of its narrow walls. Perhaps this collection was what passed for the library here.

"You all go up and choose some rooms," the domin finally concluded. "Any room with an open door is available. I'll make certain the cooks prepare enough for dinner."

Chap did not wait for the others and took to the stairs, feeling almost guilty for his earlier thoughts about Wynn. Her penchant for giving too much information had gained them comfortable, free lodgings.

Most doors on the top floor were open, and he walked over to peer inside a large room with a window overlooking the front street. When he went to the window, he could just make out a few masts in the port between the tall warehouses.

A faded four-poster bed was draped with a soft, thick quilt, and old velvet curtains graced the windows. He was tempted to settle down and rest on a washed-out braided rug at the bed's foot.

"Magiere, come look," Leesil said, stepping inside.

She followed and looked about the room. Though the furnishings had lost their former glory, this was by far the nicest place in which Chap and his two charges had stayed since leaving their Sea Lion tavern on the eastern continent.

"I hope the captain gets delayed for a week," Leesil said. Dropping the packs, he turned about and, with arms outstretched, he toppled backward onto the bed with one of his overly dramatic sighs of relief.

Magiere said nothing. She might appreciate the room for a night or two at best. But Chap knew she was obsessed with getting to the Suman coast and il'Dha'ab Najuum as soon as possible. Though it was still a long way off, there was only one thing on Magiere's mind . . . and on Chap's.

They had to learn the whereabouts of the orb of Air.

Chap looked over to see whether Leanâlhâm had followed them in, but only Brot'an stood in the doorway. Magiere suddenly appeared to realize the same.

"Where's Leanâlhâm?" she asked.

If Chap hadn't known better, he'd have thought Brot'an looked strained.

"She is looking over books in the front room below," he answered. "As she seemed settled, I did not force her away."

Magiere nodded and started for the door. "I'll go check on her."

—*No*— . . . —*Let me*—

Magiere stopped and glanced his way. When Chap met her gaze, she didn't argue. He slipped out as Brot'an stepped aside.

He heard Magiere say behind him, "Chap is—"

"Yes, I see," Brot'an cut in.

"Don't worry—he'd never force her away from a book."

Wondering about this unexpected interest of Leanâlhâm's regarding sages and books, Chap made his way downstairs. Thankfully, he discovered that any sages about had left her alone—as he peeked in through the open archway and found the girl peering about at the patched, overstuffed chairs and the old, worn bookcases.

Leanâlhâm slowly approached a case at the far wall nearer the front window and traced the bookbindings with her slender fingers.

Chap remained half-hidden beyond the archway and simply watched her.

Deceptive as it was, he would not miss a chance to dip into her memories while she was unaware of him.

The girl everyone called Leanâlhâm relished quiet and solitude in the strange and alien little room filled with books. Even while she hid herself away in the ship's cabin, Brot'ân'duivé could always return there at any moment. Here in this very human place filled with old furnishings and so quiet for the moment, she could breathe.

Books were not unknown among the an'Cróan, though they were rarely made with hide coverings. Rolled sheaves and scrolls in cylindrical cases of seamless wood were more familiar to her. She could not make out most of the words on the outer side of the books, for though written mostly with Numanese letters, the languages were often ones she did not know, had never seen, let alone heard. When she stumbled upon a spine with one poorly, incorrectly rendered word in what she thought was her own language, she pulled out that book.

It was not just oddly formed Elvish, but a word she had heard only since coming to Wynn Hygeorht's land.

". . . Lhoin'na . . ."

At best it meant something like "of the glade," in reference to the elves of this continent that, until recently, she had not even known existed. She could not make out the other words in the title, and upon opening it, she could follow only about every third word.

Even those were so oddly—badly—written for what humans called Elvish, or the language of the an'Cróan. There were many hand-drawn illustrations, some tinted with faded colors, depicting vases, bowls, cups, and such things. The more she worked out this poor Elvish, the more she saw the "mistakes" happening over and over. The text began to make a little sense.

This was not some human who could not speak the tongue well enough to write it. It was, as Wynn had once said, another "dialect." Why would "elves," no matter what they called themselves, speak some other language or form of it?

The more she picked at the words, she realized the book was a history of pottery . . . the craft work of a people like her own but so very different from them. It was hard to imagine a whole people like but not like the an'Cróan—"[those] of the Blood." She had grown up believing that her people *were* the people that humans called elves.

She sank into a faded embroidered chair and turned page after page, finally stumbling upon what seemed part of a story about a beloved set of five finely crafted urns once stolen from this continent's elven. . . .

She stopped, peering more closely at the next two words. They did not make sense at all.

The vases had been stolen from the elven . . . the Lhoin'na . . . "guild branch" by human thieves.

Leanâlhâm looked up at all the books. There was a sages' guild—or branch—for elves rather than humans?

She looked back to the story, working it out. Apparently a group of the Lhoin'na's guardians, called "Shé'ith," went after the thieves to retrieve the vases. That one term was halfway familiar.

In her tongue, true Elvish, the root word *séthiv* meant "tranquility," or perhaps "serenity," or at least by what she knew of Wynn's Numanese and Leanâlhâm's more fluent Belaskian, which her uncle had taught her. If so, that word for the Lhoin'na's guardians was strange compared to "anmaglâhk," which meant "the stealers of life." That was what those guardians did: they took back from any who would steal the people's way of life.

She turned another page and paused at a strange illustration.

Three elves in foreign attire were riding horses like humans did. Smaller still, in the image's background, was what had to be the band of thieves fleeing from pursuit. The riders must be Shé'ith, and their leader looked impressive though disturbing. He carried a sword—again, like a human.

How could any of her people have fallen so far from their ways?

Anmaglâhk did not ride horses or carry openly exposed weapons. They were as swift as a breath but as silent as a shadow. These Shé'ith appeared to be anything but that. Lifting the book nearer to her face, she studied the illustration more closely.

Compared against the rider's grip on the sword's handle, the blade was as broad as three of his fingers. It was nearly straight, until the last third swept back in a shallow arc that she guessed was sharp on the back edge as well. But two-thirds down the blade's back, a forward-leaning barb protruded slightly.

The narrow hilt was twice as long as the width of the hand that gripped it, and it curved slightly forward and then downward at its end. The wedged crossguard appeared to have a design on it, but she could not make that out. The crossguard's upward protrusion arced forward to match the back barb's lean, while the bottom one swept slightly back toward the hilt.

Like the lead male elf in the illustration, the sword seemed larger than life. It was almost unbelievable that one of her kind would carry such a strange, human thing.

Suddenly more lost than ever, she closed the book. Even so far from the land that had rejected her, even in learning there were others like her beyond the borders of her home . . . she was alone, cast adrift. Those others, the Lhoin'na and their Shé'ith, were as foreign to her as any human.

No an'Cróan would put a creature of the wild into forced servitude. None of her people would carry a heavy tool . . . a weapon . . . made purely for war. The knife, the staff, perhaps a spear, and the bow were all they needed. She closed the book, staring at its cover and thinking of a lost home and her own people . . . and the anmaglâhk. No one would write stories about them.

Well, no *elves* would write stories about them. She had seen a book once in which Wynn had written of Osha and Sgäilsheilleache.

That book had caused nothing but grief and sorrow.

Closing her eyes, Leanâlhâm fingered the book's spine and thought back to the day, the terrible day, when she had first seen Wynn's journal. . . .

Leanâlhâm hummed softly as she pulled a loaf of wild grain bread from the communal ovens in the Coilehkrotall clan's central enclave—her home. She enjoyed baking bread for her grandfather Gleannéohkân'thva, and at least in the early morning, there was no one else about.

Still humming, she wrapped the loaf in cloth to carry it back to the tree dwelling that she shared with her grandfather along with an astonishing houseguest almost too beautiful to be real.

Cuirin'nên'a—daughter of great Eillean, a greimasg'äh like Brot'ân'-duivé—was the mother of Léshil. A few like Leanâlhâm's uncle, Sgäilsheil-leache, said he should be called Leshiârelaohk, but Léshil did not like that name, given or taught by the ancestors. For Leanâlhâm, Cuirin'nên'a's pres-ence was a constant reminder that Léshil had left.

It had been a long while since Leanâlhâm had seen him, for Sgäilsheil-leache and Osha had gone to guide him on a great journey. Yes, that woman called Magiere went as well, and the odd majay-hì who followed them.

Magiere was a human like Leanâlhâm had always imagined, barbarous and violent. But for as much as Leanâlhâm would have preferred her gone at first—leaving only Léshil—there was more to Magiere. She was fierce in word, and as with Sgäilsheilleache, her word was her oath. If she gave her word on anything, it was as hard, fast, and unyielding as the gruesome sword she carried.

At first Leanâlhâm had not cared much for Magiere, beloved of Léshil.

Before he came, Leanâlhâm believed she was the only one of mixed blood among her kind. Then Léshil, knowing almost nothing of his mother's peo-ple, walked in from the outer world. He could not even speak the language. Well, he could speak it very badly. But otherwise, to Leanâlhâm, he appeared completely unburdened by the human taint in his blood. He was funny in an odd way, and he was kind . . . and handsome.

There was not a day since Léshil left that Leanâlhâm did not think of him. He was like her, and in thinking of him, those were moments that she did not feel so tainted.

Today at least the sun shone brightly through the trees, and even in miss-ing him and her uncle, Sgäilsheilleache, she felt a rare contentment. So long as Sgäilsheilleache watched over Léshil, no harm would come to him.

Leanâlhâm turned across the enclave's central green and then slowed to look hesitantly beyond the tree dwellings. She spotted no eyes watching her from the forest. No majay-hì had come to stare at her as she hurried off for home.

The dwelling she shared with her grandfather was on the enclave's outskirts. As she approached, movement among the outer trees made her freeze. She backed up, hoping it was not a majay-hì peering out at her and reminding her that she did not belong here.

Instead the great Brot'ân'duivé stepped out into sight.

Leanâlhâm's contentment did not return.

She did not exactly fear him, but like Cuirin'nên'a, he had eyes that pierced her and tried to peel her open to see all that lay within. His rare jests always seemed to mask something darker. He was anmaglâhk—and a greimasg'äh to be revered, and rightly so. But she did not enjoy his visits the way her grandfather did.

Another figure stepped from the trees, and Leanâlhâm tensed all over.

It was Osha, and she immediately searched for a sign of anyone else following the greimasg'äh. Osha had gone with Sgäilsheilleache, so where was Léshil? Had he come back?

Feeling herself flush, she could not help calling out, "Osha!"

It was an unseemly display, but again she looked out into the forest. No one else stepped from the trees as Brot'ân'duivé glanced her way. Perhaps her uncle and Léshil had fallen behind.

She did not know Osha well, though she liked him. While he was not handsome, there was kindness in his eyes, which were a bit widely set in his plain, long face. Best of all, he never stared—or frowned—at her oddly colored hair and eyes. He did not even seem to notice such things.

Osha only nodded once to her without a smile as he followed the greimasg'äh toward Leanâlhâm's home. She waited several breaths, but neither Sgäilsheilleache nor Léshil appeared out of the forest. And Osha looked awful.

His forest gray cloak was dirty and tattered. He looked thin and exhausted and . . . forlorn. Fear rose inside Leanâlhâm, and another unwanted word escaped her mouth.

"Grandfather!"

Before Brot'ân'duivé reached the entrance of her home, its front drape whipped aside, and there was Gleannéohkân'thva. His owlish face wrinkled even more under a wary frown, for she seldom called out like this.

At the sight of Brot'ân'duivé and Osha, he exhaled, "Oh, my girl, it is only . . ."

His eyes narrowed as he trailed off. She knew she should not pester the greimasg'äh, but she could not stop.

"Where are Sgäilsheilleache and . . . and Léshil?"

Brot'ân'duivé stood looking at her grandfather. But Gleannéohkân'thva chose not to start the jibes with which they often greeted each other. This frightened Leanâlhâm even more. Osha stood silently behind the greimasg'äh and looked at no one.

Brot'ân'duivé did not meet Leanâlhâm's eyes. "We can talk inside," he said.

"No!" she cried. "Where are they?"

Grandfather held out a hand to her. "Shush . . . now come."

The hint of sharpness in his voice made her feel cold. Fear turned to panic as she took his hand.

"Osha?" she asked.

He did not answer, and then her grandfather ushered her inside. While Osha and Brot'ân'duivé entered, Grandfather pulled her down beside him.

Cuirin'nên'a appeared from the back room with her shining hair hanging loose. At the sight of Brot'ân'duivé and Osha, she halted where she was, watching them cautiously.

"You have bad news," Grandfather said calmly. "Best tell us before we imagine even worse."

"There is nothing worse," Osha whispered.

Leanâlhâm pulled her hand from her grandfather's grip, set both hands in her lap, and stared at her fingers. Whatever Osha had to say, she did not want to hear it, and she wished he had not come.

"I should—" Brot'ân'duivé began.

"No," Osha cut him off. "This is my task."

As Brot'ân'duivé fell silent, Leanâlhâm glanced between those two. No one but her grandfather dared speak that way to the greimasg'äh. She became so afraid that pain filled her chest before Osha even spoke.

"Sgäilsheilleache is lost to us," he said, his voice shaking. "He died honorably, serving his oath of guardianship without wavering. I . . . I performed burial rites myself, with Léshil and Magiere's help. And I have brought my jeóin back to our ancestors."

He dropped to his knees upon the moss-covered floor. Taking a bottle from inside his cloak, he set it before himself.

Knowing it contained a small amount of her uncle's ashes, Leanâlhâm stared at the bottle.

"Where is my son?"

Cuirin'nên'a's sharp demand made Osha look up as well as Leanâlhâm. She thought she might die if Osha answered that question. She dropped her gaze again and the floor appeared to waver in her sight, though the room around her seemed to roar.

She choked and could not breathe. But if Léshil was . . .

"He is well," Osha whispered.

But that respite did nothing for Leanâlhâm now.

Whether at home or away to fulfill some necessary purpose, Sgäilsheilleache was the wall between her and almost everyone else. He was gone. How could it be?

The room fell silent, and all she did was sit there, seeing nothing, even when Osha suddenly appeared beside her on one knee. He did not touch her, but his face was close to her ear.

"I am sorry. . . . I am so . . ."

He was close enough that she could feel pain emanating from him, and for a moment she clung to it. Focused on his loss, she might not have to feel her own, but the lull did not last.

"What do you mean, he has left the continent?" Cuirin'nên'a asked quietly.

Something had passed in conversation that Leanâlhâm had missed, and she heard Brot'ân'duivé continue.

"Léshil and Magiere, and the majay-hì and the sage, have sailed for the eastern continent to hide the . . ." He dropped silent for a moment. "Or this is what Osha reports."

"It is true," Osha whispered.

"Most Aged Father will not let them go," Cuirin'nên'a countered. "He will twist the truth of Sgäilsheilleache's death into an aberration of loyalties, to a betrayal of the caste."

Leanâlhâm finally raised her head; there was more she had missed moments ago. Everyone spoke as if they all knew something that she did not.

Osha rose suddenly, pointing at Brot'ân'duivé as he spoke to Cuirin'nên'a.

"No! We have proof. Wynn Hygeorht recorded what happened. The council of clan elders have seen her . . . heard of her. By her knowledge of us, and even our language, they will believe her."

"An account?" Cuirin'nên'a asked. "Let me see it."

As of yet, Grandfather had not said a word. He sat silent and stricken, barely noting all that took place around him. Leanâlhâm longed to grab him, to curl up in his arms for comfort—and to give comfort.

"Enough!" Brot'ân'duivé barked, and Leanâlhâm flinched, looking up.

He glared at Osha with an open anger that she had never before seen him display. Had he not wanted Osha to mention this account of Wynn's? Leanâlhâm also wanted to know exactly what had happened, but Brot'ân'duivé glanced down at her once.

Grandfather reached over and grasped her hand. "The book," was all he said.

Brot'ân'duivé hesitated and then reached inside his tunic and pulled out a small book. Its blue cover was worn and creased, and it did look like something Leanâlhâm had seen the human sage carry.

Brot'ân'duivé held it out to Cuirin'nên'a. In one firm step, she took it from him, turned away, and began leafing through its pages.

Leanâlhâm was left to suffer in ignorance. It did not matter, for Sgäilsheilleache was gone. She looked to the glass bottle that Osha had left upon the moss, and then buckled with her hands over her face and cried in silence.

Outside the archway Chap stood paralyzed by all he experienced in Leanâlhâm's memories. It was like reliving the mourning of Sgäile's death all over again. He hung his head but forced himself to focus on what he had learned.

Brot'an had returned with Osha to Sgäile's home. Cuirin'nên'a had spoken of Most Aged Father with venom in her voice and had no reason to feel otherwise for all the years that he had imprisoned her. Leesil still believed that Brot'an had gotten his mother "mixed up" with the dissidents, but Chap was not so certain. From what he now pieced together, it seemed that both Gleann and Cuirin'nên'a were participants from the very beginning in whatever Brot'an had attempted.

Leanâlhâm had not been and perhaps was not even now. She had been allowed to remain that day only because Gleann was in too much grief to be without her. And poor Osha appeared to have been as much an ignorant victim as she was.

Not so for Brot'an.

The old assassin had been forced by Osha's naïve but honorable intentions into exposing the journal to the others. If Osha had not done so, would Brot'an have even shared Wynn's journal with Gleann and Leesil's mother? Perhaps—or not—but he had hinted earlier to Magiere that this journal was the crux of all that followed.

Chap still did not see how, not completely.

Leanâlhâm suddenly sat up, turned her head toward the archway, and looked right at him.

Chap froze. He'd not made a sound, not a move that could have alerted her. Yet, half-startled, she gazed at him as if she'd heard something and turned to find him watching her.

Leanâlhâm swallowed once and turned away.

Chap backed up, still distracted by what he had learned and what he had not. As he walked up the stairs, he paused once to look behind him.

Leanâlhâm didn't appear, though he lingered there a moment longer, watching for her and feeling unsettled.

The girl everyone called Leanâlhâm did not mind Chap's presence anymore. He had not tried to disturb her, tried to make her interact with anyone, or told her to make a better effort to "adjust"—as the greimasg'äh so often did.

Still, she had felt watched, like the moments in the enclave when those eyes appeared in the forest. This time, it was not quite the same.

It was as if she had been talking out loud to herself, only to find someone was listening whom she had not noticed at first. No one had come into the room, but when she had looked, Chap had been there. She hesitantly turned her head again, leaning a little to peer around the armchair's side.

Chap was gone, and she heaved a long breath in relief without knowing why.

Gripping the book tightly to her chest, she thought on that day when Osha had come to her home with that horrible news. She thought of the days that followed, some of which had slid by so slowly and yet had become dull and blurred and so hard to remember. She and Grandfather had struggled through the earliest, hardest part of mourning.

Osha, in his own grief, had been there for them. They understood his loss as well. There were strange moments she did remember. Three times she had come upon Grandfather sitting alone with the greimasg'äh, and the two had been whispering to each other. Brot'ân'duivé did not appear to be offering comfort, and Grandfather, though grieved, appeared more intense than Leanâlhâm could ever remember.

At that time, she had not thought much of this. She had been in a daze, aching from the loss and fearing a future without her uncle. And she had Osha constantly attending her. That Grandfather had his old friend to distract him with other things was a blessing she would not begrudge him. She should have paid more attention, but that time was long past.

With another deep breath she rose from her chair in the little front library and headed for the stairs. The greimasg'äh would expect her to choose a room before dinner. It was not until she was halfway up the stairs that she realized she still carried the book.

She almost turned back to put it away, then changed her mind and held on to it as she climbed the stairs to find the others.

CHAPTER THIRTEEN

On the annex's upper floor, Brot'ân'duivé felt relieved as he left Léshil and Magiere's room and they closed their door. His presence among them on this journey was necessary, but at times their company was exhausting. A few moments alone were welcome.

Walking down the hall, he peered inside various doorways. Finally deciding the choice did not matter, he entered the last room along the corridor. It was closest to the head of the stairs, and all of the rooms were equally oversoft and garish with thick quilts and heavy curtains.

Why humans lived with such cumbersome furnishings was beyond him. The life of an anmaglâhk was austere, but even his people chose possessions sparingly. Then he heard a soft *click-scratch* on the wooden floor outside the room.

He stood silently tracking the sound in his mind and knowing its every movement. From the upper steps of the central stairs to a left turn around the banister's crest and down the hall, he followed it along the path he had come moments before. A soft scratching was followed by the sound of an opening door.

Returning quietly to crack open his door, Brot'ân'duivé peeked out to confirm Chap's passage. He watched the tip of the majay-hì's tail disappear into Léshil and Magiere's room.

If Chap had come up, where was Leanâlhâm? Perhaps she was still down-stairs looking at books.

Brot'ân'duivé debated going after her. He had little experience communi-cating with adolescent girls, and especially not with an emotionally shattered orphan. Much of the time she left him feeling like an overbearing guardian to be suffered at arm's length, or perhaps like the less-than-desirable relative whom all families tolerated out of respect.

He did not wish to concern himself with such things, but he did.

Leanâlhâm was important to him, in part because Gleannéohkân'thva had been one of his only friends. He often found himself worrying, wishing to close the gap with the girl at least enough to help her find her place in this world.

Still reluctant, Brot'ân'duivé was on the verge of going to find Leanâlhâm when she came up the steps. She carried a book gripped in both hands, and stopped at the sight of him. Uncertain what to say, he sidestepped, gesturing into the room he had selected.

"Will this serve you? They are all quite similar."

She stepped closer and looked in at the huge four-poster bed.

"I will sleep on the rug," he added.

She hesitated for a few breaths. "Greimasg'äh, with so many rooms, per-haps I could have my own during our stay here?"

This had not occurred to him. Perhaps he—and not she—was the one who most viewed him as her constant guardian. He had no objection to her request, but it would be best if she took the next room so he could hear any trouble that might arise.

"Of course," he said.

"My thanks."

Her thanking him for such a small thing felt like another shove to main-tain their distance. Before she walked off on her own, he went to the next open door and gestured inward as he gripped its handle.

The room had white lace curtains and a slightly yellowed white comforter. The water basin and pitcher depicted lavender-colored roses. He did not see much difference between this room and the others, so, holding the door's handle, he waited there.

She looked inside, but her expression gave away nothing. He could not tell whether she was pleased or whether, like him, she found the place oversoft and overdecorated.

"I think . . . I think I will rest a bit before dinner," she said.

"Of course."

She hurried in, and he closed the door before she could touch it. Turning, he reentered his own chosen quarters. He would still sleep on the rug rather than smother in one of these ridiculous beds.

Crossing to the window, Brot'ân'duivé still dwelt on the girl and their increasingly empty but polite interactions. This was partially his fault, but after all she had been through, formalities might be the only anchor she had left. Should she try to tell him how she truly felt, she might open a floodgate that would not close. How would he ever deal with that?

She had always been daunted by his presence when he visited Gleannéohkân'thva in earlier days. Now she had even greater difficulty tolerating his company.

When had that begun?

Gazing out the window at the city, Brot'ân'duivé did not need to ponder for long. It was the day at the enclave, the first time he took Osha away from her. . . .

After only a short time at the central enclave of Coilehkrotall, Brot'ân'duivé became restless. Too many pressing matters, too many unknowns, could not be put off much longer. Every moment he lingered might bring another turn for the worse that he should have anticipated.

Leanâlhâm and Gleannéohkân'thva were in the worst stage of mourning. Somehow Osha's presence and shared grief were helping to carry them through. Both Gleannéohkân'thva and Cuirin'nên'a had studied the journal in private.

A part of Brot'ân'duivé was now glad they had learned of its existence. Though he was a master of gathering information, the old healer and Léshil's mother sometimes saw ways to *use* information that he did not. Until they did, he still had to deal with Osha.

He went to the guest chamber on the tree home's main floor, tapped twice on the living wood of the archway, and brushed the curtain aside. Cuirin'nên'a, more beautiful than the woman he loved and had lost, sat cross-legged upon a bedding mattress.

There was not much of Eillean in her features, yet she had her mother's determination for serving the people. If life had been fairer, kinder . . . If it had been possible for him to have bonded with Eillean . . .

"So he married—bonded—with that woman?" Cuirin'nên'a said quietly.

She was not reading the journal. It simply lay beside her as she stared at the room's blank, bark-covered wall.

"Yes, Magiere, as you read," he answered, though it had not truly been a question.

"Is he . . . happy, do you think?"

It was not the question of an anmaglâhk but of a mother. All of the caste lived a life of service. This did not change because they and others had chosen a different path against Most Aged Father. Amid a purpose, anmaglâhk could not afford sentiment, though this did not mean they had none.

"For now," he answered.

"Then he is beyond my . . . our reach."

"For now," he repeated. "But we cannot afford to wait in present matters. There is another unexpected one."

The barest crease marred Cuirin'nên'a's perfect brow.

Brot'ân'duivé dug out the smooth, roundish stone and crouched to hold it out. When Cuirin'nên'a caught sight of it, the crease of her brow vanished. Her eyes widened slightly before turning to him. She could not read its marks, though she knew from where the stone had come.

"A sudden breeze," he said.

Cuirin'nên'a slowly shook her head. It was so rare to see her baffled by anything as she glanced toward the room's curtained archway. Osha was not even present inside the tree, let alone in the outer chamber.

"That is what it may *say*," she whispered, "but what does it *mean* . . . for Osha?"

"I do not know."

"Then you have delayed too long. Act quickly!"

Perhaps sentiment and pity were the reasons he had delayed. Perhaps he had needed someone else's assurance for the cruelty he would display to the few, including her, who meant something to him. Fate was often cruel.

Brot'ân'duivé had barely risen when he heard the home's front curtain being pulled aside. Low voices rose in the outer area, and he heard his old friend, the healer.

"Set the plates," Gleannéohkân'thva said, his voice lacking all its normal biting charm. "I'll find the others."

This was followed by the sounds of two other steps and the shuffle of plates and then Leanâlhâm's shaky sigh. It would have been better if Brot'ân'duivé could have caught Osha alone.

"Now!" Cuirin'nên'a whispered.

Along with sentiment, pity had to be banished.

Brot'ân'duivé pulled the chamber curtain aside and stepped out to find Leanâlhâm sitting cross-legged, head down, as Osha spread wooden plates in a circle upon the moss carpet. Although still thin, he looked physically better. His forest gray cloak had been cleaned and mended, and several days of rest and decent meals had improved his color.

Gleannéohkân'thva was halfway up the curving steps along the wall and paused his climb to look down.

"I was about to look for you, but as you . . ."

The old healer trailed off as Brot'ân'duivé turned to Osha, now crouched beside Leanâlhâm.

"Our stay is finished," he said. "We must leave now."

Osha started in surprise. "It has been only three days. Leanâlhâm is still . . . Greimasg'äh, we cannot leave."

Brot'ân'duivé held out the stone and displayed it in plain sight with his thumb and forefinger.

"This is a summons for you . . . from the Chein'âs."

Osha rose, staring at the stone. "I made my journey to them years past to receive my weapons and tools. Why do you show me this?"

"Because they have called you back."

"No!" Osha snapped. "They call us once, when the elders of our caste approve an initiate to seek out a jeóin. The stone is a mistake!"

"There are no such mistakes," lashed a soft voice.

Cuirin'nên'a stood in the chamber archway; one of her hands held the curtain aside as she then stepped out.

"You are summoned," she added. "This is the way, based on covenants with the Burning Ones, whom we protect along with the Séyilf, the Wind-Blown. This is part of our people's ways as well. And in keeping them, this is part of what your jeóin died to uphold!"

Brot'ân'duivé clenched his jaw, for this was not the way he would have handled Osha. Years of isolation in imprisonment had hardened Cuirin'nên'a, though all she said was true. Unlike all others, she had borne a burden none of them could match.

Osha and Leanâlhâm were unaware that the other three in this chamber were part of the rumored dissidents. But in all of Cuirin'nên'a's long years alone, not one rumor had ever been proven and not one dissident had ever been uncovered because of her. She had suffered Most Aged Father's threats, taunts, and demands, his mental tortures without even being able to put her lost human mate to rest . . . until Léshil had come for her.

Cuirin'nên'a had never broken. That Brot'ân'duivé and Gleannéohkân'thva stood here still free was proof enough of this. Many might claim they could do as well as she had. Many would be liars.

Osha fell silent under Cuirin'nên'a's harsh words. Only then did Brot'ân'duivé give enough notice to the girl—too late.

Leanâlhâm's grief-strained face was filled with confusion. She sucked in a breath as if to speak. Only a sob came out as she fled, ripping through the curtained archway and out of the tree home. Osha immediately turned to follow, but the old healer blocked his way with a gentle touch.

"You have a purpose," Gleannéohkân'thva whispered. "This one must be fulfilled."

Osha stood there, slowly sagging.

"And you will guide me?" he asked, his tone unreadable.

It was obvious to whom he spoke, and Brot'ân'duivé knew the worst was over. The fire caves of the Chein'âs were a long journey away, but Osha was Anmaglâhk, and he would obey.

"Yes," Brot'ân'duivé said and headed for the outer doorway.

Once outside, he held the curtain back. Osha finally followed, as did Gleannéohkân'thva, but not Cuirin'nên'a. Osha turned all ways, looking about in a sudden return of anguish, but Leanâlhâm was nowhere to be seen.

Brot'ân'duivé's old friend nodded to him. "When will you return?" the healer asked.

"I do not know."

At that, Osha cast him a hardened glare before turning to Gleannéohkân'thva.

"I thank your enclave for its kindness and welcome," he said with a deep nod of respect to the healer. "Tell Leanâlhâm that I . . . I will see you both again."

Osha started to turn away but then froze. At that, Brot'ân'duivé spotted Cuirin'nên'a in the doorway.

As precisely beautiful as any statuette of tawny wood fashioned by the most skilled Shaper, she was equally still and watchful. Osha began to speak, but she cut him off.

"I will watch over them," she said. "No harm will come to them unless it first passes me."

With closed eyes, Osha bowed more deeply, as if in gratitude, but when he turned to leave, he would not look at Brot'ân'duivé. He strode off across the village green. Like any who had once been before the Burning Ones, he knew the general direction.

With one last nod to those who remained behind, Brot'ân'duivé took off at a trot, quickly passing Osha. Within moments, they jogged out of the enclave into the wild forests of their land. Then the two of them were alone except for the tiny hummingbirds of mixed colors darting among the large blooms in the underbrush.

Brot'ân'duivé led the way deeper into the forest.

The world shifted to rich hues pulsing in the somber light filtering down through the canopy above. Osha said nothing more for the rest of that day. Brot'ân'duivé did not give this much thought, as it would have accomplished nothing. When dusk began to gather among the trees, something else crept into his awareness, and he slowed.

If the movement of an unseen shadow could be heard, this was the only way he could have described what he felt from behind them.

Now a few steps ahead, Osha slowed to look back. "What?"

Brot'ân'duivé could not answer. When he scanned the forest, he saw nothing, heard nothing, and now felt nothing. Osha looked about, waiting for an answer. Brot'ân'duivé simply turned and ran onward.

That night when they camped, he closed his eyes but did not sleep.

For three days more, they ran deeper into the land, always heading westward and a bit to the south. No matter how far they traveled, the sense of a shadow kept returning to slowly unnerve Brot'ân'duivé. In the early afternoon of the fourth day, he stopped atop the rise of a sharp slope.

"Continue," he whispered. "I will catch up."

With a puzzled glance backward, Osha obeyed and jogged onward.

Brot'ân'duivé waited briefly until Osha was beyond sight, and then trotted down the same slope. When the sharp rise cut off his sight of the way they had come, he darted off Osha's chosen path and into the forest.

He sidled in next to a great maple tree and became as still in mind as in body. The shadows of the forest took him in, and with his thoughts emptied, his senses opened fully as he waited.

The sound of a soft step carried to his ears.

It was little more than what would be made by a leaf falling upon the earth. He saw nothing, though his eyes unconsciously followed that sound up to the trees to the right of the slope's ridgetop. His senses separated every leaf, twig, blossom, and branch until . . .

His awareness fixed on a shadow with no origin. Suddenly it changed and fit in.

Brot'ân'duivé remained hidden in silence and in shadow. Only another greimasg'äh could cause such an uncertainty to his awareness . . . to be there and then not, in a shadow. It had moved either in body or thought and betrayed itself for an instant. Brot'ân'duivé stilled his mind and emptied his consciousness before he became the one to be sensed.

"You are here. . . . I know this . . . as much as you know I am."

That whisper carried among the trees. A form suddenly took shape beside a stand of aspens off to his left. Dressed all in forest gray, this anmaglâhk was broad shouldered and perhaps short for an an'Cróan.

"Urhkarasiférin," Brot'ân'duivé whispered.

Another greimasg'äh had tracked him. This changed everything.

"Turn back," he said. "Whatever Most Aged Father has asked of you . . . your purpose ends here."

"What of the book?" Urhkarasiférin returned. "It is all I have come for, nothing more."

"Then you have come for nothing."

Still Urhkarasiférin did not move. Neither of them feared the other, and both saw death only as a necessary consequence of service. All that differed was whom they each served first, the people or Most Aged Father.

"Do you have the human sage's journal?" Urhkarasiférin asked.

It took a fateful blink before Brot'ân'duivé answered. "It belongs to me now."

That wink of a pause was enough to fail him in his lie. Urhkarasiférin was gone without a sound.

Brot'ân'duivé stood frozen for one breath and then bolted after Osha. He did not even try to move silently, and Osha came to a halt before he caught up. Brot'ân'duivé signaled to him without stopping, and Osha whirled and vanished into the trees before Brot'ân'duivé caught up and took the lead.

He changed directions often, even though he knew it would do no good if Urhkarasiférin still followed. What concerned Brot'ân'duivé more was that the other greimasg'äh might have turned back.

Patchy, lime-colored moss cushioned their footfalls until Brot'ân'duivé finally stopped. He crouched beneath the bright leaves of a squat maple, and Osha dropped beside him.

"We are followed," he whispered. "I can no longer come with you, and we must act quickly now."

Osha had been through much in the past moons. The sudden statement that he was being abandoned made him rock backward on his haunches. He braced himself to keep from toppling.

"Greimasg'äh," he whispered. "Only caste elders know the full way to the Chein'âs."

Young initiates were blindfolded for part of their journey. Even those given assent by their jeóin did not learn those last steps until many years—if ever—into their life of service.

If Urhkarasiférin was here, then Most Aged Father had sent him. There was no telling what else the mad patriarch had done. And the journal had been left with Cuirin'nên'a . . . in Gleannéohkân'thva's home.

Brot'ân'duivé would have to violate a sacred oath, and he grabbed Osha by the front of his vestment.

"Listen," he hissed. "You will travel like the wind to the coastline, to where the Branch Mountains, what the humans call the Crown Range, meet the eastern coast at the farthest corner of our territory. There you must find an elder in a coastal enclave and beg a ship to carry you south. Within three days, you will reach a large, empty shore of nothing but gray-tinged sand and seaweed. You will see the granite point of the tallest mountain from the dead center of this beach. Have the ship's crew drop you there, even if you have to swim."

"Greimasg'äh!" Osha whispered loudly. "Do not break the covenant!"

"Quiet!" he ordered. "From that beach, travel inland until you reach the base of the foothills. Head onward, looking for the shortest one, like a mountain with its top broken off. As you draw closer, it will be easier for you to see its sheared and ragged top—and the mouth of an old volcanic vent at its crest. Keep your awareness of direction, and in the line between the beach left behind and the broken peak, search along the mountain's base until you find a stone chute. Follow that to the entrance."

Osha closed his eyes. "You should not tell me these things."

"The chute leads to a tunnel," Brot'ân'duivé went on. "And the tunnel leads to the cavern. From there you will know what to do. When you reach the portal of the Burning Ones' white metal—"

"No, Greimasg'äh!"

Brot'ân'duivé shook Osha until the young one opened his eyes.

"Touch one of your blades to the portal . . . and it will open."

It was done. Brot'ân'duivé had broken one of the oldest oaths of his caste. In trusting this most inept of all anmaglâhk, he endangered a centuries-old covenant of protection for the last of an ancient race.

Osha shook his head.

"Sgäilsheilleache would have died first," he whispered. "He *did* die before breaking any oath. What have you done?"

Instead of empathy or even respect for the young one's sense of honor, Brot'ân'duivé felt only disdain.

"Sgäilsheilleache was blind," he said quietly as he rose to full height. "Ignorance to the actions of Most Aged Father is what has ruptured our caste from within . . . and my death will not help any of our people. Now get up!"

There was one more thing to be done, for Osha would not reach the coast quickly enough on his own. Brot'ân'duivé looked all around and then walked toward a patch of brighter light in a break among the trees.

"What are you doing?" Osha asked.

"Be silent and follow. Do not speak again until instructed to do so."

They were far enough from any eyes that should not see what would come next . . . what Osha should not see. Brot'ân'duivé reached the edge of the clearing, stopped, and motioned for Osha to halt.

"Stay," Brot'ân'duivé said, and he stepped out into the clearing.

Closing his eyes, Brot'ân'duivé emptied his consciousness once again, as he would to let shadow take him whole. Here in the light there were no shadows. Amid his emptied mind, he called up one image and held it until it was perfect in his silenced thoughts.

He hoped it would hear him . . . *hear* that pure apparition of its presence held with the shadow that stood amid the light. He lost all awareness, even of the moments that slipped by.

Until a heavy footfall made him open his eyes.

Beyond the clearing's far side and out among the trees, two branches in a cluster of cedars suddenly moved. They appeared to separate from the others and drift between the trees into view. Below them came a long equine head with two crystalline blue eyes larger than those of a majay-hì. Those eyes fixed on him as the creature's tall ears independently turned his way.

A deer would have been dainty next to this massive beast, for it was as large as an elk or a tall horse. Silver gray in hue, its coat was long and shaggy, more so around its shoulders and across its broad chest. What had at first appeared to be branches were two curved horns—smooth, without prongs—sprouting high from its head.

Brot'ân'duivé heard Osha's astonished whisper from behind. "Clhuassas!"

"My thanks," he murmured, for it had heard his call.

He was about to force Osha to do something else unconscionable.

Clhuassas—the listeners—were among the forest's oldest sacred ones, like the majay-hì. Desperation pushed Brot'ân'duivé to something others considered a sacrilege. But they did not understand that this was a secret of the Greimasg'äh. Only they could make a sound deep within shadow, within the emptiness of self, that could beg for such help.

Urhkarasiférin's presence was nowhere nearby as far as Brot'ân'duivé could sense. He needed to leave, and for that Osha must be taken quickly away. Then he heard Osha backstep heavily.

At the crackle of leaves underfoot, the great creature stalled.

Brot'ân'duivé could not risk admonishing Osha again.

The silver-gray clhuassas slowly walked into the clearing. Its coat glowed like threads of silver under sunlight, and its eyes seemed too bright. When it came near enough that Brot'ân'duivé felt its snorting breath upon his face, it lowered its massive head to look him in the eyes.

Brot'ân'duivé put his forehead against the bridge of the sacred one's nose. He let go of its image, and in the shadowed emptiness of his mind, he envisioned Osha and the coastal destination the young one had to reach.

The beast snorted and stamped its massive hoof once, but it did not buck its head to strike him down. Brot'ân'duivé felt its hot, moist breath as it exhaled on his chin and throat. When he opened his eyes, he was face-to-face— eye to eye—with the listener.

"Osha," he whispered, "come . . . now."

It was more than three breaths before he heard the young one's steps. Osha rounded wide to the left, his expression beyond tense.

"What are you doing?" he whispered.

"Climb onto its back," Brot'ân'duivé ordered.

"No! I will not ride a sacred one like a beast of burden!"

Brot'ân'duivé had hardly believed that an anmaglâhk of Osha's limited status would defy him, but he kept his patience.

"It has been too long since I received the stone!" he almost snapped. "This one will carry you more swiftly than you can run. It has agreed to this. . . . Now get on."

Brot'ân'duivé took out the smooth message stone and thrust it out at Osha.

Osha stared in horror between the stone and the listener. The clhuassas swung its head toward him and took a step. Osha stiffened. When the creature snorted into his face, his eyes rolled as if he might faint.

"This is its choice," Brot'ân'duivé said quietly.

Osha swallowed hard and reached out to take the stone. Turning his head away in resignation, he stepped in carefully at the creature's side. He slowly reached up to grasp its neck. Even as tall as he was, he had to jump to pull himself up and swing his leg over. Still afraid to touch it, he quickly snatched his hands back.

"You had best hang on," Brot'ân'duivé warned. "When you reach the cavern of the Chein'âs, cast the stone over the precipice's edge into the red light rising from below . . . and they will come."

Now that they were about to part, and Osha would do as required of him, Brot'ân'duivé stepped closer. He had no notion of what to say, so he fell back on all he had left.

"In silence and in shadow."

Osha would not look at him, as if the axiom of the Anmaglâhk no longer had meaning. The clhuassas lunged without warning, and Osha grabbed its neck as it raced off through the trees.

Both were quickly gone from sight, and Brot'ân'duivé turned away.

He did not know the whole purpose that Urhkarasiférin had been given by Most Aged Father. Now that the other greimasg'äh had been exposed, there was also no knowing what he would do. It was three days back to the enclave, and Urhkarasiférin might be nearly a quarter day ahead of him.

Brot'ân'duivé broke into a run through the forest.

Brot'ân'duivé started slightly at a soft knock on his door in the guild's annex.

"Greimasg'äh?" Leanâlhâm called softly from outside. "Dinner is served. Will you come down?"

He paused before answering, "Yes," and turned from the window for the door.

Brot'ân'duivé tried—and failed—to forget all he had asked of Osha, the oaths he had broken, and the far worse things he had done to save his people.

CHAPTER FOURTEEN

Leesil couldn't help enjoying the stay in Chathburh's guild annex. The comparative luxury was too enticing. The bed was so soft that he and Magiere slept late the following day and were reluctant to get up. After lunch, they took Leanâlhâm shopping, mainly to help her adjust to her new world. The girl was still timid among so many humans, but that improved so long as one of them stayed close to her. She had fewer moments of panic out in the busy streets.

While visiting a shop, she was delighted when Magiere bought her a new soft-bristled hairbrush. Apparently the girl had been using an old wooden comb scavenged somewhere along the way. Her pleasure at something so simple embarrassed Leesil slightly, or perhaps it only made him more aware that Leanâlhâm was unaccustomed to small kindnesses. But in being out and about, he also noticed a few taverns calling out to old longings he'd thought buried and forgotten.

When they returned to the annex near dusk, Domin Tamira greeted them with a smile.

"Supper is about ready," she declared. "You should call your other companions."

"Yes, of course," Magiere replied.

On the upper floor, they found Chap sitting vigil between the stairs and Brot'an's closed door. Even Leanâlhâm sighed in exasperation.

"Oh, majay-hì, you should have come with us."

Leesil wasn't so sure and stepped to the door to knock once.

"Brot'an . . . dinner."

The door opened, and Brot'an looked out, his gaze coming to rest on the girl. She held up the small object in her hand.

"Look, Greimasg'äh, Magiere bought me a brush. I will go and put it with my things."

Any response Brot'an had was left hanging as she rushed off to her own room.

"That was . . . kind of you," he said, though it sounded forced. "May I reimburse you for the cost?"

It had never occurred to Leesil that Brot'an carried any coin. Of course he would, since he'd been staying at inns with Osha and Leanâlhâm while the three were in Calm Seatt. How he'd acquired local currency was the question, and Leesil wasn't sure he wanted to know.

"It's all right," Magiere returned almost coldly.

"A message came from the ship while you were out," Brot'an said, changing the subject. "The cargo exchange is nearly complete. We set sail in the morning."

Leesil slumped in disappointment, and already his stomach felt queasy again. Dinner this night might be his last easy meal for a while.

"Let's go eat," he grumbled.

Then Leanâlhâm hurried out of her room. "I am ready."

Magiere half smiled and shooed the girl along as all five of them descended the stairs. Upon reaching the dining area's open archway, Leesil stopped in his tracks at the sight of the table. Only one aspect of their stay at the annex had been less than pleasing to him: the food.

Last night's supper had been vegetable stew and rough grain bread. They'd had watery herbed lentils and more rough grain bread for lunch. Of course he'd eaten much worse in their travels, but in a port city there would be delicacies available, shipped up and down a populated coast. And what were they having for dinner again?

As one of the robed sages set a large crock on the table and lifted the heavy lid, Leesil saw . . . lentil and vegetable stew. Big hunks of turnips floated among the carrot slices.

Five sages in different-colored robes bustled about the table, setting out bowls and mugs. He had no wish to appear ungrateful, but it was like living with five Wynns all at once. He was completely outnumbered when it came to whatever went into the cooking pot.

Brot'an ushered Leanâlhâm in, but Leesil grabbed Magiere's arm before she followed.

"Let's go out and find an eatery," he said quietly. "I want something good for my last meal . . . before I lose it by noon tomorrow on that ship."

Magiere blinked. "Leesil, this is perfectly good food. Besides, we shouldn't spend unnecessary coins."

"Don't be a miser," he whispered back.

Her brows lifted.

"We'll find a tavern," he rushed on. "Maybe I can fix the money problem as well."

This last comment was a mistake.

"Don't you even think about that!" she hissed.

They were both distracted by a fit of sniffing, and Leesil peered around behind Magiere.

Barely sticking his head through the archway, Chap stood on her far side. He sniffed again and then snorted, as if clearing his nose of something unpleasant. Chap let out a grumbling whine, and an image rose in Leesil's head.

There was an old vendor's cart in Bela, the capital of their homeland. Sausages dangled on wooden bars above a grill-covered coal pot, where the vendor was searing yet more. Leesil could almost smell them as they sizzled.

"Chap wants sausages," he whispered.

"What?" Magiere turned on the dog. "No, you don't. You two stop goading each other on!"

By this point everyone in the dining chamber was glancing their way.

"Will you join us?" Brot'an asked pointedly.

"Nope," Leesil answered. "We're going out."

He pulled on Magiere's arm, but she planted her feet. Chap took one back step and then froze, eyeing Brot'an.

"I would like to stay," Leanâlhâm said, "and go to the library again." She looked to Brot'an. "If that is all right."

"Yes," he answered. "I am staying, too."

At that, Chap's right upper jowl rose slightly.

—*If Brot'an—stays—I should—stay—*

Leesil knew this must be a disappointment to the dog, who had clearly been looking forward to eating out.

"The majay-hì is welcome to join you," Brot'an said, as if he'd guessed what Chap just related. "I do not think he will learn much sitting outside my door."

Something like a cat's hiss slipped out between Chap's teeth.

"Enough, all of you!" Magiere cut in, and then looked once at Leanâlhâm before fixing on Brot'an. "You swear to stay put and watch over her?"

Leesil didn't like the hint of a smile on Brot'an's face.

"I do so swear," he announced and settled in a chair beside the girl's.

Leanâlhâm frowned at Magiere.

"Good enough!" Leesil declared, and before Magiere started in again, he snatched the back of her belt and pulled.

"Wait, not yet—"

At least in backpedaling, she'd either follow or end up on her butt. But when Leesil reached the front door, Magiere whirled on him and almost raised her fist. Chap still lingered near the archway.

"Are you coming or not?" Leesil asked.

Chap growled once and turned to follow. Before Magiere could make any more fuss, Leesil slipped out the front door.

Exhilarated by the glowing streetlamps and the sounds of the city, he remembered one nearby place he'd seen earlier that day. He wandered happily along the cobbled ways and looked around until he pulled up short, as if stumbling upon a likely place by pure chance.

A painted sign in Numanese hung over the door; Leesil translated the words as "The Red Fox." He stayed back from the front window he had peered through during the day, as its shutters were still half open, and he turned to Magiere.

"What about this? I can smell some kind of meat being served in there."

Magiere went to the window just the same. Looking in, she probably spotted at least two tables full of patrons playing cards.

"You picked this place for the food?" she asked dryly.

Leesil feigned innocence. "What else?"

"Don't you even think of touching a single card, die, or tile."

At least this was the Magiere that Leesil remembered and back to normal for the moment. He smiled and stepped up, and grabbing the tavern door's handle, he was inside before she could catch him.

The tavern was a bit more upscale than he'd realized. A long, polished oak bar was lined with rows of actual pewter goblets and tankards. Several buxom girls weaved among packed tables with overburdened wooden trays.

But in the back of his mind, he was thinking that whatever coins they had might be multiplied a little bit—especially since he'd been the last one to have their coin pouch, and he still did.

By the time Magiere followed him, wrestling her way through the crowded room, he'd already ordered up grilled chicken, spiced potatoes, tea, and ale—and two sausages—from one of the passing girls. When he plopped into a chair, it was too late for Magiere to say anything. Only Chap still grumbled as he circled around, momentarily frightening a few patrons at a nearby table before he settled beside Leesil's chair.

A few years ago, Leesil had had to drink himself into a stupor just to sleep. Those nights were gone, and he no longer craved deep red wine. A game of cards was something else. That old itch still tickled him, and it had been too long since he'd scratched it.

Four men across the room at a table near the bar's far end appeared to be playing a card game much like Two Kings, and the dealer was a middle-aged red-haired woman. Leesil took no more than a glance before looking idly about the rest of the tavern. Soon the food arrived, along with a tankard for Magiere.

She watched him throughout the meal, but with her mouth full, at least she couldn't keep questioning him. Leesil shared his food with Chap, and every few bites he'd hack off a lump of sausage or chicken and toss it off to his right.

A clack of teeth answered, along with wet smacking and gnashing, followed by a gulp below the table. At one point there was a deep belch.

Magiere scowled in disgust, leaning back to peer under the table. When she did, Leesil arched up to look in her tankard.

More than half was gone, as fortunately the food was a bit salty—a typical trick by proprietors to sell more drink. While Magiere still scowled down at Chap, Leesil waved over one of the girls to refill the tankard. The girl was gone before Magiere looked up and Leesil quickly averted his eyes.

"What are you up to?" she asked.

He wiped his hands and stood up. "I'm going to earn our dinner back."

"Oh, no, you aren't!" She lunged, making a grab for him.

The table bucked up as Magiere's legs half straightened, and as it rocked back into her legs, Chap snarled somewhere below. Magiere tumbled back down into her chair, and so did her tankard of ale.

Leesil almost stalled. Whether she drank the ale or wore it was good enough for him to slip off through the crowd. He'd pay for that later, but right now he was eager to get in on a game.

He'd barely squirmed through the crowded room when he almost stalled again, glancing down at himself. With his hauberk of battered iron rings and both punching blades strapped on, he must look like some half-blood mercenary to the locals.

At the squeak of some serving girl when her tray of plates rattled and at least one hit the floor, he knew Magiere was coming for him. Two of the cardplayers looked up, one leaning back to glance around him at the commotion.

Leesil unstrapped both blades as he settled in a vacant chair. The instant he heard Magiere behind him, he held the sheathed blades up without even looking.

"Hang on to these for me."

"Leesil—"

"I know what I'm doing."

Before Magiere got out another word, Chap growled, followed by . . .

—*If you—cheat—do not—get caught—*

"I don't need to cheat in a place like this," he whispered in Belaskian, and when several players looked at him, he switched to Numanese. "Room for one?"

All at the table looked him over, and some exchanged annoyed glances, but he smiled at the redheaded dealer with a deck on the table before her. She studied his face, hair, and eyes for a moment.

"Do you know how to play *Vëttes*?" she asked.

Leesil's thoughts stumbled over the last word. It was somewhat similar to the Numanese word for "gate"—or maybe "gates."

"This isn't faro or Two Kings, you idiot!" Magiere warned in Belaskian. "You don't even know what you're playing."

As the dealer looked up, likely at Magiere, she smiled. She wouldn't know what Magiere had said, but the tone of an incensed spouse was plain enough. Leesil rolled his eyes, cocked one eyebrow, and winked at the dealer.

"I learn quick," he replied. "Maybe I watch first."

A few players scowled, but the dealer raised a hand to brush them off. Indeed, Leesil was left to watch as the next hand played out. He noticed a number of empty tankards that hadn't been cleared away. One young man on his right, dressed somewhat finely, glanced sidelong at him.

"I've never seen a Lhoin'na in armor before," he commented.

Leesil grinned at him and shrugged, gesturing to the hauberk. "For show."

The young man snorted with a half laugh and turned back to the game.

Leesil hoped this would lull the others into thinking he wasn't dangerous and only preferred to look that way. The fact that his wife hovered behind him in fury would add to that illusion.

He kept his eyes on the cards. They were different from the typical deck used in the Farlands. In addition to the suits' being foreign, the deck contained only what he would call "kings" and "queens," but no "princes," "knaves," or "priests." A Farlands deck had five suits, but here there were only four, which made the odds tighter and easier to calculate. Besides, even if he lost a hand or two, he could see by the coins on the table that the stakes were low.

The men made small talk as the next hand was dealt. Two bleary-eyed players ordered more ale. Leesil ignored them as he caught one twist to the game.

"Breach!" the young man on his right declared.

Leesil scanned the man's cards. After an opening bet in Two Kings, a further bet could be placed after the first two cards had been dealt, one up and one down. Winning meant coming as close to twenty points without going over. Two "kings" was the best possible hand on a first deal. But in this game of "Gates," the dealer had two cards, one up and one down. It appeared that a player had to beat the dealer's hand as well.

The young man had a nine of one suit and a seven of another; on a call for his last draw, he'd been dealt a one from a third suit. The dealer flipped her hidden card, giving her a king and a queen—and so her hand should've won. But the redheaded woman doubled the young man's bet and took away all of the other bets.

It seemed that a "one" in any suit breached the toughest "gate" the dealer could come up with. It was a long-shot play, but the game was closer to Two Kings than Leesil first thought, and he opened his pouch. To his advantage, the cards were a bit smaller than the ones he used in the Sea Lion tavern, though he'd never cheated there.

Leesil bet one silver Numanese penny, a bit much for a first hand, and the cards were dealt. His face-up card was an eight from a suit with floral leaves. Hoping for something low, he peeked at his hidden card and found a two of crossed iron bars. Calling for more cards, he kept on until the fifth took him over twenty, and he lost.

Magiere hissed behind him.

—*What—are you—doing?*—

Leesil ignored Chap as well as Magiere. What he needed most was a king or a queen. A nine would do almost as well, but not a one, for apparently that card won even if the dealer had twenty. He didn't want to win just yet.

He lost again on a hand of five cards, but therein was a nine of waves. Gathering up his cards facedown, he purposefully placed the nine on top. Before he slid them back to the dealer, he palmed the top card and kept his hands down on the table.

Yes, he'd said he wouldn't cheat, but he never said he wouldn't lie . . . about cheating.

On the next hand, he was dealt a face-up queen of clouds. He flattened the hand with the nine over his face-down card and bent its corner up for a peek: a two of floral leaves.

Leesil drew the card fully up before his face and intentionally scowled. When he put it back down, he kept his thumb over its face. Hanging onto it as he drew his hand back in plain sight, he slipped the nine, facedown in place of the two, from under his fingers.

The dealer had a seven of iron up.

Leesil placed five silver pennies atop his opening bet and passed on taking more cards. This was a fairly large bet for what the others had been wagering, and it drew more than one glance.

The dealer never blinked as she flipped her down card—a nine of clouds to go with her seven of iron.

The other men lost, two of them drawing out over twenty. Leesil flipped his hidden card for a total of nineteen. At the sight of that, Leesil felt Magiere's hand drop onto his shoulder and clench. From behind him, she couldn't have missed seeing his initial cards. But he had just doubled his wager.

—You said—you would—not cheat—

Leesil ignored Chap as the good-natured young man shrugged and looked to the redheaded dealer.

"Sorry, Merina," he said, and cocked his head toward Leesil. "He must have beginner's luck."

Leesil stored that phrase away for future use, but he was suspicious. The other men hadn't minded losing to the dealer, yet they appeared to resent that he'd won. On the next hand, the young man's first two cards totaled fifteen. He upped his initial bet of one penny with something smaller, probably equal to a groat in the Farlands. Merina was showing a six of waves, and the young man shook his head at the offer of another card.

Leesil ended up over count and lost. He hadn't drawn anything worth palming, and as he gathered his cards, he secretly discarded the floral two that he held. He won a fair amount on the third round, and his stack of coins grew. The young man won as well, but not the two drunkards.

Both cast baleful glances at him, as did Merina.

No one appeared to mind that the young man had won. Perhaps he was local, and the others only resented outsiders. From then on, Leesil made the minimum bets and lost three hands. The other players each won a hand along the way, and the mood at the table improved. It was time for one last good win.

Leesil was dealt a king of clouds faceup—and a queen of iron as his down card. Merina dealt herself a faceup nine of waves. When the others finished their draws and bets, she turned over a queen to match the nine. Leesil still won and doubled his coins again as he feigned astonishment.

"Beginner's luck," he echoed.

Merina slid over a small stack of coins, and she wasn't smiling. Only then did Leesil think about where he was . . . playing cards with a red-haired dealer in a place called The Red Fox.

It was time to get out of this.

"Enough for me," he said, sweeping coins into the pouch and glancing sidelong at Magiere. "She is waiting."

He turned away, avoiding Magiere's glare, as Chap scurried out in front, making patrons stumble into each other as they gave him room.

"We need to go," Leesil whispered, taking his blades from Magiere. "I think the dealer is the owner . . . and it appears she is well liked."

"You idiot," Magiere growled behind him.

Chap huffed in agreement as he reached the door.

They were outside and halfway down the street before Leesil slowed. He looked back, found the way clear, and started to strap on his blades. Magiere didn't say a word and stood ahead with her arms folded.

"Well?" he goaded. "Aren't you going to ask?"

"What?"

"How much I won," he said.

"Probably more than you should have!"

In truth, Leesil hadn't done a final count, but he'd turned a few silver pennies into more. Better, tonight left him feeling as if the past year had never happened—even with Magiere being grumpy with him. Or maybe because she was grumpy with him.

In the old days he'd been reckless and carefree, while she'd been cautious and conservative. He missed those days, and for a moment he'd gotten lost in the vision of how things used to be. After all, Magiere had improved some since that slip when she'd almost cut down the first mate. In part, that had been because of Leanâlhâm. Maybe he and Chap didn't have to be so vigilant about Magiere.

Following her, Leesil headed down the street, while Chap strolled at her side and made a good deal of noise licking and smacking his jowls.

"What have you done to yourself?" Magiere asked, stepping away from the dog. "You're a greasy mess. . . . I'm taking a wet towel to your face when we get back."

Still trying to clean sausage grease from all over his muzzle, Chap shook himself. Instead of growling or licking his nose by way of a retort, he suddenly stopped and looked back. His ears stiffened upright.

"What?" Leesil said, instantly on guard, and then he heard . . .

Quick footfalls—more than one set—carried from the first side street behind them.

"Move on," he said quickly.

Magiere kept pace, and as she was about to look back, someone shouted.

"There he is!"

Leesil groaned. This wasn't the first time he'd had to scurry away from a card table.

"You! Stop!" a man yelled.

Leesil was torn between bolting and facing an ugly confrontation, but Magiere made the decision for them. She halted, turned, and set herself. When her hand dropped to the falchion's hilt, Leesil's tension increased. He and Chap could hold off a few locals with no harm done, but he didn't want this going that far, not with Magiere in the middle of a public street.

With little choice, Leesil turned to face what was coming. Three men from the card table led four others, and none of them looked fully sober. A few carried cudgels, and the one in front gripped a poorly made shortsword.

"You!" the lead man shouted. "You cheated Merina!"

Words rose in Leesil's mind.

—*Do not—get—us—arrested*—

"I wasn't planning on it," he whispered through gritted teeth.

But inside Leesil wrestled for a way out of this without a fight. Magiere hadn't seemed to even hear him and focused only on the leader.

"He cheated no one," she said, lowly and breathily, as the lead one stopped just beyond sword's reach.

Leesil didn't like the edge in her voice. The leader, broad shouldered and a few days unshaven, was probably used to relying on weight and size in place of any skill.

"He cheated on the last hand!" the man bellowed, inching in as the others spread out. "I'm taking Merina's money back. Hand over the pouch now!"

Leesil didn't move. The fat drunkard reached out and grabbed him by his hauberk's collar. Leesil should've known what else that might cause, but he just shifted one foot back at the ready. A snarl broke his focus, and then Magiere lashed out.

"Don't touch him!" she shouted.

Hardened fingernails raked the fat man's face.

Leesil didn't turn in time, and Magiere slammed the man with both hands. Two other men scrambled out of the way as the bulky one flopped backward and rolled across the cobble. One spindly youth cried out in fright as the leader stopping rolling and lay prone. Half the man's right cheek was shredded.

In the dark, Leesil thought he saw exposed bone amid the blood. When Magiere snarled and hissed, he went cold as he saw her.

The whites of her eyes were almost gone under her expanding irises, and she rushed at the next closest man.

—Stop—her!—

Leesil was already in motion. He threw his arms around Magiere from behind and twisted with all of his weight. They both went spinning down onto the cobblestones. As he tried to pin Magiere, he heard Chap harrying the mob. That wasn't going to work for long.

Magiere tried to pitch Leesil off, and he almost lost his hold.

"Stop! It's me!" he shouted at her.

Several men pulled away in horror, but one stayed his ground, dropping into a half crouch and raising a cudgel. If Chap couldn't break them up, Leesil feared he'd have to release Magiere to defend both of them.

—Roll—to—your—right—

Leesil did, and when he came up atop Magiere again, he slammed his knees down on her shoulders.

"Enough!" he ordered.

Then he felt Chap's muzzle rooting around under the back of his hauberk toward his belt. Before he looked back again, he heard the clink of coins.

Chap stood beyond Magiere's feet and faced the gang of men; the pouch was in his teeth. Swinging his head, he tossed the pouch, and it landed on the cobble before the small mob.

"Take it! Go!" Leesil yelled at them. "Or pay in more blood."

After an instant of being startled by what a mere dog had done, one man snatched up the pouch as others grabbed the leader and had to drag him. They went scrambling toward the side street.

Magiere bucked again, but not with all her strength. When Leesil looked down at her, he grew sick inside. She stared up at him with fully black eyes.

She wasn't getting any better.

The only reason she hadn't given way to that other self in recent days was because nothing had threatened them . . . threatened him or Chap. And now she'd maimed a man over a few coins that he'd cheated to gain.

Leesil bent down and pressed his forehead against hers until she started to calm, and then he slid his face in until they were cheek to cheek.

"Quiet . . . Be still."

When she finally did, panting and shaking, he looked up to find Chap watching them both. She wasn't ready. . . . He wasn't ready to take her anywhere near the annex. Chap spun, hurrying off across the way.

—*Over here*—

Chap stood waiting before a cutway's mouth between two darkened shops. They needed time, and he could do little more than scout a close place out of sight.

"Come on," Leesil whispered, half pulling, half dragging Magiere.

Chap shifted aside as Leesil steered Magiere into the deeper darkness and pinned her up against the sidewall. He held her there as Chap lingered near the cutway's mouth, watching for any returning pursuit.

"It's all right," Leesil whispered.

It was not, and all Chap could do was what he always did. He turned only his head, looking to Magiere, and tried to calm her mind with the quietest memories he could find in her.

This was a slow-burning catastrophe in the making. He and Leesil had been dealing with it for more than half a year. It kept erupting more quickly each time without warning.

On their journey into the Wastes, Chap had let himself believe that Magiere's slaughter of Qahhar had been an aberration. Something that *had* to be done, brought on by close proximity to an ancient undead. Even then it was obvious that the more undead that she faced and the more potent they were, the more that inner side of her swelled to match them.

Chap had thought that was all there was to it, for in earlier times she had always come back to herself. He had been so very wrong, and his thoughts slipped back . . . back to the aftermath. . . .

Wounded, Chap lay curled against an unconscious Leesil in the sled. After the first lurch, he'd wondered how Magiere could pull it. The more he thought on this, the more often he wriggled his head out from under the tarp to watch, and the more what he saw disturbed him.

It overwhelmed any fragile hope that they might survive.

In the wind-whipped snow beyond the sled, Magiere was partially obscured from sight. She half ran, half stumbled, lunging against the sled's weight, but she never stopped as she hauled it blindly over the white plain. There was only one way she could be doing this out there alone—willfully calling upon her dhampir half.

Or was she even Magiere anymore?

He had never seen her so utterly changed, nor had he seen her maintain the change for so long. He was too broken to try to stop her, and even if he could, that would leave them all to die out here.

Chap couldn't watch anymore and ducked back under the tarp against Leesil. He must have fallen unconscious, for the next time he came aware, it was dark and cold, though he felt no wind now. Something moved nearby, as if on all fours.

He found himself on a pile of furs and covered in even more of them, and realized he was inside the shelter they'd used along the journey. Leesil breathed behind him under the furs, but that movement, that crawling scrape, came from the other direction. It stopped, and he caught the sound of ragged breaths.

All he could think was that somehow Magiere had managed to erect the shelter and then drag all of them inside. At least she had to have come back to herself for that, but it was fully dark. The oil lantern was not lit.

Chap huffed once to get Magiere's attention. No answer came, and so he huffed again.

A long, guttural hiss, as if grating out of an animal's throat, answered him. Then silence.

It was a long, cold night as he listened for any hint of Magiere's movements. He heard nothing more. Sometime before dawn, fatigue must have driven him down into a fearful sleep. He awoke to dim light leaking into the shelter.

"Where . . . where's Magiere?" Leesil asked weakly.

Chap did not see her inside the shelter. There were slates of dried fish laid out beside the furs. The oiled cloth on which the fish lay looked as if it had been ripped wide instead of unrolled properly. He snapped a piece of fish in his teeth and squirmed over to drop it beside Leesil's head.

Leesil grimaced, weakly turning his face from the smell.

At that Chap took a deep breath of relief. If Leesil could be that picky, he would live.

Chap found he was still wearing the fur that Leesil had rigged for him, and he wanted to find Magiere. First he ate a piece of smoke-cured fish. It crackled as he chewed, and its cold made his teeth ache. When Leesil still refused to eat or sit up, Chap snapped up another piece. With a snarl, he dropped it on Leesil's face.

Leesil grunted at him but grabbed the piece.

They needed water as well, but without the oil lamp's minimal heat, any water skin would be frozen solid. Still, Chap rooted around trying to find one, if Magiere had even brought one in.

"Here," Leesil groaned, and Chap looked up.

Leesil, still in his coat and clothes, dug weakly under the furs. He pulled out a water skin, though he could not have put it there himself. With his good hand, he pulled its stopper with his teeth and drank a little. When it came time for Chap, there was nothing in which to pour the water. Chap tilted his head back and opened his jaws, and Leesil splashed water into his mouth.

Chap finally raised a memory for Leesil of the sled laden down with all their belongings. Leesil nodded, and with labored effort they crawled outside. The sky was calm but gray, and the first thing Chap spotted was the sled.

It was a ways off, and someone had dug it out of the night's drifts, though it was still caked in crystallized snow crust. Chap looked out along the sled's ice-coated lines of frozen, empty dog harnesses.

Magiere stood with her back to them with the end of those lines perhaps gripped in her mittened hands. She didn't move when Leesil weakly called out to her. When he tried to stumble toward her, Chap cut him off. Leesil looked down in confusion, and Chap barked once for no.

He turned, slowly approaching Magiere, and made it halfway along the sled lines before he heard her hiss. Even then she didn't turn her hooded head to show her face.

Chap backed away, not taking his eyes off her until he reached the sled.

"What's happened . . . to her?" Leesil whispered.

Chap did not want to guess. Instead he raised Leesil's memories of watching Ti'kwäg dismantle the shelter. Weak as Leesil was—and with only one usable arm—it took him a while to complete this task, and he was shaking by the time he helped Chap aboard the sled and then climbed in himself. They never had a chance to call out that they were ready before the sled lurched forward.

All that day, as Leesil slept again, Chap pondered the worst of what had taken place. He could not understand what was happening to Magiere. He kept remembering the sight of her clutching Qahhar's head, her face half-covered in gore as black as her eyes. The leaking of the ancient undead's fluid from her mouth begged the worst worry. She had vomited some of it up, and that meant she had swallowed it . . . drunk it.

Could that be what affected her now?

Before, whenever she let her dhampir half rise, the aftermath when it receded left her exhausted, sometimes collapsing. Chap couldn't see how she still maintained her dhampir state for this long. But she was out there pulling the sled at half the speed of a dog team.

When they stopped at dusk, she stayed out in front and would not come nearer nor look back, no matter how Leesil shouted at her. When he tried to go to her, Chap stopped him.

Chap dragged whatever he could of the shelter's fixtures off the sled as Leesil worked with one arm to assemble them. It was not well-done, and when they crawled inside, the shelter was dark and the temperature unbearable. Leesil fumbled one-handed to light the oil lamp, as Chap watched the shelter's entrance.

Magiere couldn't stay out there, not even as she was. He finally howled, making Leesil jump and twist about. Long moments passed before they heard snow crunching outside under footfalls, and Chap backed up.

The canvas flap pulled aside a little under the grip of a fur-mittened hand. Dim light within the shelter exposed a white face looking in and partially dusted with frost. Some of the black stain over Magiere's mouth and jaw remained, with spidering cracks from its having dried on her face in the frigid air.

"Get in here," Leesil whispered.

She stared at him with her fully black eyes.

"Now, Magiere."

She crawled inside.

"Why are you doing this?" Leesil whispered. "Let it go . . . and come back."

A sliver of white appeared on either side of Magiere's irises. Chap thought her irises might finally be contracting, and then Magiere shuddered. She toppled where she knelt, catching herself at the last instant with both hands flattened on a fur hide on the floor. Her whole body shook as if she might collapse completely.

Leesil grabbed her shoulders.

Magiere shrieked so loudly that Chap went deaf for an instant, and she lurched, shoving Leesil off.

Leesil fell back with a yelp of pain. Before Chap could lunge in, Magiere scrambled to the shelter's wall, turning around, and pressed up against it until the canvas bowed across her back.

Her eyes had flooded fully black again.

At the sight of Chap watching her, she ducked her head. Even as she cowered from him, wrapping her arms over her head and face, a growl shook her whole body.

Leesil struggled up to his knees and tried to go to her, and Chap cut him off again. When Leesil would not stop, Chap had to snap at his face. Leesil finally gave up and dropped where he knelt and hung his head.

Chap was at a loss. He lay down upon the shelter's fur-covered floor and soon felt the cold from the packed snow beneath seeping into him. But he would not move, would not leave Magiere unwatched . . . would not leave her to suffer alone.

The worst of it was that although he did not know *how* she did this, he understood why. So long as she held on to that other half of herself, she might keep going. She was the only chance they had to get the orbs—or themselves— out of the Wastes.

But when she finally let go, what would it cost her?

Worse, what would it cost if she did not—and soon? What might be the lasting effects of her having swallowed Qahhar's black fluids?

It was another long, cold night for Chap, even after Leesil dragged over hides to cover them both and tried to push two such toward Magiere. She would not look at them.

The next morning she was gone.

Chap rose in a panic, having fallen asleep sometime in the night. He quickly roused Leesil and then bolted out of the shelter. There was Magiere, waiting with her back turned at the end of the sled's empty dog lines.

Two more days and nights came and went, and Chap and Leesil took to struggling along on their own, decreasing the weight that Magiere had to pull. On the third day, Chap made Leesil harness him to the sled, and they both pulled as well. On the sixth night, Chap collapsed in the shelter and lay watching Magiere again.

Her breath came in ragged, grating hisses. He couldn't tell whether they were from exhaustion or from holding on to the barest control over her dhampir half.

Chap forgot about the need to hide the orbs. He no longer tried to raise calming memories for Magiere. That was now as much of a danger to her as anything else. She'd been in this state for far too long. If—when—she finally let go, he now worried that it would kill her.

He saw no way to stop her, and if he did, he had no way to save her.

The next dawn, Chap was too exhausted to help pull the sled. Leesil was no better, and Chap bullied him onto the sled before turning to trot beside it. There was nothing but endless white all around them.

Then the sled suddenly stopped.

Chap staggered three more steps before he saw the sled lines lying limp in the snow. He quickly looked ahead, terrified that Magiere had finally let go. But she stood there, perfectly still except for the rising wind pulling at her coat's fur. Another storm was coming. Chap lunged toward her but halted before getting far enough to see her face.

Out beyond Magiere was a cluster of small domed ice dwellings. A group of dogs were curled up in the snow beside the largest dome. It was a camp of Wastelanders, likely on their way to the coast.

One dog raised its head and looked out at them. It began to growl and then snarl. Another looked up, and then another.

Leesil called out, "Why have we stopped?"

Magiere bolted over the snow.

Chap froze an instant too long in indecision, and Magiere charged at full speed without the weight of the sled holding her back.

Leesil shouted this time. "Magiere!"

Chap had no time to warn Leesil and took off running. He should have known what could happen.

Magiere knew him, knew Leesil, and that was all that kept her in check. With that other half of her dominant for so long, the real half of her had weakened, grown exhausted. The dhampir within her could feel this.

She dove straight for the nearest dog.

Leesil got out one hoarse, cracked shout as the world in front of Chap exploded into yelps and snarls. Magiere went rolling in a tangle with a dog amid screeching yelps and the sound of breaking bones. All the other dogs leaped up in fear, thrashing against their leashes.

Magiere came up atop the first one, slammed its head down, and bit into its throat.

Another dog attacked her from behind.

She lashed back at the second dog, snapped upright on her knees, and took it head-on as the first one lay limp and twitching in the snow. The second tried to snap at her face, and she grabbed its snout. A muffled crackle of bone was smothered in a squeal of pain. When she wrenched its head aside to get at its throat, its neck broke, and it went silent.

She hesitated, staring at the lifeless corpse in her grip no longer able to feed her. With a jerk of her head and her blood-smeared face, her fully black eyes fixed on another dog trying to get out of reach. She dropped the corpse and scrambled on all fours.

"No!" Leesil screamed from somewhere close.

Chap charged in and threw himself at Magiere. It was not the dogs he feared for but something—someone—else that would be called by their noise.

Even as he tried to get his teeth into the back of Magiere's coat, she fell atop the third dog, pinning it amid snarls. It yelped and growled, thrashing beneath her. Chap latched his jaws on Magiere's shoulder and bit as hard and deep as he could.

Something struck his side, and she bucked him off. He flopped across the snow, and when he struggled up in renewed pain . . .

People stood outside the main dome.

Magiere whipped around and focused on them.

Short and covered in bulky fur clothing, they looked at her twisted white features, spattered and smeared in their dogs' blood. Magiere shot to her feet, and as she lunged, Chap scrambled in behind her.

He'd barely gotten a grip on her ankle when Leesil cut around in front of her and struck out with his fist, catching her across the jaw. That would not have done anything if Chap had not wrenched her leg as well.

Magiere toppled over Chap and crushed him down as she fell. He thrashed out from under her legs.

Leesil stood there panting and shuddering in the icy wind. He already had one winged blade gripped in his good hand as Chap wheeled to face Magiere.

She rolled to her hands and knees among the corpses of the dogs. All of the other animals had run off. Drops of blood fell from her hanging head to spatter the snow-crusted ice between her mittened hands. Chap could not tell whether the blood was hers or that of her prey, even when she lifted her head and . . . there was white around her large black irises.

She swallowed hard in confusion and then gagged. Chap stiffened when he thought he saw the whites of her eyes vanish. She looked aside at the bloodied, twisted body of a dog, and she screamed, heaving out gasps as she tried to scuttle away only to encounter another corpse.

Her eyes rolled up, and she collapsed.

Leesil rushed in as Chap looked all around. There was no sign of the inhabitants of this place. He spotted only dim forms in the distance that vanished amid snow whipped up by the wind. He had no time for self-loathing at what he'd let happen to them.

Chap barked loudly at Leesil, lunged toward the ice dome's entrance, and returned to help Leesil drag Magiere. There was an oil lamp still lit inside. A half-eaten meal lay out on wood planks, and the floor was covered in furs and bedding. Using his one good arm, Leesil managed to get Magiere's prone form laid out and covered with furs.

She was barely breathing.

Leesil tried to wipe the blood off her face. All Chap could do was watch, not knowing which half of her would be there when—if—she opened her eyes again. He glanced once toward the shelter's entrance.

Somewhere out there, families fled in terror amid a rising wind and falling darkness. They would only run all the more if he went after them. A monster, like those shadows in the blizzards spoken of by their ancestors, had come for them. And he had let it happen, acting too late.

By dawn the dogs would not be the only victims of his failure.

Chap laid his head upon his forepaws and watched Magiere as Leesil tried to rouse her. It did not—would not—work. Chap could not be certain, but he feared that swallowing the ancient's fluids had done something to Magiere. How else could she have remained changed for so long?

But the instant she had reverted to herself, horror at what she had done struck her. And the worst of it was that after remaining in such a state for so long, feeding on the dogs was the only reason she still lived . . . for now.

Chap would never tell her about the villagers, and neither would Leesil. This would not stop her from knowing, if she ever awakened and saw where they were. It wasn't her fault, and yet it was. Was she even two halves anymore, or now the whole of something else?

"Where's Chap?"

His head snapped up at that weak, faltering whisper. Leesil quickly leaned in where he knelt next to Magiere.

"He's here," he said. "We're both right here."

Without rising, Chap scrambled closer and shoved his muzzle in against Magiere's cheek. No matter Leesil's attempt to clean her—he still smelled blood on her breath.

"Why did you do this?" Leesil whispered in anguish. "Why didn't you let it go and come back sooner?"

Chap felt Magiere's fingers trying to tangle in his fur.

Her voice grew even weaker as she answered, "I couldn't lose you . . . either of you."

Chap buried his head in the crook of Magiere's neck. He heard only Leesil's shaking breaths as he laid his head on his wife's chest. Any relief was short-lived, for Chap couldn't stop thinking of all that had changed.

Dawn came late.

Still weakened, Magiere rose with Leesil's aid, but this only confirmed Chap's decision. For all he could think of was a delusion left behind in Magiere's homeland.

He had seen an image of her in that sorcery-induced state, as she stood in black-scaled armor before a horde of undead and other creatures in the dark. She had led them into a forest where everything died in their—her—wake.

He knew of her birth and how it had been accomplished through sacrificing one member of each of the five races, along with her undead father. He knew her birth had been intended to create the impossible, a being of both life and death who could match even the most potent undead. And the Ancient Enemy of many names had wormed into her dreams to lead her to the first orb.

Hiding the orb from their enemies was no longer Chap's only concern.

Magiere could never know where the orbs were hidden, and that meant that Leesil couldn't know either.

The next two moons blurred by, as they lived on stores taken from a village left empty, until the endless white broke upon the edge of the western ocean. For the most part, all Chap remembered was cold and pressing Magiere and Leesil onward. The sun rose for shorter and shorter times, and the world had seemed harried by night, as though a creeping darkness ate away the light a little more each day.

Then somehow, ahead down the shore, lay White Hut, the trading post where they had hired Ti'kwäg. Nothing seemed to matter after that but rest, at least for Leesil and Magiere. They set up a shelter and never spoke, especially not Chap, about tomorrow or what lay ahead. One afternoon, while Magiere slept, Chap dug in Leesil's pack.

"What are you doing?"

Chap withdrew his head with the "talking hide" gripped in his jaws, and found Leesil sitting up and watching him. Leesil had made the hide with Belaskian letters and short common words to replace the one Wynn had written up in the Old Elvish of the an'Cróan.

Chap cast Leesil a huff, muffled by the hide in his mouth, and pushed out under the shelter's flap. He waited outside until Leesil followed, now frowning in puzzlement. Chap dropped the hide, pawed it out flat, and then nosed and pawed its letters and symbols.

Hire me a guide with a dog team.

Leesil looked physically better, but his mental state was less certain.

"A guide?" he whispered, crouching beside Chap. "I'm not taking Magiere back out there."

Chap pawed again. *I will hide the orbs. Do it now while she sleeps.*

Realization flooded Leesil's face, though he frowned in worry as he glanced back at the shelter.

Chap didn't need to explain; Leesil was no fool. Magiere was somehow connected to the orbs. Even in their current situation, she might not let Chap go if she knew what he was about to do. Leesil had always wanted the orb—now orbs—out of their lives.

"Even if we had enough money or trade goods," he whispered, "how could you possibly do this on your own? What are you going to do, dig a big hole and bury them like a bone?"

Chap growled at him.

"You can't carry them . . . and any outsider will know where you hide them."

Chap would not tell Leesil how he would address this problem, and he pawed at the hide for much longer this time.

Hire someone to go inland, not north. Trade Ti'kwäg's travel gear. No one knows it is not ours. No one will know what was lost in the journey when we turn over what remains.

Chap sighed in frustration at having to paw out so much.

Leesil sighed right back, shaking his head, but he stood up and walked off. Chap peeked back into the shelter to find Magiere still asleep.

It took longer than expected for Leesil to come back, and Chap worried that no guide might be willing, now that they had returned without Ti'kwäg. But Leesil returned in success.

Later that night, after Magiere went back to bed, Leesil called Chap outside. He shared the arrangements that he had made. Leesil could be quite cunning when properly motivated.

The next morning, Leesil suggested Magiere go with him for a walk along the shore. It was the first time he had asked anything of her since leaving the icy crags. So she agreed quickly and went off with him.

Chap remained behind on the pretense of giving them privacy. He would not be there when they returned. Magiere would have no chance to argue—or worse.

A stocky man arrived with a sled and looked none too happy at being instructed to follow the lead of a wolf bigger than any of his dogs. Grunting and straining, he took up the chest with the first orb, and then the second, hidden in wrapped furs by Leesil.

Once all was secured, Chap turned away, heading inland.

When Leesil returned and Magiere learned what had been done, it would drive a further wedge between them . . . and between her and Chap. This could not be helped. Hiding the orbs from their enemies—and her—mattered more. Leesil would face even worse once he told Magiere the rest.

All that he would have to show her was Qahhar's *thôrhk*. That could not be left with the orbs, in case by some slim chance they were found. And he and she were to head south along the shore to get clear of all eyes in White Hut. This way Chap could find them again later, far from any who might see him return . . . alone.

Chap loped ahead of the dog team and the sled but already dreaded what would come. The next three days proved less difficult than expected. The new local guide was chattier than Ti'kwäg—only this one talked to his dogs. He talked to Chap as well, and he had a strange habit of referring to himself in the third person.

"Nawyat get you supper," he would say.

Chap could not help liking the man, which only made what was coming, what would be necessary, worse to contemplate. With the journey under way, he did not know for how long Nawyat would follow him, and in the end he would need complete control.

On the fifth morning, he searched the landscape and saw that much had changed the farther they went inland. Snow and ice broke where the land underneath was rugged and exposed. When he spotted a large patch of dark gray rising well above the snowpack, he purposefully veered away. Nawyat could not have any clear memory of this place, if he remembered anything at all.

Chap led the dogs and guide onward for another quarter day before he stopped. At first, hearing the sled halt, he couldn't bring himself to look at Nawyat.

"You lost now, big wolf?" the guide called out. "No lead Nawyat more?"

Chap's every instinct wailed that what he was about to do was wrong. If this act was what he suspected, having never done so before, it was a . . . sin.

When he turned, Nawyat was already walking toward him.

"What you do?" the guide asked, peering down at him with a frown that scrunched the brows of his dark-skinned face.

Drawing upon the element of Spirit within him, Chap closed his eyes. His body felt suddenly warm amid the cold. From Earth beneath his paws, and Air all around him, and Water from the snow, and Fire from the heat of his flesh, he bonded with the elements of Existence. These mingled with that of the Spirit within him—and he began to burn.

The guide would not see the blue-white vapors rising around his form like flame. Normal eyes could not see what was happening to him—only eyes like Wynn's, with her mantic sight that separated the presence of the elements in all things.

Chap opened his eyes to look into Nawyat's puzzled dark ones. He felt for any rising memories in the guide as something to snatch hold of. When he found them, the whole world suddenly swam like warped oil upon water.

It had been so—too—easy.

Nawyat would not know until too late—no one would.

The world appeared to double in Chap's sight, as if he saw it from two different places. He saw through his own eyes . . . and then also Nawyat's . . . and then through the guide's eyes only.

Chap watched his own majay-hì body collapse upon the snow.

He began shaking, feeling hands, feet, arms, and only two legs, all wrapped in heavy fur and hide clothing. He dropped his eyes to look down at . . . Nawyat's hands . . . his hands now.

Chap raised his gaze again, staring at his own limp form upon the snow. He tried to find any lingering memory not his own—and could not. There were only his thoughts inside the guide's body. The world blurred before his eyes, and it took moments before he understood why.

He was crying.

Stumbling out, he worked hard to control this human body. He fought to drag his own and heave it aboard the sled. Then he watched the breath, so shallow and weak, slowly escaping his body's muzzle.

How long could he remain inside the guide's flesh before it was too long?

Not knowing how to use hands, Chap had to wrestle at gripping the sled's lines. Even if he had ever felt what it was like to speak with a mouth, he did not know the guide's language to command the dogs. It took longer to return to the spot he'd chosen than it had to leave it behind. When he found the gray rise, a dome of granite with one side sheared off, he took out the shovel and pickax that Leesil had instructed the guide to bring.

Chap began to dig, fumbling, stumbling, and falling so many times in losing his balance on two legs instead of four.

This place was not as far as he would have preferred, but in the past two days he'd seen no signs of anyone coming or going this way. He had at least five days to survive in his return to the coast, and more to find Leesil and Magiere. Inside the guide's body, he kept hacking and shoveling snow, and then ice, and then frozen ground at the base of the dome's sheered side.

He kept going deeper. The day was almost gone by the time the hole was deep and wide enough for both orbs.

Chap returned to the sled and uncovered the second orb. It was so heavy that he fell twice, jarring his left knee the second time. When he finally dropped the orb in the hole, he limped back for the first one—the one in the chest.

He could not get the chest open and had to strip off his mittens. His fingers grew numb in the cold. When the latch was finally undone, he lifted the lid and brushed aside the covering to grab the orb with both hands.

A shriek echoed everywhere.

Chap didn't realize it came from him, for it was Nawyat's voice that tore out of him. He found himself sprawled on the snow beside the sled, shuddering from . . . that one touch. It had been like . . . when he touched someone's rising memories, when he touched a part of that being.

Something had touched *him*.

His thoughts went numb for an instant, and he scuttled in retreat across the snow. When reason returned, he tried to deny what he had felt. In all the time since the first orb had been found, he'd never touched it. He couldn't handle it in his own body, so there had never been reason to do so. But if he had felt . . .

It was impossible. Leesil had helped rig the sling and poles by which Magiere and he carried the first orb from the six-towered castle. Leesil had touched the orb and would have instantly mentioned feeling anything—but he had not.

Chap crawled to the sled, pulled himself up, and stared into the chest. The orb lay there as moments before, dark and rough surfaced and inert. Even its spike was flush with its exterior, as if all of it were one piece. No *thôrhk* had lifted the spike free. Chap reached down, his—Nawyat's—shivering fingertips hovering for an instant, and then he touched it.

Memories carried the presence of the one from whom they came—and the *presence* flushed through Chap.

Something was *alive* inside the orb.

That was the only way he could define it, and, at a loss for what it meant, he jerked his hand away. He looked back toward the base of the granite dome's sheer side.

Chap staggered to the hole's edge, dropped on his knees, and flattened on the snow to reach down into the hole. He hesitated again before touching the second orb, but with his bare hand this time.

And there it was again . . . a presence.

Magiere had felt something, but only when she opened an orb with a *thôrhk*. So why did he feel something now? And the thought of her *thôrhk*, or the other one he had left behind with Leesil, lingered in Chap's mind.

If he had kept it with him instead . . .

Chap pushed up, away from the hole. There was no more time to linger, though he was now plagued with more burdens.

Although he got both orbs into the ground by nightfall, he'd barely finished filling in the hole when it became too dark to see. Assembling a shelter was easy in theory, for he'd seen it done many times. Doing so in this body in the dark was another matter. He managed it and threw food out for the dogs before dragging his true body into the shelter.

In the morning, he shoveled snow and ice across the filled-in hole and hoped for foul weather to soon obscure any evidence that someone had been digging there. Well after midday, he took down the shelter, returned to the dogs and sled, and then drove them back to the place where he'd taken Nawyat's body.

When—if—the guide awoke, he would see no more than in the last moment he remembered.

Chap hesitated. He could already feel that something was wrong.

He was shaking and not from fatigue. There were moments when the world appeared hazy and dim. What if his return to his own flesh was worse than possessing that of another? He took time to assemble the shelter again and dragged his own body into it.

The breath from his muzzle was even weaker now as he watched.

Chap stripped off Nawyat's gloves. Taking his own head in Nawyat's hands, he pushed up the lids of those majay-hì eyes. The pupils were no more than black pinheads at the center of crystal-blue irises, but he looked into those eyes, trying to find Spirit again . . . not his individual spirit but the elemental Spirit of flesh itself.

Everything went black before his—Nawyat's—eyes.

Chap felt his head hit the hardened ground as he collapsed, and then he was struggling to breathe.

His chest burned. Cold air stung his dry throat. Every muscle ached as if he'd lain in illness too long without moving. He had to fight to open his eyes, and even then everything was so dark. It was more than a dozen breaths before he made out a mute form before him.

Everything in the shelter appeared turned sideways where Chap lay with his head against the ground. Beyond his nose was a dark-skinned hand . . . and beyond that was Nawyat's face.

The guide lay on his side, eyes half-open and unblinking in his slack-featured face.

Chap tried to get up—in his own body—and could not even lift his head. He tried to bark, to paw, to do anything to rouse some reaction from Nawyat.

In desperation he reached for the guide's memories, searching for anything that rose there now that he'd vacated the man's body.

There was nothing.

He had gone too far, lingered too long in that man's flesh.

Chap lay there through the night. By dawn he was able to roll onto his belly, though at first he couldn't bring himself to look upon his victim. When he did so, the light outside was bright enough to filter through the shelter's canvas.

Nawyat's eyes were still half-open and empty. Though he breathed, it was no more than Chap had seen in his own body through the guide's eyes. Was there anything left of the individual spirit Chap had pushed down so completely that he had taken the man's flesh as well?

He tried again to find any memory in Nawyat, but the darkness in the guide's mind was so complete . . . and then something flickered in Chap's awareness.

It was only one image, and it did not move like the memory of a past event. Chap—Nawyat—saw himself in the moment when he had fixed upon the guide and taken the man's will so completely that he took his flesh as well.

The image of himself in Nawyat's memory did not move. It lingered, frozen, capturing the moment of Chap's sin.

When Chap had been born into flesh, he'd not known how much of his memory of being with his kin, the Fay, had been torn out of him by them. He had not even remembered that they had done this to him. Only later had he suspected, and even then he had difficulty fully fathoming any fragments of memories left inside him.

Among those had been—was—a notion of sin, the first sin. Until now he had only suspected what it was, but the hint of possibility must have been retained out of all that had been lost in *being* one with the Fay.

Somehow he knew their sin, though not why they called it such.

Their—his—first sin had been domination, a slavery so utter and complete, but he could remember no more than this from his time as part of them.

Was the one memory, that last image of his *own* sin, all that was left of Nawyat?

Perhaps it was a sign that the guide was still there and would return to his own flesh. Perhaps that was just a pathetic wish spawned in guilt and self-loathing he could have never imagined.

Chap slipped from the tent and hobbled at first until he regained control of his own body.

He began running for the coast.

Each dusk he burrowed into the snow with only the fur hide Leesil had fashioned around his body. He was left to fitful sleep, plagued by what he had done to a man as Fay and what he had felt from the orbs.

Each dawn he hunted for any wild game until the day fully came. Whether he had eaten or not, he ran onward. When he finally saw the ocean in the distance, he turned southward along the shore. On the seventh day, in the late afternoon, he spotted a canvas shelter upon a small knoll above the rocky beach. Down near the water, someone stood looking out over the ocean.

Chap saw white-blond hair blowing in the wind—and he howled.

Leesil twisted around and, as Chap bolted onward, Leesil shouted. "Magiere!"

Chap stopped ten paces off when Magiere thrashed out of the shelter. She went running toward Leesil until she saw Chap. He'd known they would wait for him, though he was uncertain how Magiere would react now. She only studied him through unreadable eyes.

"Is it done?" she asked.

He huffed once for yes.

"I want to go back to Calm Seatt," she said. "I want to talk to Wynn."

Chap huffed once, again. Then Leesil was on him, wrapping both arms around his neck as Magiere joined them.

In the mouth of the cutway off a street in Chathburh, Chap looked back and locked eyes with Leesil. As before, as on the ship, perhaps they remembered some of the same things . . . but not everything.

Leaning against Leesil's chest, Magiere breathed heavily and raised her right hand. There was still blood on her fingers, like there had been the moment in the Wastelanders' camp among the corpses of the dogs.

"What did I—?"

"It's all right," Leesil interrupted, stroking her hair.

Nothing was all right. All three of them knew this, though Chap knew two things that were far worse. He looked away from Magiere and then hung his head.

She was not the only one who had changed for the worse.

The first sin of the Fay was not his only burden, though he did not yet understand why and how they had come to name it so. It was one thing no one else could ever know until he understood what it meant.

Leesil had felt nothing from touching the orbs. Magiere had felt something only when she opened one or touched a *thôrhk* to it. The only difference between them and Chap was that he was a Fay born into flesh.

And he did know exactly what he had felt.

A Fay had been imprisoned inside each of those two orbs.

All the hate that Chap bore them for what they had done him and those he cherished did nothing to smother his second guilt. What he had done, he would not even wish upon Brot'an.

Chap had buried alive two of his forsaken kin in a frozen grave to be forgotten.

CHAPTER FIFTEEN

Returning to the annex, Chap followed Leesil and Magiere through the reception area and up the stairs. As they passed, two sages sat reading in the library, but neither looked up. When they reached their room, Chap paused.

He was too weary with his own burdens and, even though Magiere needed tending, he did not want to spend the night watching Leesil soothe Magiere. When Leesil ushered Magiere in, Chap remained in the hallway. Leesil looked back in puzzlement.

—I will—stay—out here—for a while—

Leesil half turned to Chap but then glanced at Magiere collapsed on the bed. Leesil pursed his lips and was perhaps ready to argue, but instead nodded and closed the door.

Chap looked down the hallway. Both Leanâlhâm's and Brot'an's doors were closed. Chap quietly approached the latter and sniffed at the space near the bottom. The scent was faint, but he could tell that the old assassin was inside. It was the only scent he picked up, so Leanâlhâm must be in her own room. And suddenly Chap no longer wanted to be alone.

Leaving Magiere and Leesil to each other, he went to scratch softly on Leanâlhâm's door. Light footsteps sounded inside, and she opened it and looked down. Her hair hung loose down her back.

"Majay-hì?"

—May I—come in?—

Leanâlhâm blinked, glanced about the upper hallway in puzzlement, and then stepped back.

"Please," she answered, pulling the door wide for him.

He entered, and after closing the door, she scurried in her bare feet back toward the bed. The book he'd seen her with earlier was lying open and propped up on a pillow.

—Were you—reading?—

"I have been trying, but the pictures keep stopping me. My people do not make drawings like this in their texts unless necessary."

Chap was slightly taken aback by the ease with which she talked to him. Perhaps having her own space to control made her more comfortable. Anything that made her treat him less like an aberration of her homeland's sacred guardians was a relief to him.

She clambered up onto the tall bed, settled before the book, and turned a page.

"Are you coming up?"

He leaped up after her, stumbling a bit when his paws sank into the quilt and mattress. He stretched out, and she pointed to an illustration of a young elven female dressed in a sage's robe and holding an etched wooden plate.

"I think she was doing travels and uncovered artifacts, but I do not know why she was traveling."

Chap glanced over the story.

—She—was—a journeyor—

Leanâlhâm looked up at him in surprise. "You can read this book?"

—Some— . . . —words are—different—for elves—in—this land— . . . —I know—only—the way—your people—speak—

Leanâlhâm's brow wrinkled for a moment at that, and Chap hoped she would not start treating him with awe once again. Thankfully, her curiosity overrode all else.

"What is . . . a journeyor?"

—Like Wynn— . . . *—a rank—among the sages—* . . . *—They go—away—
after learning—much—to learn—more—* . . . *—to prove—worth—and bring
back—knowledge—to their guild—*

"They must be so brave to go to strange places all alone."

—Not all—journey—like Wynn—did— . . . *—Most—go to—other—
branches—annexes—settlements—in their—region—or—places—to work—*

Leanâlhâm grew quiet and still. "She is very brave, and now she will
journey again with that other man and your daughter . . . and Osha?"

—Hopefully—

It seemed a strange thing to hope for. Chap said nothing about the hope
that any of them would survive to return home. Leanâlhâm pulled her knees
up against her chest and studied the image of the young elven sage, and Chap
dipped lightly into her mind for any surfacing memories.

He—Leanâlhâm—saw Wynn back when the young journeyor had first
visited the girl's land with Magiere, Leesil, and himself. Then came flashes of
the moment Osha had arrived with Brot'an . . . and Wynn's journal.

Chap had already been through too much this night. But now he was
isolated with a pensive, lonely girl cast adrift without a destination of her
own. Another opportunity like this might not come anytime soon.

—Brot'ân'duivé said—Wynn sent—him—a journal—through—Osha—

Leanâlhâm's gaze turned farther from him. "He told you this?"

—What—became of—the journal?—

She turned fully away from the book and him. "Do not ask me. I cannot
break my promise—my oath—to the greimasg'äh."

The question still worked, though this brought Chap no pleasure and
only more guilt and shame in reigniting Leanâlhâm's painful memories. . . .

In the three days after Osha departed with Brot'ân'duivé, Leanâlhâm hardly
left her home. She had no interest in baking grain bread or working on em-
broidery. It was difficult enough not to weep.

Sgäilsheilleache had gone to the ancestors. It seemed impossible that

Léshil would ever return. Now even Osha had been taken from her. She even grew fearful whenever Grandfather, so weary himself, left their home. But she could not bear to go after him and hid away from a world that grew ever smaller with each loss.

Grandfather was also in pain, yet somehow performed his daily tasks. He spoke to other clan members about the weather or goods that had arrived or were sent off for trade. She did not know how to do this, though he would rise from bed the next day to do the same.

She knew that anger was a sign of bad manners, but deep inside she was angry. Not with Osha, who had left her like this, but with Brot'ân'duivé, who had forced him away.

Cuirin'nên'a was the closest thing Leanâlhâm had to another woman in her life, but Léshil's mother was quiet, guarded . . . and cold. She had not loved Sgäilsheilleache and viewed death as a part of life—part of the way of the Anmaglâhk. Leanâlhâm wondered whether the woman even understood grief.

As a result of buried anger and sorrow, Leanâlhâm began doing odd things.

Besides spending most of her days in bed, when she did get up, she carried the bottle with Sgäilsheilleache's ashes into whatever room in which she settled. Those ashes needed—deserved—to be carried to the ancestors' burial grounds, but she did not want to let go of that last part of him. While in bed, fearful of falling asleep and losing sight of the bottle, she placed it beside her mat.

On the third day, Grandfather woke her earlier than she wished and would not leave until she rose. He insisted that she bathe and dress, and she could not believe what more he expected of her. He wanted her to attend a celebration.

Reavrahkrijha—Heart of Spring—had arrived, and the Coilehkrotall, like all clans, celebrated the true birth of a new year. A feast would be prepared with smoked fish brought from the coast to be served with the most tender first growths of the harvest and the last of winter's stores. All in the enclave would sit together at tables upon the green and visit and offer good wishes to one another. This was a common tradition of the an'Cróan; it would be taking place in enclaves throughout their land.

But it did not feel like a day of new beginnings for Leanâlhâm, as she stood in the main chamber of her home with Grandfather under the watchful eyes of Cuirin'nên'a. All she had to cling to was the small bottle of her uncle's ashes tucked inside her tunic against her stomach.

"Come, my child," Grandfather said. "It will do you good."

How could he think this? How could he force her to mingle among people who did not believe she belonged here, who *knew* Sgäilsheilleache was gone. She had no one but Grandfather now to stand between her and their judgments.

"I do not think—" she began.

"We are going," he interrupted firmly, and then looked to Léshil's mother. "And you, too."

Cuirin'nên'a raised one feathery eyebrow. She had never shown interest in the company of anyone outside this home. Grandfather was head of the household and a clan elder whose presence was required on such occasions. Even Sgäilsheilleache had never dared disobey Grandfather in anything but his caste duties. This was the way of their people.

But Leanâlhâm hoped Cuirin'nên'a would decline. That might give her a chance to do so as well. Instead Léshil's mother nodded respectfully, and Grandfather shooed them both out and off to the feast.

Everyone was dressed finely, with tiny colored cords of shéot'a cloth woven into their braided hair. Long tables set out were laden to their edges with honey cakes, spring berries, fresh mushrooms, dried fruit stores, and leafy greens. There was barely room for cups, plates, and utensils, and it should have been a pleasant sight.

Leanâlhâm shied away from anyone, from accepting their polite but brief condolences or their well-mannered but halfhearted wishes.

She busied herself at the oven only to carry food to tables and get away from anyone trying to approach her. When there was no more to be done, she sat between Grandfather and Cuirin'nên'a and pretended to eat. Grand-father offered blessings and formal wishes and smiled forcefully and carefully at every jest, friendly chat, or raised cup. After a while he looked at Leanâl-hâm sadly.

"Is this so difficult?" he asked.

"Could we go home?" she whispered.

The look on his wrinkled old face, so broken and disappointed, made her regret even asking. But he immediately rose. And even Cuirin'nên'a's con-trolled expression betrayed relief as they followed him and left the feast long before anyone else would consider doing so.

They made their way past the other tree dwellings, to the outskirts where their large one awaited. Leanâlhâm ached to rush ahead and return to her room.

A strange birdlike whistle rose sharply out in the forest as she reached the curtained doorway of her home. A chirp followed three times after that.

Leanâlhâm stopped because her grandfather was no longer beside her. She looked back to find that he had turned—and they both stared at Cuirin'nên'a.

She was frozen in place farther back with her head tilting slightly.

Leanâlhâm stiffened as those beautiful but cold eyes suddenly narrowed. She followed that gaze out among the trees but saw nothing.

Cuirin'nên'a rushed straight at Leanâlhâm and snatched her wrist. Before she could even think to resist, she was whipped around away from the door-way and shoved down into the brush at the base of an oak.

"Stay!" Cuirin'nên'a ordered in a whisper.

Leanâlhâm cringed, and her wide-eyed grandfather trailed Léshil's mother in a rush through the curtained doorway. Too much had happened lately that Leanâlhâm did not understand. This time she would not be shut out.

She climbed out of the brush, hurried to follow, and pulled aside the doorway's curtain. Then she halted, her thoughts blank in confusion.

She barely noticed Grandfather or Cuirin'nên'a, each standing to one side of the doorway and partially blocking it. Leanâlhâm's eyes fixed on the main chamber of their home, torn apart and in complete disarray. Dishes had been knocked from shelves. Seating mats were cast aside in rumples. Pillows had been shredded or cut open and their grass or feather stuffing scattered about, some still floating on the air. But most of all Leanâlhâm stared at . . .

Two tall figures in forest gray, with matching cloaks tied up around their waists, stood at the chamber's rear. Inside their hoods both wore wraps over the lower halves of their faces. The anmaglâhk on the left, nearest to Cuirin'nên'a's guest chamber, held something in his hand.

It was the journal.

"Lapdogs!" Cuirin'nên'a spat. "You disgrace a holiday to do his bidding?"

Leanâlhâm was utterly confused. Anmaglâhk protected their people. Why had these two come to destroy her home?

"We are here to serve," the one with the journal answered. "You will not interfere with our purpose. Step aside, or be proven the traitor that you are."

Leanâlhâm's gaze shifted as Grandfather took a step forward. She had never seen him so angry.

"True guardians do not turn on their people," he accused. "Leave my home and everything in it at once—or face sanction before the elders' council of the clans."

The second anmaglâhk, slightly shorter than the first, had eyes so lightly colored that they were nearly yellow. Neither reacted to Grandfather's demand.

"Step aside," the first one repeated, tucking the journal into his tunic.

Leanâlhâm grew fearful amid confusion. No one spoke to a clan elder this way. No anmaglâhk was above the people's ways, not even Most Aged Father.

Cuirin'nên'a became a sudden blur.

Leanâlhâm blinked in a flinch.

When her eyes opened, Léshil's mother had crossed the entire chamber. The shorter anmaglâhk stepped out to cut her off, and they tangled in a flurry of limbs. It was so rapid that Leanâlhâm could not follow any one movement.

The other anmaglâhk bolted straight for the doorway.

Leanâlhâm lost sight of the room as Grandfather sidestepped in front of the doorway. Almost instantly he was gone, knocked to the floor. The anmaglâhk rushed straight at her, and she froze.

He slammed her chest with one palm.

She went spinning, toppling outside the tree's entrance. The ground rushed up, and she hit it on her left side. The strike had already taken her breath, and the impact made it worse. She fought to breathe, trying to get up, and then Grandfather stumbled out of their home.

His expression was dark with rage, and he had barely cleared the drape when Leanâlhâm heard a commanding shout.

"Gleannéohkân'thva, no!"

Grandfather did not heed Cuirin'nên'a and rushed by toward the forest's edge. Leanâlhâm then remembered the strange chirps heard out in the forest. A wave of fear rushed through her.

"Grandfather!" she gasped out, struggling to her feet.

There was no sign of the anmaglâhk who had struck her. There was only a brief sound like someone whipping a stick through the air. And it cut off instantly.

Grandfather halted short of the forest's edge, and Leanâlhâm swallowed in relief.

All was quiet. Not even the sound of a struggle rose out of her home. Grandfather took a small step back in retreat. He began to fall.

His back hit the turf, his eyes wide, and they did not blink when his head bounced on impact. A short arrow stood erect from the center of his chest.

Leanâlhâm screamed, the sound ripping from her throat as she rushed in.

No matter how she shouted at him or rubbed his face, he would not answer. His unblinking eyes stared upward. She felt no breath from him and grew numb.

Leanâlhâm did not twitch when Cuirin'nên'a suddenly crouched beside her. The woman was stained in spatters of red . . . and a blood-drenched stiletto was in her narrow hand. Leanâlhâm looked back only once.

No one else came out of the draped doorway.

She looked down at Grandfather, the last of those who truly cared for her. This could not be real.

"Why?" she whispered.

Cuirin'nên'a did not answer.

In confusion Leanâlhâm grabbed her grandfather's tunic and tried to drag him toward their home. She could not leave him here, but she barely moved him at all. A slender tan hand closed around her wrist, and something broke inside Leanâlhâm.

"No!"

She released her hold on Grandfather and struck out at Léshil's mother.

Cuirin'nên'a's head snaked aside, and Leanâlhâm's small fist passed harmlessly away. She was jerked to her feet, and the grip on her wrist released briefly. Cuirin'nên'a's bloody hand clamped over her mouth.

"Quiet," she hissed. "We run now!"

Before Leanâlhâm could say a word, she was pulled into the forest at a wild pace, and Cuirin'nên'a dragged her on and on. For how long Leanâlhâm did not know. Everyone who loved her had been taken from her. She wept in flight and was unable to stop, even when Léshil's mother halted and pulled her up short.

There was a large redwood almost as great as the tree homes of the enclave. Though no Shaper among the people had guided the growth of this tree, there was a natural cavelike hollow between two of its huge roots mounding the forest floor.

Cuirin'nên'a glanced all around. "We are unseen. Get inside."

Leanâlhâm did not understand.

"In!" Cuirin'nên'a ordered, pushing Leanâlhâm down between the roots.

She shrank back into the dark and dank hollow. The notion of being left here without anyone, even Léshil's mother, was too much.

"Do not leave me!" she begged.

Again Cuirin'nên'a did not answer. She dropped the stained stiletto and began tearing her own gown apart. She shredded it into strips, which she bound around her legs, arms, and torso. Taking up mulch and earth from the forest floor, she smeared it over her whole lithe body, then dropped to her back to writhe and cover it as well.

"Please," Leanâlhâm whispered.

Cuirin'nên'a rolled up to a crouch and retrieved the stiletto; leaves and soil now clung in the blood upon it. She wiped the blade clean across her thigh. All of her unsettling beauty was masked, like some creature rising from the dead leaves and needles of the forest floor. All that remained clearly visible were her alluring, beautiful eyes . . . coldly fixed upon Leanâlhâm.

"I must get the journal," the woman whispered.

Leanâlhâm did not know why such a thing mattered. Panic rose at the idea of being left truly alone. She tried to crawl out, and Cuirin'nên'a rushed in on her.

"Stay—and do not step into the open!"

"Please . . . no."

Léshil's mother grew so still. Her face was too masked by smears to make out her expression. Only her eyes appeared to soften.

"I will return," she whispered. "Stay where I can find you."

She lunged off through the forest. No sound carried from a single footfall as she flitted from shadow to shadow and was gone.

Cowering between the roots of the great redwood, Leanâlhâm pulled her knees against her chest. She clamped a hand over her abdomen and pressed the bottle of her uncle's ashes against her stomach. All she could do in the fear that rose over her grief was to watch the trees and wonder whether the murdering anmaglâhk were near.

To know fear of them was a madness as great as her love for her uncle, Sgäilsheilleache.

And somehow all the horrors of this day had to do with Wynn's journal.

Somehow Brot'ân'duivé and Cuirin'nên'a were at odds with their caste— and they had gotten Grandfather involved. Even Osha had been taken from Leanâlhâm by the greimasg'äh. Because of Brot'ân'duivé and Cuirin'nên'a,

Leanâlhâm was wholly alone in a world with no one to love her, to protect her even from those who were supposed to protect her people.

Afternoon turned to night, and still Cuirin'nên'a did not return.

Leanâlhâm's thoughts grew dull and tangled. She began to piece together all those times she had been sent away . . . whenever the greimasg'äh came to visit. How many times had she returned from little errands she had been sent on, only to find Grandfather whispering with Brot'ân'duivé? And that had only increased after Léshil's mother came to live with them.

Anger rose again.

Leanâlhâm had no one left to trust, had been intentionally sheltered, kept ignorant of . . . things she should have been allowed to know and understand. She looked about the darkened forest. Still afraid, she rose, bracing against the great redwood.

The last time she had seen Sgäilsheilleache, he had promised that he would finally take her to the ancestral burial grounds. All young an'Cróan undertook that journey before reaching adulthood. Sgäilsheilleache and Grandfather had always advised her to wait.

They did not have to say why. She knew it was because of her . . . tainted blood. But Léshil had gone there, guided by Sgäilsheilleache. And Léshil had come back.

He had more human blood in him than she did, but, even so, Sgäilsheilleache had guided him.

Leanâlhâm looked about the forest. She knew only that the burial grounds were far north, and then east of Crijheäiche. If that was all she knew, how could she find it on her own? For the first time she almost wished she found majay-hì eyes watching her from the forest—anything not to feel so alone and lost.

Leanâlhâm heaved a gasp as she flattened against the tree in terror.

There were eyes watching her—but not those of a majay-hì.

They peered around thickened ivy crawling up the trunk of a gnarled and twisted oak . . . but they were green like hers, and not pure crystal-blue. And more, the face around those strange eyes was too pale beneath the leaves.

The eyes shifted, as *it* began to move.

Leanâlhâm looked about, trying to see which way to run in the night.

Something light in color stepped out around the ivy-shadowed oak . . . on long legs that ended in paws. Leanâlhâm stared, her whole mind empty.

There stood a female majay-hì.

Delicate and small boned, it had a coat so pale it looked cream white in the scant moonlight. After a long pause, it padded slowly forward, and Leanâlhâm looked frantically about again.

There was nowhere to run that it could not easily catch her.

The female stopped where the redwood's huge, long roots sank into the forest's floor.

Leanâlhâm simply stood there, watching. The longer she looked into this sacred one's eyes, the more she saw that their color was not truly green. Nearer now, they were more the crystal sky blue that she knew, but with irises that sparkled with hints of yellow.

The female lowered its head slightly, as if it was looking down Leanâlhâm's body. Its gaze stopped midway. Leanâlhâm had no idea at what it was looking at as she closed her arms around herself, feeling exposed under the scrutiny.

The bottle of her uncle's ashes pressed firmly against her stomach.

The white majay-hì turned and walked off through the trees to the north. Without knowing why, Leanâlhâm took a step, and the female halted.

The majay-hì looked back at her, then took two more steps and paused again.

Leanâlhâm did not know what to think of all this. Majay-hì always moved in packs, and there were no other eyes out in the forest. She took another step . . . and then another for every one the white female took.

At least she was heading the way she thought she needed to go.

Inside Leanâlhâm's room at the annex, Chap lay upon the bed. He no longer watched the girl, as in the memories she had seen something—someone—he too often had to push from his thoughts.

His own mate, Lily, had come for the girl.

How was that possible? Why had it been Lily? Where was she now? And what of their daughter, Shade, or any of their other children? Chap was so lost in more guilt that he could barely think on anything else he had learned through Leanâlhâm.

Brot'an had taken Osha somewhere. The Anmaglâhk had murdered Gleann, though Nein'a had done all she could to stop them and was likely hiding away among the dissidents. Leanâlhâm had lost everyone who cared for her.

All because of Wynn's cursed journal, the one she should never have written in the first place.

If only it had never reached the blood-soaked old assassin, let alone Most Aged Father.

"What are you doing?"

That frightened hiss of a whisper roused Chap.

Leanâlhâm, with her legs curled up and clutched to her chest, had scooted back against the bed's headboard. He had not noticed her move, and at first he didn't understand her question. But she kept staring at him . . . in the same manner she had when he'd peeked in on her in the annex's little library.

"What were you doing?" she whispered.

Chap stiffened.

No, this was not possible. She could not know he'd touched her rising memories, but it was clear he had pushed her too far. In truth he was uncertain he could handle any more himself.

—*Come and*—*look at*—*this book*—*with me*— . . . —*I will help you*—*read*—*more*—

She hesitated, lost either in the past or some other unexplained fright—perhaps both. Finally she scooted across the bed but still watched him out of the corner of her eye as she pulled the pillow holding the book closer to her.

Chap remembered that she liked learning about the sages.

—*If*—*there is more*—*about*—*sages*—*we can*—*start there*—

Soon she was distracted from the past in reading onward. He clarified what words he could, for the dialect was not the one he knew. When she yawned too many times, he pawed the book closed, and he slept there with her upon the bed. He looked up only once in the night, when Leesil cracked the door to check on them.

The next morning they all headed back to the *Cloud Queen* and set sail. Captain Bassett declared their next stop was a port called Drist. Even as the ship sailed out of Chathburh, Chap couldn't stop thinking of Leanâlhâm's memories from the night before.

He believed Cuirin'nên'a had taken a blade from the anmaglâhk inside the tree dwelling and killed the man with it. What had been the ramifications of that? She had also abandoned Leanâlhâm in the forest and given precedence to recovering the stolen journal.

Gleann died with an arrow in his chest. Had the council of clan elders learned of an anmaglâhk murdering one of them, a healer and onetime Shaper, in cold blood?

For the first time since seeking the truth of what had happened among the an'Cróan, Chap was uncertain of how much to share with Leesil and Magiere—especially Leesil.

And what had become of Chap's mate, Lily, mother of their daughter, Shade?

CHAPTER SIXTEEN

Midafternoon, as the *Bashair* approached Chathburh, Én'nish was on deck with the rest of her companions. All six anmaglâhk stayed out of the crew's way and scanned the approaching port for any large ship bearing painted Numanese letters for the *Cloud Queen*. Dänvârfij had led all of them to believe their prey would still be in this port and unknowingly waiting to be captured.

Hungry for any hint of the quarry that had eluded them much too long, Én'nish leaned far over the rail. She anticipated pulling her blades for such a purpose and was equally eager to watch Rhysís put one arrow and another into Brot'ân'duivé's chest. There was only one thing she wanted more—the blood of Léshil on her blade for the loved one he had taken from her.

Disguised in human clothing, she was not likely to be spotted from a distance. Yet as the ship made port and docked, she stepped back from the rail and peered around in dismay.

"It is large," Tavithê said, voicing Én'nish's thoughts, as they both took in the sprawling harbor.

Numerous piers had clearly been built over many years, and not with much planning other than to fit in one more. Én'nish began counting ships but soon gave up.

"We have to disembark and search," Tavithê added.

"No," Fréthfâre said, leaning hard on her walking staff. "Eywodan, go and find the harbormaster. See what you can learn first."

As soon as the ramp was lowered, Eywodan headed off down the pier and vanished into the crowd. A somewhat uncomfortable silence followed.

Tension between Fréthfâre and Dänvârfij had grown, though Én'nish blamed the latter for their failures. Dänvârfij was too cautious, too hesitant to shed blood. They should have taken this ship the first day out of the isle. Had they done so, they might have caught the *Cloud Queen* long before now.

Only Fréthfâre had the strength of spirit to lead this team. But so far Dänvârfij remained the one to give orders and make tactical decisions, if not all strategic ones.

Én'nish often wished Fréthfâre would simply take control, but perhaps it no longer mattered if they could trap their quarry by tonight.

"Help me with my arm," Rhysís said to her.

She tried not to show pleasure at his request. For much of this journey she had barely noticed him. That had changed somehow. He had taken an arrow in the shoulder of his bow arm back in Calm Seatt. Though the wound had healed, his arm needed strengthening. He had taken to holding it out, and she would grip it, and then he would try to bend it and lift her.

Stepping close, she grasped his forearm.

"Tighter," he said.

Én'nish learned Rhysís's one weakness among all his skills: he needed to take care of someone. For the better part of their journey to this land, Wy'lanvi, the youngest member of the team, had fulfilled that need almost as a younger brother.

In Calm Seatt, Brot'ân'duivé had killed Wy'lanvi, and Rhysís had taken this hard.

Én'nish understood the anguish of loss, and she tightened her grip on Rhysís's arm.

Shortly after Wy'lanvi's death, Rhysís had shifted his need to care for someone to her. At first she had not known what to think of this. He was never overt, but he took notice of her extra duties in caring for Fréthfâre. He tried to lighten her burdens in small ways.

Én'nish had never valued kindness, had even learned to distrust it, for there had been so little of it in her life. But coming from Rhysís, she did not mind it so much.

"Plant your feet more firmly," Tavithê growled at her good-naturedly. "Make him work harder . . . or perhaps I should be the one to dangle from his weak limb?"

"I do not think so," Rhysís answered with a slight smile.

Tavithê was wiry but muscular, by far the best of them in hand-to-hand combat. It seemed both strange and oddly comforting that they joked with each other while Eywodan located their quarry. Humor was another challenging thing to Én'nish, but again, with these two companions, she had come to neither despise nor distrust it.

Dänvârfij and Fréthfâre stood apart and separate, waiting in silence.

Én'nish was not tense. They were within reach of the half-dead monster, Magiere; her murderous consort, Léshil; and the traitorous Brot'ân'duivé. Soon the first two would be suffering and the last would be dead—finally.

They passed the time in this manner, though at each effort, Rhysís barely lifted Én'nish's feet off the deck, but he managed it five times in a row. As her feet touched down a sixth time, Eywodan came striding up the ramp. In her hunger, Én'nish tightened her grip on Rhysís's arm, and she did not wait for her superiors to ask.

"Where?" she blurted out. "Where are they docked?"

Eywodan hesitated.

"What?" Dänvârfij nearly barked.

Eywodan shook his head. "We missed them by less than half a day. The *Cloud Queen* sailed this morning."

Those words did not register over the roar of pounding blood in Én'nish's ears. When they did, she wanted to shriek in fury. She kept silent, swallowing the pain and frustration, and then found Rhysís frowning at her—or rather at her biting grip on his arm—and she let go.

This was all Dänvârfij's fault for not letting them take the ship.

Dänvârfij's jaw muscle clenched, and Fréthfâre smoldered with visible anger.

But it was Rhysís's expression that kept Én'nish grounded. She could only describe it as . . . dark. Normally a stout supporter of Dänvârfij, he now glared at her.

He wanted the traitor's blood as much as Én'nish wanted Léshil's. They both sought payment for the loss of someone cherished.

"We take the ship?" he said flatly, only half questioning. "As soon as we are out of harbor?"

Dänvârfij dropped her head in brief contemplation. "Yes."

The following morning the *Bashair* left harbor, resuming its journey south.

Dänvârfij stood on deck with her team spread out to strategic positions and awaiting her command to act. Only Fréthfâre remained below in one of their cabins, and Dänvârfij knew how that grated on the crippled ex-Covârleasa. But it could not be helped; she would be less than useless up here.

Dänvârfij maintained her calm disinterest, though she was well aware how the others felt—that they should have taken the ship before now. They did not understand how difficult it would be once they did so. There were not enough of them to sail this vessel, even if all of them had known what was needed. And only one of them had such skill. Revenge clouded their reason.

All Dänvârfij's instincts and experience told her this choice was wrong, that waiting would be better, but she could not put it off any longer. Rhysís, Én'nish, and even the good-natured Tavithê had made their positions clear. They had lost too many comrades to Brot'ân'duivé. They had been humiliated in being outmaneuvered by the monster and her half-blood consort. They were failing in their purpose given by Most Aged Father.

Still, questions plagued Dänvârfij. Eywodan was the only one who also hesitated at this impending action. He stood silently near the ship's prow, and she strolled casually along the port rail to join him. He had experience with sailing vessels, as had some others originally assigned to the team, but they were all dead now. Perhaps that also had been a calculated choice by the traitor.

"If we leave half the crew alive," she said quietly, "but find we cannot trust them to assist us, can you bring this ship into a dock with only our help?"

Eywodan did not answer at first, and then, "No."

This concerned Dänvârfij greatly. It was one thing to manipulate a captain into serving their needs and entirely another to force a crew to obey. Her team could kill two-thirds of the men and lock up the others with little effort. That would be over in moments, but what then?

She could terrify enough of the remaining crew into service moment by moment, but they were loyal to Captain Samara. That created an unknown variable. Killing the captain might intimidate them into submission, but for only so long. Keeping the captain as a hostage might prolong their obedience, but eventually they would try to free him. Either way, her control would eventually falter, and going by Eywodan's word, there were not enough of her own, skilled or not, to handle this ship.

"Hold off and wait," she whispered. "I am going to speak with the captain."

Eywodan cocked his head with a quizzical lift of one eyebrow but then nodded. As he flashed subtle hand signals to the others, she headed off down the deck's center. Rhysís frowned as she passed, but she ignored him.

Shortly after leaving the harbor, Samara had gone below. She made her way down through the narrow passages to his cabin and knocked softly. Beyond the door, he called out a single word in Sumanese that she did not understand. Taking it as an invitation, she opened the door.

His cabin was tiny, and he sat at a built-in desk shelf that lowered from the hull wall on two braided silk cords. He did not hide his surprise at the sight of her.

"Pardon," she said quickly. "May I enter?"

"Of course. Is something wrong?"

She stepped in and closed the door. He was a slender man with dusky skin and dark eyes.

"Nothing," she said, and then purposefully faltered, displaying all the hesitancy of someone pressed to a hard choice. Depending on what he told her in the next few moments, she might have to kill him.

"I have not told you, but we are trying to"—she struggled for the correct term—"catch up with another ship. We hoped to do so in Chathburh . . . but missed it."

He shook his head. "I do not understand."

"We have family aboard a ship called *Cloud Queen*. We were . . . to board that ship but missed it at the isle."

He relaxed at that and stood up. "You should have told me sooner." Walking to a map on the wall, he asked, "What kind of ship is the *Cloud Queen*?"

"Very large . . . for large cargo."

"Do you know by how long we missed it?"

"A day . . . maybe more."

Samara turned back to his desk and spread out one roll of canvas to reveal another map. He tapped one point on it. "We are here, just south of Chathburh. The next port for a vessel of that make and size would be Drist." Looking to her, he pursed his lips. "Normally I advise passengers to not disembark there, for it is an unlawful place. But a large cargo vessel has to sail farther out from shore, in deeper water. I keep the *Bashair* closer to shore, and she is swifter. We should pass this other vessel by tomorrow at the latest. We will make Drist well before she does."

Samara paused again, and this time, taking a deep breath, he folded his arms. "But I won't keep my ship there long. If you want to wait for your family, you will have to find lodgings . . . and I do not advise that in a place like Drist."

Dänvârfij nodded, suppressed any visible relief, and even tried to smile.

"We will manage. And thank you."

But her thoughts were turning as she left. If the *Bashair* overtook the *Cloud Queen* and reached Drist first, there was no reason to seize this ship yet. And if Drist was the lawless place Samara described, so much the more in favor of her purpose.

On deck near the aftcastle, Én'nish grew restless. The plan was to kill and toss overboard anyone in the open and then silently work their way down through all entrances, until the remaining crew below were cornered and locked in. They could then decide how many to keep alive to man the vessel.

Too many days of inaction—other than caring for Fréthfâre—had left her half-mad to do something. She had bitten back a hiss when Eywodan had signaled everyone to wait as Dänvârfij walked off below, alone.

Én'nish looked to Rhysís, standing at the opposite rail near the forward mast. He glanced more than once toward the aft, where Dänvârfij had vanished, and then shook his head slightly. He kept clenching the hand of his recovering arm.

Én'nish was thankful when Dänvârfij reemerged, and set herself, ready to pull her blades. She picked out the closest sailor checking rigging near the rearward mast, and she looked for the next signal.

Dänvârfij stopped, barely beyond the rearward entrance to below. She leveled her left hand at her side, palm down, and slowly swept it outward away from her thigh.

Én'nish clenched all over.

Why had Dänvârfij called off the attack and ordered them to go below?

Tavithê straightened where he leaned against the forward mast, sauntered idly toward Dänvârfij, and headed below. But, like Én'nish, Rhysís stood his place and stared at Dänvârfij. Only then did Eywodan walk away from the prow.

Rhysís did not move, and neither did Én'nish.

Eywodan traversed the far rail and came up behind Rhysís to settle, leaning on the rail with his elbows as he looked out to sea. A slow turn of his head brought his gaze around to fix on Rhysís's back, as if he might pierce his comrade with only his eyes. As Eywodan shifted, his eyes turned on Én'nish with equal warning.

Rhysís lowered his head and only half looked back, as he was well aware that Eywodan stood behind him. With a slow breath, he headed after Tavithê and never once looked at Dänvârfij.

Still Eywodan watched Én'nish—and did not move until she did. Unlike Rhysís, Én'nish never flinched from looking Dänvârfij in the eyes as she passed.

*　　*　　*

Dänvârfij ignored Én'nish's glare and did not even follow the young one's path below. Instead, she stood waiting as Eywodan drew near. They had no one except for him to manage this vessel. With Samara's assurance of overtaking the *Cloud Queen*, seizing the ship was not the expedient strategy.

Likely Fréthfâre would hear a jaded and inaccurate account before Dänvârfij even reached the cabin. That was acceptable—this time. In correcting the facts, Dänvârfij would put Én'nish in her place and thereby warn Rhysís against further insubordination. Dissension was unacceptable in their purpose.

Eywodan came up beside her. Glancing about the deck, he cocked his eyebrow again.

"Am I to assume you have something better in mind?" he asked.

Dänvârfij was grateful for his show of support but did not say so. This was expected of all who shared the purpose given to a team's leader, but she gave him a nod of respect.

"Yes," she answered.

"Should I come with you to report to Fréthfâre?"

"No, watch the crew . . . and anyone else who comes on deck."

Eywodan nodded and wandered off. He settled where Rhysís had stood stubbornly a moment ago and leaned against the rail. Dänvârfij turned to head below.

What she did now was best done alone, for authority. There would be no further open defiance, regardless of anyone's rightful desire for revenge . . . even her own.

CHAPTER SEVENTEEN

The next day, Leesil was on deck, and for once the ship's rolling didn't make him quite so miserable. Though he certainly didn't feel normal, at least he'd kept breakfast down. Magiere, having recovered for the most part from that bit of ugliness in Chathburh, sat on a barrel behind him. She was still unsettled, but as so often before, they'd chosen not to talk about it.

Leanâlhâm was kneeling by Chap, and the two were obviously in some kind of "chat," though Leesil heard bits from only the girl's side. It struck him that those two had been getting awfully chummy lately, but at least Leanâlhâm wasn't hiding away as much.

Still, he worried about her future. For someone so young, she'd lost too many people in her life. What would happen when it came time for her and Chap to part ways?

Leesil knew full well that they would eventually. All that remained to figure out was where Leanâlhâm should go. The sight of her beside the dog as the two huddled against the rough breeze only made such a notion worse.

Leanâlhâm was Sgäile's niece, and just as with Magiere, Leesil wasn't about to let anything happen to her. That also meant getting her somewhere well away from Brot'an. And the old assassin was a bigger problem.

Brot'an stood hulking over the rail and gazing toward the distant shore.

Leesil noticed an almost imperceptible stiffening of Brot'an's shoulders. Anyone else might have missed it, but he had received too much dark tutoring from his mother. Slipping to the rail, he followed Brot'an's gaze.

Under the steady wind, a small two-masted vessel sailed along nearer the shoreline.

Leesil glanced sidelong at Brot'an, who gripped the rail with both hands.

"You know that ship?" he asked.

Brot'an didn't flinch or look at him. He didn't even blurt out a "What?" and instead answered flatly. "No."

"Then what's wrong?"

Brot'an pivoted halfway and looked to where Chap and Leanâlhâm huddled.

"Leanâlhâm," he called. "Go below and see what the cook is preparing for lunch. Wait for it and bring it up to us."

Normally Magiere would've gone at Brot'an for ordering the girl about. Instead she moved to the rail behind Leesil. Something was happening, and she must have sensed it.

Leanâlhâm frowned, as if knowing she was being sent off for some reason other than biscuits, dried fruit, and probably salt pork left over from last night. Rising, she headed for the door below the aftcastle, and Chap didn't follow. They all waited until Leanâlhâm was out of sight.

"All right, out with it," Leesil said, glancing at the small vessel growing smaller in the distance. "Why are you watching that ship?"

Brot'an shook his head and stepped closer to tower above Leesil.

"I do not know. Perhaps it is nothing."

The four of them were almost alone. Only the ship's pilot at the wheel was close enough to hear. So long as they spoke Belaskian, that wouldn't matter.

"You think we're being followed," Leesil accused.

"What?" Magiere asked angrily.

Leesil swung his arm back to keep her away from Brot'an, but he, too, was tired of Brot'an's never-ending string of secrets, one leading to the next.

"What do you know that we don't?" Leesil paused. "It's anmaglâhk out there on that ship, isn't it? How did they learn enough to follow us?"

Brot'an still didn't answer, and Leesil's frustration grew. Standing a few steps off, Chap rumbled softly.

—Ask him—why—he is—at odds with—his caste— . . . —What caused— this breach—

At Chap's suggestion rising in his thoughts, Leesil didn't take his eyes off Brot'an. Chap was after something, perhaps knew something.

"What did you do?" Leesil asked. "What caused the break between you and Most Aged Father, between you and your caste?"

"Not with my caste," Brot'an returned, and there was an uncommon edge to his so carefully controlled voice. "Only with Most Aged Father's blind fanatics, only with the loyalists."

"The what?" Magiere asked.

Brot'ân'duivé briefly closed his eyes at Magiere's question. He had known this moment would come, and *something* pulled at him, telling him what—who— was likely on that other ship. That too had only been a matter of time, for he had put it into play himself. When he opened his eyes again, he fixed on Léshil.

"It was from Cuirin'nên'a," he began, "that I learned the true depth of the breach. For I did not cause it."

Léshil's features flattened. "My mother?"

No one spoke. Not even Brot'ân'duivé broke the silence. As yet he could not see how much or how little he would have to give up.

"I answered your questions," Magiere said, barely above a threatening whisper. "Now you answer Leesil."

Brot'ân'duivé did not need her to remind him of their bargain. . . .

Once Osha had gone off with the summoned clhuassas, Brot'ân'duivé ran for the central enclave of the Coilehkrotall. It was a three-day journey, but he cut that time short by resting only briefly along the way and even traveling by night. Near dusk on the second day, something disturbed him.

He slowed and heard movement ahead, soft-footed but in haste. A familiar whistle carried on the air. Someone was trying to catch his attention.

He rushed onward, swerving into the trees and away from any open paths. It was not long before that someone appeared.

Cuirin'nên'a came over a gradual rise and halted. She crouched, studying the earth in tracking, and Brot'ân'duivé hurried into the open. That she was here and not with the girl and his old friend unsettled him. Cuirin'nên'a rose at the sight of him.

Besides wearing an anmaglâhk's cloak over her shoulders, she was covered in soil, leaves, and tree needles amid dried smears of earth. She had shredded her gown to wrap up her limbs and torso. Older, dried blood crusted on her hands, though there were signs she had tried to clean it off. In surveying her whole form, he saw no wounds.

"Brot'ân'duivé," she breathed, but that was all she got out amid panting from a long, hard run.

He had known her since she was a girl, and had never once seen relief in her eyes, not even when he had helped to free her from a glade where Most Aged Father had imprisoned her. Brot'ân'duivé pulled her to the base of an ash tree, made her sit, and then waited.

"Gleannéohkân'thva is dead," she finally managed to say.

A hint of pain slipped into her voice and struck him as well, though this barely registered in his mind. Gleannéohkân'thva was like the forest's highest trees . . . seemingly eternal no matter how old he grew.

Strands of silky white-blond hair were stuck in a smear of blood on Cuirin'nên'a's cheek. Brot'ân'duivé reached out and pulled them off, and still he could not respond.

"Assassinated," she went on quietly, "by loyalists."

He half turned and sank on his heels; his back struck the tree's trunk as he settled beside her to stare out at nothing.

"Three," she said. "One hid in the forest while two entered to search for the journal. We were at the feast, and I should not have left it behind. They took it before I could stop them."

She paused as if reliving the moment. Details were missing, but only one thing mattered.

"The one with the journal ran," she continued. "Gleannéohkân'thva followed and would not heed my warning. When I had finished with the other, it was too late. Gleannéohkân'thva lay outside, an arrow . . . an anmaglâhk arrow through his heart."

Brot'ân'duivé still stared outward. If he looked at her, either of them might lose control of their grief.

"What of Leanâlhâm?" he asked. "Where is she?"

"I hid her in the forest well beyond the enclave. Then I went after the two who fled with the journal. In place of catching them, I . . ."

At her sudden silence, Brot'ân'duivé had ample time to guess at the rest.

"Who did you meet?"

"Urhkarasiférin," she whispered, "returned from following you and Osha."

It was as he had guessed, though it made no sense. How did she know this other greimasg'äh had tracked him? Urhkarasiférin would fulfill any purpose set by Most Aged Father that served the people. He was as devoted—and perhaps as naïve—as Sgäilsheilleache, and neither a dissident nor one of Most Aged Father's blind followers.

Had that now changed? Had another greimasg'äh taken sides?

"He did not," Cuirin'nên'a whispered.

Brot'ân'duivé glanced at her. That she followed what he would reason, without his saying anything, testified to his trust in her.

"I would not have found him," she went on, "except that he let me. I attacked him on sight even so, thinking he had been the one to lead those sent by Most Aged Father. I knew I would not survive, but I did not care, so long as neither did he."

"Why did he let you live?"

She sighed. "He had nothing to do with what happened, leaving the other three behind to only watch—and wait for his return. I assume the enclave has been under surveillance. When he saw you there and then leaving again, he must have wished to speak with you . . . or at least understand your intentions before anything was done. Killing had never been part of his purpose. He did not order them to break into Gleannéohkân'thva's home."

"And you believe him?"

Cuirin'nên'a glanced at Brot'ân'duivé. "He gave me his cloak, let me go, and told me to find you."

The ramifications of everything set in.

Most Aged Father had sent four of their caste, including a greimasg'äh, after the journal. They must have watched the enclave for some time, likely even while Brot'ân'duivé had been there. Urhkarasiférin had waited for a clear opportunity with no complications, no unwitting harm to anyone. When Brot'ân'duivé had left, taking Osha as well, perhaps the overly quiet shadow-gripper had not been satisfied, and so followed.

If Brot'ân'duivé had been given such a purpose—and accepted it—this was what he would have done. Urhkarasiférin would do no more or less.

Most Aged Father would have known this, so it begged two more questions.

Why was Urhkarasiférin selected for this? And had the others of his team been given a second purpose unknown to him, or simply chosen to act on their own?

Whether the three had waited for an opportunity or had been secretly ordered to act mattered little. There could be only one reason for Urhkarasiférin's presence.

Most Aged Father had known where Brot'ân'duivé would be and had sent another greimasg'äh in ignorance to deal with him, if necessary. That ancient worm in the wood of his people had used a shadow-gripper as an unwitting accomplice in his subterfuge.

Most Aged Father's loyalist fanatics had broken into the home of one of their people. They had stolen from an elder of the clans and killed him.

"Where is Urhkarasiférin now?" Brot'ân'duivé asked.

"On his way back to Crijheäiche for . . . clarification."

No doubt he would receive only more lies. This time Urhkarasiférin would not be fooled, but what he would do then had yet to be seen.

"And Leanâlhâm?"

Cuirin'nên'a closed her eyes. "She was gone when I returned for her . . . before coming for you."

"Gone?"

"I found no sign of a struggle and so searched. I tracked her path for a ways before deciding to come for you."

Yes, though one word did not make sense. "What *path* and to where?"

"Not *where* . . . but after whom."

Brot'ân'duivé shook his head in puzzlement.

"I am not fully skilled in the wild," she explained. "It is not my expertise. For as far as I went, her course remained true north alongside the paw prints of a majay-hì. To my eyes, its tracks were as fresh as hers. She may have even been following the sacred one directly."

This troubled Brot'ân'duivé even more, but he had to act. Too much time had been lost. He needed to hunt Most Aged Father's agents and retrieve the journal before it reached Crijheäiche. Failing in that would necessitate drastic measures to remove it from Most Aged Father's possession.

The journal had become a tool of fear. Amid bloodshed, it could serve either him or the old worm in pulling down the other.

With its hints of an artifact from the time of the Ancient Enemy, the journal could be used to sway the caste in one of two directions. Worse, that it had been found secreted in the home of the old healer and in the hands of Cuirin'nên'a—once imprisoned as a traitor—would make it proof for Most Aged Father to do as he wished in hunting down every dissident.

If Brot'ân'duivé could not retrieve it, then Most Aged Father had to die.

"Can you travel?" he asked.

"Of course."

"Find Leanâlhâm and get her to safety."

"And where would that be?" Cuirin'nên'a asked dryly, sounding more herself.

Thinking, he tilted his head. "Take her to Urhkarasiférin's clan. He has proven he will not turn you over to Most Aged Father, regardless of his allegiances. He would never allow an innocent to come to harm, so he will protect the girl. Once she is safe, spread the word through our cells. Every dissident must go into hiding and wait for instructions. Most especially all among the Coilehkrotall."

"What are you going to do?"

"What I have to."

He thought she might argue, insist upon coming with him. Instead she nodded. A moment later she was gone, and he stood gazing at the spot where she had vanished. But before beginning his hunt, he had one more thing to do—an unavoidable, undesirable task.

On the edge of dusk on the third day after leaving Osha, Brot'ân'duivé walked silently into the home enclave of his lost old friend. He made his way unseen to Gleannéohkân'thva's tree dwelling and slipped inside.

The interior was in shambles, with blood dried on the moss floor, but the body of the anmaglâhk whom Cuirin'nên'a killed had been removed. The people here would know to send for one of the caste to retrieve it, and so would prepare it for return with their own hands. Brot'ân'duivé could only imagine their dismay at finding an anmaglâhk slain in the home of one of their own.

They would have already seen to the body of Gleannéohkân'thva, their treasured elder.

Brot'ân'duivé had not even been present for this. Gleannéohkân'thva had been more than an ally. Perhaps aside from the lost Eillean, the old healer had been Brot'ân'duivé's only friend in a life that did not leave room for such things.

He swallowed down that pain and buried it. Within a few steps, it resurfaced against his will, but he had come here for more than a last farewell.

This tree had belonged to a Shaper turned healer. It was one node in a living and hidden method of communication traditionally reserved for the Anmaglâhk and the council of clan elders. And now this enclave would be watched by Most Aged Father's agents. This home would be stripped for further evidence that worm-in-the-wood of his people could use to vilify any dissident—or anyone charged as such—before the council of elders.

Brot'ân'duivé knelt in shame for what he was about to do. After taking out his flint and one stiletto, he paused.

It was not enough to make certain that Most Aged Father's agents found nothing of use. He went into the guest chamber, where Cuirin'nên'a had stayed, and he began tearing up the living moss carpet to dig into the earth until he found what he sought.

Earth-stained oval nodules lumped out of the base of one great root—new word-woods not quite ready for those who would need to communicate with this tree. Brot'ân'duivé gouged them off the root with his blade and returned to the main chamber, then searched the place for lantern oil and found two small bottles.

Once the torn pillows, wall hangings, and blankets were burning, he tossed the unfinished ovals of wood into the fire and waited until the flames grew enough that smoke filled the room and stung his eyes. When he turned to leave with both oil bottles in hand, he spotted Gleannéohkân'thva's satchel against the wall near the door.

It was always there, waiting for when the old healer's skills were desperately needed. Brot'ân'duivé picked it up, a foolish and sentimental act, but he could not let it perish.

He stepped out of the home of his old friend with smoke already billowing around the doorway's drape. He pulled the drape aside enough to heave the oil bottles in and hear them break.

Someone would soon spot the blaze in the night.

The enclave would be roused and cleared as some took to controlling the fire. The damp spring would do most of that for them. All that truly needed to be destroyed was whatever was inside the tree's hollow part at its broad base.

Still, to murder a living home was something he could not take lightly.

Brot'ân'duivé ran into the night forest, not bothering with stealth as he headed for Crijheäiche. He did not—could not—look back.

Chap listened with rapt attention to every word Brot'an spoke. He almost didn't believe Most Aged Father had given orders that allowed the deaths of his own people—all for the sake of a small journal. Yet when Brot'an spoke, Chap believed him.

He knew there were missing details—which Brot'an either didn't know or had left out. Such as all that had truly happened with . . .

One tiny glint caught the corner of Chap's eye, and he turned his head slightly. There in the shadows inside the doorway below the aftcastle was a glimmer in a verdant green eye.

Leanâlhâm crouched upon those inner stairs with her head barely high enough to peek out. She was flattened close to one sidewall, listening and watching. She had never gone below as instructed.

Chap was careful not to let her know he had spotted her. He pretended to eye Leesil and Magiere while keeping the angle of his head where he could see the girl.

"What happened to my mother?" Leesil demanded.

Brot'an's hesitation almost made Chap look back at him.

"It was not until later that I rejoined Cuirin'nên'a."

Leanâlhâm flinched and cowered at the mention of Leesil's mother, and Chap became warier.

He casually turned, stalking up the deck to stand off behind Brot'an. That would unnerve the old assassin, though it was not Chap's reason for doing so. From there he could see Leanâlhâm without looking directly at her.

Cautiously Chap reached for whatever memories rose in Leanâlhâm's mind at the mention of Cuirin'nên'a.

The girl everyone called Leanâlhâm crouched on the steep steps below the aftcastle and listened to Brot'ân'duivé, who so coldly and flatly related the events. How could he speak of burning her home—her grandfather's home—so calmly, as if it had been only one more task to complete? When he had finished, at the mention of Léshil's mother, Leanâlhâm could not help but picture Cuirin'nên'a in her mind.

Leanâlhâm had been moved when she heard how quickly Léshil's mother agreed to come after her. She had not known this before and, at that time, had not wanted that woman anywhere near her. For Leanâlhâm had already found another guide. . . .

The white majay-hì remained barely within Leanâlhâm's sight. The more she tried to catch up, the quicker the female pressed on, though it never abandoned her. Its very actions confused her after all the times she had feared finding those eyes watching her from out of the forest. But Leanâlhâm blindly followed the female through the night, into day, and then through another night.

By the following dusk, she was aching in exhaustion when the white majay-hì suddenly veered and vanished.

Leanâlhâm grew frantic. She stumbled to the last place she had seen the female. No matter how she thrashed through the surrounding brush, she found nothing. She was crying and did not even know it until she stopped and stood helpless, ready to drop on her knees.

"Leanâlhâm!"

Her head whipped around at the shout.

Favoring her right leg, Cuirin'nên'a weaved closer through the trees.

"I had thought to catch you before now," she said, and then demanded, "Where are you going?"

Cuirin'nên'a was disheveled, still covered in shredded cloth wraps stained with soil and mulch, though most of that on her face had dried off or been wiped away. And now she wore an anmaglâhk's cloak. Spots in her bound-up silky hair were crusted with dried blood. The sight of her was unsettling compared to the woman who had come to live in Leanâlhâm's home . . . so perfect and beautiful.

All Leanâlhâm saw now was a living reminder of loss, blood, and death. She spun, looking again for the white majay-hì, but the female was still gone.

"You . . . you frightened it off," she whispered.

"Frightened what off?" Cuirin'nên'a asked.

Leanâlhâm turned back and then retreated, swallowing hard in her dry throat. A majay-hì had run from this woman.

"Go away and leave me alone!" she shouted. "You care nothing for me, nothing for those I loved. All you care about are your whispers and schemes with the greimasg'äh!"

"I am to take you to safety. At least you were heading in the correct direction."

Leanâlhâm had no idea what this meant. Who besides her grandfather or Sgäilsheilleache—or Osha—would willingly take in a mixed-blood girl without even a true name? All of them had left her, and any other place would be empty, devoid of love and loved ones.

She had followed the white majay-hì only because it appeared that the sacred one had *wanted* to lead her somewhere. Had it known where she wanted to go? Because of Léshil's mother, even that had been taken from her.

"Go away," Leanâlhâm warned.

"That is not going to happen," Cuirin'nên'a replied quietly, and took two more steps.

Leanâlhâm backed up and almost tripped.

"This is your fault, yours and the greimasg'äh's!" she shouted. "Because of you two, Grandfather is dead. What did you do? What did you drag him into?"

At that, Cuirin'nên'a froze.

"I will go nowhere with you!" Leanâlhâm ranted on. "Find another way to ease your conscience . . . or go on suffering, if you even can. I am going to the ancestors to deliver Sgäilsheilleache, even if I cannot bring Grandfather to them. I am taking my true name. Now get away from me and do not—"

Cuirin'nên'a was suddenly right in front of her.

Leanâlhâm struck out without even thinking. She felt no more than the touch of fingertips on her wrist, and her fist struck nothing. In an instant, she was pinned facedown, and an angry whisper rose near her ear.

"Unless Sgäilsheilleache or Gleannéohkân'thva told you more than they should, you will never find the way. They had reasons for keeping you from that place, and I will honor their wishes. There has been enough loss in losing them . . . and I will not see you lost as well!"

Before Leanâlhâm uttered another word, she was heaved to her feet and pushed onward in a silent walk into the trees, until Cuirin'nên'a found an open space. All Leanâlhâm could do was sit against a cedar's trunk and watch while the cold-blooded woman made a fire.

"In the morning we go to the Hâjh River," Cuirin'nên'a said, adding more twigs to the small flames. "I may be able to influence a river barge master to carry us partway. I am taking you to the clan of Urhkarasiférin, where you will be safe."

Leanâlhâm sank in upon herself, hanging her head. She was to be imprisoned among the people of yet another greimasg'äh. The weary night dragged on.

She touched little of the travel rations Cuirin'nên'a laid out on a fresh maple leaf. Thirst made her drink too much water, and her stomach began to ache. She gave in to exhaustion and squirmed around to rest her head against the cedar. But . . . she lifted her head and peered off into the forest.

The campfire's soft yellow-orange light glinted upon blue eyes that pulsed to green, like her own.

The white majay-hì watched Leanâlhâm between the bush's leaves. Suddenly its head turned as it looked more toward the fire. Leanâlhâm did not wish to do anything to alert Cuirin'nên'a to the female's return.

That did not matter, as Cuirin'nên'a stood up and stared at a guardian of their forest.

"Is this the one you followed?" she asked.

Leanâlhâm hesitated to say anything. The white guardian pushed her head out of the leaves and studied Léshil's mother, and then turned back to Leanâlhâm.

"Yes," she finally answered. "She wanted me to follow." It was a half truth, for she knew no such thing, but she wished it to be true. "I did not remember . . . that I had seen her before," Leanâlhâm went on. "Not until daylight came and I saw her clearly."

"Before?" Cuirin'nên'a asked, still watching the majay-hì.

"When your son, Léshil, and his friends came to us," Leanâlhâm explained, "and Sgäilsheilleache took us all toward the Hâjh on the way to Most Aged Father. The strange majay-hì with Léshil sometimes went off with this one's pack."

"My son?" Cuirin'nên'a whispered. "You are speaking of the majay-hì they call 'Chap'?"

Leanâlhâm flushed at the thought of anyone putting a name upon a sacred one. Wynn Hygeorht, the funny little human called a "sage," had also done that to this white female. Leanâlhâm would not repeat such an offense.

"It is a rare thing," Cuirin'nên'a whispered, continuing to watch the majay-hì. "Rarely . . . if ever . . . is someone singled out by one of them."

Leanâlhâm did not think so, not after what the others had done to her. She looked to the white majay-hì watching Cuirin'nên'a, but she could not understand what Léshil's mother meant.

Cuirin'nên'a glanced away. "Very well," she whispered.

The white female wheeled and vanished into the forest.

Leanâlhâm clawed up the cedar, scraping her hands on the bark as she pulled herself up to stand, and lunged after the majay-hì in a panic. She was snatched by the back of her tunic and pulled short. All hope vanished, and she did not struggle this time. She stood weeping yet again at another loss.

"I will take you to the ancestors."

Leanâlhâm spun around, numb with shock, and then relief overwhelmed her.

"Do not thank me," Cuirin'nên'a warned. "There are other things that need my attention, which are now dangerously delayed by my choice. And when we have reached the burial grounds, you will have never run so long and hard in your life."

And so, although Leanâlhâm had never expected help from Léshil's mother, the two of them traveled together. In some ways Cuirin'nên'a's presence made the journey easier than it would have been in following the white majay-hì.

The people of the Hâjh knew her as the daughter of great Eillean—another greimasg'äh. Comfortable transportation and good meals on a barge were provided without barter. Due to spring swells, the current was faster than at any other time of the year. The barge swam with great speed, as a "living" vessel of the people, and carried them swiftly down the river for days. But they did not go all the way to Crijheäiche, Origin-Heart.

Much to the confusion of the barge master and his awestruck attendants, Cuirin'nên'a requested a stop where there was no known settlement for leagues. After disembarking, she led the way through the wild with the confidence of someone who knew exactly where she was going.

Leanâlhâm followed without question, and the running soon began.

Her only relief came when the thickening woods slowed them enough that they had to find a way through. Wherever Cuirin'nên'a was taking her, it was on a direct course rather than an easier path.

In daylight, Leanâlhâm harbored little doubt the ancestors would accept her, for they had accepted Léshil. But that night in the dark, as she lay weary and aching upon the ground, questions and fear crept in.

What if the ancestors rejected her?

At dawn she pressed onward, following Cuirin'nên'a, who never appeared to tire. The next afternoon the forest around them began to change.

There were no flowers here, only an overabundance of wet moss that clung to tree trunks and dangled from branches overhead in dark, wet curtains. The trees were older and gnarled, their bark darkened by moisture that was thick in the air. On that bark were growths of fungus in earthy, sallow colors. A rain began, its drizzle pattering against the leaves.

The farther they went, the less Leanâlhâm could see the way out when she looked back. Until it was completely dark, she could not even tell when night drew close. The sky had long past been blocked out, and it seemed they walked for so long in a perpetual dusk.

Leanâlhâm felt as if the trees, so old and tangled with each other, were aware and did not want her here. She had always felt like an outsider among her people, but now the an'Cróan forest itself closed in on her as though she was a trespasser.

"Keep up," Cuirin'nên'a commanded.

It was long past dark with they stopped. Leanâlhâm waited, but Cuirin'nên'a did not crouch to prepare a fire this time and simply stood there with her back turned. Finally Leanâlhâm stepped closer.

The forest ahead thinned, its branches screening an open space. It was so dark that the masses of leaves and trailing moss were little more than shapes of pure black. Yet beyond and through the spaces between them was a soft light, perhaps a little brighter than a full moon might provide.

Leanâlhâm tried to make out what was hidden beyond in the clearing, but she caught only a hint of glistening yellowish brown limbs beyond shapes that might be more moss-draped oaks.

"Enter there," Cuirin'nên'a whispered. "Do not move. Do not look for it. It will come to you."

Leanâlhâm glanced up, but Cuirin'nên'a did not look at her. Then she heard something sliding heavily up the wet forest mulch.

The faint, soft sound carried from directly ahead. For the first time since this journey began, Leanâlhâm's fear grew beyond that of being rejected.

Was there danger in what she did now?

The sound grew louder, as if something circled around the far clearing instead of passing through it. Wet dragging came between rhythmic pauses.

"You will say these words exactly as I speak them," Cuirin'nên'a whispered.

But Leanâlhâm was frozen with fear.

"Father of Poison," Cuirin'nên'a began.

Leanâlhâm tried to choke out the words, but nothing came from her mouth. The dark base of one oak bulged near the ground. The swelling rolled and flowed on the forest floor, and came toward her across the nearer clearing. It turned in to the path between her and that farther half-hidden clearing. The soft glow from that place caught on a piece of slithering darkness.

Its surface glinted to iridescent green.

A long body, thicker than her own, was covered in tight-fit scales. Their deep green shimmered to opalescence as it came closer. The yellow glint of two eyes marked its approaching head, like gems bigger than her fists in an oblong boulder pushed along a hand's breadth above the ground.

"Repeat my words!" Cuirin'nên'a hissed.

Leanâlhâm shook so hard that her teeth clicked. She fumbled in the tunic's front to pull out the bottle of her uncle's ashes for something to hang on to.

"Father of Poison," she uttered in a shaky croak.

The slithering mass upon the ground began to twist and roil no more than four strides ahead.

Cuirin'nên'a took a quick breath. "Who washes away our enemies with Death."

Leanâlhâm struggled to get out those words. The mass in the dark began to rise . . . like a snake too huge to be real.

"Let me pass by to my ancestors, first of my blood," Cuirin'nên'a whispered. "Give me leave to touch the Seed of Sanctuary."

But then Leanâlhâm lost her voice.

The serpent's body knotted and coiled, gathering into a mass beneath the last of it, which raised a scaled and plated head to hover in the dark and sway gently. Slit-irised eyes like spiral-cracked crystals fixed on Leanâlhâm.

"Say the words!" Cuirin'nên'a ordered.

"Let me pass by . . . to . . . my . . ."

The serpent's jaw dropped open.

She saw in that night-shadowed mouth the shapes of glistening fangs longer than an anmaglâhk's blades. The widening maw could swallow half of her before she screamed.

She had come for two reasons, and for either she would rather die than fail to try. Closing her eyes, she struggled on.

"Let me pass by to my ancestors, first . . . first of my . . . blood. Give me leave to touch . . . the Seed of Sanctuary."

A horrid, cold breath washed over her face.

Her fingers began to ache in clutching the bottle.

That breath came twice more, stronger each time . . . and then stopped on an inhale.

Leanâlhâm's legs nearly buckled as she waited to be swallowed alive. A soft grating sound in pulses broke over the noise of blood pounding in her ears. She heard the coils grating upon wet mulch.

The sound grew strangely softer, more distant, until it was gone, and still she could not open her eyes.

"Now enter," Cuirin'nên'a whispered.

Leanâlhâm shuddered, not only at those sudden words but the quaver in Cuirin'nên'a's voice.

This was the woman who had come out of Leanâlhâm's home blood-stained from having killed one of her own without hesitation, and later gone after the others all alone. There had been no fear in her hard, beautiful eyes back then.

Leanâlhâm looked up to find Cuirin'nên'a's features visibly tense.

"Are you not coming?" she whispered, her own fear growing again.

"You must enter alone."

"But I heard about . . . Sgäilsheilleache went with Léshil."

"Go."

Leanâlhâm hesitated in looking to the glow beyond the oaks. No matter what waited there, she could not turn back now. Taking her first hesitant steps, she peered about for any sign of the Father of Poison. She never stopped looking as she walked, until the glow ahead grew too much to ignore.

She found herself standing between the surrounding oaks on the edge of the inner clearing. Before her was an enormous glistening tree not quite as large as those that surrounded it. She knew it only by a name, for no one would have dared to describe it.

Roise Chârmune—the Seed of Sanctuary.

All her fear faded as she stepped closer and gazed up into its wild branches filling the night above her. It was not shaped like the tall and straight ash trees she had seen all of her life. From its thick trunk, stout branches curved and wound and divided. A soft glow emanated from all of its fine-grained tawny wood and dimly lit the entire clearing.

Leafless and barkless, yet alive—she could *feel* that much, and this must be what all those before her had felt upon coming here. From its wide-reaching roots lumping the earth to its thick and naked pale yellow body and limbs, the tree's softly rippled surface glistened beneath its own glow. Warmth spread from it that she could not describe, as if its light sank through her skin.

Leanâlhâm held up the small bottle.

Before her own need came that of someone she loved. Carefully removing the stopper, she crouched, uncertain whether she did any of this correctly. She slowly tapped the ashes out and spread them at the base of the tree.

"You are home," she said, closing her eyes and wishing the ancestors would keep Sgäilsheilleache among them forever. It seemed so long before she rose and, with her head still down, tucked the bottle away in her tunic. Then she looked upon Roise Chârmune.

"I am here," she whispered.

Nothing happened. Had she done something wrong, or was there something she had not done? She hesitantly stepped closer, reached out, and her hand stalled with her fingertips shy of that bare, tawny trunk. Swallowing hard, she touched the glistening wood.

The world darkened and grew cold.

Leanâlhâm's breath caught as she felt a hand overlie hers against the tree . . . and then she saw the hand take form. It was long fingered and glimmered like the tree, and she could see her own hand right through it. Leanâlhâm turned her head to look upon . . .

A ghostly golden an'Cróan woman, her slender face lined by age, sternly watched Leanâlhâm. The woman's robe over her gown might have been blue, but Leanâlhâm could not be certain as she began shivering in the sudden cold. The way the woman's long hair moved in some unfelt breeze reminded Leanâlhâm of long grass blades caught in a river's flow.

She could not help but think that . . . she looked upon one of the ancestors.

With a sharp flash of pain in her heart, she blurted out, "Is Grandfather with you? Could I see him once more? I never told him good-bye."

By way of an answer, the elder woman placed her other hand upon Leanâlhâm's cheek—and pressed, forcing her to look back to the tree.

Roise Chârmune began to swell before Leanâlhâm's eyes, as if she were falling face-first into its trunk. An instant before impact, she thought she saw translucent leaves sprouting from its limbs. Then she saw something more . . . through and beyond it.

She looked out upon a land she did not know, as if she stood upon a high precipice, about to fall. Beyond a broken expanse, where a ragged terrain spread between ranges of woods, was the richness of a deep and dark forest.

Leanâlhâm felt herself teetering on the edge.

She arched back, stumbling in an awkward retreat, and spun about. Everything around her had changed. The burial grounds . . . the glowing tree . . . were gone.

Across an open grass plain that strangely frightened her was a forest's edge with trees that dwarfed the dwellings of her homeland. They were so impossibly tall. But that plain between them terrified her for some reason, as if a violent event had happened there that she could not remember.

She backed away, but then the grass clung to and snagged her clothing, as if trying to stop her. With her breath quickening, she thrashed around, ripping her cloak from the grass's grip.

Leanâlhâm froze in place, for there at the edge of the plain stood the ghostly elder woman.

"Where am I?" she cried out.

The ghost said nothing. Perhaps a brief sorrow passed across her features. If so, it was quickly gone, replaced by stern watchfulness.

Leanâlhâm turned to the right to run. There beyond her stood the ghost, closer now. She retreated and then whirled to run the other way along the plain. Again the woman was there, closer still. Leanâlhâm stumbled in trying to stop and fell face-first into the tall grass.

Rolling, she tried to escape the clinging strands. She fought to get to her feet, and this time ran for the far tree line, but that ghostly woman appeared again . . . out on this plain and far from that massive forest that was not her own.

Leanâlhâm pulled up short before stepping over the precipice.

It was suddenly there before her again. Beyond it was now only choppy water as far as she could see, but it was not the rich blue-green of the bays of her people. Crashing waves of dull gray and foam broke upon the rocks far below her. Backing away, she turned more slowly this time and . . .

She found herself in a dark forest of vines and enormous trees. The sky was no longer visible above, blocked out by intertwined branches. Spinning around, frantic at being lost, she stopped.

There was a glow far ahead of her, but she could not see from where it came. It could only be Roise Chârmune, and so she ran for it, slapping her way through the brush until her clothes were soaked by droplets on wet leaves. She broke upon a narrow path and could not see the light in the forest anymore.

Turning both ways, she saw it at last.

There stood the woman, pointing the other way along the path, away from herself. Or was she pointing at . . .

Leanâlhâm backed away. All that she knew was gone and lost. She recognized nothing here.

"Where am I?" she cried again.

Down the path by which I came . . . to a lost way.

Leanâlhâm shuddered so hard that it nearly pushed her to convulsions. She had heard those words, mournful in the woman's voice, though the spirit's lips had not moved. Cowering, as the woman pointed beyond her and back toward the precipice, Leanâlhâm raised her hands to cover her eyes but never touched her face.

Her fingers and palms, all the way to her wrists and beneath the edges of her tunic sleeves, were lit from within by a pale glow . . . like that of the woman pointing at her. She choked, unable to breathe, and then turned and fled.

Was she to die for having come here? Was that what all of this meant?

She was in an open grassland and running as fast as she could, but another forest loomed ahead, smaller and sparser than the great one. She broke through, and there was the woman, watching and pointing, among the trees. Beyond and ahead was that other glow in the forest's depths, so like that of the ghost.

Trying to catch her breath, Leanâlhâm swerved away at a run . . . and found herself in a different forest of red and orange leaves . . . then down a stony shore . . . and through a world of white ice . . . and then a place of nothing but sun and burning sand . . . and then another foreign forest.

She tried to find anything familiar—her homeland, the dark silhouettes of the burial ground oaks, the draped moss beyond that . . . anything.

In terror, she coughed out, "Grandfather! Sgäilsheilleache! Help me!"

There was no answer, not even the voice of the ghostly woman.

Everything blurred and darkened before her eyes.

Leanâlhâm's next footfall landed on something that turned under her weight. As she fell, she called out the only name left that she could remember. "Cuirin'nên'a!"

The world went black and silent . . . for who knew how long.

A glimmer of dull flickering light, which danced in umbers and oranges as if seen through something in its way, grew as Leanâlhâm struggled to open her eyelids.

The whole world was dark—and sideways—but for a small fire upon the forest floor. Beyond that crouched a slender figure in a travel-stained cloak of forest gray.

Cuirin'nên'a raised her head, and her beautiful, cold eyes widened as Leanâlhâm struggled to sit up. Only then did Leanâlhâm see that she was somewhere else, no longer within sight of the burial ground. All around her were the dank, mossy trees of the forest along the way to that place.

She breathed in and out through her mouth. What she had seen there had felt so real.

"And what do I now call you?" Cuirin'nên'a asked.

Leanâlhâm was struck mute at such a question. Did Cuirin'nên'a not wish to know what had happened? Obviously she had come when Leanâlhâm called out for her, so she must have seen something while carrying away a collapsed unconscious girl.

Leanâlhâm did not want to think about a name and began, "I saw—"

"No," Cuirin'nên'a commanded. "We do not speak of such things. That is only for you to know . . . and to choose a name, as you see fit, by what you learned."

Leanâlhâm shrank upon herself. At her touch, Roise Chârmune had turned into a common leafy tree, as if it had lost all that it had once been. She had found herself in an endless stretch of foreign lands, one after another, as she tried to find her way home . . . and could not.

The truth of that much almost broke her.

She did not belong among the people.

No matter how much Sgäilsheilleache and Grandfather had tried to make a life for her here, it was not what should be. She began to weep. Had Sgäilsheilleache seen anything such as she had? Had he seen his death upon facing the ancestors? Had he seen his flesh glow like the ghosts of the dead long gone from this world?

All she knew was that he had not seen what she had.

She had seen a world without her home, and the ancestors wanted her gone.

"I cannot . . . not . . ." Leanâlhâm stuttered out. "Not choose . . . from what she said . . . to me."

Pulling up her knees and burying her head, she broke into sobs.

"What?" Cuirin'nên'a whispered too sharply.

Leanâlhâm weakly lifted her head. Through tear-blurred sight, she found Cuirin'nên'a watching her intently. Fear, more than anything else, quelled her sobs.

"She . . . one of them?" Cuirin'nên'a struggled to get out. "You saw . . . heard the ancestors? That does not happen!"

Leanâlhâm grew still, for this was not exactly true. She had heard hints that the ancestors had spoken to Léshil. Cuirin'nên'a had to know this much and more.

Did the ancestors not speak to all who came for their true names? How much the worse for her, if they did not? Grandfather had once mentioned that Léshil refused to accept his true name.

Leshiârelaohk . . . Champion of Leshiâra . . . Champion of Sorrow-Tear, one of the ancestors.

She suddenly knew who that ghost of a woman had been. Only the one who had given Léshil a name he rejected could have cursed her in this way.

"What did she . . ." Cuirin'nên'a began and then pulled back. "No, do not tell me. But you must take a name."

"No!" Leanâlhâm shouted.

If Léshil could deny his, so could she choose . . . not to choose.

Cuirin'nên'a was on her and grabbed her by the shoulders.

"This does not happen without cause," she snarled, but then she began to falter. "Not to anyone but . . ."

She did not need to finish, for Leanâlhâm knew how those words would end—*not to anyone but my son.*

Leanâlhâm wondered at the *given* name of Léshil, which was a very old one meaning "colored by rain," or, by the symbol of rain, "tinted by the world's tears." Why would a mother do that to her son?

Léshil—Leshiârelaohk—and Leshiâra . . . the one of the world's tears to champion one of sorrowful tears.

What of that mother's own *taken* name, Cuirin'nên'a, the Water Lily's Heart? What had she seen in the burial grounds to take such a name, so much better than the one she gave her son at birth?

"Listen to me," Cuirin'nên'a began again with restraint. "The ancestors do not interfere in our lives, our choices, without great need. For such an effort, at such a cost, when they speak to you . . ." She stalled, shaking her head. "You must listen, you must hear them, and you must choose."

Leanâlhâm had already borne the cruelty of her birth name—Child of Sorrow, given by a mother who had run off in the madness of grief.

"What is your name?" Cuirin'nên'a asked.

Dwelling in sorrow . . . remembering what the ghost had said to her, she finally whispered, "Sheli'câlhad."

Any few words or a phrase, once turned into name, could require a moment to unravel their meaning. It was such a moment before Cuirin'nên'a leaned away a little and exhaled a slow breath, the closest to a sigh that Leanâlhâm had ever heard uttered by this woman.

"Lie down and rest," Cuirin'nên'a said.

Léshil's mother remained at Leanâlhâm's side and was always there in any moment when she awoke in fright amid the dark. She awoke the last time well before dawn, though she did not open her eyes. Still, as if knowing, Cuirin'nên'a spoke.

"I will take you to Urhkarasiférin's clan, where you will be safe."

Leanâlhâm did not miss that Cuirin'nên'a never used her true name, and she did not argue. Where she was taken, led, or left in a land in which she no longer belonged did not matter.

The trek was not as long or grim as the one to the ancestors' burial grounds. They were intercepted and guided by a team of warrior-hunters from Urhkarasiférin's clan. It took much explaining by Cuirin'nên'a as to why they had come, for word of what had happened at Leanâlhâm's home had already spread. Why it had happened did not seem to be known by anyone as yet.

Leanâlhâm said not a word.

Cuirin'nên'a left her with Urhkarasiférin's sister, as the greimasg'äh was not present. There were few words of parting between them other than a promise from Léshil's mother that those who had killed Grandfather would not be allowed to live.

It meant nothing to Leanâlhâm.

Cuirin'nên'a's last words were not even to her, but to Urhkarasiférin's brother.

"I need a bow. Preferably small, but any will do."

And then . . . she was simply gone.

Alone in the night within a strange home that she did not know, the girl called Leanâlhâm chose not to wait for the ancestors to cast her out. Stealing what food she could, she slipped away from the enclave and headed for Ghoivne Ajhâjhe with little notion of what to do when she got there. But in all that she had lost, how fitting that she had taken a name even worse than the one given at her birth. . . .

. . . To a lost way . . . *d'shli calhach* . . . Sheli'câlhad.

Chap watched as Leanâlhâm's verdant green eyes closed. The girl crumpled down the stairwell's wall below the aftcastle until he lost sight of her.

He could not fathom what had happened to her in the burial grounds. Somehow, for some unknown reason, his own beloved Lily and Leesil's mother had made this come about. An innocent, naïve girl had lost everything because of all she did not know . . . because of the dissidents and what had happened surrounding Wynn's journal.

CHAPTER EIGHTEEN

As Leanâlhâm disappeared down the stairs, Chap, concerned about her and overwhelmed by what he had learned from her memories, started to hurry after her.

"Did you get it back?" Magiere demanded. "Did you get Wynn's journal before it reached Most Aged Father?"

Chap stalled, waiting on the reply.

"No," Brot'an answered.

Chap had been distracted for only moments by Leanâlhâm's memories. He did not think he'd missed much of Brot'an's story. Much as someone should go after Leanâlhâm, Magiere's question and Brot'an's answer held him in place. He needed to hear more.

"What happened when you got to your caste's settlement?" Leesil asked.

Brot'an closed his eyes. "I started a war."

He paused for a long moment, and then began to speak again. . . .

If Brot'ân'duivé had known he would not catch the loyalists on foot, he would have headed for the river and taken a barge. For much of the year an anmaglâhk could travel faster overland, so long as he or she did not stop to rest. But in mid- to late spring, when mountain runoff was strongest, river currents became swift, smooth, and strong.

Taking a barge would have been faster, as the living vessels swept along with their small crews rotating both day and night. But Brot'ân'duivé sought to catch his quarry—and the journal—before they reached Crijheäiche. If he did not, the journal would be in Most Aged Father's hands, so he ran, always checking for tracks.

His quarry remained out of reach all the way to the outskirts of Crijheäiche.

Brot'ân'duivé lingered in the forest outside the settlement. It would gain him little to let his presence here be known—except as a last resort to make his enemies scurry in a hasty frenzy. For the present it was best to stay hidden until he obtained more information.

If Urhkarasiférin had returned here by now, Most Aged Father would know that his prime enemy would come for the journal. In that event, "Father" would keep the journal hidden elsewhere until it was needed, for Brot'ân'duivé would have done no less if they exchanged places.

The small book was important as a tool, rather than for what little it held. Only when the time was right would it be thrown in the faces of the council of elders as proof of the patriarch's paranoia. . . .

That humans posed a great danger to all an'Cróan.

That Magiere should have never been allowed to live.

And that she, who shared part of a nature with the undead, had sought out and obtained a device likely fashioned by the Ancient Enemy itself.

Brot'ân'duivé could imagine how that worm-in-the-wood of his people would use Wynn Hygeorht's naïve words to justify more unspeakable acts. For Brot'ân'duivé himself had carried out some of those acts in service to his caste, his people, before he had met Eillean.

Not all of this he regretted, and of what he did regret, most was due to the excess of what Most Aged Father had "requested." This excess would only become more extreme once the journal was exposed to the council. Already, carefully manipulated wars were spreading in patches throughout the Far-lands' inland and southern reaches.

Brot'ân'duivé slipped from the shadow of one ringed oak to the next, until he reached the rearmost position behind Most Aged Father's massive oak. There he climbed, working his way through the interlinked branches above, until he gained a clear view of the entrance into Most Aged Father's massive oak.

Settling there, he watched and waited. Over the following two days, his confusion and suspicion grew.

Few in Crijheäiche ever came or went from the great oak, for the old worm preferred to cultivate his image of mystery. But over those two days, his home was as busy as a workday morning in a port. It was not the number of anmaglâhk who arrived and later left that caused the most concern, but rather *who* was coming and going.

On the first day, Dänvârfij spent half the morning within Most Aged Father's home. When she reemerged, another named Rhysís, whom Brot'ân'duivé knew only slightly, came to meet her.

"We will have a team of eleven," she told him. "Gather supplies for a long trek following our ocean voyage to the central continent. Get started on basic necessities and have them barged up to the coast."

Brot'ân'duivé remained still among the leaves as Rhysís left. Eleven anmaglâhk were to cross the ocean to the central continent, but to what purpose? He was even more taken aback by the next visitor's arrival.

Crippled Fréthfâre, once Covârleasa to Most Aged Father, hobbled into the green between the encircling oaks. An attendant followed, always tensely ready should she falter or lose her grip upon her short staff. Fréthfâre entered the tree, left her attendant outside, and did not emerge for the rest of that morning.

With what little Brot'ân'duivé had heard earlier, he wondered of what use she could be.

In midafternoon, an old comrade named Eywodan arrived, followed shortly by the tempestuous young Én'nish—who had recently been cast aside by her jeóin, Urhkarasiférin. How she had first attracted the attention of that greimasg'äh still puzzled Brot'ân'duivé.

Anmaglâhk of various aptitudes continued to appear throughout the next day. Most Aged Father's sycophant and new Covârleasa, Juan'yâre, busily shuffled them in and out. It was unprecedented, and Brot'ân'duivé's frustration grew.

He had learned nothing of the journal's whereabouts, though he suspected all of this activity was connected to it. It was not difficult to reason that Most Aged Father was in a panic. Something more had happened for him to summon such disparate members. What were the connections?

Én'nish could be linked to Léshil, who had killed her betrothed.

Fréthfàre was linked to Magiere, who had crippled her.

Dänvârfij could be linked to Magiere, Léshil, and Chap through her failed mission to intercept and seize the "artifact"—and through the death of Hkuan'duv.

These facts combined with Dänvârfij's orders to gather supplies for a long journey left Brot'ân'duivé with only one conclusion: Most Aged Father was sending a large team after the artifact. Worse, he had chosen members motivated by personal vengeance.

At the second day's end, all who had visited were long gone and had not returned. Brot'ân'duivé knew they were on their way to Ghoivne Ajhâjhe to catch a ship. His urgency grew, but he waited, remaining focused on his own purpose.

Of all who had entered the tree, only one had not reemerged this day.

Juan'yâre was still inside with Most Aged Father.

Brot'ân'duivé counted two sentinels before the great oak's entrance. No others were in sight, and this disturbed him. If the journal was within, there should be more guards, but he had no more time to waste.

It took him longer than expected to work along the branches of the ringed oaks and leap to the lowest limbs of Most Aged Father's home. As he landed, the branch's leaves shivered and rustled. He quickly turned inward to flatten against the tree's immense trunk.

One anmaglâhk sentinel rounded the trunk below him and peered about. Brot'ân'duivé stilled both mind and flesh . . . and let the shadows take him.

The anmaglâhk below tilted his head toward the branches above and stared upward for too long. Finally he turned, lowering his head, and looked out across the green to the ring of other oaks.

Brot'ân'duivé waited, though he was so tired that his mind lost its stillness. The only sentinels "Father" would have near him now were those most loyal to him—like those who had not hesitated in killing Gleannéohkân'thva.

Brot'ân'duivé would not hesitate either and did not risk the sound of drawing a blade as he stepped off the branch.

Something caused the anmaglâhk to look up.

Brot'ân'duivé landed with one foot on his target's shoulder and folded his leg upon impact. His other knee struck as his weight crushed his target to the ground face-first. At a muffled crack of ribs breaking, he struck with one fist into the back of his target's neck.

A crackle of vertebrae made his target go limp.

Brot'ân'duivé heard fast footfalls coming the other way around the tree. Amid too much hatred and anger to let shadow take him again, he ripped down the wrap across his face.

A greimasg'äh came to kill his own, and in exhaustion, he did not even try to hide. When the other sentinel appeared, he lunged from his crouch.

The fast rhythm of the anmaglâhk's feet barely faltered at the sight of him, but it was enough. Brot'ân'duivé dropped low at the man's delayed thrust.

A stiletto's tip entered the side of his cowl instead of his chest. He straightened before the tip fully pierced the cloth. The forward edge of his right elbow rammed upward into his target's jaw. The anmaglâhk's head had not fully whipped back when Brot'ân'duivé's left hand struck the man's throat with two rigid fingers.

It all took less than a breath.

Brot'ân'duivé stepped back as his target fell prone upon the ground.

One anmaglâhk lay dead, and the other mutely struggled for air through a collapsed throat as he choked on blood filling his mouth. In a time to come, Brot'ân'duivé would look back and question which death was worse.

Even then he would not care. All that would disturb him in reflection was his loss of self-control. Without a sound, he rounded into the great oak and down the stairs toward the large chamber surrounding the heart-root. When he was halfway down the steps, a voice carried from inside the heart-root.

"I will not be long, Father, and I will bring fresh tea when I return."

It was the sycophant, Juan'yâre.

Brot'ân'duivé froze with nowhere to hide. Immediately the boyish form of Juan'yâre appeared out of the heart-root and trotted for the stairs—and he stopped at the sight of Brot'ân'duivé six steps above. His lips parted below widening eyes. There was more fear there than in the last one who died.

Brot'ân'duivé descended six stairs in a single step.

The Covârleasa's right hand flashed up on instinct to block—and failed.

Brot'ân'duivé's fingertips struck the soft hollow of the sycophant's throat. Juan'yâre toppled down the remaining stairs, and Brot'ân'duivé did not wait.

Secrecy was lost, and he dropped off the stairwell's side to run for the entrance to the heart-root's chamber. He halted before the heart-root's opening and looked in.

Inside, Most Aged Father lay in his bower of living wood and dead moss, and stared out through milky irises. There was not a trace of surprise in his eyes at the sight of Brot'ân'duivé.

"My *son!*" the old one bit off in his creaking voice. "You are ever predictable."

Brot'ân'duivé's right hand flashed to the sleeve of his left wrist to pull a stiletto.

"Your too-long years end . . . *Father*," he said. "And the ancestors will not take you in as they have Gleannéohkân'thva."

Most Aged Father smiled, exposing yellowed teeth in their shrunken gums.

In the corners of Brot'ân'duivé's sight, the walls of the outer chamber began to move . . . and silver glints appeared from three directions.

He lunged rearward as three anmaglâhk melted from the main chamber's walls: two anmaglâhk on the left, one on the right, all holding bows with nocked arrows pointed at him. Each had a stiletto gripped between his teeth, at the ready once their shots were fired. A fourth figure stepped out of the heart-root chamber's rear wall with a single blade in hand as he stood beside Most Aged Father's bower.

Brot'ân'duivé had not seen any of them upon entering. None of them were greimasg'äh, and he looked to that old worm still smiling at him. How all this had been done, he did not know, but *who* had managed it was obvious.

He had been so focused on reaching Most Aged Father that he had not thought to sense for anything else.

"I am of the ancestors," Most Aged Father said softly. "I was one of them, led here long ago to our land. You are the one who will never meet them when you die."

Brot'ân'duivé's mind went still, his heart and breath slowed, and calm returned.

He could take any one archer, but not all three, before a shot was fired. If he turned to run, he would not make it to the stairs without being hit by one, if not all three, arrows. Standing in the open, he had no opportunity to let shadow take him without his opponents still firing upon his position.

"Shoot," Most Aged Father whispered in the silence.

At the sound of bowstrings releasing, Brot'ân'duivé twisted and snatched the edge of his cloak.

He tore it loose from around his waist in a spinning arc. A rush of air passed below his chin as the first arrow missed. His cloak jerked in his grip as the second arrow pierced it below his left arm at chest level. He finished that twist as the sound of a third bowstring released.

But Brot'ân'duivé felt—heard—no arrow strike him.

"Run, you old fool!" a female voice shouted.

One of the archers to his left, nearest to the stairs, whirled around as the other slid limply down the chamber's wall. An arrow protruded from the center of the second's chest.

Cuirin'nên'a stood atop the steps with another arrow drawn back, and she fired again, hitting the first one, who had whirled toward her.

That one fell as she reached for another arrow.

Most Aged Father stared out through the heart-root's entrance at Brot'-ân'duivé still standing there. Then the ancient creature shrieked in rage as the anmaglâhk beside him rushed toward the heart-root's opening.

Brot'ân'duivé heard an arrow's release and glanced to the right as the third archer—the only remaining archer—fired. The arrow flew past toward the stairs, and Brot'ân'duivé flung his stiletto.

It cracked against the anmaglâhk's bow. In reflex, the man dropped the bow in a back step, and Brot'ân'duivé drew his second blade. Then he heard Cuirin'nên'a suck in a sharp breath behind him on the stairs.

Before he could glance back, the anmaglâhk in the heart-root chamber came through the opening and collided with him. The impact drove him back as he grabbed the blade thrust at his throat. Its edge bit into his palm. Before he could counterstrike, his opponent grabbed his other arm at the elbow and tried to puncture the joint with a thumb.

Brot'ân'duivé met his opponent's eyes.

There was no fear of death, not even in facing him, in this one. This was a true anmaglâhk but with a twisted purpose. He would willingly die to kill one of his own simply because Father had told him this was right.

Brot'ân'duivé had long mourned the decline of his caste and the corruption of it by their patriarch. It was no longer defiance or even hate that drove him. There was only overwhelming grief in looking into the amber eyes of a fanatic.

He saw no sacrifice and service to the people in those eyes. He saw only the death of Anmaglâhk virtue, murdered by Most Aged Father.

And he heard the one who had dropped the bow coming in on his right. It did not matter whether he died, so long as he ended this here and now.

Brot'ân'duivé slammed his forehead into the fanatic's face, and the man's head lashed back. Brot'ân'duivé twisted aside the stiletto blade he still gripped, and it bit deeper into his palm. Wheeling away, he kicked into the knee of the archer charging in on his right. As that one stumbled, Brot'ân'duivé rammed his stiletto through the throat of the fanatic and then slung his impaled opponent at the archer.

He put aside all else, exposing his back as he looked into the heart-root chamber, still gripping the hilt of his own stiletto with one hand and the blade of a dead anmaglâhk's in the other.

Not the slightest trace of fear haunted Most Aged Father's milky eyes.

Brot'ân'duivé knew he had failed on one count. The journal was not here; it was beyond his reach. It would not matter if someone else put the journal before the council of elders, for he would silence the one voice that could truly twist Wynn Hygeorht's words.

Most Aged Father smiled.

This was one of the only moments in which Brot'ân'duivé had ever truly hesitated, and he would regret it for the rest of his life. The entrance to the dark wood of the heart-root trembled like a mouth made of flesh.

It snapped closed before Brot'ân'duivé's eyes.

"No!" he shouted, and slapped his bloodied hand against the wood as he dropped one blade. Even the pain of that did not break through the shock.

"Do not move!" Cuirin'nên'a shouted.

Only that violent command broke through to him. He turned to see the last archer, the last anmaglâhk, rising as he pushed off the corpse of his ally. Both other archers lay upon the chamber floor; both with arrows dead-center in their chests. The feathers of those arrows were not those of an anmaglâhk.

This one remaining anmaglâhk, with the lower half of his face still obscured by a wrap, continued backing away to the main chamber's far side. But his eyes were focused on someone else.

Brot'ân'duivé followed the path of that gaze.

Cuirin'nên'a crept in around him with a stiletto in her right hand and the feathers of an anmaglâhk arrow protruding from below her left shoulder.

"What part of 'run' did you not understand?" she hissed at him, and then looked beyond him to the heart-root.

Brot'ân'duivé could not look at it again. Astonishment passed quickly across Cuirin'nên'a's face and was replaced by a trace of anguish.

"We are undone," she whispered. "You have ruined and exposed us. There is now no doubt that we stand against *him*."

He said nothing. There was only the need of this moment to which he could attend. They must flee and warn all those who stood with them to go deeper into hiding, and Cuirin'nên'a was wounded.

Brot'ân'duivé turned away, reaching for her, but she lifted her blade to point the stiletto at the last anmaglâhk backed against the far wall.

"I know your eyes, Mähk'an'ehk!" she said. "Do not follow us . . . and you may live a little longer."

Brot'ân'duivé pulled her away, and, leaping over Juan'yâre's slumped form, they fled up the stairs.

There was no one outside in the green between the great oak and those who ringed it. He bolted north, leading the way deep into the forest and putting as much distance as possible between them and Crijheäiche. Later he was unsure how far they had run when he heard Cuirin'nên'a stumble behind him.

Slowing, he forced her to rest, hidden beneath the low branches of a fir tree while he backtracked to make certain they were not pursued. Returning, he knelt beside her to inspect the arrow she had taken in defending him.

"What did you think, if anything?" she asked. "That you could break in there, into his home . . . and kill him? Why do so with so many present? Even you could not have reached past them to him in such a space."

It had not occurred to him until then that she had not seen what he had. When he told her of anmaglâhk stepping out of the walls like spirits, she only stared at him.

"And what were you thinking," he added, "when you killed an anmaglâhk in Gleannéohkân'thva's home?"

She glanced away.

Brot'ân'duivé sighed. The situations were not truly comparable, for she had probably had little choice—unlike him. But there was still the question of the sentinels hidden like greimasg'äh in the shadows of the walls.

"How could we . . . at least you . . . not have known this?" she asked, as if knowing his thoughts.

Brot'ân'duivé had no answers for her. Most Aged Father was too long-lived. It appeared that time and the tree of his home allowed him to do more than thrive beyond his fair share of years.

"It is done," he said, "and we have killed our own, regardless of the fact that they are counted as enemies. Any uncovered dissident, anmaglâhk or otherwise, will suffer for that as much as we will . . . if we are caught." He paused. "And I may also have killed a Covârleasa."

"Juan'yâre still breathes," she replied flatly. "I checked him on my way in to make certain."

Brot'ân'duivé raised an eyebrow.

"I left him alive for the fear he may spread," she explained before he asked. "The dead do not spread that as well as the terrified living. I knew what you attempted before I entered. Juan'yâre, sycophant that he is, will know fear in that Father could not protect him . . . from us." Cuirin'nên'a looked up at him. "And that lackey will chatter," she added, her voice turning bitter. "So will Mähk'an'ehk. Let them fear us even in failure. For the sake of the others we have now exposed to open persecution, let them flinch at every shadow in the silence."

Brot'ân'duivé grew still, watching Cuirin'nên'a glare off into the dark.

The war in silence and in shadow had begun this night, yet she thought of those she was born to protect. Like his lost Eillean, she thought of her people, and in that she was her mother's daughter. For all of his failures this night, he could not have had greater pride in her if she had been his daughter as well.

Brot'ân'duivé turned his attention to Cuirin'nên'a's wound and peeled away layers of shredded and earth-stained cloth. The arrow had gone through but, judging by its angle, had only pierced flesh and not bone. Gripping the shaft's front close to her skin, he snapped off the protruding point at her back and jerked out the shaft all in one movement. She barely flinched.

"I will dress it with moss and try to stop the bleeding," he said.

They were both quiet while he tended her. When he finished, he rocked back on his heels and was uncertain what to say.

"We cannot risk a fire," he finally said.

She tilted her head to one side, and some of her anger had faded. Like him, she understood that the past could not be changed. What was done was done.

"Were you truly going to kill him?"

Puzzled by such an afterthought, Brot'ân'duivé studied her. "I came for the journal and failed in that, but knowing he would use it against us . . . yes."

He was still stunned by the sight of the heart-root's entrance closing before him.

Cuirin'nên'a struggled to sit up, and he almost stopped her. All she did was reach behind herself and dig beneath her cloak. When she withdrew her hand and settled back, she thrust something at him.

It was the journal, and in all his long life he had seldom been at such a loss for words.

"How . . . Where?"

"From Juan'yâre," she said. "I told you I checked him. He was carrying it."

In near disbelief, he slowly reached out for the book. She did not release it when he pulled.

"I did not do this for you, but for those who walk with us," she said, and then let go.

When he fully held the journal, he felt an awkward bulge in its worn cover. Flipping it open, he found a small polished oval of dark wood . . . a word-wood.

"A number of dissidents sought haven with the Âlachben clan," she said. "They are with us and have escaped suspicion so far. One of their Shapers could rival Gleannéohkân'thva in her skills. As with all of our groups, she has been making these from a tree home in one of their own outer enclaves."

He closed his hand around the word-wood. There was at least some relief in the fact that they might still communicate as needed.

"You and Gleannéohkân'thva knew of this?" he asked.

She had the good grace to pause before saying, "He felt it best to keep such knowledge limited, for the protection of individual factions among us, especially the Âlachben. Of all the dissident factions, those among that clan have succeeded in escaping Most Aged Father's scrutiny."

Though troubled by being kept ignorant of this, Brot'ân'duivé turned his thoughts to greater matters.

"Did you find the girl and get her to safety?"

Another pause followed. "Yes."

Her hesitation meant not all had gone as planned. "Did you see Urhkara-siférin?"

"No. His sister and brother offered their assistance. They took the girl without reluctance but clearly desired me to leave."

"Why?" he asked, and when she did not answer, "What happened?"

She looked closely at him, and it was clear that the answer troubled her.

"Urhkarasiférin denounced all sides in this conflict," she answered. "He will not allow either dissidents or loyalists in his clan's territory. He has left the caste, and only because I delivered an innocent was I tolerated among his clan."

Brot'ân'duivé could not see all that this meant other than that their people had begun to fracture even further. Perhaps Cuirin'nên'a was the wise one, and he had indeed been a fool. It was possible now that many of the clans would turn against both dissidents and loyalists.

"Listen to me," he said. "There is more that I have learned."

He told her what he had seen and overheard while watching Most Aged Father's tree for the past two days. As she listened, her alarm increased.

"A team of such size . . . going after my son!" She pushed herself up. "They must be stopped at any cost."

He had to step in her way, and she tensed as if she might go at him. He held up his empty hands.

"I will leave for Ghoivne Ajhâjhe tonight," he assured her. "They are already well ahead and will likely be gone before I reach our port. But I will pursue them . . . alone."

"No! Now get out of my way!"

"Cuirin'nên'a!"

Though she stalled, he knew that his next words, both a truth and a trick, were all he had to keep her from the one thing that mattered more to her than pulling down Most Aged Father.

"Someone must remain—an anmaglâhk must remain—to coordinate those from inside the caste who have joined us with the greater number of dissidents among the people."

"There are others!" she snarled at him and tried to push past. "This is about my son and our greater hope in him."

Brot'ân'duivé did not relent. "Anmaglâhk have killed their own! And they have killed a healer, a Shaper . . . an elder of a clan. Among those who have joined us, what will they think of this? They will look upon *any* anmaglâhk with suspicion as their world fractures around them. There is only one among us they would trust."

Cuirin'nên'a's jaw clenched as she shook her head.

"You were imprisoned for ten years," he went on, "yet Father gained nothing from you . . . not even enough to hold you once your son returned. You are known—and trusted—for this among our own."

Her fury escaped in harsh breaths through her nostrils.

"You must hold us together in my absence," Brot'ân'duivé whispered, and he watched her face as his words sank in. "Spread word of what truly happened among the Coilehkrotall . . . and why I acted as I did."

Cuirin'nên'a's breath hissed out between her clenched teeth. It was not at all like an anmaglâhk to be so affected, but on this night he was unsuited to admonish her.

"You may reach me among the Âlachben," she whispered, "by the word-wood you now have."

In relief Brot'ân'duivé nodded and began to turn away. A hand latched on to his arm.

"Find my son—protect him! And if the chance comes, guide him to his purpose . . . or whatever happens here will not matter."

Brot'ân'duivé offered a slow bow of his head. Then he turned, running north for Ghoivne Ajhâjhe.

*   *   *

On the deck of the *Cloud Queen*, Brot'ân'duivé fell silent. He could recall every detail of what had come next, but he said no more. He had not related all the finite details in his story, only the general truth of what had happened. He had not mentioned anything concerning . . .

Léshil was not ready, as yet, to face his fate.

"You sent my mother back among your dissidents?" Léshil asked in shock. "You left her there in the middle of what you'd stirred up?"

Brot'ân'duivé did not answer. Along the run to Ghoivne Ajhâjhe, he had hoped fervently that word of his "treachery" would not reach the port by the time he arrived.

"You left her," Léshil pressed, his anger growing, "in the middle of a civil war . . . that you started!"

Brot'ân'duivé looked upon the grandson of Eillean.

In retrospect, he wondered whether all their efforts to train Léshil in secret, away from all ties, could serve the purpose they intended. They had attempted to cultivate someone capable of cunning, with skills outside of any allegiances, to be the weapon of their need. Léshil was not as skilled as most anmaglâhk but skilled enough. Unlike the Anmaglâhk, his mind was undisciplined, thereby creative, ungrounded, and unbiased—as a living weapon should be.

Brot'ân'duivé still did not believe in portents, omens, and revelations, but he was learning to in the hardest of ways. And perhaps, if necessary, another way, another weapon might yet be found.

The orbs.

Perhaps the weapon needed to kill the Ancient Enemy was one of its own making. What other reason could have led Brot'ân'duivé to this moment? But as he looked upon Léshil, another uncertainty flickered through his subtle machinations. Perhaps the weapon that had been made, the one standing before him, would need to use the weapon that had yet to be found?

He knew now that he would have to follow Magiere, go through her to procure this artifact, this key, this orb. And that itself might be enough. With it he might find a way to claim the other orbs that had been hidden away. He might have a weapon suitable to Léshil's final purpose.

"Well?" Léshil demanded.

Magiere was silent, just watching, but Chap circled slowly, threateningly around Brot'ân'duivé.

"Your mother is strong," he answered. "She is needed where she is. We must all follow our separate paths, each to our separate purpose."

Léshil turned away, as if overwhelmed by all that had been said . . . and all that had not been said.

CHAPTER NINETEEN

Magiere wasn't sure what to think while listening to Brot'an on deck. It didn't surprise her that Leesil focused on his mother.

Nein'a's situation certainly wasn't good, but Magiere saw larger issues at stake. Standing behind Leesil, she carefully put her hand on his shoulder and closed it.

"So you started a war, you and Most Aged Father," she began.

Brot'an shifted his attention from Leesil to her. "Wars begin well before anyone chooses to declare so."

She wasn't going to argue with that evasion. "What happened when you got to your people's port?"

At the sound of a stumbling footstep, Magiere looked back to find that Leanâlhâm had returned. The girl stood outside the aftcastle door with a tray of food in hand. Her eyes were reddened and puffy. Had she been crying?

How long had she been there listening? And Brot'an still hadn't answered Magiere's question.

"Are you going to tell them?" Leanâlhâm asked, looking to Brot'an.

It was unusual for Leanâlhâm to speak up like this. Would Brot'an try to worm out of her question, too? Magiere turned to watch him and looked for a crack in his armor.

"Or not, because I am here?" the girl added. "You have no secrets to keep from me in this, Greimasg'äh. I was there!"

Leanâlhâm's tone surprised Magiere even more, but she didn't take her eyes off Brot'an. She wished she could've, just for a smile and a wink to the girl. It was the most backbone Leanâlhâm had shown in a while—and it was about time.

Magiere was also puzzled. How could Leanâlhâm have been at the port with Brot'an if she'd been stowed away with Urkhar's people?

—Do not—ease up— . . . *—You have them—both—ready to—tell all—*

At Chap's instructions, Magiere knew he was right, despite the risk in dredging up more pain for Leanâlhâm. None of them could truly help the girl until they understood more of what had happened to her. Still, Brot'an said nothing—fair enough!

Magiere glanced back at Leanâlhâm. "Why don't you tell us, if you were there?"

This time she did wink at the girl.

"And you can keep quiet," Leesil snarled, likely at Brot'an, though the shadow-gripper hadn't made a sound.

Leanâlhâm swallowed hard. Stepping a little closer, she set the tray atop a water barrel. She hesitated again, watching Magiere with those suddenly frightened, and reddened, green eyes of hers.

Magiere didn't like having to do this, but she nodded slowly, urging the girl on, and Leanâlhâm began to speak. . . .

It took the girl that everyone called Leanâlhâm almost eight days to reach the coast. She had barely eaten anything. What little food she carried was gone, and she knew almost nothing of how to find more in the wild. Upon reaching the inland outskirts of Ghoivne Ajhâjhe, the one true city of her people, she hung back among the trees.

Cuirin'nên'a must have learned by now of her disappearance. Would Léshil's mother have guessed where she had gone? Was Cuirin'nên'a already here, somewhere in the shadows, waiting to take her back? The possibility did not seem as unlikely as it once had been.

Exhausted and hungry, with no notion of what to do, Leanâlhâm was certain only that she did not belong among the people anymore. Never having begged for anything in her life, she begged a wheat roll from a small baker's shop—as she had nothing to barter.

She had never seen anything like this city.

To her knowledge, all inland an'Cróan lived in cultured wild groves of living tree dwellings. This place, which stretched so tall and wide, was made of ornately carved wood, some stone, and other materials she could not name. As she peeked out at the great piers down the beach, wild arrays of structures were spread along the shore above, amid sparse but massive trees. There were even more structures beyond the broad mouth of the Hâjh River spilling into the bay.

She shrank back from this overwhelming sight and realized how little of the world she truly knew outside the limits of the enclave where she had grown up. Then she scurried away, trying to find some quiet corner.

Beyond one living structure, a tree more massive than that of Most Aged Father, with curtained openings into its huge trunk and walkways the size of bridges among its branches, she found an open garden. Settling near its central pool, she looked down to where fish of glittering colors swam in dusky water. After using her cupped hands to take a badly needed drink, she bit into the roll.

Its crust was hard from having sat out all day, but there and then it tasted like the best thing she had ever eaten. Upon finishing, she returned to the waterfront and walked down the shore toward the beach and the long piers stretching out into the still bay.

The ships of her people were harbored here and there. One of those would be the best way for her to leave, but how would she know whether any of them were sailing into human waters? How could she even gain passage in order to obey the ancestors?

"Are you lost?"

Her breath caught at the voice, and she turned.

A young fisherman with a string of flounder over one shoulder walked toward her. If he noticed her darker hair, her green eyes, he did not show it. Still, she was filthy and tattered and had no idea how to answer.

Lost? She was more lost than anyone could be.

"I . . . I need . . ." she began, and could not get out anything more.

"A ship? Passage?"

She nodded. "North, and then around to human waters."

He straightened. "No ships, not even for cargo, go as far as human waters, unless they carry emissaries with clan warriors . . . or the Anmaglâhk."

She looked forlornly about the bay. How was she to ever leave here? She was trapped between mountains on the western and southern sides of the territory and an ocean to the east and north.

"You do not want to go among humans," he admonished. "My father sells our fish in the city, and we need someone to help clean fish. Do you need dinner and a place to stay?"

He was kind, but he was an'Cróan. She did not belong with his family.

"No. Thank you."

With a frown, he nodded to her and walked away. She went off the way he had come, up the shoreline and keeping to the rocky slope above the sand so she might not be easily spotted by anyone along the city's front. The only thing she could think of was to sneak aboard one of the ships, but which one? And what would happen if she was caught? It would have to be a large one, maybe military. That sounded like the only kind that would leave an'Cróan waters, but what did one of those even look like?

The only other way was to cross the mountains, and even from a distance they looked impossible to breach on foot. Desperation made her wonder if she should try. She might have to steal more food, clothing, and possibly a bow, if she could figure out how to use it. The thought of theft, and the shame of it, frightened her too much. When she spotted a small cleft in the rocky slope, she crawled in to hide.

Should she just sleep here? The air began turning awfully cold, and an inbound wind blew straight into the cleft. Her only other choice was the city, and she did not like that place, with its structures of dead wood and stone.

Perhaps she closed her eyes a bit too long while her chin rested upon her pulled-up knees. When she opened them again, night had fallen and . . .

A large ship—bigger than anything else in dock—was coming into the harbor. Would a ship of this size be the kind that the fisherman had spoken of, one that would eventually head for human waters?

Crawling from the cleft, she stood watching as the ship settled in near the pier's end. She wondered about its *hkomas*—what humans might interpret as a "captain." If he would give her leave to board, she might soon be away from this land—perhaps by the next dawn, and she would not even have to watch as the coastline faded from sight forever.

Once the vessel docked, a ramp was lowered. Within moments a tall man walked down and onto the long pier. Even from a distance she could see there was something unusual about the way he moved. She could not hear his footfalls upon the planks, and the manner in which his left arm swung with his loose white-blond hair pricked her awareness.

When he passed beneath a lantern along the pier, her breathing quickened.

Strangely, he no longer wore an anmaglâhk's garb but only the breeches and tunic of a coastal clan. His cloak was brown, and the end of a long and narrow canvas-wrapped bundle, tied to him by a cord, protruded over his shoulder. With his gaze fixed hard upon something beyond the pier's end, he did not see her until she cried out.

"Osha!"

Magiere stiffened as Leanâlhâm fell silent.

"What?" she asked. "What was he looking at?"

Leanâlhâm pointed to Brot'an without a word, and Brot'an sighed. Magiere could see this was taking its toll on the old shadow-gripper as well.

"What happened?" Magiere insisted.

With a brief pause for another breath, Brot'an picked up where the girl left off. . . .

Brot'ân'duivé had been in Ghoivne Ajhâjhe a full day as he waited in the shadows and watched the smaller docks at the mouth of the Hâjh River. His quarry would have taken a barge and most likely had already arrived, but there was always a chance that part of the team had been delayed somehow. He wanted to explore all possibilities before taking action blindly.

If he could put an end to their purpose here, then there would be no need to leave. He could stay to attend to other matters, to finish what he had failed to accomplish: to remove that worm-in-the-wood of his people at any cost. But no anmaglâhk arrived at the barge docks.

The team had already come and gone. His only option was to follow—to track them. As darkness fell, he slipped from cover and went to the harbor to look for any ship he might know with a *hkomas* who could be trusted for both information and passage.

He kept to the rocky upslope along the shore for its darker cover, far from both the dock lanterns and those along the city's frontage. It took him a while to spot a suitable vessel, but in that he finally had some luck. His gaze came to rest on a midsized ship in the harbor—with a *hkomas* who knew him.

Brot'ân'duivé also noticed a larger ship settled in at the longest pier, but he did not give it much thought. He had taken only a step toward the smaller vessel when a tall man disembarked from the larger one.

The way the man walked down the pier gave him away. The smooth gait of an anmaglâhk was broken by a slight awkwardness others would not notice. He did not wear a forest gray cloak, and something long and narrow was lashed over his back with its cord bound across his chest.

Brot'ân'duivé stepped through the sand toward that other pier as Osha, now dressed like a coastal dweller with a traveler's cloak, neared the shore.

Whatever had been required of Osha by the Chein'âs, the Burning Ones, must have been brief. Even for all the time that had passed, he could not have come all this way otherwise. Why had he not returned to the inlands, to the caste, or even to the ruin of Sgäilsheilleache and Gleannéohkân'thva's home enclave?

Osha passed beneath a dock lantern. Its brief light exposed his lost, grieved expression.

Then came a sudden change.

His head barely turned, or perhaps it was only his eyes that did so.

Sorrow shifted to anger so spiteful that Brot'ân'duivé knew the young one had spotted him, though he did not know what he had done to deserve such venom. Then a cry broke over the soft lap of water upon the shore.

"Osha!"

Brot'ân'duivé's gaze shifted to the cry's source.

Leanâlhâm came out from the shadows of the rock clefts and ran toward Osha.

Brot'ân'duivé stalled where he stood. How could the girl be here? Osha halted, eyes widening at the sight of her, and another movement in the night pulled Brot'ân'duivé's focus.

Three forest gray forms, nearly black in the darkness, rushed out of the trees between two buildings up the shore. Leanâlhâm was only halfway to Osha when they leaped, clearing the rocks to land upon the sand, and they raced to close in on the girl.

"Leanâlhâm!" Osha shouted.

He glanced once more, accusingly, at Brot'ân'duivé and broke into a run.

Brot'ân'duivé quickly scanned the city's front.

Only three anmaglâhk were visible, but he had no notion of how many Most Aged Father had sent—as they were no doubt after him. Perhaps upon not finding him, they had instead focused on the girl.

He knew he should flee. He should do anything necessary to remain out of their sight until he caught a ship to pursue his quarry. His purpose was worth more than two lives among the people . . . even two lives he knew well.

One anmaglâhk caught Leanâlhâm up in his arms, lifting her off the ground. She kicked and squirmed in fright as Osha shouted something. The other two closed in to cut him off.

Brot'ân'duivé unsheathed a stiletto and palmed it with the blade's tip between his fingertips and its handle flattened against his forearm.

Brot'ân'duivé paused, looking beyond Magiere and Léshil to Leanâlhâm.

"The rest is yours, if you wish," he said quietly.

As the girl gazed back at him, some of her tight anger vanished. If nothing else, perhaps speaking the end of it all—for her—might serve more than one purpose here.

Magiere twisted about, taking a protective step toward the girl. Leanâlhâm raised a hand to hold Magiere off.

"It is all right," she whispered, and just as quickly, she picked up where Brot'ân'duivé had left off. . . .

Running wildly toward Osha, the girl suddenly felt herself whisked off the ground, and impossibly strong arms held her in the air. On instinct, she kicked and struggled, but her captor did not appear to notice.

Panic engulfed her, as she had no idea what was happening . . . until she saw Osha nearly flying toward her up the shore. Then she caught a glimpse of forest gray sleeves on the arms pinning her.

The Anmaglâhk were supposed to protect her, protect all of the people. She had no faith in that anymore, not after the loss of Sgäilsheilleache and the way her grandfather had died.

"Let go of me!" she shouted, and then suddenly feared for more than herself.

Osha had no weapon in his hand as he charged in. She caught glimpses of forest gray on each side of her, and realized there were more of them. Without warning, the one who held her suddenly dropped her feet to the ground. She was so shocked that she tried to bolt too late.

One of his arms whipped around her and pinned both of her arms to her sides.

Osha skidded to a stop just out of reach.

Why was he wearing that strange cloak and clothing? Where were his stilettos?

"Release her!" he ordered. "Do you know who you assault? She is kin to the great Sgäilsheilleache."

"That is why we take her," a voice answered above her head, "and Sgäilsheilleache is great no more . . . not after killing one of his own, a greimasg'äh more honored than ten of him!"

"We will keep her from the *traitor*," added the one to her right. "This is the wish of Most Aged Father."

Lost and terrified, she did not understand any of this. Who was this "traitor" they spoke of?

"Do not ally yourself with *him*," warned the one holding her as his grip shifted slightly.

Able to turn her head, she glanced both ways.

Osha did not appear to know the other three, though all had their face wraps pulled down.

The one to her right bore a jagged scar from the corner of his mouth to his cheekbone. The one to her left, unlike most anmaglâhk, had his hair cropped short beneath the upper edge of his cowl. She could not see the one who held her, but judging by his voice above her head, he was quite tall.

She watched Osha, and his brow furrowed in the same confusion she felt. What could Most Aged Father possibly want with her? And who was this traitor?

"So the caste now makes hostages of the people?" Osha nearly shouted back. "Yet you dare claim Sgäilsheilleache has fallen from honor in upholding the people's way in a sworn oath? You know nothing of what happened at his death . . . *liar*!"

The girl's fear only grew. She respected Osha, but her uncle had never finished training him. Osha was no match for these three . . . but even so, he took a slow step forward.

He spread his arms slightly, as if daring the three to come at him, and the sides of his cloak fell from his forearms. Moonlight, or some lantern at the city's front, caught on his left wrist. She should have seen a sheathed stiletto there, but instead . . .

There was only the sheen from burns on his palms and wrists already beginning to scar. It must hurt even now, though he did not appear to feel it.

She saw something else—perhaps a pain that had nothing to do with flesh—beneath the fury in his eyes. She had suffered enough to recognize that.

"Stand down," the short-haired one ordered. "Or we take you to have sided with traitors . . . and we will kill you."

"Kill me?" Osha repeated, his voice quiet at first. "Look in my eyes and see if that matters to me anymore. Release her. *Now!*"

A shadow rose out of the darkness behind him.

She saw it in the last instant only because of the pier's lantern, and she almost shouted Osha's name in warning. A scarred face with burning amber eyes inside a cowl appeared over Osha's shoulder.

Brot'ân'duivé snatched the neck of Osha's cloak and jerked him back.

The girl felt her captor's grip tighten as he dragged her a short ways in retreat. The other two anmaglâhk shifted into readied crouches. But from behind the tattered and bloodstained greimasg'äh, a change in Osha's face caught her gaze.

Osha's plain, long features twisted in near hatred. He glared at Brot'ân'-duivé's back as if he might strike at the greimasg'äh first of all. Brot'ân'duivé did not notice and stood erect but relaxed, as if disregarding the three anmaglâhk before him.

"Release her," he ordered, "and walk away."

"On your word . . . traitor?" replied the tall one holding her.

At the greimasg'äh's silence, waves of sickness swelled in the girl. This would end in more blood and death—and Osha would not back down, either.

"Stand off," warned the one with the jagged scar. "Killing you would increase our advantage in breaking the rest of your kind. But we are taking the girl either way."

At first Brot'ân'duivé did not respond in any fashion. Starting with the anmaglâhk on his left, he looked slowly from one opponent to the next and finished with the scarred one.

"In the span of several nights," he began, dispassionate and clear, "I have been forced to begin killing our own, something unheard of since the first of us took guardianship *in silence and in shadow*. I have spilled blood all the way to the chamber of Most Aged Father himself."

He stood as if waiting for a response. His eyes flickered slightly, as if he watched for something, perhaps a move on their part, or as if he was simply noting their positions.

"Stained as I am in their blood," he went on, "would your stains even be noticed among the others?"

The shorthaired one went for a stiletto up his sleeve.

Brot'ân'duivé lunged in one long step as his right hand whipped up, dragging the edge of his cloak. His opponent jerked backward at some impact she did not see. That anmaglâhk hung in stillness . . . and then dropped to his knees.

In the blink that it took him to choke once, Brot'ân'duivé lashed his right hand out.

As if from nowhere, a stiletto shot from his hand toward her legs. She did not have time to pull aside.

She felt no impact or pain, but she heard—felt—the one behind her shudder. She began to topple as her captor stumbled and his weight came forward. She tried tearing away from his grip, but he was still strong and still on his feet.

A narrow white metal blade appeared out of the corner of her eye.

In the hand of her captor, it came around the side of her head and level with her throat, and she was too lost and frightened to cry out.

Another hand latched upon the wrist of her captor, and she later remembered seeing the shiny scars of burns in four lines.

Osha, his face in frightful rage, loomed before her. He wrenched the anmaglâhk's wrist aside, turning the blade outward, and she saw Osha's other hand thrust suddenly over her head with thumb and first finger spread wide.

The hand passed so fast that she heard the whip of air from his sleeve.

Her captor's breath caught suddenly. As he choked, the stiletto fell from his grip. She jerked herself free, ducking around behind Osha.

The anmaglâhk toppled, holding his throat as he gagged for breath. A stiletto like Brot'ân'duivé's was deeply embedded in his right leg above the knee.

Still hiding behind Osha, she cast her gaze about, looking for the greimasg'äh.

Leanâlhâm fell silent on deck, standing almost directly in front of Brot'ân'-duivé now.

"The rest was all yours," she said quietly.

She was right, and he knew it. Exhausted and drained, Brot'ân'duivé began again where she had stopped . . .

As he faced his last opponent upon the beach, he whispered loudly, "One crippled . . . one down."

And the anmaglâhk with the jagged scar struck forward.

A stiletto passed a finger's breadth before Brot'ân'duivé's left eye as he lightly turned his head away. Even without a line of sight, he needed only the angle of his opponent's arm and shoulder.

Brot'ân'duivé rammed the heel of his left palm into his opponent's jaw before the blade withdrew. The anmaglâhk's head snapped back. All of them were trained to withstand blunt impact so long as they survived it. At the crack of bone, that one crumbled upon the sand.

But then the short-haired man rolled to one knee and thrust a blade upward toward Brot'ân'duivé's abdomen. He parried with his empty hand, deflecting the blade. In the same motion, his left hand came back, fingers curling in to pull the leather tie string at his wrist. His other stiletto slipped free of its sheath under the momentum of his arm's movement, and the blade's hilt hit his palm.

The short-haired anmaglâhk whirled around on his knee and came back for another thrust.

Brot'ân'duivé steered his opponent's arm upward and rammed his second stiletto through the man's wrist.

It happened so fast that his opponent did not even cry out. The only sound was the wet crackle of cartilage.

"And another hobbled," Brot'ân'duivé whispered, jerking his blade out.

"Break off!" someone shouted.

Brot'ân'duivé slapped the anmaglâhk away and turned to find that the one who had held Leanâlhâm was limping backward up the shore. Osha had retreated to the water's edge and was holding the girl behind him.

The one with the scar struggled up as well, shaking his head to clear it. Blood ran freely from his mouth and down his chin. Teeth lay in the sand at his feet.

"Go!" the tall one shouted again.

The short-haired one backed rapidly away, clutching his maimed and bleeding wrist. As all three fled, they did not take their eyes off of Brot'ân'duivé until they had to scurry over the rock slope like so many gray rats. They rushed for the city and vanished between the buildings and into the forest beyond.

Brot'ân'duivé let them go for now.

Let them run in fear, wondering when he would come again. Let them whisper that fear to Most Aged Father. In this, Brot'ân'duivé purchased Cuirin'nên'a time . . . until the loyalists learned too late that he was gone. And then would Most Aged Father truly know the worst of fear.

Brot'ân'duivé—the Dog in the Dark—hunted those that the worm had sent out into the world.

He turned to the young pair staring at him, one with fearful green eyes and the other with spiteful hate he did not yet understand. He pointed toward the far pier and the midsized ship that he had sought.

"Go and board. Tell the *hkomas* there that I sent you. Wait below deck until I come."

"I am not going anywhere with *you*," Osha hissed. "I have lost everything, so it costs me nothing to be rid of you as well."

Brot'ân'duivé had no notion what this meant. The mere look of Osha—from the young one's plain attire to his missing weapons and the strange parcel on his back—raised a dozen questions leading to a dozen more.

Brot'ân'duivé did not entertain even one.

"Then you will be dead, if you wish it," he returned, pointing with his blade at the girl cowering behind Osha. "You will be hunted as much as she is . . . more so for having been seen with me. You will be pursued as much as any true dissident."

That final word did not appear to register at first. Confusion certainly filled the girl's green eyes. But finally Osha's features went slack as realization appeared to sink in.

"Yes, I am one," Brot'ân'duivé confirmed, "and now I am more than that, a traitor. So there is nothing left here for either of you, so long as Most Aged Father lives."

Osha looked him up and down. "What have you done?"

Brot'ân'duivé closed on him. "Get to the ship—now!"

The girl shrank back.

He had no authority over her. She was not and never had been anmaglâhk, dissident, or loyalist. But she was no longer innocent, whether she wished to be or not. He had done difficult things in recent days, but he could not force her on this journey . . . overtly.

"It would be dangerous for you here," he said to her. "You may stay if you wish to risk it."

The very words implied that she would be a fool to do so. He could only hope that after all she had been through, she could take the pain of such a hard choice.

She looked up at Osha. "I would go if you will."

Osha hung his head, and Brot'ân'duivé knew he had them both, whether he wanted them or not. Though a burden to him, they would be safer abroad than they would be remaining here.

Osha turned away, grabbing Leanâlhâm's hand as he headed toward the piers.

"The rest you know," Brot'ân'duivé finished, looking at Magiere. "We followed the team hunting you. Once they reached this continent, I began eliminating them at any opportunity until I tracked them to you in Calm Seatt."

"That's everything?" Léshil asked.

Before Brot'ân'duivé could reply with a nod—a lie—Magiere came at him.

"No, it isn't!" she insisted. "What about Osha? In all this time you must have learned something. Why did he run into you at the port? What did they—the Burning Ones—do to him? And why did you cast him out of . . . your caste?"

"I did not cast him out," Brot'ân'duivé answered.

"Then what?" Léshil asked.

"I know far less of what happened to him than you wish," Brot'ân'duivé replied, "so it is his to tell. I will say no more on that."

If either Léshil or Magiere thought of forcing the issue, neither did so. What he had said was the truth for the most part. There was much concerning Osha that he did not know or understand. But at least those here were distracted from what more he had left out. He had given only the details that served him and not what had come next.

He did not tell them that he had waited until Osha and Leanâlhâm were safely aboard the ship and then changed his mind concerning one thing. He did not tell them that he had turned his eyes upon the forest as he had run through Ghoivne Ajhâjhe.

Only one survivor need reach Most Aged Father.

The old worm would hear but one voice carrying the fear of three after watching the other two die in the dark. It would be—had been—a long while before anyone knew that Brot'ân'duivé left his people's land.

Most Aged Father would have a new fear to grow into a new paranoia. But long before that, Cuirin'nên'a would be in hiding with the others.

In silence and in shadow, fear was a weapon of the Anmaglâhk, though none had ever wielded it against their own until Brot'ân'duivé.

Leesil was quiet as every word spoken about his mother stuck in his head. That world was no part of his. He understood it a little because of her, what she had taught him in his youth, and how she had trained him. But he'd never understood her ways, her people, and didn't want to.

Just the same, he couldn't stop the guilt over what had happened to Leanâlhâm.

Another innocent was caught in the middle. How many others had suffered because he, Chap, and Magiere—and even Wynn—had passed through their lives? Then it struck him that Chap had been quiet during this entire exchange.

—*The girl—went—for—name-taking—*

Chap's sudden words made Leesil feel as if he'd been punched.

"What?" he exhaled, turning on the dog.

—*Before—she went to—Edge of the Deep—*

It took a moment before that last part made sense; it was the meaning of the name for the an'Cróan's one city by the bay.

Facing the serpent, the "Father of Poison" guarding the burial grounds, had been a terrifying moment for him—mostly because Magiere's life had depended on his not failing to get in there.

He turned to the girl. "Leanâlhâm, you went to your ancestors?"

With a sudden expression of horror, she quickly looked at Chap. Then came the panicked anger of her fast breaths.

"What?" Magiere whispered, and then louder, "When?"

Still breathing too hard, the girl looked from Chap to Brot'an, who said nothing. Magiere closed on the girl.

"What were you thinking? Your uncle had his reasons, Leanâl—"

"Do not call me that!" the girl shouted, and backed away. "Do not call me *anything*. I want no more names!"

Leesil was at a loss as the girl glared at Chap, and there was no awe for him in her face this time. There was only panic amid accusation—but for what? Perhaps all this brought back too many memories from which she'd been hiding. Something had driven her to leave her people after the death of Gleann, her grandfather.

Something to do with the ancestors.

They all knew what the name Leanâlhâm meant: Child of Sorrow. How any mother could do that to her child was beyond understanding. She had lived with that name on top of being one-quarter human among a people who distrusted—or hated—anyone who wasn't purely an'Cróan.

If she could choose a new one, what could be worse than that name?

To Leesil's best reckoning, aside from his own experience, all who went for name-taking in the ancestors' burial ground saw visions by which they chose a name to replace the one given at birth. He hadn't been so lucky; those damn ghosts had *put* a name on him.

Leshiârelaohk—Sorrow-Tear's Champion.

"It is time . . . Sheli'câlhad," Brot'an whispered.

Leanâlhâm stiffened all over and screamed something in Elvish at Brot'an.

"Yes, now," Brot'an returned flatly. "You can no longer run from who you are."

Leesil couldn't possibly pronounce the name Brot'an had just spoken. Out of everyone here, someone else had been holding back, and Leesil turned on Chap.

"Out with it! What do you know about this?"

Chap retreated a step. —*Not—my—place—to*—

"Don't give me that," Leesil cut in. "You've been digging around her memories. Now, what did Brot'an call her?"

"To a Lost Way," Brot'an supplied.

Leesil looked up in bafflement. "What's that supposed to mean?"

"It is her name," Brot'an answered, "rendered in your tongue."

Leanâlhâm buried her face in her hands, and Magiere grabbed the girl by the upper arms.

"Look at me!" Magiere said, but the girl wouldn't. "Don't you listen to those ghosts. There's nothing in a name, especially from them. You don't have to be anything—*anything*—you don't want!"

The girl wouldn't lift her head.

"It is her name," Brot'an said, "given by—"

"Shut up!" Leesil shouted.

This was why Leanâlhâm had run from her people—the ancestors had driven her out. She was lost in a world not her own, lost between a name that cursed her from birth and another that banished her. Yet she was still an'Cróan, a people for whom taking a name meant everything about their identity.

And Brot'an had done nothing for her suffering.

Leesil had to find her a way out quickly, and he turned on Chap again. "You give me something else!"

Chap blinked, looking between him and the girl, and not a word rose in Leesil's head.

"Don't play dumb with me, mutt!" he warned. "All those years with my mother, being born among those elves, you speak their tongue as well as they do. Give me something better than Brot'an's meaning!"

Chap snarled at him, clearly no happier about this, but as much at a loss as Leesil. Something had to be done if Leanâlhâm was to find even temporary peace.

—*Way*— . . . —*to—a way*— . . . —*Way—toward*—

"What?"

Magiere looked at Chap as her head filled with his fumbling attempt to find another meaning. Then she turned back to the girl and shook her once.

"Listen to me, please," she whispered.

"No names!" the girl cried.

Magiere knew what it was to be exposed for something she didn't want to be—that other half inside of her. Even the old word from her land's folklore revolted her—*dhampir*.

Everywhere that she went, it followed her. Any stranger who learned of it, and understood it, looked upon her as only that. It was what she saw whenever she glimpsed her own reflection.

She didn't want this for Leanâlhâm, and "To a Lost Way" was worse than "Child of Sorrow." But to the an'Cróan, that second name they chose—or had forced upon them, as Leesil had—meant everything about who they became. They couldn't let go of it.

Like Leesil and then Chap, Magiere wanted some better meaning for a name the girl couldn't bear or deny. She ran through every name or title she could remember. All she could think of from Chap's failed suggestions was an old word in Droevinkan, her native tongue. She carefully pulled the girl's hands down.

"Listen to me . . . Chi'chetash," she whispered.

The girl's tear-streaked face wrinkled in confusion, but there was still fright in her reddened eyes. Magiere faltered, and then Chap barked.

—*Yes but—too—foreign—* . . . —*Simpler—*

Magiere kept her eyes on the girl as she explained. "Chi'chetash are wanderers with purpose. They find new or even lost paths . . . and some map their travels. They find ways so others do not become lost. They're way finders . . . who can always find their own way home."

Leesil and Chap were quiet, but Magiere didn't dare look away. The girl everyone called Leanâlhâm opened her eyes wider, though tears still ran down her tan cheeks.

"Wayfarer," Leesil said.

Magiere didn't know that word. At her glance, he nodded, and she hoped her fumbling had led him to something better.

"You're not lost . . . Wayfarer," Magiere said, still holding the girl's face. "I will never let that happen . . . by any name."

The girl was still too much an an'Cróan and still too young to see she could make any choice she wanted. She didn't have to be shackled by a bunch of ghosts, and almost anything had to be better than what Brot'an . . . what she had called herself.

"Wayfarer?" the girl whispered.

Magiere grabbed hold of her and pulled her close.

"Yes," she answered in exhaustion. "Not to a lost way but toward a new one . . . that you find for yourself . . . starting from me. I am your home now, to always return to."

Magiere cast a dark glance at Brot'an. All he did was look out over the water rushing by the ship's hull.

"You will call me this?" the girl whispered. "Only this name?"

"Only this . . . Wayfarer," Magiere assured her.

CHAPTER TWENTY

As the *Bashair* entered the harbor in Drist, Dänvârfij kept her expression impassive, though she was tense. All of her team except Fréth-fâre was up on deck and awaiting her orders. Dusk had come, and daylight was fading quickly.

On the journey from Chathburh, they had passed several large cargo vessels but from too far to read the names painted on their hulls. She had delayed her team from taking this ship and staked everything on beating the *Cloud Queen* to this destination. If she had miscalculated, the ramifications could be severe.

Fréthfâre would likely wrest control from her with the support of all but perhaps Eywodan. Dänvârfij cared nothing for herself in that, but Fréthfâre would lead them only to failure in their purpose.

As the *Bashair* drifted into the docks, Dänvârfij focused on what lay ahead. Under the light of massive pole lamps, six long piers jutted from the waterfront, and vessels filled nearly every available space. A massive ship flying a yellow-and-green flag was docked at the third pier's end, and its name was painted on the prow—the *Bell Tower*. She had rarely seen ships so large allowed to dock rather than anchor farther out and use skiffs for transport. Other differences here became readily apparent.

Chathburh had been a sprawling port city; this place was compact but unnervingly busy, even with nightfall coming. Dockworkers and sailors clambered along piers, ramps, and decks: hauling cargo to and from vessels, teaming the moorings and riggings as they shouted over the general dull din. The milling crowds might prove an advantage or obstacle.

A small schooner pulled away from the far side of the second pier and drifted out to sea. Down on the pier, a dockworker waved and shouted to the *Bashair* to take the open spot.

"Gently in!" Samara called.

His pilot cranked the wheel hard, and the crew prepared lines to cast. It took little time to settle the small Suman vessel, and then half the crew began strapping on cutlasses distributed by the first mate.

Normally the crew settled down once they reached a port, or prepared to go ashore in shifts. Something was different about Drist.

One sailor scrambled up the central mast to a watchman's platform barely big enough to sit on with dangling legs. With a case of quarrels strapped to his shoulder, he began cranking back the cable on a large crossbow. As soon as the ramp was lowered, two armed sailors ran down to take posts at its bottom and watch everything around them.

Dänvârfij saw similar safeguards on all the other docked vessels. Perhaps Samara's mention of an "unlawful place" had been more serious than she first thought. She leaned out over the rail.

The city loomed between high, dark hills cresting above the shore to both north and south. Buildings of mixed sizes and shapes, dingy and worn by coastal weather, were so closely mashed together that only a few inward roads showed between them. Typical for a port city, the air was tainted by the stench of fish, salt brine, livestock, and smoke.

If she stayed on this continent a hundred years, she would never grow accustomed to the smell. This place was the worst by far.

"Look at them."

Dänvârfij resisted being startled, finding Rhysís suddenly beside her. Arrays of people hurried along docks or milled about the bay doors of large warehouses. Carts and bearers vied to get in and out. Every color and form of attire that Dänvârfij could imagine was scattered among them.

Caramel-skinned Sumans in earthy-colored garb led goats harnessed in lines. A small number of even darker-skinned people, with tightly curled black hair, were dressed in one-piece shifts of cloth, or in pantaloons and waist wraps of stronger colors beneath black patterns. These tried to navigate a cart of shimmering cloth bolts around clusters of armored men.

The number of Numans was almost overwhelming. Some dressed like vagabonds, while others wore finery beneath voluminous cloaks.

Dänvârfij heard clear footsteps coming across the deck.

"We will not stay long," Captain Samara said as he approached. "I hope to resupply and finish a small cargo exchange by midmorning tomorrow. If you wish to stay here and wait for your family, you should disembark and find lodgings by then." Glancing at the city, he shook his head. "But I do not recommend it. Perhaps you could catch your kin at the next port?"

Dänvârfij had no intention of disembarking, but she feigned a polite smile.

"No, we wait here, but can we spend tonight . . . on the ship? Leave . . . tomorrow before . . . you sail?"

Samara nodded. "Of course. It is senseless for you to go out there at night."

"My thanks," she said.

The captain walked away, and Rhysís whispered, "When?"

Dänvârfij returned to watching the port. "Not until the crew is asleep, those on watch grow weary, and fewer people are . . . out there. Can you kill the one up in the mast without him falling?"

"Yes."

"Én'nish and I will handle the two at the ramp's end. The rest should be simple."

Én'nish had seethed over the pointless delay in taking this ship. Now she partly saw how they had a better opportunity. Halfway between the mid of night and dawn, the piers were almost empty. Well before that, most ships, including the

Bashair, had pulled up their ramps. Besides the armed lookout up in the mast, only three humans, two on the aftcastle and one at the prow, were on deck.

Dänvârfij had asked the three on watch whether she and hers could stay up and observe incoming ships to spot the one bearing their "family." The guards did not find this strange and assented without even bothering to ask their captain.

Perhaps Sumans valued kin and blood more than Numans did, and Én'nish committed this to memory for future use. The rest of the small crew was below, likely asleep, and the captain was in his own cabin.

Eywodan and Tavithê stood near the aftcastle door to below, and Én'nish, with a blade held reversed and hidden behind her forearm, waited beside the aftcastle stairway. Rhysís leaned against the starboard rail with his assembled short bow hidden beneath his traveler's cloak. He looked up now and then to the sailor with the crossbow upon the mast's platform above.

Én'nish watched Dänvârfij near the prow and waited—longed—for the signal to act. She slipped her other hand around her back and beneath her tied-up cloak to grip the handle of her bone knife. Tension was not appropriate, but it quivered in all of her muscles.

A soft chirp carried across the deck.

Eywodan and Tavithê slipped below for the sleeping crew. Rhysís nocked an arrow, raised his bow, and fired.

Én'nish heard a soft thud from above, but the man did not fall to the deck. She spun and rushed up the ladder steps onto the aftcastle. Neither sailor on watch would be alarmed.

She had purposely done this several times in the night—always hurrying to the ship's rear as if she had heard the snap of sails in the wind or the call of a crew inbound from the open waters.

The two sailors stood close together at the aft with their backs turned. Only one glanced aside at the last instant.

Én'nish thrust her stiletto through the base of his throat before he offered a greeting, and she slashed the other's throat with her hooked bone knife. The latter's eyes turned vacant as he dropped.

It was over too quickly. She should have volunteered to go below instead of remaining up here. Not risking the noise of toppling the bodies overboard, she left them and hurried down to the deck.

Dänvârfij, with a bloodied stiletto in hand, came toward her. Then Rhysís joined them.

"Weight the bodies," Dänvârfij instructed, "and lower them quietly over the far side, away from the dock."

Rhysís nodded and turned toward the aftcastle. Én'nish followed. By the time they finished and returned, Eywodan and Tavithê had emerged from below. Even in the dark, Én'nish could see they were stained.

"Ten left alive for our need," Eywodan said, "including the cook. They are locked up, and I convinced them of the wisdom of silence."

"The captain?" Dänvârfij asked.

"Still asleep in his cabin. We made little sound."

"He knows too much about us." Gripping her stiletto, she started for the stairs. "He should be silenced. Then I will report to Fréthfâre."

Én'nish watched her go. It was done, and they had finally taken the ship. But she raised her bone knife and studied the streaks of blood across the silver-white metal. It had all gone perfectly, quickly, and quietly . . . with too little satisfaction for her.

And it was not the right blood on her blade.

Two evenings later, the *Cloud Queen* reached the harbor in Drist. Leesil stood beside Magiere and stared out at the mass of activity, with its assault of colors, noises, and smells.

"Ah, dead deities," he murmured. "I thought Chathburh was crowded. Where's the captain going to dock this hulk in there?"

Magiere shook her head. "I don't know."

Wildly busy, the port boasted only six overly long piers. All of the docked vessels except for one were smaller than the *Cloud Queen*. But Leesil's question was soon answered.

He noticed that larger ships were docked at the piers' ends, and one spot at the end of the second pier was open. Captain Bassett shouted orders, and it wasn't long before the crew threw mooring lines over the side.

Chap, Brot'an, and . . . Wayfarer crossed the deck to join Leesil. At the sight of crowds all over the waterfront, the girl clutched Magiere's arm. When she spotted a massive vessel, so big that it looked close enough to touch, docked at the end of the third pier, she flattened in against Magiere. As Magiere wrapped her arm around the girl's shoulders, Leesil looked to that behemoth of a ship.

It was flying yellow and green colors, which he hadn't ever seen before. Probably from some other nation in the region besides Malourné. The name *Bell Tower* was painted on the hull's front end.

"Where does that ship come from?" Brot'an asked a nearby sailor.

Leesil wondered how that vessel's captain had even gotten permission to dock such a monster.

The sailor glanced the same way and spat in disgust. "Witeny."

Leesil shrugged at Magiere. Witeny must not be popular with the people of Malourné. But any chance to converse with the crew vanished as men on deck began strapping on weapons and loading crossbows.

"What now?" Brot'an said, watching it all closely.

Leesil was baffled, as the crew had never done this at any other stopover. As soon as the ramp was lowered, two sailors with loaded crossbows jogged down to take positions at the bottom. He noticed the same at every other ship in sight, and he started to get a bad feeling about this place.

Captain Bassett came striding over, and Magiere intercepted him.

"What's going on?" she asked sharply. "Why are your men arming themselves?"

Bassett scowled, and it wasn't hard to guess that he didn't care much for her attitude.

"A brigands' port," he answered, "but still worth the stop. Goods traded here are hard to find elsewhere along the coast."

Leesil didn't like the sound of that, either.

"We have major cargo to exchange," the captain went on. "Several days' worth, so it would be best if we weren't juggling a big job around passengers."

Magiere raised her brows and glanced at Leesil. Wayfarer had already tucked in beside him as Chap started grumbling. Again, Leesil understood Numanese better than he could speak it.

They were somewhat politely being told to go ashore for a few days.

Much as the others weren't happy about it, he wouldn't argue. They could take care of themselves, and he couldn't wait to get off this ship. He hoisted up his pack, already prepared to disembark.

"Not . . . problem," he said quickly. "We . . . go."

At Leesil's assurance, however, the captain nodded and strode off.

Magiere pierced Leesil with an annoyed glance. This was likely a mix of uncertainty in taking Wayfarer into such a seedy-looking place and the captain rushing them off. She wasn't one to be pushed anywhere.

Brot'an peered around the harbor as if looking for something specific. Wayfarer backed up, crouched down behind Chap, and planted herself so firmly that Leesil wondered whether he'd have to pick her up and carry her off the ship.

Chap looked up at him. —What—advice—for here—from—Wynn—

Leesil unslung his pack. "Hang on."

He dug inside and pulled out the scant papers Wynn had sent with them. Paging through notes scrawled in Belaskian, he found something and frowned.

"Someplace called Delilah's. She says it's expensive but the safest, although . . ."

—What is wrong?—

He wasn't about to read the rest out loud and quickly stuffed the pages into his pack.

"Nothing. Just more boring stuff about the place's history, nothing of worth."

Magiere stepped closer. "Nothing . . . else?"

Leesil sighed. "Just two short lines. She said when we get to the front desk, whatever Mechaela asks us to do, we have to *do* it. Apparently it's the only safe place here."

"I do not like this," Brot'an put in.

Frankly, neither did Leesil, but the captain had made it clear he wanted them out of the way—and Leesil wanted off the ship for a few days at least.

"Let's go and get some rooms. As annoying as Wynn can be, she's usually right about these things."

When he looked down, Wayfarer's breath was coming short and fast. He flipped a hand toward Chap and Magiere.

"You think anyone's going to bother those two?" he asked, grinning at the girl. "Even if so, who do you think would get the worst of that mistake?"

Chap licked his nose at him and glanced down the ramp.

"You're not funny," Magiere growled over her shoulder at Leesil.

"No, indeed," Brot'an added.

With a wink, Leesil whispered to Wayfarer, "I am so."

She rolled her pretty eyes, but at least he'd broken her panic, and he held out his hand. She took it, and he pulled her to her feet and kept her hand in his grasp. Shifting his pack, he started down the ramp into the crowds.

"Don't let go," he said.

"I will not," the girl answered, a bit of a quaver in her voice.

Moments later they wove down the pier between sailors and dockworkers. The crowds grew only worse as they neared the waterfront. The people of various races and occupations—not to mention goats, sheep, and several large dogs on leashes—were almost more than Magiere could navigate out front without stalling again and again.

On their way, they passed a small, odd vessel with its ramp drawn up and *Bashair* painted on its side. Something about it stuck in Leesil's head, as if he had seen it before but couldn't remember where. He held tightly on to Wayfarer's small hand as Magiere and Chap cut them a path and Brot'an followed behind.

*   *   *

Én'nish crouched on a warehouse roof and watched the port. In two days her team had accomplished much.

Rhysís was positioned a few rooftops to the south. Eywodan and Tavithê remained on the ship to keep it secure. At regular intervals Eywodan would bring a few of the crew on deck to feign duties and maintain an appearance of normality.

Én'nish had no idea what he had said to them, but they obeyed without question. He kept the ramp up, but a number of ships in harbor did so as well, so it did not appear strange. For the most part no one even glanced at the *Bashair*. Humans here kept to their own, in personal and other matters.

The team had also arranged quarters on land, and Fréthfâre and Dänvârfij were now in a filthy two-story inn at the port's north end. Eywodan was certain he could manage the vessel with a crew of ten. The team was prepared to either abandon the ship or use it in pursuit, as need be. Fréthfâre and Dänvârfij wanted all possible outcomes covered.

They could not fail again, and this time their quarry would not escape.

Still, confidence in their arrangements did little to quell Én'nish's urgency. The traitor must die. Léshil and his tainted mate must be taken for their secrets. And she would make Léshil watch his love die, as hers had at his hands. Only then would she take his life.

A large cargo vessel drifted into port and docked at the end of the second pier. Every nerve in Én'nish vibrated once she made out the Numan letters on the hull's prow.

The *Cloud Queen* was here.

Én'nish remained crouched, waiting and watching. A light sound reached her ears as Rhysís landed beside her on the rooftop. Neither spoke yet. Eywodan and Tavithê would have seen the ship as well but could not leave their posts.

"I will report to Fréthfâre and Dänvârfij," Rhysís whispered. "Follow any of our quarry if they come ashore. Learn their final location . . . but do not engage them alone."

She nodded once, and then he was gone.

Én'nish watched for anyone familiar among the crowds on the second pier.

Leesil pressed on behind Magiere and Chap, and pulled Wayfarer along as he studied their surroundings. When they reached the waterfront, he spotted a floating walkway along the rock wall beneath the piers. Between every other pier post were switchback ramps and ladders leading upward from lower floating platforms for small boats.

With little choice, they pushed through the throngs until their group reached the city's edge. A few streets in, they left the thickened masses behind for more sparse passersby in the growing dusk. Wayfarer had kept pressing up behind him along the way, but now she peered about, a little more curious.

"Better now?" he asked.

"Yes," she said barely loudly enough to hear.

Chap watched everywhere as well, turning all the way around at least once. It was pretty clear to Leesil that the dog was less than pleased.

—*Which—way—now*—

Leesil took a breath to remember Wynn's instructions. "Inland a few blocks and then to the left."

The farther they went, the fewer people they saw, and after a little while this began to concern Leesil. Where was Wynn sending them? It was getting darker, and once they made the left, within a block and a half down a poorly cobbled street they passed only hard-looking, worn women in faded, low-cut gowns, sailors swilling from clay bottles, and a mix of what might have been merchants, both prosperous and shabby.

Leesil kept an eye on both sides of the street and noted eateries, taverns, and inns along the way. There was little to tell by the bland and dilapidated buildings, but he had an idea of what kind of illicit endeavors went on behind those closed doors. This was the hinterland between merchant and laborer districts, always the same in any city.

It was just darker and dingier than most he remembered. He had a hard time picturing what had brought Wynn of all people here. Looking ahead, he quickened his pace, nearly passing Magiere.

"I think that's it."

Beyond the next intersection, on its far left corner, stood a large, well-situated three-story building that covered a fourth of the next block. Its blue paint, at a guess in the dark, didn't look too badly cracked, but the white shutters—around iron grates over the windows—were stained and filthy.

Leesil didn't like the look of this. What was hard to break into was also hard to get out of in a hurry.

The building sported a sweeping ground-level terrace with two armed and lightly armored guards by the front columns. He took their measure.

Their leather outer tunics didn't hide the chain shirts beneath. Though properly closed, the tunics were both worn in a loose fit. The guards hadn't limited their mobility for the sake of appearances. They wore their swords low rather than cinched up to their belts. They were both ex-military or experienced mercenaries.

Well, Wynn was right about one thing: if this place hired such, it wouldn't be cheap.

Both guards were watchful but relaxed as the quintet approached. A white sign above the door held one gilded word in Numanese: DELILAH'S.

"May we pass and take rooms?" Brot'an asked, never ceasing to amaze Leesil with how polite and harmless he could sound. If those guards only knew the truth about what was walking into their establishment.

"By all means," one said. "Please see Mechaela at the front desk."

Leesil hesitated again, and then Chap huffed and started for the front door.

Én'nish had trouble controlling herself as she silently slipped along rooftops to follow her quarry. The sight of Léshil and the traitor was almost too much for her.

She took note of their number: five in total, with Magiere, Leanâlhâm, and the majay-hì. Neither Osha nor the little human sage appeared to have caught up. This was useful and preferred: the fewer, the better. The necessary targets were present, and Brot'ân'duivé was the only anmaglâhk.

Én'nish kept well behind, fearing that the greimasg'äh might sense her, but she did not let them out of her sight. Not far into the city, they approached a three-story building with worn sky blue planking and soiled white shutters. Én'nish hesitated at the sight of iron grates across all of the windows.

The guards out front mattered little compared to those. The place was large and extravagant . . . and fortified.

Her team had chosen a tiny hole of an inn where they might vanish. Yet this place would not be so easily invaded, and likely not in stealth. She waited as the quintet stopped, all gazing upward. Finally the majay-hì took the lead toward the door.

Én'nish lingered until they entered and then fled through the night on her way to report to Fréthfâre.

CHAPTER TWENTY-ONE

As he passed between the two guards, Chap was somewhat hesitant, wondering what kind of place Wynn had sent them to. But Leesil moved out ahead, opened the door to Delilah's, and pulled Wayfarer inside.

Upon stepping through the doorway, Chap found himself standing on a huge deep brown oval rug with a border pattern of white flowers. The foyer walls were a rich shade of cream, and dark amber curtains framed the grated windows from the polished wood floor to the high ceiling. Soft tones of a skillfully played flute floated from somewhere unseen, and the air smelled lightly of sandalwood.

"Oh . . . oh, no!" Magiere whispered, jabbing Leesil in the back. "Do you know how much this is going to cost?"

Leesil frowned as Wayfarer glanced up at Magiere in confusion.

Chap glanced left at a solid walnut counter with gold inlay. Behind it, a young man in a white linen shirt and black satin vestment looked expectantly their way. Chap heard Wayfarer whispering to Leesil.

"He looks like . . . like . . ."

The young man had the look of Wynn, with an oval face of olive-toned skin and light brown eyes and hair to match.

"May I help you?" he asked. "I am Mechaela. What do you seek this evening?"

The question was oddly phrased. What would travelers seek here but lodging? Two men dressed similarly to Mechaela passed by into a wide parlor on the right. Neither was armed, and Chap stepped forward to peer after them.

Low, plushy padded couches around small tables bearing glass or crystal vases with fresh flowers filled the room. On the walls were painted seascapes of detailed clarity, and he spotted another archway opening into another room at the chamber's far side.

Therein, four well-dressed men sat playing cards at a polished black table, while a tall, lovely woman circled them and poured wine. Her gown of layered gauze was . . . a bit too revealing.

What kind of place was this?

"We would like two rooms," Brot'an said, striding to the counter.

"Of course," Mechaela answered, picking up a quill and opening a very large black book.

Chap was more aware of their financial situation than Leesil or Magiere realized. They *had* coin, but they also had to make it last. A few nights here would take a sizable stack.

After scribbling whatever names Brot'an gave, Mechaela looked all of them over.

"You will need to relinquish your weapons while inside the establishment," he said politely. "You can retrieve and return them upon coming and going."

Magiere stared at him. "I don't think—"

"That is acceptable," Brot'an cut in, and he pulled a small pouch out of his shirt.

Chap had never seen this before. So, the old assassin carried some coins. How he had acquired such was better left alone.

"I'm not turning over my sword," Magiere stated flatly.

Though he hated it, Chap was in agreement with Brot'an, and he looked up at Magiere.

—Guards—at the door— . . . —Guards—inside—and—grates—on all—windows— . . . —Wynn—sent us—here—with—good reason—

Magiere made no move to hand over her falchion. "I want to talk to the owner, this . . . Delilah," she demanded.

"I'm sorry, but madam is not available," Mechaela answered. "I assure you, the rule is without exception. I also assure you that first and foremost of all services to our guests is their safety." He paused briefly and became firmer. "You are safe here. Now . . . please?"

The young man held out his hand. It was directed toward Magiere's falchion, and he did not retract it at her hesitation.

"Oh, just give it up already," Leesil muttered, but, strangely, he locked eyes with Brot'an, not Magiere.

Chap neither liked the house rule nor Leesil's duplicity. Certainly the old assassin's own weapons were well out of sight—unless the host called the guards to search him.

Leesil broke the standoff and unstrapped his blades to drop them on the countertop. When he turned back, Magiere followed suit—but with obvious resentment. Leesil joined Wayfarer, who was now staring off into the parlor.

Mechaela cleared his throat audibly, and Magiere halted. Her unnaturally pale face darkened, but she finally reached behind her back, beneath her cloak, for a weapon the young man must have spotted. Magiere pulled out the white metal battle dagger, sheath and all, at her back and slapped it down on the counter.

Chap looked back over his shoulder and . . .

With Wayfarer hanging on Leesil's arm, they both gazed through the parlor into the room beyond it. Chap peeked around the girl's legs as he heard Mechaela say, "Very good. I will show you to quiet rooms on the upper eastern floor."

In the parlor, the woman gowned in gauze stood beside one gentleman and rested her hand on his shoulder. As the man dropped two more gold coins on the table and added to a startling amount already wagered, the woman glanced aside and noticed those watching her.

She smiled softly and winked at them before turning her attention back to the game.

Chap went cold inside.

Worse still, though Wayfarer straightened in bafflement and looked up at Leesil, all he did, still watching, was raise an eyebrow in response. Whether that wink had been for Leesil or Wayfarer—or both—Chap hoped that . . .

A vicious exhale sent a chill down his spine to his tail.

"It's . . . it's a *domvolyné*!" Magiere snarled right behind him.

Wayfarer flinched and looked back at her as Chap was trying to think of a way to head off what was coming.

"What?" Leesil exclaimed, still looking through the parlor. "No . . . Wynn would never—"

Magiere's hand smacked the back of his head.

As Leesil spun, he nearly jerked Wayfarer off her feet. "Hey! What was that for?"

Chap grabbed the girl's other wrist in his jaws and tried to pull her toward the stairs, where their host waited and watched. At least he could get the girl out of the way and thereby perhaps draw Magiere off.

Wayfarer clung to Leesil's arm in confusion and looked between him and Magiere.

"Majay-hì . . . Chap—stop!" she said. "What is . . . dom . . . domvol . . . ?"

Even for the girl's good grasp of Belaskian, it was an old and obscure term.

Chap tugged on Wayfarer again as he warned Leesil. —*Do not*—

Brot'an cut in. "Let us go to our—"

"It's a 'house of leisure,'" Leesil idly answered the girl.

Magiere, incensed, shot back at him, "It's a brothel!"

Chap wanted to groan.

"What is a brothel?" Wayfarer asked.

Everyone, even Magiere, stalled in silence, and then she stormed off up the stairs past a visibly uncomfortable but smiling Mechaela. Wayfarer glanced after Magiere, looked at Leesil, and then stared once more at the scantily clad woman in the far room.

The girl's mouth slowly dropped open.

"Oh . . . oh . . . you!" she gasped.

Leesil frowned and then suddenly turned aghast. "No, wait . . . I wasn't looking at the—"

"You . . . you . . ." Wayfarer sputtered at him in outrage. She snatched her hand from his arm and whirled to rush off. She grabbed Magiere's arm along the way and pulled her in a race up the stairs.

Brot'an unfolded his arms with another long exhale and followed them. Mechaela hurried upward, not looking at Leesil even once, though he still had that sly smile on his olive-toned face.

Leesil stood in shock, mumbling, "I wasn't looking at—"

Chap stalked away up the stairs.

Leesil did not catch up until the host had walked them to their two rooms down a long hallway. Mechaela opened both doors and handed a key to Magiere and then Brot'an.

"Please let me know if I can have food sent up or anything to make your stay pleasant."

Brot'an stepped into the first room. Magiere entered the second, and Wayfarer followed her. But when Leesil tried to enter, the girl turned on him through the half-opened door.

"You . . . shame!" she accused. "And Wynn, too . . . shame for this place . . . and you for . . . Oh, you!"

Wayfarer slammed the door in Leesil's face.

—*Half-wit*—

Leesil stabbed a finger at Chap's nose. "Don't you start. You know exactly what I was—"

Chap snapped at the extended finger. Leesil jerked his hand back, and Chap scratched at the door. Before anyone answered, Leesil opened it and stormed inside—and stopped cold.

Wayfarer sat on the end of a huge, fluffy bed, while Magiere stood beyond, with her back turned, at the grated window.

"I wasn't looking at the woman!" Leesil shouted. "Did you see the amount of coin on that table?"

Magiere turned her head, narrowing her eyes.

—*We*—*know*— And Chap hopped up on the bed behind Wayfarer, but the girl did not know Leesil as well as he and Magiere did.

"I do not believe you," Wayfarer said coldly, looking away as she crossed her arms. "You were . . . are unfaithful."

At that, Magiere's ire faltered. She swallowed hard, fighting to suppress a smile, before she said to him. "Either way, it's not going to happen. So don't you even think about it!"

Leesil looked around at all three of them and slapped his hands to his head.

"We're running out of coin!"

"Humph!" Wayfarer twisted away from him a little more. "Liar!"

Chap couldn't help a little ambivalence. That Wayfarer still did not believe Leesil might be amusing, but what he'd said was true. They were low on money. However, they also could not *afford* another of Leesil's fund-raising schemes.

Magiere took a deep breath and rubbed her face. "We'll figure something out," she said. "But not—"

Two knocks at the door were followed immediately by the twisting of its handle. Brot'an entered without invitation and looked at the bed. Stepping closer, he pressed his hand down until it sank into the puffy bedding, and he shook his head in disgust.

"Worse than the annex at Chathburh. How do any of you sleep?"

Chap ignored him.

Leesil only frowned. "The price of having any meals brought up may cost more than the rooms. We should go out and bring something back."

Being frugal didn't carry any weight with Wayfarer. "I will stay here," she declared.

"Brot'an stays with you," Magiere added.

—*Then*—*I*—*stay*—*and watch*—*Brot'an*—

Magiere eyed Chap, and Brot'an frowned, likely wondering what he had said to her.

"Perhaps Magiere and I should go," Brot'an offered. "We speak the local language best."

Chap didn't care for that. Brot'an was after two things: getting Magiere alone for more questions and getting her out of Chap's sight for that. Magiere apparently came to a similar conclusion.

"Leesil likes to pick out his own food, as does Chap," she said, and looked at him again. "So we'll bring him with us. Yes?"

This was clearly not a request. Chap wrinkled his jowls at her and wondered when she had become subtle about anything. She was quietly telling Brot'an that she would not go anywhere without Chap. At the same time, she would get Chap off the old assassin's back.

"Well enough," Brot'an answered.

With a grumble, Chap steeled himself to go off into another foreign city and leave Brot'an unwatched.

While Magiere didn't particularly like this cesspit called Drist, she was relieved to have her weapons back as she walked the dark streets with only Leesil and Chap. Much as she'd come to care for Wayfarer, perhaps more than was wise, the girl was too easily frightened.

"What's it going to be?" Leesil asked. "We could probably get anything we fancied around here."

True enough, for Magiere had never seen so many races and cultures mingled in one place. The choices for warm, prepared food would be broad. She tried to smile at him.

"Just follow your nose," she quipped, and then added more seriously, "but don't think you're settling in for anything else."

Leesil snorted and sauntered onward. "Never crossed my mind. I'm sure half the citizens in this port can cheat better than me."

Only a block away from the hotel, Chap's ears rose. He began drooling like a hog at the sight of a slop bucket, and Magiere shook her head. Leesil wasn't the only one to get them in trouble; she hoped Chap hadn't picked up the scent of some rolling sausage cart. Instead, he steered a quick course and trotted out ahead.

Magiere hurried after, and around one corner she spotted a little brick eatery enveloped in a delicious aroma. Chap was already there by the time she and Leesil caught up. Once inside Chap again caused a fuss by just being a "wolf" . . . or just being Chap. It didn't help when he panicked a couple of old men by sticking his nose over the edge of their table, where they were trying to finish off their meal . . . of sausages, of course.

"Stop that!" Magiere warned, grabbing him by the scruff and hauling him off to where Leesil had found an empty table.

As a dusky-skinned proprietor passed by with a tray, Leesil stopped him to inspect what he carried. Leesil pointed to a plate of skewers, each loaded to the ends with roasted chunks of meat, red potatoes, bits of onion, and sweet peppers.

"Five," Leesil said, holding up a hand with outstretched fingers and thumb. "Five . . . those . . . to take away."

Magiere shrugged at Chap. Leesil might be a disaster when it came to any tongue but his own, yet in this he didn't need her to translate. The proprietor came back so soon that it was startling, which made Magiere wonder how long ago that food had been cooked and left to sit. Leesil gave it no mind, paid the man, and scooped up the five skewers, wrapped loosely in some strange flimsy waxed paper.

Their errand was finished faster than Magiere expected, and they were all outside once again. Part of her wished they'd stayed out a little longer, but they had what they were after, so they might as well go back and eat.

"Those do smell good," she said.

Chap huffed, and instead of stalking ahead, he trailed Leesil closely.

"Will you get off my heels?" Leesil grumbled.

Chap grumbled right back as they headed to the . . . *hotel* where Wynn had sent them. Magiere wouldn't forget to have a word with the sage about that. Suddenly Chap wasn't on Leesil's heels anymore. Magiere slowed and looked back.

There he was, stalled just short of a cutway between two shops they'd just passed; his ears were perked up. Leesil slowed ahead and turned at finding that no one was beside him anymore.

"What's the matter?" Magiere called to Chap.

Leesil stepped back past Chap to look into the cutway's mouth just as Magiere heard the sound of running feet. A small, dingy form burst out and slammed straight into Leesil. Skewers went flying and rolling across the cobbled street.

"What in the seven hells?" Leesil choked out.

Magiere looked down at a boy of about twelve, sitting on his butt and staring up at Leesil in terrified shock. He was pale and thin, his hair was filthy, and his short pants and stained shirt were severely tattered. He wore nothing else against the cold night except a pair of hide-and-twine sandals. Stranger than that, he was soaked from head to toe.

The boy scrambled into a crouch, and before Magiere could ask him anything, he looked wildly about, the whites of his eyes exposed in the dark. He glanced once into the cutway and then bolted down the street before anyone could stop him.

The boy skidded to a stop after only four lunging steps.

Magiere heard shouts and more running feet off in that direction.

The boy whirled around and stared at the two people in his way. He didn't even flinch at the sight of Chap, but he was shaking either from cold or fright or both. He fixed on her.

"Help . . . please," he begged.

Another set of running feet echoed out of the cutway.

"What did you do?" Magiere asked.

He wasn't carrying anything, but that didn't mean he hadn't tossed aside something he'd stolen. Thievery was likely in a port like this.

"Nothing!" he nearly shouted, and then covered his mouth in panic.

Leesil stepped closer. "Answer her," he managed to say clearly. "What you do?"

As he looked into the boy's eyes, an uncomfortable feeling grew in Leesil's gut. He'd seen that haunted—no, hunted—look too many times in his life before meeting Magiere. Where he'd grown up in the Warlands, it was so common that everyone there learned to glance away and hurry off before it was too late.

"Nothing!" the boy whimpered. "I haven't done anything wrong!"

Shouts and pounding footfalls grew. Chap began rumbling, watching the cutway's mouth and the open street, but he glanced once at Leesil.

—Whatever—you do—do not—let—Magiere—act—

Leesil lunged in and grabbed the boy's shirt. He pulled the urchin around and shoved him off into Magiere's hands.

"Up against the wall, and watch him!" he ordered in Belaskian. "You guard him and leave the rest to us."

At least in that she might stay out of whatever was coming.

Magiere shook her head. "What are you going to—?"

"Do it . . . please!"

With a frown, Magiere backed to the street's side and pulled the boy out of sight into the shadows of a shop's landing. She pushed him down behind a railing and remained there. Almost in the same instant, a taller form shot out of the cutway. Leesil was already crouched, playing at picking up the scattered skewers.

Chap snarled and snapped, and the man pulled up short, scrambling backward at the sight of a huge wolf.

"You . . . slow!" Leesil snarled in Numanese. "Break my food!"

Three more stocky men rounded the corner from out of a side street down the way. They stalled at the sight of him and the other man held at bay by Chap. As they came up the street more slowly, Leesil whispered to Chap in Belaskian.

"Put that one down if he moves!"

All of them were dressed alike in leather and canvas attire. They didn't strike Leesil as constabulary, if this port even had such. Two of the three carried wooden cudgels in hand, and all wore sabers or shortswords sheathed on their heavy studded belts.

He'd seen their kind before—too many times—in childhood.

"Did a boy run past here?" the first man barked, his stubble-shadowed face twisted in suspicion.

Leesil scoffed, as if annoyed. "Boy? Yes, boy. Little beast knock . . .

food . . . over." He rose with only two skewers in hand and pointed off beyond the trio. "Went there."

At a mumble from the one without a cudgel, the other two took off down the street. The one giving the orders lingered, looking Leesil over from his slightly slanted amber eyes and white-blond hair to the strange weapons strapped to his thighs.

"Come on," he barked at the one Chap had cornered. "Stupid runt doubled back toward the docks without knowing it."

The one at the cutway's mouth inched away but kept his eyes locked on the large, growling wolf, and then he took off after the other two. The apparent leader looked Leesil over once more and followed the rest. Soon they were gone from sight.

Magiere came out into the street, pulling the boy along by the shoulder of his shirt.

"Why are they after you?" she asked him.

"I jumped ship and swam for shore," he whispered. "I couldn't sneak off and take the pier, so I jumped."

"So you are . . . deserter?" Leesil asked, but even then he didn't believe it.

The boy's mouth opened, but all he did was shake his head.

Leesil looked down the street. Four armed sailors were chasing a boy for jumping off a ship? The uncomfortable feeling in his gut began to burn with anger.

"Why you on ship if not want be?" he asked as best he could, not certain he wanted the answer. "Where family . . . Where you live?"

At the mention of "family," the boy winced. Leesil waited for Chap, whose eyes fixed on the boy's face.

—*I think*—*those men*—*were*—*slavers*— . . . —*We*—*should not*—*get*—*involved*—

Something inside Leesil snapped. "We're taking him with us."

Magiere's brow wrinkled. She glanced once at Chap, likely when he was explaining to her, and she exhaled, shaking her head. But Leesil knew *she* wouldn't argue.

—No—we have—enough—problems—

"Those men will find him," Leesil countered in Belaskian. "The boy hasn't got a wit in his head the way he's running around instead of finding a hiding-hole!"

The boy appeared even more leery at Leesil's talking to a wolf in some strange tongue. He clutched himself in his wet clothes.

"What your name?" Leesil asked.

"Paolo," the boy whispered.

"Come. You safe."

Dänvârfij hoped they might turn failure into success this night, but she held that hope at bay. There was much to do. She had been more than relieved when Rhysís had earlier arrived at the shabby inn to report that the *Cloud Queen* was in dock and Én'nish was watching for their quarry. Soon they would know how to proceed.

Even Fréthfâre was less free with her barbs and focused on their purpose. Hunched in the room's one chair and obviously in pain, she listened silently to everything Rhysís reported. Perhaps the ex-Covârleasa might for once use her influence to genuinely help.

While waiting, the three of them talked of possible tactics, depending upon what Én'nish reported upon her return, to trap their quarry. Dänvârfij's relief came when Én'nish finally swung in through the open window.

"They are on land," she said immediately and looked to Fréthfâre.

Dänvârfij swallowed an irritated reply to this obvious comment; otherwise the small one would still be watching the port.

"Is the traitor still with them?" Fréthfâre asked.

"Yes, but they are only five. The traitor, Magiere, Léshil, Leanâlhâm, and the majay-hì."

"Not Osha?" Dänvârfij asked.

"No."

This troubled her. An outcast anmaglâhk was loose, unwatched and unaccounted for, in the world.

"There are issues with their quarters," Én'nish went on. "It is a large hotel of three stories. I do not know their location inside, and there are iron grates on all windows and armed guards at the entrance. We cannot take the guards without being noticed. Their presence—and the windows—suggests further security within."

Dänvârfij took a slow breath. If this was the case, their quarry could not be attacked within the building, even if the targets were located before Dänvârfij's team entered. She glanced at Fréthfâre.

"What do you counsel?"

Fréthfâre hesitated. "Additional surveillance. We must know more, such as their length of stay. One on watch there, one at the port, and one to gather information regarding their ship's schedule. If the vessel is to remain several days, we have time to study our quarry's movements and plan their capture in the open."

"Agreed," Dänvârfij said, for it was what she had calculated, and that boded well for later cooperation. "Én'nish, watch the hotel. Rhysís, to the port. I will check in with Eywodan and Tavithê, and then gather information about the *Cloud Queen*."

One by one they left the filthy inn. While it was clear they would not fulfill their purpose tonight, Dänvârfij took relief in knowing that they would soon enough.

Chap sat on his haunches in one of their luxurious third-floor rooms and could not believe Leesil had brought the boy here. Magiere appeared unsettled but did not argue. Brot'an stood near the window and stared hard at Leesil as if he'd lost his mind.

Perhaps Leesil had.

Only Wayfarer took direct action where the boy was concerned. Upon seeing his dripping clothes, she pulled back the bed's plush quilt and stripped off the blanket beneath to wrap around Paolo. At least her presence distracted the urchin, for he kept staring at her in wonder.

"We must find him some dry clothes," Wayfarer said, looking to Magiere.

Those words broke the tense silence. Brot'an began pacing in irritation, while Leesil unwrapped the skewers and held one out. Paolo's hollow eyes fixed on it, though he hesitated until Wayfarer encouraged him. Then he grabbed it and tore into the meat and vegetables with his teeth like a starving cub.

Wayfarer watched him with a startled expression, but for once she did not appear remotely afraid of a human stranger. Paolo finished every bite off the skewer and licked the stick itself. Leesil shooed Wayfarer up, turned her to face away from the boy, and stripped the blanket off him.

"Take off wet clothes," he instructed.

Numbly obeying, the boy relaxed slightly once he was wrapped in the warm blanket again. He dropped onto the floor and leaned against the wall beyond the bed's foot. Wayfarer turned around with another judgmental glance at Leesil, likely about the woman in the foyer.

Now that he and Magiere had taken on the girl as their responsibility, whatever infatuation she had once carried for him had transformed into something else concerning his fidelity to Magiere. But Leesil didn't notice Wayfarer's misguided judgment.

He appeared caught in the throes of an overwhelming flash of protection concerning the boy. Chap knew better than to argue with him and looked to Magiere instead.

This boy was not their prime concern, but for the moment Leesil had forced the issue.

—*Time for—answers—from—the boy*—

Magiere glanced down at him.

—*I saw—memories*— . . . —*Men—women—locked in—a ship's hold*—

Magiere poured water from the porcelain pitcher into a waiting cup on the side table and brought it to Paolo. She waited until he finished.

"Why were those men after you?" she asked. "It's no crime to leave a ship, that I know of."

Paolo looked up at her, hesitated, and appeared to grow more aware of his surroundings.

"It is, if you're property," he said quietly, setting the cup on the floor and pulling the blanket tighter.

Even Brot'an stopped pacing. "What do mean by 'property'?"

Paolo looked up at the tall, scarred elf, and his mouth closed.

"From what Wynn's told us," Magiere said, "slavery is illegal in the Numan lands. The captain of a ship can't own him."

"When have most humans ever obeyed their own laws?" Brot'an countered.

"Drist is not in the Numan countries," Paolo said quietly. "It is a . . . free port. I was traded away to cover a debt, and the captain now owns me."

Chap closed his eyes. They were up to their necks now—the boy was an indentured servant or laborer. Leesil had broken what constituted law here by harboring stolen property.

Leesil crouched down. "What you mean?"

"My father was unable to pay our tithe for the last three years. Our chief covered the debt in exchange for services. Father couldn't leave the farm with no one else to work but my mother and three younger sisters. So our chief sold me into service to cover the loss—sold me to a captain bringing workers and laborers up north."

"Sounds like slavery to me," Magiere said.

Chap clenched his jaws. Now Magiere was turning to Leesil's side.

"In my years among human nations, I have seen this arrangement often," Brot'an said. "Indentured servitude is a binding agreement. If what the boy says is true, we are now thieves in possession of stolen property."

Chap concluded this as well, but Leesil whirled on the balls of his feet.

"Legal or not, it's slavery!" he shouted back in Belaskian. "The strong—the rich, the so-called nobles—controlling the weak and poor . . . like livestock!"

Paolo, not understanding what was said, shrank against the wall in confusion. Even Wayfarer winced at the open anger in Leesil's voice.

All this was getting out of control, though Chap was at a loss for how to stop it.

Leesil knew what it meant to be a slave and worse. He had grown up as a spy and assassin, like his father and mother, serving Lord Darmouth in the Warlands. He'd betrayed peasants and nobles alike, and had even killed them upon the warlord's command. Only one, perhaps two at most, of the three members of Leesil's family were ever allowed—at the same time—to go beyond their home on the lake's edge below Darmouth's keep. If any one of them disobeyed, the others' lives would be forfeit.

"The captain let me up on deck to help scrub," the boy blurted out in Numanese. "That's how I jumped overboard. But there are many others . . . in the hold."

Leesil turned on the boy and demanded, "What ship?"

Chap tried to interrupt. —No—

Paolo looked around at everyone. "A big one, from Witeny, at the end of the third pier."

No one spoke for a moment. They had all seen that ship.

"Leesil?" Magiere finally whispered.

He turned his head, and his eyes narrowed in warning.

"Where were they taking you?" Magiere asked the boy.

Paolo shook his head slightly. "Somewhere north, farther. The crew was set for a long journey. That's all I ever learned, except that we stopped at every port along the way, sometimes for days. Some crew always came back with more people. A few in the hold mentioned a camp . . . and . . ."

He paused, lost in thought.

"And what?" Magiere asked.

Paolo looked uncertain at first, as if whatever he thought of confused him. "Some were kept apart. Somebody said they were craftsmen: carpenters and smiths. One time they pulled someone out to help mend the bonds. I think they called him a . . . a ropewalker?"

Chap did not know that term.

"A shipyard," Brot'an interrupted. "A ropewalker works the lines and machines that make the heavy cables for ships. The indentured servants in the hold are to be used for labor in a shipyard."

"We're getting them out," Leesil said, switching back to Belaskian. "I don't care what else is going on. I'm not letting that slaver leave the harbor with anyone in its hold!"

Chap had had enough. —*No*— . . . —*I feel—for them—but we cannot— stray from—our purpose*—

Leesil ignored him and turned to Magiere. "I'm going to check out that ship. Are you coming?"

Chap eyed Magiere, who stood watching Leesil. She didn't need to answer. She would never refuse her husband, even if a part of her disagreed, here and now. Chap struggled for any way to stop them, for as much as he, too, wished to help, he could not risk either of them being lost.

"Wait!" Brot'an barked, and he looked at the boy. "When did your ship dock?"

"Two days ago."

"While on deck, did you hear of how long it would remain here?"

Paolo nodded. "Some of the crew said this was a good place for their . . . needs. Maybe a while."

Brot'an turned to Leesil. "That ship is not going anywhere tonight. Let me look it over in the morning. I can accomplish this without being noticed and return with what I learn. I can gauge the size of the crew and their capabilities better during the day."

Leesil didn't say anything, and his expression was unreadable.

"That does sound best," Magiere put in. "We'll have a better chance, if any, if we know what we're up against."

"All right." Leesil finally answered, "but we will have a chance . . . one way or another."

CHAPTER TWENTY-TWO

By midmorning the follow day, Dänvârfij made one change in the watch rotation. Rhysís remained atop a warehouse and watching the port, while Eywodan and Tavithê held the *Bashair*. But Fréth-fâre's pain had grown worse in the night, so Dänvârfij had sent Én'nish to the inn. She took Én'nish's place watching the hotel from a nearby rooftop.

As yet nothing useful had been learned regarding the *Cloud Queen*'s length of stay. This made Dänvârfij anxious. Her quarry could be packing to leave even now, and she could not let them escape to open waters. Worry had plagued her since dawn as she tried to formulate alternatives.

Én'nish had not exaggerated about the hotel; it was a fortress. While watching the guards and the barred windows, Dänvârfij toyed with the notion of direct infiltration.

No, it was still better to set a trap for their quarry in the . . .

The hotel's front door opened.

A tall, cloaked figure emerged. Male, judging by height—excessive height for a human—he stepped out past the guards. Even though he was heavily cloaked, his movements were unmistakable.

Dänvârfij tilted her head to one side as she watched Brot'ân'duivé walk up the street.

If she could kill him now, Magiere and Léshil would be more vulnerable. This thought faded as quickly as it formed.

She could not take Brot'ân'duivé alone. Such an act would likely end in her death and leave her purpose unfulfilled. It was better to learn where he went and why, which might lead to solutions for getting their quarry into the open. She rose slightly, preparing to follow.

Brot'ân'duivé was walking the wrong way.

Dänvârfij had expected him to head toward the port. She stared in puzzlement as he moved inland. What other purpose could he have in this lawless human city? After letting him get one cross street ahead, she leaped silently to the next rooftop. A greimasg'äh could sense pursuit more easily than most, and she could not allow him to become aware of her.

He turned right down the next side street.

Dänvârfij dropped off the roof into a cutway and hurried for the back alley to which it connected. She peered around the corner to the alley's intersection with the side street, and she watched every passerby crossing the far view.

Brot'ân'duivé never appeared, and her throat went dry.

On instinct, waiting, she looked back up the cutway. There was no sign of his having doubled back. She almost bolted down the alley toward the side street, but that would put her in the open in trying to find him. Instead, she spidered up a rear wall onto the rooftops and scanned the city in all directions.

Even if he had scaled a building to a roof along his way, it might mean she had been noticed. She saw no one in the heights. Could he have entered a building?

Crawling low to the rooftop's edge, she looked down upon the side street lined with small dwellings—no shops or eateries. The other possibility was the alley along the backs of the buildings on the street's far side. An unwanted fear washed over her.

Following this greimasg'äh into a shadowed place was unwise. It occurred to her that no matter what, the traitor would assume he might be trailed—it was in him both by his nature and training. He might have gone inland simply to throw off any hidden pursuit. There was only one way to be certain, and it was a blind choice.

Dänvârfij continued along the rooftops until she was forced to take to the streets, and then she raced for the port. If she could not find him, the others needed to be warned.

A greimasg'äh, now their enemy, was on the move.

Crouched in the far alley's shadows, Brot'ân'duivé pulled a hidden bundle from under his arm and took off his heavy dun-colored cloak.

Earlier that morning, Mechaela had allowed him to go through a surprisingly large array of clothing "abandoned" by patrons over the years. He had borrowed a few things, including a bright cerulean cloak of light wool, more garish than he normally would have desired. The owner had been quite tall for a human, and so the cloak's hem reached Brot'ân'duivé's shins—adequate enough. He had also borrowed a pair of cream-colored suede boots, useless for anything besides fashion.

In most ports the vivid blue would have called attention to him—but not here. This harbor was a cacophony of wild attire from many lands, and he would blend even more easily than he would in anmaglâhk garb.

Wrapping his own boots inside the dun cloak, he pulled the cerulean cloak's hood low over his eyes and stepped into the street. He kept his knees bent, adopting an affected slouch to minimize his notable height. At best he would be half a head shorter. That was all he could manage in his hurry, as he took a roundabout way toward the harbor's southern end.

Brot'ân'duivé already knew he had been followed out of Delilah's.

A change of clothing, stature, and gait might throw off pursuit once he mingled among the locals. As he neared the waterfront, the number of people in the streets multiplied. He slipped among them and shadowed a pair of overdressed gentry accompanied by heavily armed escorts. Peering from under the hood, he watched the rooftops and knew exactly where he would have placed sentries—if he had been in charge of hunting himself.

The barest hint of a figure wearing dark blue rose slightly over the crest of a warehouse roof.

It was sensible to assume that his enemies had abandoned their attire for disguises as well. What mattered was that the team was here in Drist. Their presence was no longer a guess.

He carefully repeated checks as he walked, but the figure in dark blue did not rise any higher. He briefly lost sight of it until his angle improved when he reached the waterfront's southern end. The figure still had not moved, which meant whoever was there had not left to report in.

He had not been spotted as yet.

Brot'ân'duivé slowed amid the dodging masses of dockworkers, the finely dressed, and those selling goods off their backs or begging on the boardwalks. Among the flowing crowds, he drifted to the waterfront's edge and stepped down along the stairs to below.

The *Bell Tower* was docked at the third pier's end. He needed a place to vanish with a decent vantage point. Once on a floating walkway, he quickened his pace and then stopped among the shoreward pilings of the fourth pier. With a good view of the third pier above, he unrolled his dun-colored cloak and pulled it over the cerulean one.

He swung around a tall pier post and onto a low beam between it and the next one outward in the water. Flattening against that support, he looked to the massive ship marked as the *Bell Tower*. It was a good distance away, but he saw all movement along its rail, its ramp, and the pier.

Brot'ân'duivé stilled mind and body and let shadow take him once he had set his purpose deep within himself. With his gaze locked upon that vessel, all that he would see and hear would fall into the back of his mind, beyond conscious thought.

Sometime during the morning, a dog wandered down the walkway and passed into the periphery of his sight. He did not look directly at it . . . did not move . . . did not think. The dog never paused, and the click of its claws continued until even that faded from his stilled awareness. He continued taking in all movements and changes upon the *Bell Tower* until a thought rose to break him loose from shadow.

He refocused his gaze.

Dänvârfij descended the ramp of a much smaller ship on the second pier and stood brazenly in the open, staring toward . . . the *Cloud Queen*. Dressed in breeches and a dark vest, she no longer wore the forest gray of the anmaglâhk, but it was she.

This could be no coincidence. She and her team not only knew the vessel on which Magiere traveled, but their own ship had docked only a few vessels away. He could not have anticipated this last detail.

Dänvârfij turned and walked toward the waterfront.

Brot'ân'duivé decided to keep this information to himself, as he was uncertain how he would use it. Though he pretended to assist in Léshil's foolish pursuit, he still hoped to put an end to it.

There were four to five armed men always walking the deck of the *Bell Tower*. Separate from the other crew, those appeared to have no other purpose but the vessel's—the cargo's—safekeeping. Léshil and Magiere would not be able to board by the ship's ramp, not even under a ruse. The moment they tried, they would be stopped and unable to fight their way past.

Skiffs had come and gone below the piers. Some were tied off nearer the lower walkway. He had seen a few other ways to board the vessel, but he would not suggest such. He had enough—more than he would tell—to make the chance of infiltration sound rationally hopeless.

Stepping back onto the walkway, he stripped off the dun cloak to wrap it around his boots again. Up the stairs, he slipped in among the shifting, noisy masses, but he paused a final time upon the waterfront. He looked from the *Cloud Queen* to the *Bell Tower* . . . and to the smaller ship that Dänvârfij had left.

A new strategy, wrapped around Léshil's present fixation, began to form.

Most Aged Father's team of loyalists and fanatics were far from home. Brot'ân'duivé saw a way to add to the number who would not return.

The fewer the better, and as he followed Magiere to an orb, he could then freely watch for the time and place to put Léshil to his destined purpose. That purpose had been foreseen by lost Eillean, prepared through a mother's sacrifice by Cuirin'nên'a, and marked by the ancestors with a name.

Leshiârelaohk.

Dänvârfij wasted no time in hurrying back toward the three-story hotel with barred windows. After contacting Rhysís and Eywodan, she had been relieved, though troubled, that no one had spotted the traitor. Perhaps he had been playing decoy. A similar ruse had been used to steal away Magiere and her companions in Calm Seatt. By the time Dänvârfij reached a vantage point to look up at the hotel, her anxiety faded.

If Magiere and hers had booked passage on a ship all the way to the Suman Empire, she would not likely travel by land in leaving Drist. No, when she left this place, she would intend to board the *Cloud Queen*. So wherever else she or Léshil went in this city, to whatever purpose, did not matter . . . except if it put them in easy reach.

Crouched on the roof, Dänvârfij noticed someone tall, but perhaps not tall enough, dressed in a bright cerulean cloak. The man stepped straight between the front guards and to the front door without challenge. In the last instant as the door closed, something changed, as if the man looked taller next to the door's closing edge. Then he was gone from sight.

Dänvârfij knew such tricks of posture. She had no certainty, but if what she had glimpsed was true . . .

She could never forget that the treacherous greimasg'äh was among the best of her caste. Where had he gone, if that had been he who had entered a moment ago? If he had slipped to the waterfront, then for what reason?

Dänvârfij lingered a moment in indecision before she fled back toward the filthy inn to speak with Fréthfàre. Contingencies needed to be prepared.

In the inn's room, Én'nish sat listening to Dänvârfij report on Brot'ân'duivé's possible deception.

Dänvârfij, for all her disrespect of Fréthfâre, seemed certain of her assumptions, and she was not given to groundless speculations. In this, excitement built within Én'nish as she listened.

"I agree this is a temporary stop for our quarry," Fréthfâre said, sitting bent over in her chair. "They will not continue via land but—"

"They will return to the *Cloud Queen*," Dänvârfij finished.

"From what you and Én'nish have described, this hotel where they stay is unbreachable."

"It is."

"Then the only option is to abandon the *Bashair* and take the *Cloud Queen*. We lay our trap for when our quarry returns to leave port."

Dänvârfij hesitated, and then nodded. "Agreed, but that ship has a larger crew. Taking it may not—will not—be as certain or clean as taking the *Bashair*."

"Of course," Fréthfâre confirmed flatly. "And?"

After another long pause, Dänvârfij answered with equal coldness. "I will need Én'nish."

"When do we move?" Én'nish asked too quickly.

"Near mid of night, when most of the crew is asleep," Dänvârfij answered. "Though waiting that long troubles me. We do not know when the vessel's captain plans to depart. The others must watch that ship as well for any sign."

"Agreed," Fréthfâre said.

For once she did not sound bitter in dealing with Dänvârfij's overly cautious ways, not that Én'nish blamed the rightful, *true* Covârleasa for her bitterness. But she sounded pensive, as if she wished to take part in the night's task.

"Go now," Fréthfâre continued. "Prepare Rhysís, Eywodan, and Tavithê for infiltration. Tonight, kill the *Bashair*'s remaining crew, dispose of the bodies, and take the *Cloud Queen*."

Anticipation of nightfall, and what would come, quickened Én'nish's breaths.

CHAPTER TWENTY-THREE

After nightfall, as Leesil prepared to leave with Magiere, he was still suspicious of Brot'an's change in attitude. The old assassin seemed far too willing and helpful in devising a plan, though he refused to take an active role—not that Leesil would have wanted him along anyway. Besides, someone had to watch over Wayfarer and now Paolo.

Chap was another matter, and Leesil already had a headache from the dog's badgering.

"Are the rope and hook packed in easy reach?" Magiere asked.

"Of course." But Leesil checked again and made certain all other gear was accounted for, stowed away in his pack. Their plan was sound, though there were always risks—more so this time.

Chap rumbled where he lay on a rug near the bed.

"No more!" Leesil growled back. "And you know why you're staying behind."

The dog snorted twice in place of huffs or barks, but raised no memory-words in Leesil's head.

In fact Chap had stopped talking to anyone. That wasn't a good sign. He was to remain behind to help guard the young ones in case anyone came searching for Paolo. More to the point, tonight's attempt to rescue a ship full of slaves was going to involve climbing up the hull. They didn't have time to hoist an oversized wolf in complete silence.

It had taken both Leesil and Magiere to argue this point, with Chap nearly throwing a full tantrum and calling up memory-words that had previously been shouted at him . . . and shouting the words back in pieces that suited his own point. It was the most bizarre, irritating, tiresome argument Leesil had ever had. One more reason to give Wynn a kick—or two—for teaching Chap such a trick.

The real problem wasn't that Chap wanted to come along; he didn't want anyone going at all.

"You can change now," Wayfarer said.

The girl laid out two sets of clothes on the bed. Brot'an had somehow borrowed them from Mechaela that afternoon. However, Magiere frowned as she looked over the new attire.

"What makes you think we might be watched or followed?" she asked Brot'an.

"You should take precautions, regardless," he answered. "This establishment is busy at night with people coming and going. In those clothes—and in following my instructions—you should reach the waterfront unnoticed and then return as someone else to any watchful eyes."

Magiere frowned, unconvinced.

Leesil would never admit it, but he found Brot'an's suggestions sound. He began unbuckling his hauberk as he joined Magiere beside the bed. A stylish black velvet tunic, well-tailored breeches, a charcoal cape, a hat, and a polished walking stick awaited him.

Wayfarer politely turned around while he and Magiere began assisting each other in removing their hauberks. Once he was in the tunic and breeches, she helped arrange the cape. Then he sat down on the bed, and she twisted his hair into a tail and tucked it all up under the hat.

Paolo stood by, watching all this with quiet interest. He'd said little all day but had eaten every bite of food offered.

Magiere studied Leesil. "You look like a dandy."

"That's the idea," he answered. "Your turn."

Her mouth tightened under a scowl.

They'd both agreed not to wear any armor. If things went badly, they'd have to jump overboard and swim for it. And they needed absolute silence while skulking about—a creak of leather or click from hauberk rings or studs could give them away.

"Only down to your shirt and breeches," Wayfarer told Magiere. "Step into this, and I will fasten it."

Wayfarer picked up a voluminous skirt of purple silk, and Magiere reluctantly obeyed, glowering the whole time while Wayfarer dressed her. Once the skirt was in place, the girl draped a crimson velvet cape over Magiere's shoulders and closed the front so that it covered the white shirt. The skirt wasn't quite long enough, but at least it covered most of Magiere's high leather boots.

Wayfarer turned for the last item on the bed.

"I'm not wearing that," Magiere warned through her teeth.

"Oh, yes, you are," Leesil warned back. "Now sit down!"

Fuming, Magiere dropped onto the bed's edge.

Wayfarer arranged Magiere's long, loose hair around her shoulders and picked up a delicate silver tiara. The girl set it atop Magiere's head and began pinning it into place.

At night, her red tints wouldn't show much except in some lantern's light. Leesil had already noted a number of lovely, overdressed, pale-skinned women floating in and out of the hotel. Up close, Magiere wouldn't likely be mistaken for one of them, but someone watching from afar wouldn't notice any difference.

Brot'an had advised that if they tried a full hood, she might stand out as someone attempting to hide. Dressed like this, she fit in as a patron—or someone who worked here—leaving for the night.

"Perfect," was all Leesil said, appraising her disguise.

Without answering, Magiere rose, so Leesil grabbed his prepared pack and the walking stick. He almost thanked Brot'an for the arrangements but then thought better of it. The notion that Brot'an was up to something still nagged him. Instead, Leesil turned and found Wayfarer watching him with worried green eyes.

"If we're successful," he said, "this shouldn't take long. We'll be back before the mid of night." He looked to Chap. "We've managed worse than this, and you know it."

Chap didn't respond, and Leesil headed out. Nothing was going to stop him from freeing those slaves. Magiere pulled the door closed, and they made their way to the stairs.

Once they reached the front desk and retrieved their weapons, Leesil strapped on both of his blades beneath his cape. They were still visible to anyone looking closely enough, but most "gentlemen" here carried weapons.

Magiere put her battle dagger at her back inside the velvet cape, but there was no way she could completely hide the sword as well. Leesil held on to her falchion under his cloak, and they were ready.

"You're up first," she said.

"You know the tavern Brot'an mentioned?"

She nodded. "I'll see you there."

Mechaela looked over the front desk and assessed her attire.

"Very nice," he offered.

Leesil swallowed hard, hoping the man didn't get punched. Leaving Magiere behind, he walked out the front door and headed off into the night. Events were under way.

He carried the walking stick in one hand and clutched Magiere's sword beneath his cape in the other; he carried his pack over one shoulder. Half a block down the street, he spotted three well-dressed young men coming toward him. They were a bit loud and wandering in their course.

He instantly affected the dandified movements of an overbred nobleman who'd had too many drinks.

"Gentleman," he slurred. "One of you . . . help?"

Taking in the sight of him, they stopped, swaying a little.

"Can you point . . . Three-Leg Horse . . . tavern?" he asked.

The second one, the most steady on his feet, raised an eyebrow.

"Are you certain, sir? That is too uncouth a place . . . by the look of you. And you are obviously not from around here."

Perhaps that one wasn't as drunk as he'd seemed. Leesil blinked twice, feigning a bit of trouble in understanding. In truth he did have trouble understanding some of those words, but he nodded.

"A . . . *lady* . . . wait for me," he whispered. "We do not"—and he faltered—"want be see by others."

At an added wink by Leesil, the third young man choked back a snicker, slapped the second on the back of the shoulder, and nearly missed.

"Oh, for the sake of saints, just help him out, Ogas."

The first merely chuckled, nodding, and almost lost his footing.

"Ah, grief!" said the second. "Get Hines off to Delilah's . . . before he falls on his face! I'll show this foreigner the way and meet you there."

As the other two wandered—and weaved—off the way Leesil had come, the one who remained bowed slightly to Leesil.

"I am Viscount Ogastino."

"Please to make ac . . . ac-guain . . ." Leesil fumbled, intentionally this time.

"Yes, yes, come along now."

Leesil strode off with the reluctantly helpful young viscount, and together they looked like nothing more than two gentlemen out for an evening's entertainment. The Three-Legged Horse was almost on top of the harbor, and as they stepped inside, Leesil agreed with his companion's earlier assessment.

Viscount Ogastino then surprised him. "Shall we order an ale? I'd rather like to see this *lady* who agreed to meet *here*."

Leesil had only wanted male company for the walk, to help him blend in.

"Um . . ." he began, not certain what to say.

Then the door opened, and Magiere stepped in.

"That her," he whispered.

As she stood in the doorway in her crimson cape and a small silver tiara holding back her dark hair, the viscount's eyes fastened on her pale face.

"Oh, blessed deities of woods," he murmured. "There's a forest bride I'd have met up with anywhere!"

Leesil didn't like that insinuation about his wife—not at all.

"Yes . . . forest . . . bride." He tried agreeing with that lewd remark. "She want not be seen. You go?"

With that, the viscount composed himself and nodded. "By all means. Have a *pleasant* night."

Magiere was already on her way through the smoky tavern. As Ogastino passed her on his way out, he looked her up and down with a smile that made Leesil tense.

"What was that?" she asked as she joined him.

"Forget it," Leesil grumbled. "Just something to throw off anyone watching."

"Let's get out of here," she whispered. "I want a dark alley to get out of this damned dress . . . and get my sword back!"

Leesil loved her fierce side as much as he did the rest of her. For the first time since launching this undertaking, he looked into her eyes and was unable to forget what happened in Chathburh.

"There are lives at stake," she whispered, as if knowing his thoughts. "I'm in control."

Leesil tried to smile. "I know," he agreed, hoping they were both right.

Once Dänvârfij gauged that enough of the night had passed, she led her team down to the floating walkways below the waterfront. All were once again garbed in their traditional forest gray of light wool. With matching scarves over their faces and only their eyes visible, they slipped among the deeper darkness below.

Rhysís untied a skiff beneath the first pier, and they boarded. Tavithê and Eywodan oared the small vessel, making barely more sound than a seagull swimming upon the briny water. They worked the small craft out beyond the first pier's end into open water and kept well clear of all docked vessels. Earlier Dänvârfij had noted that the men on watch up in the masts kept their eyes on the waterfront and other ships, and almost never looked out to the open sea.

The skiff slipped by unnoticed all the way to the starboard side of the *Cloud Queen* at the end of the second pier.

Dänvârfij's confidence in their plan grew a little with each passing moment. Of all that Brot'ân'duivé might suspect, he would least fear allowing Magiere and hers to reboard their own ship. They would be taken in complete surprise.

A number of the *Cloud Queen*'s crew had been seen going ashore earlier that day; they had not been seen to return as yet. Dänvârfij estimated that less than two-thirds of the crew remained aboard. Before embarking this night, Rhysís had climbed the *Bashair*'s central mast for a look. He had reported only six men, counting one up the main mast, on deck and watching over the *Cloud Queen*.

Rhysís and Tavithê had their short bows assembled and quivers of short arrows fastened to their hips under their cloaks. Both shouldered their strung bows, and, once the skiff floated up beside the vessel's hull, Rhysís took the end of a rope and hook in his teeth. He pulled his bone knife, took the one Dänvârfij handed him, and began the painful process of scaling the hull as quietly as possible.

They could not risk throwing the hook over the rail; silence in that was impossible. In addition, should any sailor come along, this way he would not see a hook and line or hear Rhysís until too late.

Once he was up and over the rail, he set the hook and dropped the rope over the side. Én'nish climbed up to join him. Tavithê went next, followed by Dänvârfij, who had a stiletto already clenched in her teeth. The last to follow was Eywodan, as Dänvârfij retrieved her bone knife from Rhysís.

After that they made no effort to remain unseen, and events sped up quickly as they came out into the open on both sides of the aftcastle. A sailor at the prow on the forecastle spotted them first and shouted. Rhysís ignored the man and aimed his bow up along the main mast.

As soon as a sailor above looked over the crow's nest wall, Rhysís's bowstring thrummed.

Dänvârfij was already running.

The first crewman who had shouted never reached the main deck. Intercepting him, Dänvârfij drove her stiletto inside his guard and through the hollow of his throat, and then watched him drop. From the top of the steep forecastle steps, she looked away from his corpse to survey a silent ship.

Only the forest gray forms of her own team moved among motionless human bodies lying upon the deck. All of the anmaglâhk were barely visible by the light of two hanging lanterns, and the smallest was the first to reach the portside door below the aftcastle.

Én'nish stood waiting, flattened against the wall. As the door opened, voices could be heard before anyone came out.

"I'm telling ya, I heard Ethan shout," one said.

Two disheveled men stepped out, and Én'nish let them both fully emerge. She sidestepped in around the open door and slashed open the second man's throat. As the first one turned at the wet sound, Eywodan appeared from the door's other side and struck the man's temple.

The crewman's eyes rolled up, and his back hit the deck. Such a strike would render him half-unconscious, and Én'nish, with her wet blade still in hand, was instantly on top of him.

Dänvârfij quickly closed, but Eywodan was quicker.

"*Bithna!*" he hissed at Én'nish.

The crewman's eyes fluttered as Én'nish's slash halted with her blade merely hovering near his throat.

"Is your captain here?" Dänvârfij demanded.

The man's eyes finally widened. He looked up at her, and then at Eywodan, and then at Én'nish, whose half-covered face was barely a forearm's length above his.

"In . . . in his cabin," the man answered.

Dänvârfij scanned the deck and glanced back to see Én'nish clamp her free hand over the man's mouth and thrust her blade between his ribs.

No more footsteps carried from below, and the deck was theirs.

All of the team gathered around Dänvârfij.

"Rhysís, Eywodan, and Tavithê, go below and finish this," she instructed.

"Lock the captain in his quarters. Én'nish and I will stand watch here to take any crewman who might return from onshore."

All three men slipped through the door to the stairs. Half the crew would be kept alive to rotate up here for the illusion of normality. But Én'nish, who glared in hungry rebellion once they were alone, clearly wanted to take part in the killing below.

For a moment Dänvârfij thought Én'nish might argue, even now that they were halfway to completing their purpose.

Én'nish finally dropped her gaze and looked away.

When Brot'ân'duivé could no longer hear Léshil's and Magiere's steps on the outer stairs, he turned to Chap.

"I am going down for a moment. Keep watch on the young ones."

Snarling as expected, the majay-hì jumped to his feet, and Wayfarer flinched, as did Paolo. Brot'ân'duivé merely waited, knowing he would never hear Chap's argument in his own thoughts.

"He says you . . . you are not . . . going anywhere," Wayfarer related, visibly embarrassed or perhaps shocked, as she swallowed hard. Perhaps she had not repeated Chap's exact words.

Brot'ân'duivé responded directly to the adversarial majay-hì. "Stay with the young ones, and I *will* return in moments. Magiere and Léshil could not be stopped, so they must be guarded without their knowledge."

Chap fell silent, and his flattened ears rose slightly.

Brot'ân'duivé took that moment of stunned confusion to slip out. Quickly descending the stairs to the last landing above the entryway, he hovered around the stairway's turn to watch below.

Magiere stood with her back to him, and somewhere off to her right was the front counter. Brot'ân'duivé could not hear whether their olive-skinned host was down there as well, but Magiere remained, perhaps counting under her breath.

Léshil was nowhere in sight and had likely already left, beginning the night's plan. Magiere suddenly stepped toward the front door in her crimson cape. Her long gait did not match the look of an elite woman seeking a night's pleasure.

As soon as she was gone, Brot'ân'duivé descended and found Mechaela on duty behind the counter. It would seem the man rarely slept, for he had been there at dawn that morning.

"I need another room, possibly for half the night, in the most secure part of the inn," Brot'ân'duivé said. "Cost is irrelevant."

He felt no pride or shame at theft but had put his skill to use several times in Calm Seatt. The pouch he carried held more than sufficient coins, though he had kept this information, like all else, to himself unless otherwise necessary.

Mechaela tilted his head in puzzlement. "I assure you, the rooms you were given are quite secure."

"I need to leave the young woman and a boy behind tonight. I want no one outside of the staff to have any chance of knowing where they are. Another room, please . . . now."

Mechaela hesitated and then curled a finger, motioning Brot'ân'duivé around the counter. The host gestured toward a set of small bells below the counter.

"This way," he said, and stepped to the door at the counter's far end.

Brot'ân'duivé followed as Mechaela opened the door and passed through into a dim, plush hallway. Almost immediately Mechaela turned aside to open the first door to his right. Brot'ân'duivé entered a bedroom with paintings of beautiful but scantily clad women on the walls.

"These rooms are for patrons who require extra privacy," Mechaela said as he stepped near the bed. "I seldom need to . . . intervene for those who work here, but it has happened."

He pinched a dangling end of a ribbon near the headboard that tied back one corner of the bed's canopy curtain. The ribbon slid without untying the curtain and retracted when released.

Out of the room's doorway, Brot'ân'duivé heard a small bell ring lightly.

"Should one of our employees require assistance," Mechaela explained, "I can be inside the room before the bell fades. Other interior guards will follow quickly." He paused. "I assume this is safe enough for your need?"

"You will be at the desk all night?"

"Yes."

Brot'ân'duivé nodded and pulled out his pouch.

Chap bristled as he waited for Brot'an's return. The old assassin had counted on his being unwilling to leave Wayfarer and Paolo alone. Brot'an had something in mind and knew Chap would wait, caught unaware and baffled.

Chap hated being played so easily.

"It is all right, majay-hì," Wayfarer whispered as she knelt beside him. "The greimasg'äh wishes to protect Magiere and Léshil in all that he does."

Chap did not snarl at her gullibility. He cared for and worried about her too much for some angry retort.

Brot'an was not gone long, and when he hurried back in, he left the door open. Before Chap could even snarl . . .

"We will place Wayfarer and the boy in a safer room," Brot'an said. "Then we go after Magiere and Léshil. Now."

Chap glared at him. With no way to speak directly into Brot'an's mind—having never dipped into the man's memories for words to use—he was not about to use the girl again for some long attempt at getting answers.

"The team of anmaglâhk is here," Brot'an said flatly. "I have seen them in port."

Chap's rage erupted, and he snarled, baring his teeth.

Wayfarer drew away in fear, and Paolo jumped up from the floor and flattened against the wall.

Chap ignored them, for everything was now clear. Brot'an was using Leesil and Magiere as bait in a trap for his enemies.

"There is no time for this!" Brot'an snapped. "Neither you nor I could dissuade Léshil. I watched you try—and fail. We have a chance to pass unnoticed, as our enemies will focus on them."

These anmaglâhk were not Leesil and Magiere's enemies as much as Brot'an's. Chap lunged, snapping for Brot'an's leg.

"Majay-hì, no!" Wayfarer blurted out.

Brot'an hopped to get out of reach and stood in the open door.

"They were coming sooner or later," he said. "Better that they come on our terms. We have a chance to take them unaware and end this . . . if we act *now*."

Chap hesitated. Brot'an was using Magiere and Leesil because he had not been able to stop them. Now he wanted to go after his enemies while they were distracted . . . in going after Leesil and Magiere.

Brot'an looked to Wayfarer. "Come."

"But . . ." Wayfarer stammered in confusion, and Paolo didn't move.

In two strides Brot'an swept in, not even glancing at Chap. He grabbed Wayfarer's hand and snatched up Paolo in his other arm. The boy looked so frightened that he didn't struggle.

"There is a safer place for them downstairs," Brot'an said and, turning his back, he slipped out the door.

Chap followed with no other choice.

CHAPTER TWENTY-FOUR

Leesil reached the waterfront while still wearing his fine breeches and tunic, but along the way he'd left the cape, hat, and walking stick behind. The clothes were loose enough for him to move easily, and his tool kit from his early days was stowed in the back of his tunic. Magiere was down to her breeches and shirt, with her long falchion strapped over her back and out of the way.

They headed quietly down the shoreline stairs to the walkways below the piers and the skiffs tied off below.

Though there were some people still about on the waterfront and many of the ships, Leesil and Magiere found themselves completely alone down below. It took no time to find a small, manageable boat under the third pier where the slave ship was docked. Magiere climbed in while Leesil untied it from a piling.

They ignored the oars and instead pushed the skiff along between the pilings; sometimes they had to duck all the way down to slip under a cross support. They remained hidden from sight by anyone above on the docks, and even those along the shoreline would not be looking for anything below.

They reached the pier's end without hearing a warning call or spotting a single person stopping to look their way. As they floated out into the open, Leesil leaned his head close to Magiere's.

You ready? he mouthed, and she nodded.

The bay was calm, and they pushed off around the last piling to hand-walk the skiff along the back of the *Bell Tower*. Ripples from the skiff's movement spread around the ship's greater hull with no sound at all.

Leesil looked upward, listening, but neither of them saw nor heard anyone up on the aftcastle. As they rounded to the starboard and the open side, he glanced about for anyone watching.

There on the end of the next pier was the *Cloud Queen*, and he sank low in the skiff and motioned for Magiere to do the same. He couldn't see much more than the hull and the masts above. No one walked the ship's near-side rail.

Lantern light didn't reach the crow's nest on the central mast, though he knew someone was likely up there. Here in the dark, next to the slave ship's hull, he hoped they wouldn't attract any attention.

Leesil dug into his pack and pulled out a coil of thin rope that ended in a plain metal hook he'd wrapped with strips of cloth. Magiere tried to steady the skiff as he rose carefully to his feet and looked up. Even if he'd borrowed Brot'an's hook-bladed bone knife to match the one he carried, that kind of climb wasn't like scaling a stone wall with cracks and mortar lines. Leesil wasn't sure he could manage it quietly enough, so he'd opted for a different strategy. Right now he simply hoped the padded hook would make little noise when it passed over the rail and banged against the deck's sidewall.

Even so, he worried about what would happen after that.

The problem was that once he and Magiere freed the prisoners, they had to get a large number of people up on deck, deal with any sentries while not rousing the rest of the crew, lower the ramp, and get everyone off.

No small task—but he believed it *could* be done if executed quickly, before any guards realized what was happening. He and Magiere would leave last in order to help hold off any pursuit. He also hoped to find makeshift weapons in the hold—anything to arm the stronger prisoners and put them out in front of the escape . . . in case all of this did come down to a fight.

After that there was still one more consideration.

Paolo had suggested that the slavers were here to gather more prisoners, and the ship had already been here for three days. Odds were that by now someone in the hold was from Drist. Once the prisoners made it off the ship, their only option would be to run to whomever or whatever passed for the authorities here, even if that proved to be only the harbormaster.

Leesil believed that most harbormasters would have a problem with the transportation of human cargo. Would it matter here, where even people became property? Someone in the hold had to know, and Leesil had to learn, before even one prisoner stepped off the ship.

"Leesil?" Magiere whispered.

He flinched, looking down to find her watching him. He shook himself to clear his head and slowly swung the hook on half an arm's length of rope, then whipped it upward along the hull. With the rope sliding through his hands, he prepared to stop it when the hook dropped over the rail so that he could pull it short of striking the deck.

Én'nish surveyed the *Cloud Queen*'s deck as Tavithê and Eywodan walked opposite circuits three strides in from its rails. A few terrified crewmen stood in plain sight of the shoreline and remained obediently silent. With the ship secured and its ramp lowered, any returning crew might find the lack of sentries at the ramp's base to be odd. But they would simply come up to see what was wrong instead of calling out from below. And they would be dealt with.

Everything was quiet and controlled as Én'nish glanced shoreward in anticipation. No one worth noting wandered the waterfront, but after two steps toward middeck, she stopped and looked shoreward again.

Something had not been right.

Moving closer than she probably should to the rail, she realized it was not the waterfront wanderers that had caught the corner of her eye. As if gliding upon the water between the pilings, shadows moved beneath the base of the next pier. She was not even certain what it was as she walked rearward until she had to stop at the aftcastle wall.

A bulky, low shadow glided along beneath that other pier and vanished behind the massive vessel docked across the way.

"Tavithê," Én'nish whispered sharply, not looking away.

"What?" he asked, now standing beside her.

Én'nish kept her eyes on the other ship. "Find Dänvârfij. . . . Something strange is happening over there."

His soft steps rushed off, and she walked back along the rail and peered all ways and over the *Cloud Queen*'s side, in case this was some human criminal element working to raid ships in the harbor. She found nothing until she raised her eyes again and froze.

A skiff slipped out around the huge ship's rear end.

She heard no oars dipping the water. The shapes of two figures, as best she could see, were pushing the skiff along the waterline of the *Bell Tower*. Én'nish could not make them out, but who would round a ship in the dark in such a fashion?

She watched to see whether the little boat would keep on along the ship's hull. The skiff stopped at a point directly below where the towering aftcastle's wall met the deck. One figure remained low, perhaps seated, but the other rose.

Én'nish heard something like a soft whirl of air in the night. Then the standing figure began climbing up the ship's outer hull. His white-blond hair gleamed as his head rose above the rail's edge.

Leesil grabbed the rail and pulled himself up to peek over the edge for any crew nearby. There would be one in the crow's nest above, but most likely all eyes were turned to the ship's dockside or toward the waterfront. With no one close in sight on the deck, he slipped over the rail and tugged the rope sharply twice.

The rope pulled tight.

He looked over the side and watched until Magiere rose from the darkness below and climbed upward. He glanced out over the port for anyone watching, and as he was about to look down again, he noticed something that startled him—as if he'd walked into a dark room and caught the reflection of something there in a mirror.

Across the way, another skiff floated at the waterline of a large vessel. It took him a blink to remember that the vessel was the *Cloud Queen*. He couldn't see the ship clearly, for there were fewer lanterns hanging over its deck than there were on the other ships about the port. It was too dark to spot anyone in its upper crow's nest.

Magiere's hand grabbed the rail next to Leesil's. He reached down to help pull her up and over, but he left the rope dangling by its hook. It could serve in a hasty retreat if necessary and was less noticeable than if coiled on the deck.

A door waited three strides away along the aftcastle's front wall. Looking toward the nearest mast, he spotted the first of three broad hatches along the deck's center. Those probably dropped directly into the hold, or an upper one if the ship's belly was multileveled.

If only he and Magiere could reach the first hatch unseen.

"Now?" Magiere whispered.

He was pondering their next move when a stocky man with a cudgel tucked in his wide belt came around the mast. The man stopped at the sight of them. Perhaps this ship had never been boarded before, for he just stared.

The last thing Leesil wanted was a fight attracting other sentries.

The man's shock passed—and Leesil charged.

As the crewman grabbed the head of the cudgel to pull it, Leesil ducked into a slide across the deck. His right foot extended first, with his booted toe outward. As that foot passed the man's right boot, the man faltered with his cudgel half-drawn. Perhaps he was caught between shouting, pulling the weapon, or even trying to hop aside.

Leesil twisted to the right on the deck. As he flopped over, his extended foot hooked the back of the man's right boot. Leesil flattened his hands to the deck and pushed up as his left foot shot upward.

His left heel slammed in under the stocky man's chin.

The maneuver was among a few that his mother had taught him in his youth, though he hadn't learned a name for it until later. She, with her long legs, could use it to even greater effect as an anmaglâhk. Sgäile had once called it "the cat in the grass."

The stocky guard never even grunted. The worst of the noise was the guard's body toppling on the deck. That couldn't be helped, and Leesil rolled into a crouch and listened carefully as he looked about.

All he heard was Magiere scurrying in low behind him. He saw no one else, even up in the rigging. Magiere helped him shove the unconscious guard in against the first cargo hatch's frame sidewall.

The hatch wasn't that large. In place of netting or a grate, it was covered with a lashed-down canvas. Leesil undid one corner to peek in, and Magiere tapped him on the shoulder.

She pointed around the hatch's side, and there was a rolled-up rope ladder.

Dänvârfij stood beside Én'nish at the rail and stared toward the great ship at the end of the next pier.

"What do you mean, someone with white-blond hair climbed that hull?"

"Yes," Én'nish answered sharply, "and when they were under the lanterns, I knew the second one by the sword on its . . . *her* back. Léshil and his woman are aboard that ship, unguarded by the traitor!"

"There," Rhysís said, pointing.

A loose skiff floated at the waterline of the *Bell Tower*, and Dänvârfij was at a loss. Though she believed what Én'nish claimed, she did not understand it.

Léshil and Magiere had boarded another vessel in secret. Had they arranged other passage in trying to flee the port unseen? Were they after something on that other ship? The latter seemed unlikely, and either way, why had Brot'ân'duivé let them go alone? Or had he?

It left only one tentative conclusion.

"They know we are here," Dänvârfij whispered.

Worse, there was only one way they could have found out: Brot'ân'duivé must have spotted her when she had tried to follow him. But why was the traitor not with Léshil and Magiere? Had they tried to leave the greimasg'äh behind? If so, why abandon the majay-hì as well?

"If they are not fleeing by arrangement," Eywodan posed, "then they are at risk of discovery. If they are killed before we can extract the information they have, then we fail in our purpose."

Dänvârfij had contemplated this as well. Even if Léshil and Magiere were only captured, they could be locked away out of easy reach. That they had pulled their skiff around in plain sight of the *Cloud Queen* suggested one useful thing.

They did not yet know their own vessel had been taken.

"Rhysís, get over into that ship's crow's nest," she commanded. "Cover us from above as we board it. Eywodan, remain here and lock up all of the crew. We need somewhere close to bring captives and quickly take them out of sight." Glancing at Tavithê, she added, "Bring your bow, remain out of any conflict, and wound either of our quarry for easier capture."

The team broke apart as Rhysís rushed to climb the *Cloud Queen*'s main mast and Eywodan began herding the few crewmen below deck.

Dänvârfij led the way as Én'nish and Tavithê followed her over the side, into the water, and then into their own waiting skiff. Once aboard the skiff, they pushed off with their hands and drifted to the starboard side of the *Bell Tower*.

Boarding was easier for the rope that had been left dangling, but Dänvârfij did not climb over the rail when she reached the top. She hung there against the hull and out of sight from its deck, and looked back to the *Cloud Queen*.

It was too dark to see Rhysís go up into its rigging, but she heard the whir of a rope followed shortly by a quick clatter overhead. Rhysís had already gained the heights and had cast a line between the two ships. Before the lookout in the crow's nest of the *Bell Tower* even saw him, the man would be silenced with an arrow.

Dänvârfij rolled over the rail into a crouch and waited for Én'nish and Tavithê to follow.

Magiere would do anything Leesil asked of her, but as she climbed down the rope ladder into the ship's hold, she wondered about the wisdom of what he did tonight.

He knew what it was to be a slave in the Warlands—to be used as a weapon. Once he'd escaped that life, he'd drunk himself to sleep for so many years, even after they'd first met. Dreams of his victims could be smothered only by strong wine or worse.

Magiere knew something of servitude from her own youth as a peasant caught between the feuding would-be grand princes of Droevinka, her homeland. She understood the guilt that now drove her husband, determined to carry this through. Foolhardy or not, she loved him for this as well, but they had their own task to complete.

The weight of that grew each time they thought they had finished after too many years far from home. And now here they were, risking their lives to free indentured servants off a ship. Much as she would have done the same at some other time and place . . .

Magiere kept silent as her right foot stepped down and found the hold's floor.

There were no lamps, and barely any light from the deck filtered through the corner of the peeled-back hatch cover above. She saw the barest movements, like black shadows deeper than the dark, in the hold. She pulled her falchion over her shoulder, and then she clapped her other hand over her nose and mouth.

The place reeked like a fetid pig barn, with the stench of urine, filthy and sweating bodies, and rotten swill or food. All of her senses began to sharpen, and she swallowed hard.

A whimper, like crying, rose from somewhere in the hold and then choked off in a fearful draw of breath.

"Who's there?" a frightened voice whispered.

The voice sounded young to Magiere, belonging to someone no more than a child.

"We hadn't done nothin'," the tiny voice whispered. "We been quiet . . . so quiet . . . please."

Magiere felt tears start rolling down her face as her irises expanded. The scant light slipping through the opened canvas above showed *them* to her eyes.

Dozens and dozens of bone-thin people, young and old, in threadbare clothing, huddled against the walls and between the barrels and crates. Tight and thick ropes were knotted about their arms and ankles. Four, five, or more were bound together to iron rings bolted into the hull walls or floor. There was no way of knowing how long some of them had been held down here.

Magiere's gaze fell upon one face with skin so taut that the man's cheekbones and jaw looked sharp.

He wrapped his arms around a woman and tried to pull her farther back between a stack of lashed-down casks and the hull wall. When his gaze dropped down, Magiere remembered the falchion gripped in her hand. She pulled it behind herself and hid the heavy blade with her leg as she looked at all of them trapped here in the darkness . . . which slowly grew brighter in her sight.

Her jaws began to ache under a fury-fed hunger. She wanted to kill someone for what had been done here.

A hand latched down hard on her shoulder and jerked her around.

"You keep yourself whole!" Leesil whispered. "If we have to kill, we do it cold and quick . . . my way! You understand?"

Magiere looked into his amber eyes. He was right. The last thing he needed now was her losing control.

"Yes," she got out in a stuttering breath.

Leesil released her and looked about the hold.

"We not guards," he whispered loudly, struggling with his Numanese. "Any here know Paolo?"

Magiere was unable to help him for a moment, and he went on as best he could.

Someone shifted in the hold's dark rear. "Yes," a young boy's voice answered. "Is he all right? He didn't come back after they took him up."

"He with us and safe," Leesil answered. "He sent us to you. Any here from Drist?"

No one answered. The man with the woman between the casks and hull eyed Magiere with open fear, as if she and Leesil weren't to be trusted. Leesil didn't appear to notice and had already cast about for anything that might be used as a weapon.

"It is . . . all right," Magiere struggled to say, hoping no one saw her eyes in the dark. "We came . . . to get you out."

"Get us out?"

This voice was stronger. She half turned to see a tall man standing bound to the hull's right wall. His wrists and ankles were tied separately, and his face and dull gray eyes were calm. Leesil turned from scavenging, holding a flat-bladed shovel pulled from a crate filled with tools.

"Yes," he said. "We free you . . . to leave."

The gray-eyed man shook his head. "I will not."

Magiere's shock made her anger grow.

"The village chieftain agreed to forgive my debt if I worked for seven years," the man went on. "If I break my word—that contract—my wife and children will be homeless."

An unbound young woman stood up. "The captain paid my father's tax upon our farm. If I run, my father will be guilty of theft."

Leesil looked about, as if searching for anyone to deny what the man and woman had said, but no one spoke up. "This . . . wrong!" he insisted harshly. "No one . . . own you!"

"I signed myself over," a young man added. "I'll not be branded for escape if we get caught. I could end up working more years, if not worse."

There were more who began murmuring—not all, but most. Magiere watched in frustration as Leesil's eyes filled with pain. Of all that might go wrong, this wasn't something either of them could have imagined.

"I'll come."

Magiere's head snapped around as Leesil spun toward the voice.

A filthy man with no shirt and dark hair down to his shoulders rose from the floor. His eyes were so dark that their irises could have been black. His shoulders were wide, and he was well muscled all over, unlike the others, who were mostly withered.

"They took me out of a prison in Sorano," he said, "charged and locked up for something I didn't do. I owe no one anything." He pointed at a small boy huddled behind him. "But he comes, too. He was brought in with his mother, and she died a half moon ago. I won't leave him."

Magiere saw panic drain from Leesil's face at those words. This was what he'd come for. She stepped in before he even moved, and hacked straight through the thick rope binding the man's ankles to the floor.

"Any other?" Leesil called a bit too loudly.

Several more stood up or reached out.

Leesil drew a winged punching blade and hurried among them as Magiere rushed the other way through the dark hold. In the end a dozen or more gathered around Leesil at the ladder. The shirtless man used the shovel Leesil had dropped to pry open several crates before stopping at the third one.

"Here," he whispered.

Leesil went to the crate and began lifting out more tools to hand to the others as weapons.

Magiere stopped short of joining him and looked to the shriveled man hiding the woman behind the casks. The man lowered his eyes and curled away from her. She wanted to drag them out of this place whether they wanted to come or not.

"Dirken, you're going to bring trouble down on us."

Magiere turned toward the tall man lashed to the hull wall; his eyes were looking upward toward the hatch's opening. The shirtless one, now holding a pickax, took a step toward him.

"Shut your mouth! You call out to the guards, and those'll be your last words."

Leesil grabbed the shirtless man and pulled him back.

"You lead . . . take fighters," Leesil ordered him, and then gestured to the women and children in their small group. "They stay middle. Magiere and I . . . rear, fight guards who follow."

Dirken nodded, gripping his pickax.

"But you must run," Magiere got out. "We cannot . . . protect you all, so run to the city guards."

A half-starved woman blinked at her. "City guards? In Drist? There ain't no such thing here, and anyway, holding us here ain't no crime. The captain's got papers on all of us."

Dirken nodded, turning his dark eyes on Magiere. "I've been here before. There's no law in Drist. This ship was taking us all up to the Northlander coast to work in some shipyard. We're indentured workers, not slaves, so it's legal. Even if there was a constabulary, they'd turn us back over to the captain."

Leesil went quiet at this, and Magiere knew his desperation was growing again. Something else Dirken said bothered her enough to clear her mind a little more.

The Northlanders that she'd met used only longboats. Why bring so many to build longboats? It didn't make sense. Unless these slaves were to build something else, something that required a good deal more labor, in a true shipyard?

Leesil appeared to waver, looked to her, and switched to Belaskian. "I'm not sure about this now. I won't break them out just to get them killed or imprisoned again. Where can we send them?"

Magiere didn't know, but she wasn't leaving anyone who wanted out. Quickly she counted those willing to try to escape.

"We only have fourteen," she answered, "and Wynn said our hotel is safe."

"For anyone who can pay," Leesil answered bitterly, and then he grew too quiet again.

Magiere knew he was scheming and, desperate as he was, that could be trouble.

"What about the *Cloud Queen*?" he said. "Bassett may be hard, but he's no slaver. Maybe he'd offer them a short refuge, hide them in his hold until the next port."

This was possible, but Magiere still felt trapped in not having a better answer. The scant light above, shining down upon Leesil, suddenly grew slightly brighter.

Magiere barely looked up when . . .

"Down!" Leesil shouted.

She caught a glimpse of a glint before he shoved several prisoners aside. A thrum in the air caught in her ears, and then a shriek of pain pulled her eyes. An arrow stuck out from the leg of a half-starved woman, who crumpled right beside her.

"Hide!" Magiere called, backing away from the ladder. Any who weren't chained or tied scattered as she stepped in front of the wounded woman.

Leesil was nowhere to be seen.

Falchion in hand, Magiere crouched, reached back for the woman, and then heard someone else behind her drag the woman off. Her hand slipped up to the small of her back, and she pulled out the white metal dagger.

Unless she stayed near the ladder, there wouldn't be enough room to use her sword, but she could be easily picked off from above. She sidestepped, inching around the open crate of tools, and crouched lower.

At another thrum, she shifted left.

An arrow suddenly quivered in the edge of the crate's opened top. She looked up, her sight widening.

The hatch's cover had been fully pulled back, and the silhouette of a form knelt up there. It took less than a blink for Magiere to make out its cowl and a matching wrap over the face of the archer.

That anmaglâhk drew back another nocked arrow.

Magiere couldn't scale the ladder quickly enough. She and Leesil were trapped and pinned down—and where was he? She couldn't turn her eyes away to look for him. All she could do was wait for the bowstring's thrum and charge the ladder whether she was hit or not.

The light above on deck suddenly dimmed . . . as if something passed between the archer and a lantern.

The anmaglâhk hesitated. Perhaps his head turned, though she couldn't be certain, as the shadows within the man's cowl deepened in that instant.

A darker shadow enveloped the anmaglâhk's head.

She made out an arm that wrapped around his neck.

The anmaglâhk's neck and head slammed against the hatch's edge, and a muffled crack echoed in the hold, but the shadow that had appeared above him continued to drop.

Both forms passed through the open hatch and fell through the dark air. Magiere watched in silence as one form landed lightly in a crouch like a man of immense height. Magiere saw amber eyes inside his hood . . . and that one was looking out at her through bars of scars on his face.

Then a body slammed upon the hold's floor. The archer lay still, with his head twisted at an unnatural angle.

"One," was all that Brot'an whispered as he rose before Magiere.

Prisoners began screaming and scattering amid the sound of strained chains and ropes.

"On deck, now!" Brot'an ordered. "Chap is outnumbered."

Magiere heard snarling above, and Leesil had reappeared, already scrambling up the ladder. She rushed after him with no time to ponder Brot'an's sudden appearance.

Dänvârfij saw victory within reach for but a moment.

Her team had seized the *Bell Tower* and eliminated any crew on the deck. They prepared to slip into hiding to search for the quarry, and Tavithê had pulled back a partially opened canvas atop a cargo hatch.

He had looked to her and nodded, and she had known they had their quarry—and so quickly. She had nodded back, and he aimed and fired, intending to wound for easier capture.

Shouts rose out of the hold as he drew another arrow.

It should have ended there, with either Léshil or Magiere incapacitated and the other unable to save either of them.

An enraged snarl rose somewhere behind Dänvârfij. Before she could turn, Én'nish cried out. Savage snaps, scraping claws, and shattering wood rolled across the deck just before . . .

A shadow fell through the light of a lantern dangling beyond Tavithê.

Dänvârfij never finished her turn.

Tavithê was slammed headfirst against the hatch's edge. She lunged for him and then heard his neck snap. He fell from sight beneath the form of an immense shadow, and both vanished into the hold.

Dänvârfij's heart seemed to stop. She wanted to scream Tavithê's name, but she did not dare do something so pointless.

The traitor was among them again.

True anger, so rarely felt, surged inside her. She whirled to run toward Én'nish's shouts but gained only three strides before she heard a door slam open.

Two humans with cudgels and sabers rushed out of the aftcastle's left doorway. One instantly grunted and fell, and momentum slid him across the deck with an arrow protruding from his back.

Dänvârfij did not glance up toward Rhysís in the crow's nest. She set herself for the one human coming at her. More shouts carried across the deck.

"We've been boarded!"

A white-blond head of hair popped out of the hold's hatch.

Léshil rolled out into the open with his monster of a mate right behind him.

Chap rammed Én'nish again and sent her bouncing sideways off a water barrel. He was on her before she could right herself.

Throwing his bulk atop her, he clawed her arms and tried to pin at least one as he snapped for her throat. Instead he had to clamp his jaws on her wrist when she tried to slash a blade at his face.

Chap ground his teeth through forest gray wool until Én'nish let out a savage scream, and then a sharp pain burned across his right shoulder, and his hold faltered. His snarl turned into a yelp when he twisted away and stumbled off as she tore her wrist from his jaws. A stiletto came at him again in her other hand.

Chap had to duck, and Én'nish rolled away to her feet and ran off. He lunged after her but faltered as the open deck filled his view.

Dänvârfij kicked a crewman, who staggered off to her right and nearly fell. The man then stiffened, arching, and toppled forward with an arrow through the back of his neck. Chap could not tell from where that arrow had come, and Dänvârfij bolted straight at Magiere.

"Do not fire at the quarry!" she shouted out in Elvish.

Before Chap could blink, Dänvârfij and Magiere went at each other . . . and Én'nish closed on Leesil in a maddened rush.

Where was Brot'an? This was all his fault. If they survived this, Chap would make certain Brot'an never had such a chance again.

As if summoned, the old assassin appeared to leap from the uncovered hatch. Three crewmen came running out of the aftcastle's far door, though they faltered at what they saw. They would have no idea who was with whom or that more than one faction had boarded their vessel.

"We're under attack!" one of them shouted.

They would simply kill anyone viewed as an intruder.

Én'nish and Leesil slammed together, falling to the deck in a flurry of blades.

If either Magiere or Leesil was taken, one hostage was all these anmaglâhk would need to control the other.

Chap stalled too long in choosing either Magiere or Leesil to aid first. Heavy footfalls came at him from behind. He lunged aside, and the head of an iron mace cracked the deck boards.

Én'nish saw no one but Léshil . . . the one who had killed her beloved, Grôyt'ashia.

She barely heard the guttural shrieks of rage from Léshil's monster of a mate, or the click and screech of Dänvârfij's blades off the heavy falchion. She had barely heard Dänvârfij call to Rhysís not to fire.

Én'nish's orders were to take Léshil alive. Once, the thought of his being tortured had held her to obedience. The hope of him watching his mate die would have even been enough.

She rushed at him and drove a stiletto straight for his throat.

Léshil twisted as her blade point nearly touched his flesh. The stiletto's tip caught and tore a hunk from his tunic's collar, and suddenly he was gone.

Én'nish leaped, tucking her legs up in midair.

Léshil attempted to lash his leg across her shins, but his foot passed below her raised ones. Then he was up again, spinning away across the deck and pulling one of his winged blades as her feet touched down.

Magiere tried to hold on to reason as she fended off a double slash of white stilettos with her falchion's tilted blade. She couldn't let the hunger overwhelm her; she had to stay sane. None of them could falter here and now if any of them were to escape alive. And it wasn't her own life that she feared for.

She could kill this woman, this anmaglâhk, but if she lost all awareness of Leesil, or Chap, or what she had to do to back them up, someone might die.

As the woman's double slash passed off her sword, Magiere dropped to one knee and swung with her white metal dagger.

The hair-thin black line down the blade's spine lit up with orange-red heat. Humid air sizzled in its passing. The blade missed her opponent's right thigh . . . and grazed the left.

Forest gray wool split, smoke rose from the gap, and Magiere heard a sharp suck of breath. She quickly pulled the falchion's blade up and across. Two more screeches rose on the steel under the flash of white stiletto blades.

Magiere slashed again with the dagger. Her opponent twisted out of the way this time, and she straightened up, looking into the woman's amber eyes. They were somehow familiar, though she couldn't place them above the wrap across the woman's face.

A trace of smoke from the woman's wound blew away in the breeze, and her eyes betrayed no pain. She came again so fast that Magiere barely blocked.

Fear, not anger, let hunger begin to escape.

Magiere's jaws ached under the change in her teeth. Everything in the world but her own body suddenly slowed. She dodged and chopped down with the falchion at the anmaglâhk's shoulder.

The woman leaned under the sword's path and pulled her left wrist out of the way last.

A glint of white passed before Magiere's face.

She barely saw her opponent's right hand finish its swing as a burning sting rose along a line from her left temple to the center of her forehead.

Blood ran down into Magiere's left eye and half blinded her.

Leesil knew exactly whom he fought. Above the wrap that hid the rest of her face, her slanted eyes were sick with fury. He knew the depth of her pained hatred for him and knew the reason for it, but he felt no pity for her anymore.

Én'nish and her kind had come at him and Magiere too many times. It would end right here.

He held on to control and grew coldly calm, as in his youth. He could taste those nights that had haunted him for so many years after. Carrying a thin blade between his teeth or a garrote wire coiled between his gloved fingers, he would crouch in the dark or scale a wall to slip into a bedchamber.

Én'nish tried to get inside his guard, to strike for his throat, his heart, his abdomen, and finally the inside of his thigh to pierce an artery. He kept her going with feints of his own but had no chance to pull his second blade.

When her speed waned, when the fury used her up . . . he feinted straight at her this time, as if to aim a kick and expose his left side.

She took the bait and lunged.

Leesil spun in his false kick and turned his back to her. The winged blade he held in his right hand swept around, and he heard his blade clink against one of her stilettos.

She had tried for his heart again, as he knew she would: it was the only kill point of which she could be certain in a fast attack from behind.

He dropped to one knee as he came around with Én'nish's blade still grating on his own, and he punched his free hand under as he swept her blade upward on his. His fist cracked against her small knee, and she began to buckle as he slashed down.

The point of his winged blade tore open her tunic, down her abdomen, and off her right hip.

She staggered back. Shock rather than pain washed the malice from her eyes.

Leesil felt nothing as he pushed off, rising to finish her.

An arrow hit the deck right in front of his foot, and he jumped back, looking up.

Never looking at the man, Brot'ân'duivé rammed two straightened fingers into the right eye of a crewman. As his target fell, dropping both cudgel and sword amid a scream, he unfocused his sight and took in the whole deck at once.

He had expected Dänvârfij to send two, perhaps three, to take either Léshil or Magiere. Only one need be seized to subdue the other. He had taken out one anmaglâhk, but two were left: Dänvârfij was obviously one and Én'nish the other.

Brot'ân'duivé had planned to take those two and then kill the others one by one when they came to investigate. Now the crew had been alerted, and two more men rushed out of one aftcastle door.

He saw Dänvârfij's blade slash Magiere's forehead.

Léshil split the front of Én'nish's tunic and stepped after her as she retreated . . . and an arrow sprouted from the deck at his feet.

Brot'ân'duivé ducked under one crewman's cutlass as he kicked out the knee of another. He rammed an elbow into the back of the first one's neck and peered upward into the rigging.

Four, not three, anmaglâhk had boarded this ship. There was an archer above.

Everything had come apart for both sides. In these circumstances, if he were the one coming after Léshil and Magiere, at this point he would try for a kill instead of a capture—at least of one of them.

Brot'ân'duivé crushed the throat of the second crewman wavering on an injured knee, rushed for the base of the main mast, and climbed fast up into the dark.

*   *   *

Dänvârfij saw blood run down Magiere's forehead and into her eye. She had faced the monster before in the Everfen, but the sight of Magiere still unnerved her. She was fighting something unnatural.

Magiere's one clear eye suddenly flooded black, as if the iris had swallowed all of the white. Her face twisted up and her mouth gaped, exposing teeth like a beast's.

Dänvârfij fought for calm, for focus. She needed another crippling blow to put this *thing* down. Her left thigh burned from the dagger of white metal no human should possess. And she now wondered about the wisdom of having ordered Rhysís not to fire.

He might have ended this already, but from his distance above, he might kill Léshil or Magiere. That could not be risked; then again, both Léshil and the monster were within reach. Only one need be left alive, and this creature before her was insane.

Madness spawned mistakes.

Dänvârfij tensed as Magiere roared from pain. Dänvârfij feinted with her right blade toward Magiere's blinded side. Trying to see with her clear eye, Magiere twisted her head and raised the dagger to defend.

Dänvârfij spun and kicked Magiere's cut temple.

Magiere's head barely snapped aside. Though she lost her grip on the dagger, that same hand came slashing back with hooked fingers. In the same instant, Dänvârfij glimpsed a shadow racing up the main mast. Then she felt the impact on her neck.

Fingers—nails as hard as claws—raked her skin but failed to dig into her throat.

A shout sounded from high above in Elvish.

"Abandon!" Rhysís cried out.

Brot'ân'duivé closed on the crow's nest as he heard the shout. The one up here must have spotted him somehow. He gripped the lookout's edge and pulled himself up, but all he saw was an anmaglâhk sliding away along a rope by a short bow's haft gripped in both hands. Brot'ân'duivé grabbed for the rope's anchored end to wrench it and throw his quarry off balance.

The rope went limp in his grip.

He watched half its length fall, severed somewhere out there in midair. A splash came between the ships and piers, and his own half of the rope fell to dangle.

Brot'ân'duivé looked where that rope had led a moment before. Across the water at the next pier was the *Cloud Queen*. Wrapping the corner of his cloak around the rope, he vaulted the crow's nest wall as he slid quickly toward the deck of the *Bell Tower* along the rope's length.

Leesil heard one word shouted in Elvish.

He barely took a quick glance to see where the arrow had come from, and then he fixed on Én'nish again. He couldn't risk looking for Magiere or Chap. If he did, Én'nish might not come after him but instead go after whomever he couldn't save.

The look of shock in her eyes at that shout from above almost stunned Leesil.

There was such a loss of hope amid her fury.

Before he could go at Én'nish again, a slender forest gray form rushed in from the corner of his sight. That other one snatched Én'nish by the back of her cowl and dragged her in a race for the ship's starboard rail.

Leesil almost went after them . . . until Magiere, with blood covering half her twisted face, charged after the pair. He grabbed the back of her shirt, and his feet slid as she tried to rush on. Trying to make her stop, he pulled hard and threw himself onto her.

Then he spotted Chap, penned in near the rail by a large crewman with a mace.

A small number of prisoners from below must have come up the rope ladder, because Dirken and two other raggedly dressed men were on deck and trying to clear a path for the others through the remaining crew.

"Help wolf now!" Leesil shouted at them.

That was all he could do as he dropped his winged blade and wrapped his other arm over Magiere's shoulder to pull her back. He heard splashes in the water below.

The pair of anmaglâhk had jumped overboard.

Chap dodged a falling mace and looked for an opening to lunge in and rip out his attacker's knee.

A dull clang rose as a shovel blade rebounded off the back of the crewman's head.

The man's eyes and mouth went slack, and Chap quickly leaped aside before the crewman fell on top of him. Once clear, he looked up into the face of a shirtless, thickly muscled man watching him warily.

Chap spotted Leesil struggling with Magiere and rushed away down the deck.

Leesil looked wildly around while still trying to control Magiere. The ship's boarding ramp was up. Most of the crewmen who had appeared were down, and the freed slaves outnumbered the rest. Then two more armed sailors came out of the aftcastle's far door.

"Valhachkasej'â!" Leesil cursed.

A large form dropped from the aftcastle.

Never slowing, Brot'an flattened both crewmen as he landed, and rushed toward the port side.

"Off—now!" he shouted, as at a full run he snatched up Leesil's abandoned blade.

Leesil reversed his effort and wrenched Magiere on her own force to the rail. He looked over the top of it and down it at the pier. It was a long jump but straight down. Magiere twisted suddenly, breaking his hold. All he could do was stun her with a slap across her cheek. She whirled on him; half her face was coated in blood, but her one clear eye showed white around an enlarged black pupil.

"Over!" he shouted at her. "Onto the pier!"

Magiere froze as if confused.

From out of nowhere, Chap hit Magiere in a leap with his whole bulk. Both went over the rail. Leesil shook off his surprise and snatched up Magiere's dagger.

"Dirken!" he shouted in Numanese. "Your people . . . jump! To pier!"

Leesil vaulted the rail as Brot'ân'duivé cleared it beside him.

The world went black as Magiere hit the dock and air rushed out of her under Chap's crushing weight. When her sight returned, Chap was gone, and someone grabbed her arm and shouted at her, "Get up!"

She heard others landing roughly on the dock as she was hauled up. Her scalp and forehead burned as if she'd been cut, and through one eye only, she saw Chap take off down the dock as ragged people rushed by, following his path.

A vaguely familiar shirtless man carried a boy in his arms.

"Run!" Leesil ordered, shoving her. "Down the pier and up the next."

She didn't question him and started to race after Chap. Too little of what had occurred was clear in her head. The last thing she remembered was the pass of a white stiletto . . . and then pain . . . blood . . . hunger had followed. She couldn't even look at Leesil as they ran.

She had failed him, left him, in losing herself again.

They ran onto the waterfront, hurried to the second pier, and broke into a full run again. But as they approached the end of the second pier, everyone began to slow. Through her one clear eye, Magiere took in the sight of the *Cloud Queen*.

The ramp was down, and it shouldn't be at night. As Leesil halted beside her, she saw no sentries up on deck.

The ship looked deserted.

CHAPTER TWENTY-FIVE

After leaping over the side, Dänvârfij hit the water. Impact broke her hold on Én'nish as seawater closed over her head. She kicked to the surface and looked about in the dark. Panic came briefly until she saw Rhysís swimming toward her with Én'nish in tow.

Dänvârfij glanced up at the ship's rail. She saw no crewmen, though she heard running feet on the dock beyond the *Bell Tower*.

"Get under the pier," Rhysís whispered, and he went off, swimming with one arm and dragging Én'nish's limp form by her collar.

Dänvârfij followed. There was nothing else she could do. The side of her neck burned, and more so the wound on her thigh, even with the water's chill. The latter injury might be deeper than she had first thought. Even pulling Én'nish, Rhysís outdistanced her. He stopped, treading water, to look back.

"Can you make it?" he asked.

"Go," she urged.

He kicked onward, swimming around the ship's prow and in between the dock pilings. Exhausted and wounded, Dänvârfij followed him. It seemed far too long before they reached the shoreline and the walkway below the waterfront.

Rhysís pulled Én'nish out of the water as Dänvârfij barely got herself onto the floating walkway. Breathing heavily, they both knelt beside the young one.

Én'nish opened her eyes slightly and looked up at them. Rhysís pulled back one side of her bloodstained, split tunic. Dänvârfij had no idea how bad the wound might be, but regardless, the night's failure turned her thoughts down darker paths.

Tavithê was gone, taken by the traitor and left lying in a ship's hold. Two more of them had been wounded, and though she had done the same to Magiere, their quarry had escaped again . . . because of the traitor.

Dänvârfij grabbed Rhysís's wrist. "Brot'ân'duivé will go for the *Cloud Queen*. Eywodan is alone there. Go now, and I will watch over Én'nish."

"No," Rhysís said and continued attending Én'nish's wound.

His abrupt disobedience struck Dänvârfij mute at first. "Rhysís—"

"No!" he nearly snarled, looking her in the eyes. "Én'nish is down, and you can barely walk. Do you think I will leave either of you? And what if the traitor does not go for the ship but comes after us? I would, in his place."

Dänvârfij stared at him as he turned his attention back to Én'nish. She could not force him under the circumstances, and in truth, he could be right.

"If any of us can face the greimasg'äh alone," Rhysís added, "it is Eywodan. They were old friends once, and they know each other's ways." He glanced at her thigh. "Get something to tie around that leg."

Dänvârfij was at a loss as to what to argue anymore. She tore a strip from her soaked cloak and began wrapping it around her wound.

Magiere was numb as she leaned against Leesil and looked up at the *Cloud Queen*, deserted from what she could see. She tried with the back of her hand to wipe away the blood in her left eye. She barely remembered what had happened on the other ship.

Chap stood at the boarding ramp's base. A dark stain matted the fur on his right shoulder. It looked worse than what she suffered; a scalp wound always bled too freely at first.

Brot'an, as well as Dirken and some of the others wishing to escape, had collected around her and Leesil. Most appeared uninjured other than minor cuts and bruises. They were lucky in getting off the ship before too many of the crew had been roused. And she wondered whether the crew would be coming soon, searching for their lost "cargo."

She touched her forehead and tested with her fingertips to see whether the wound had stopped bleeding. Leesil let go of her and reached under his velvet tunic to tear off a piece of the shirt beneath it.

"Press that on the wound," he said, and she did so as he looked to the ship. "Where is everyone?"

Brot'an stepped past both of them. "The ship appears deserted because it was taken by those who came after us. I saw a line in the rigging between the two vessels. Some, at least one of them, may still be aboard the *Cloud Queen* . . . as I counted only four aboard the other ship."

A more frightening thought struck Magiere. "Where's Wayfarer?"

"Safe," Brot'an answered. "I arranged for her and the boy to be hidden away under watch."

Magiere wasn't certain what that meant. But if Brot'an and Chap hadn't come, she and Leesil could have been taken or killed. Still, it angered her that the old assassin had left Wayfarer with strangers. What had motivated him to come in the first place?

Magiere peered at Chap. How Brot'an had gotten the dog aboard the slave ship would wait until later.

"Chap, you lead," Leesil said, and then switched to Numanese. "Brot'an, Dirken . . . follow. All other come last."

As the dog, with Brot'an and Dirken behind, stalked up the ramp, Leesil tried to lift Magiere's arm over his shoulders, but she held him off. She could fight if need be—if he let her.

Perhaps he was too distracted to argue, for he turned silently up the ramp, and Magiere followed him.

When they reached the deck, Chap, Dirken, and Brot'an had spread out. Chap returned first and huffed twice for no, which meant he'd found nothing. Brot'an and Dirken returned with the same result. Leesil motioned the rest of the freed slaves toward the bow, and they did as he directed.

"Stay—hide," he told them, and turned to Magiere and switched to Belaskian. "Stay here and guard them, no matter what you hear."

That jolted her, and when she opened her mouth, he shook his head.

"I don't want to bring them below until we know what's happened here," he whispered.

That wasn't the only reason, although maybe he was right.

"Keep Chap with you," Magiere told him. "He and Brot'an might sense anything wrong more quickly than anyone else."

Leesil nodded, handed over her white metal dagger, and turned away. Chap was already waiting at one aftcastle door. Magiere stood pressing the piece of shredded shirt cloth against her scalp as Leesil motioned Brot'an toward the other door. Dirken followed that way as well.

With reluctance, Magiere backed toward the huddle of freed slaves. Leesil and the others were gone, leaving her dizzy, bloodied, and guilt ridden on deck.

By Brot'ân'duivé's count, only one anmaglâhk remained here, if Fréthfâre was secreted elsewhere in the port. He had counted four on the *Bell Tower*. He killed Tavithê and flushed another from the crow's nest. The two who'd been wounded on deck were both women, so he knew who they were.

The one here had to be either Rhysís or Eywodan.

The human called Dirken followed at his heels as they headed down the stairs beneath the aftcastle. Brot'ân'duivé saw Léshil and Chap step into the passage's far end, and each pair turned its separate way into the ship's depths. When Brot'ân'duivé reached the hold and continued into its darkness, Dirken followed him.

At a click of tin, light glowed in the space, and Brot'ân'duivé glanced back to see that Dirken had grabbed a lantern off the deck along his way.

"You are Lhoin'na?" Dirken asked.

"No, I am . . . something else."

"Those others, on the *Bell Tower*, looked like you . . . darker than a Lhoin'na."

Dirken said no more as Brot'ân'duivé walked into the ship's hold and stopped midway to close his eyes. He listened to every sound and tested every scent in the stale and musty air. Then he pointed.

"That way."

They exited through the hold's far door and made their way down a short passage Brot'ân'duivé had not visited before. This was the lowest deck—down below the passenger's quarters. At the passage's end, a thick door was barred from the outside. Iron braces had long ago been installed on both sides; the door had been designed to lock something or someone in if necessary.

Brot'ân'duivé did not wonder why.

He heard movement beyond the door. Someone—more than one—was locked in there now. He looked sidelong at Dirken.

"Be ready to step past me. It would be best for those inside to see a human face first."

Dirken frowned as he nodded.

Brot'ân'duivé hefted the bar from its brackets. He ratcheted the lever handle and stepped aside as he pulled the door outward. Sounds of rapid movements, those of bodies rustling and pushing past each other, came immediately from inside.

"Settle down!" Dirken barked. "We're here to get you out."

Brot'ân'duivé stepped around behind Dirken but held back. Several men in the room gasped or cursed.

"It's one of them!" a man called out.

"Don't be a fool!" Dirken shouted over the rest as he held up the lantern. "Or do you think just one would open the door for all of you?"

Some of the crew did not appear to listen. The panic and arguing grew louder. Then a young man stepped forward, squinting; there was a bad bruise on his forehead, and his right eye was swollen shut. It was Hatchinstall, the captain's first mate. Through the dim light, he peered at Brot'ân'duivé's face.

"It's one of our passengers!" he called back to the others.

As Brot'ân'duivé had feared, at first the frightened sailors had seen only a tall an'Cróan in the doorway. More squinted at him, perhaps noted his scars, and began to quiet.

"What happened?" Brot'ân'duivé asked.

The young mate's good eye was glazed. "A group, looking like you, boarded and killed half the men. We couldn't stop them. . . . Nothing we tried did any good."

"Where's your captain?"

Hatchinstall shook his head. "Don't know. They dragged me down here but . . . not him. Maybe they locked him in his quarters."

Brot'ân'duivé took a slow breath. That was where Léshil would go first.

"Get them up on deck," he told Dirken and then turned down the passage at a run.

A hostage kept separate in upper quarters accessible to the deck would be guarded.

Leesil hadn't expected to find anyone in the passengers' cabins. He and his companions *were* this ship's passengers. But as he and Chap turned the other way from where Brot'an had headed, the notion of where to look first came to mind.

Any crew left alive for future needs would be locked away below. Less than a handful would be needed to manage the vessel. But one, most of all, would know the routes and ports along this coast.

Silence in the first level below deck ate at Leesil's nerves.

Chap was the first to creep in on the door to the captain's quarters. Leesil waited as Chap sniffed the space below the door, and the dog lifted his head back up.

—*Two—inside—* . . . —*One—elf—*

Leesil wondered how Chap could know that by smell, though the dog probably could tell by strength of scent whether anyone was in there. Then again, if even one was an'Cróan . . . well, one of *them* wouldn't be here unless someone else was present.

Leesil reached back and under his velvet tunic for his box of lock picks.

—*No—a blade—*

Leesil blinked—Chap couldn't possibly know the door was unlocked.

—Why—lock?— . . . *—A blade—now—*

Leesil reached for his right winged blade.

—No— . . . *—Anmaglâhk—blade—*

Leesil hesitated. In Calm Seatt, Brot'an had given him anmaglâhk weapons—a stiletto and a curved bone knife—when they'd gone to get Wynn out of her own guild's keep. He hated those weapons and had disposed of his own long ago. For some reason, he'd kept the ones Brot'an had given him.

The stiletto was hidden in a sheath in his boot.

Leesil had to trust his old friend's greater instincts. He drew the stiletto and palmed the hilt, with the blade flattened behind his wrist and forearm. Exhaling slowly, he reached quietly for the door lever and turned it with a light push.

The door opened, and he fixed on two figures before a porthole at the chamber's rear.

Beyond the broad desk covered in charts, Captain Bassett stared at him with wide eyes. Someone nearly as tall as Brot'an stood behind him and held a curved bone knife against his throat.

The anmaglâhk, with a long braid of hair, looked at Leesil and then glanced down at Chap. He had to have known someone was outside the door, but clearly he hadn't known who would enter.

Leesil realized Brot'an had been right, that the anmaglâhk team had taken their ship and likely murdered half the crew to set a trap for Magiere and him. More people suffered and died because of them.

"Let him go," Leesil said dully in Belaskian.

Chap entered the cabin and veered left as Leesil followed, sidestepping the other way.

"You for him," the anmaglâhk answered in perfect Belaskian. "A fair trade . . . and I let him live. But the majay-hì leaves now."

Leesil took another step along the cabin's far side. Hope and fear crossed Bassett's face, and Leesil shriveled inside. He could not imagine the cruelties that had taken place on this ship. One more innocent suffered because of him, because of a task Magiere felt compelled to complete. . . .

Because of those damned orbs.

"Let him go with Chap," Leesil said. "And I'll leave with you."

The anmaglâhk's expression remained unreadable. When Leesil glanced aside, Chap's eyes were already on him.

—Save—the captain—if you must— . . . —But—you are—an assassin— facing—an assassin—

Those words, what Chap had called him, made Leesil sick inside.

—Act—like one— . . . —You—we—are—better than him—

It took great effort for Leesil not to let his expression change. Could he save the captain *and* kill an anmaglâhk?

"If we are agreed," the anmaglâhk said, "discard your weapons."

—Wound—the captain—

Again Leesil fought to kept his expression blank, but a part of his old self began awakening.

—Do—this— . . . —I will—go over—the desk—before—the anmaglâhk— can react—

In years past, serving Lord Darmouth, Leesil had helped hunt down the warlord's enemies. Now and then one of his targets took a hostage as this one did now, someone Leesil didn't need or want to kill to get to the one he'd been ordered to kill. He knew what to do and needed no further prompting from Chap.

"All right," Leesil answered.

He leaned down, unstrapped his left winged blade, and let it drop to the floor. As it fell, he watched for the anmaglâhk to relax even slightly. It didn't happen. He twisted over the other way, but because of the stiletto hidden behind his right hand, undoing that other sheath wouldn't be easy. He feigned difficulty and leaned farther across to work the straps with his left hand.

His right blade started to come loose.

"Kick them away," the anmaglâhk ordered.

"All right, all right," Leesil grumbled.

The right winged blade hit the floor, and the stiletto slipped down his right wrist. He snatched its tip as he toed a fallen winged blade as if to nudge it away.

Leesil shifted his weight in a step and snapped his right hand out as his eyes locked on Bassett's shoulder.

The stiletto struck low, piercing the captain's upper right arm.

Bassett cried out, twisting from the wound. His left shoulder struck the anmaglâhk's chest as his legs buckled, and his weight dropped. The anmaglâhk automatically tried to get a grip on his crumpling hostage.

Chap was already in midleap as Leesil scooped up his right winged blade.

Chap landed atop the desk and lunged. He hit the captain's chest and slammed Bassett and the anmaglâhk back against the central porthole in the rear wall.

Leesil rushed in as Chap and the captain tumbled away, and the anmaglâhk had no choice but to turn on him. Leesil's first swing missed, and he hadn't even had time to strip the sheath off his blade. In the same instant, he saw two straightened fingers thrust toward the hollow of his throat, and he barely twisted his head away.

The strike hit the hollow between his collarbone and shoulder, and his left arm went numb. The pain came as the force made him topple against the desk. One thought filled his awareness in that instant.

The anmaglâhk didn't use his bone knife.

Leesil knew his opponent wanted him alive; he had no such notion in kind.

The space between the desk and rear wall was tight, and he let himself fall back atop the desk. The pain in his shoulder told him that the muscle had been torn by that finger-strike. Wounds didn't matter—all that did was who died.

Leesil saw the anmaglâhk's empty hand lead the man's next attack. The bone knife came as well, but wide and to the side. That was a mistake, for Leesil wasn't alone in this. He kicked at the man's hand, and his foot slid in along that forearm to the anmaglâhk's elbow.

That stall was all Chap needed as the dog lunged up from behind the desk.

Chap's jaws snapped closed on the wrist above the bone knife. As the anmaglâhk tried to wrench free, Leesil levered himself up off the desktop.

The sheathed point of his winged blade rammed the base of the anmaglâhk's throat. Force made the sheath's tip split. Blood squirted across the leather.

Leesil grabbed the man's other wrist and threw his weight against his blade to grind the tip in. The anmaglâhk tried to gasp but only choked, and his eyes filled with shock. The wrist in Leesil's grip began to go limp.

The tall anmaglâhk's eyes never closed as he slid down the wall.

Chap released his grip, but Leesil did not until . . .

—*Enough*— . . . —*It is*—*done*—

Still the man's eyes were open, staring out.

Leesil didn't know what to feel as his other arm weakened. His sheathed blade merely slid from the bloody gash in the man's throat and down his *victim's* chest.

"Léshil!"

When he spun, Brot'an was inside the cabin door. Dirken followed with a few others behind him.

The shadow-gripper's gaze dropped, likely looking to one of his own left dead against the back wall. Something flickered across Brot'an's face. Was it pain or regret?

No, neither, not in him.

"Captain!"

The first mate pushed around Brot'an and rushed to crouch near Bassett, but Leesil found the captain glaring up at him. Pain didn't hide the wounded man's growing fury.

"They were after you?" Bassett accused, his voice sharpening. "Those killers were after you . . . on my ship!"

"They saved us," the first mate said, tilting his head at Brot'an as he pulled Leesil's stiletto from the captain's arm. "This one let the rest of the men out."

It was all too much for Leesil. He didn't want to recognize what was inside him: put there by his mother and his father, used by Brot'an to kill a warlord, and still lingering even though he tried to smother and forget it.

The need to protect his own had called up the assassin in him.

In that, old habits—old ways—made him wonder at Brot'an's timely arrival.

"Set sail," Leesil told the captain, but like Chap's, his gaze remained on Brot'an. "There are more of them here in port . . . and they'll be coming."

"You brought this down on us," the captain whispered.

"Get the ship ready!" Leesil shouted back.

"How? A third of my crew is onshore and another third dead!"

"I'll help," said Dirken, halfway behind Brot'an. "I've got a few more with me who can do the same."

Hatchinstall stood up. "I'll go get the rest of the crew. Most will be drinking at the Three-Legged Horse or playing cards at Ancient Annie's."

"What about Wayfarer and Paolo?" Leesil asked, stepping around beside Chap.

"I will retrieve them," Brot'an said quietly; these were the first words he'd spoken besides a name since he'd appeared in the cabin. "Do not let the captain sail until I return."

To Leesil's surprise, Brot'an stepped around him and went to crouch down and heft the body of the dead anmaglâhk. The anmaglâhk master walked out without looking at Leesil again.

Chap took a step to follow, but Leesil put a hand on the dog's back.

"No, that's enough . . . for now."

All he wanted was to go to Magiere.

Brot'ân'duivé strode down the boarding ramp with Eywodan's body over his shoulder. For the first time since leaving his homeland, he was numb and yet felt pain as well.

Once on the pier, he had no wish to lead any remaining anmaglâhk back to the hotel. It might be the first place they would look, all the same. He needed to retrieve Leanâlhâm . . . Wayfarer and the boy, and leave this pit of a city behind.

Brot'ân'duivé crouched on the pier and lowered Eywodan's body into the water, and then he slipped over the side. With the body floating on its back, he pulled it as he swam beneath the second pier. He did not wish to be seen, but there was something fitting in taking Eywodan to water.

Eywodan knew—had known—how to sail. He liked the rivers, the lakes, and the sea. Once, when a coastal enclave had flooded during a storm surge, Eywodan had rushed to aid their people—as had Brot'ân'duivé that same night. When nearly everyone had been evacuated, swelling water had smashed debris against Eywodan's knee. Brot'ân'duivé had carried him through the water in search of a healer.

It would not have mattered whether Brot'ân'duivé had reached Eywodan before Léshil this night. The outcome would have been the same, and still . . .

Brot'ân'duivé halted to float in silence with only his eyes above the water as he fixed on the foot of the third pier.

Above on the waterfront's edge Dänvârfij and Rhysís crouched beside a prone form that must be Én'nish. He could not hear what they whispered, but with their attention diverted, he swam to the base of the second pier and outside of the support beam closest to the shore.

There he heard them.

"It is not as bad as I feared," Rhysís said, "Her organs were not cut, but Fréthfâre will need to stitch the wound."

Dänvârfij rose with an audible sigh in the dark. "Thank the ancestors."

"Go . . . help Eywodan. . . . He is alone."

At Én'nish's weak whisper, Brot'ân'duivé could listen no more. They were broken, reduced to being thankful for injuries that were not lethal. He could take Rhysís or Dänvârfij right now if he wished. The two loyalists would not be able to fight well enough for both to survive.

He *could* finish this.

But Brot'ân'duivé looked into Eywodan's dead eyes. He reached out with two fingers and closed them. He quietly rolled the corpse up onto the floating walkway below the shoreline.

After one final look at an old comrade who had become an enemy, he sank beneath the water and swam away. When he emerged farther on, climbing out below the waterfront's southern end, he waited for water to finish dripping from him before he silently crept up the stairs.

Brot'ân'duivé peered over the waterfront's edge. When Dänvârfij and

Rhysís crouched to gather up Én'nish, he slipped into the streets and headed for Delilah's.

Dänvârfij did not allow herself to think on what happened this night as she helped Rhysís lift Én'nish. He would have to carry the young one back to Fréthfâre.

They needed to regroup, heal, and plan yet again.

Dänvârfij had never seen enough value in Én'nish to outweigh her faults. But as Rhysís picked up the youngest among them, Dänvârfij took Én'nish's hand.

"Rhysís will take you to Fréthfâre to be tended. I will go for Eywodan."

Én'nish squeezed her hand.

Wounded as Dänvârfij was, she could accomplish that much. But when she turned to head up the waterfront, the flapping of a gull below on the walkway pulled her attention.

The bird stood perched on a large bulk and pecked at it.

Dänvârfij squinted in the night. The whole waterfront except for the bird's squawks grew too silent in her ears. She drew a stiletto and let fly.

The gull's piercing screech was cut short as the stiletto struck and its body skidded along the walkway.

Dänvârfij stood there breathing too quickly as Rhysís stepped near. When he saw what she did, he spun, looking all ways. Dänvârfij never took her eyes off Eywodan's body.

"The traitor is here," Rhysís said quietly.

"No, he is gone," Dänvârfij whispered, numb, shaking her head.

Had Brot'ân'duivé left the body as a warning? Proof that he could slaughter any of them anytime he wanted? Or had he simply had his fill of killing his own for one night and made the choice to slip away?

She did not know the answer.

CHAPTER TWENTY-SIX

Three days later, Magiere stood near the front mast of the *Cloud Queen* as the ship sailed south on its long run toward the port of Sorano. The deep cut above her temple was healing quickly, though not immediately as had other wounds she'd taken before.

Her world had settled into a brief calm.

"No, not like that," Wayfarer said. "Use smaller stitches."

"I am!" retorted the small boy who was sitting beside her and helping her mend a fishing net.

"He's doing fine," Paolo put in, sitting on her other side and peeling potatoes. "Stop bossing him around."

"He needs to learn," the girl insisted.

Magiere almost smiled. On that last terrible night in Drist, Brot'an had retrieved Wayfarer and Paolo—and all their gear—with astonishing speed. Not long after, Hatchinstall had returned with the crew who'd been onshore. Dirken and a few freed slaves had filled in the lighter duties requiring less skill. With a skeleton crew, the captain had set sail.

Paolo had taken over as the cook's assistant, along with the boy, named Alberto, whom Dirken had brought. For some reason Alberto was quite taken with Wayfarer; he was likely charmed by her strangeness and beauty. When Leesil mentioned trying to get the two boys home, Dirken had shaken his head.

"Alberto has no home," Dirken explained. "And Paolo can't go back to his. If he does, his village chief will have proof that he broke his contract."

Magiere had bitten down anger upon hearing this. Even freeing the boys might not stop what would come—only delay it. There seemed to be no answer that wouldn't leave more victims.

However, when Captain Bassett expressed an interest in keeping Dirken as a deckhand, the man made it clear that if he stayed, so did the boys. Paolo didn't object, and in truth, Magiere thought he was better off with Dirken than with parents who'd sell him to pay a debt.

So . . . it seemed one worry had been settled.

Thinking on other worries, Magiere touched her forehead lightly.

Back on the night of the rescue and reclaiming of the *Cloud Queen*, when she had gone down to her cabin, she'd found Leesil and Chap waiting for her.

Leesil sat in silence on the bunk's edge. At the sight of her, he began mothering her obsessively, trying to dress the wound in her scalp. It made her shrink in shame, and she pushed his hands away. If she'd only stopped at that. She'd made a bad mistake again in thinking . . .

If she could just make that wound go away, it would be as if it had never happened, as if what she'd done—losing herself again—had never happened. She could let her hunger rise, let it fire her flesh, until the wound was gone without a trace.

But she didn't even get the notion out before Leesil came at her and pinned her against the cabin wall.

"Don't you even try," he warned. "You let it scar."

Chap was watching the whole time. His silence was enough for Magiere to know that he agreed.

How many scars did Leesil have for being there beside her? She couldn't even count them from memory. There and then she hadn't been able to look either Leesil or Chap in the eyes, and had hung her head and hid until Leesil's arms closed around her.

Now Magiere looked toward the bow. There sat Chap a few paces behind Brot'an; he was watching the shadow-gripper's back. Brot'an had been nearly

silent ever since returning from the hotel back in Drist, and she was beginning to understand how much his determination to protect her mission was
costing him.

If Chap had been suspicious of Brot'an before, it was worse now. Apparently Brot'an had known the anmaglâhk team had reached Drist to hunt her
and Leesil again. He'd kept this to himself, using it and all of them to trap
their enemies . . . his enemies. But the old assassin had closed his own trap at
the right moment.

He always did what he believed was right—whether or not it was. She
could hardly fault him, considering how often she'd done the same. And now
she was back on course, heading for the far-off Suman Empire.

At the bang of a door, Magiere looked back.

Leesil stepped out of the nearer aftcastle door. He was slightly pale and sick
already, but being back at sea hadn't put him down as it had before. Perhaps
he'd kept his sea legs in their short stay in Drist. Spotting her, he crossed
quickly and put his arms around her to pull her back against his chest.

That was what she needed now most of all.

He said nothing for a while, and when she tilted her head aside to look at
him, he was watching Wayfarer and the two boys chatting away at their
work. He looked around until he spotted Dirken repairing a sail. The man
looked much cleaner, dressed in some borrowed clothing.

"Is there anything he can't do?" Leesil asked.

"Not that I've seen yet," she whispered.

Perhaps these moments were all about avoiding what they didn't want to
talk about anymore—the orbs.

"You did a good thing," she added, nodding toward the boys, "in getting
them off that slave ship."

"Anyone would have done the same."

No, they wouldn't have, and he knew it, but she didn't argue. He'd never
known how to take a compliment—and she didn't often give them. But she
could tell he had something else on his mind.

"Bassett blames us," he finally said, "for so many of his men being killed.

I don't think he'll forgive or forget. He wasn't in a position to throw us off in Drist, but he suggested we leave at the next port."

She couldn't blame the captain. A third of his crew had been murdered.

"It doesn't matter," she said. "We'll find another ship."

Turning around, she pressed her face into his shoulder. They'd survived another day, and he was still here beside her. A shortsighted way to look at things, but she didn't dare say or even think more than that as she held on to him.

Right now this moment was the only thing that mattered. Not the orbs, not Wynn's warnings of a war already coming, and not that all Leesil wanted was to take her home.

Chap watched Brot'an's broad back and wondered how to rid himself of the aging assassin. No matter the end result, Brot'an had intentionally used Leesil again, and Magiere this time, in a ploy of his own. And what angered Chap more was that Magiere still seemed willing to keep company with Brot'an. She believed Brot'an's thin excuse—an obvious lie—that he was here to protect her and her "purpose."

Chap settled upon the deck and lowered his head upon his paws.

The crux was that he did not yet know Brot'an's true agenda. He needed that to prove to Magiere that Brot'an served only himself. He needed to learn Brot'an's every secret, all the reasons why he was truly here. And worse, Chap remembered what Wynn had secretly revealed to him concerning the orbs.

Wynn was now under the protection of a premin named Hawes. And Hawes had theorized, from the way the first discovered orb of Water had eaten the moisture from the icy stone cavern in which it was found, that each orb by its Element might be able to do the same. Everything in Existence was composed of those metaphoric Elements, and if all orbs could be used at once and focused on one chosen target . . .

Chap did not want to imagine what could be done with such a "weapon" as that. He kept eyeing the back of the old assassin, who was now at war with his own caste . . . with Most Aged Father.

Brot'an could never be allowed to lay a hand on a single orb, or use one to go after the others that had already been retrieved. Brot'an could not be there when the next orb was found, though until its location was known, removing him was not possible. Not until he'd been stripped of every secret.

Until then Chap lingered in the dark.

What was in a name? Everything.

Brot'ân'duivé had not always believed this. The life of an anmaglâhk balanced upon the invisible shifting line between life and death, whether it was that of one's self or another. Pragmatism was required in all things within silence and shadows.

Even in youth, when he had first gone before the ancestors, he had no interest, let alone belief, in omens, portents, and fates. That had come later, under the tutelage of Cuirin'nên'a's mother, Léshil's grandmother . . . his beloved Eillean. But she had only nurtured what was seeded in him on the night he went for name-taking in the ancestors' burial grounds.

All who went in youth took a name by what they experienced there. The ancestors had not appeared to him as they had to Sheli'câlhad. The ancestors had not spoken to him as they had to Léshil . . . Leshiârelaohk. All he had seen . . . was a dog.

A great mastiff with a near-black coat, so dark he did not see it at first, came snarling out of the shadowing oaks surrounding the tawny glowing tree called Roise Chârmune. A broad, iron-spiked collar was buckled around its thick neck—it was a human war dog.

And he was afraid.

In a lunge, it snapped at him, kept coming, until it drove him away from the tree of his people's ancestors. Then it twisted and rolled upon the earth in a snarling mass until it tore the collar off and left it lying on the ground.

The mastiff came at him again.

He fled backward, farther and farther, until he stopped between the ringed oaks. It lunged in close enough to snap at his face in a sudden rise upon its hind legs.

Awash in fear, he refused to yield any more ground.

The mastiff turned away. It went to Roise Chârmune, curled up with its head upon its huge paws, and went to sleep.

None of this made sense, and he crept in on the dog below the tree; he was close enough that it could have pulled him down and killed him.

The mastiff opened its eyes without a sound, looked up at him, and he froze.

He did not dare take his eyes from its dark ones as he watched for any sign of an attack. Then the mastiff, with the glow of the tawny wood upon its dark coat, raised its great head and eyes to Roise Chârmune.

The mastiff settled into a peaceful sleep . . . as if it had served its purpose.

He had not understood what it had meant. Back then the dog seemed only the shadow of a father who had vehemently denounced his choice to seek a place among the Anmaglâhk. Not even that would turn him from a life of service, and he chose a taken name out of spite.

Brot'ân'duivé had not known then what was in a name.

A name had . . . purpose.

Leanâlhâm, the Child of Sorrow, had become Sheli'câlhad, To a Lost Way. What that meant had yet to be seen, needed to be seen, regardless of the fact that she now hid behind the name of Wayfarer.

Osha, the Sudden Breeze, had fallen from the ways of the Anmaglâhk and bore a sword of a strange make, though it had been created from the same metal as the weapons and tools of an anmaglâhk. And with that, he had also returned with a handful of black feathers, now fletched to his arrows' shafts, and five arrowheads made of the white metal.

Even this Brot'ân'duivé did not yet understand.

But he knew his name.

Like the mastiff that turned upon him, he had turned upon his own and been branded a traitor by his own caste. Like the mastiff, he guarded something more precious than himself in breaking free of his master.

Most Aged Father, that worm that ate the wood of his people, remained among them while Brot'ân'duivé had been driven from them.

Still, this, too, had a purpose.

Somewhere there was a way to end that sickness, that *thing* who would end his people for no other reasons besides paranoia and madness. There was no cost too high to stop that.

Brot'ân'duivé, by his taken name, would follow this course, alone if need be and cast out like . . . the Dog in the Dark.

EPILOGUE

On the same night that Leesil, Magiere, and Chap escaped from Calm Seatt to sail for the Isle of Wrêdelyd, Wynn Hygeorht returned to the Guild of Sagecraft and took refuge in the main library. She missed her three friends—and Osha and Leanâlhâm—but greater concerns wouldn't let her rest.

The others had gone in search of the orb of Air. Her task was to remain and use the guild's resources to locate the orb of Spirit.

She hadn't parted on good terms with Magiere, let alone Leesil or Chap, for she'd accepted the protection and companionship of a Noble Dead, Chane Andraso. Magiere might never understand or forgive that choice. The rift left Wynn with a weight she had to put aside.

Chane had proven his worth time and again. She wouldn't part with him now simply because he was undead or even because of unforgiveable things he had done in his past. Not even Shade, a majay-hì sent to guard her against the undead and worse, would have asked that of her now.

They had a final orb to locate and retrieve.

But upon returning to the keep this night, Wynn had badly needed a moment to herself—or perhaps with just Shade. Wynn longed to sit among the books of the library in a moment of quiet relief . . . as if she were just a sage again. So she'd made her excuses to Chane, and he had politely agreed. Maybe he'd wanted time to himself as well. Now she sat in a chair on the first floor of the library, with Shade at her feet.

Wynn was supposed to be searching the most recent maps of the Numan Lands and beyond—in case she, Chane, and Shade ended up traveling by land. All she did was lean down and stroke Shade's charcoal black head.

Solitude with only Shade wasn't as comforting as she'd hoped.

Shade whined and licked her hand. —*Wynn—safe—now—stay—here.*

"For a little while," she answered.

She wasn't up to arguing with Shade again, so she picked up her elven quill off the library table and tried to focus on one map laid out before her. There were a number of routes through Witeny and Faunier, but in her research she'd run into several issues. The shortest ways weren't necessarily the quickest, and it all depended on where and when one passed through.

And upon wherever one was going.

Wynn's thoughts began wandering again. How would Magiere, Leesil, and Chap fare on their journey to the Isle of Wrêdelyd and beyond? How was Osha doing? Had he been sad to have to leave her so quickly?

She pushed that thought away. Osha was a serious tangle out of her past, and, much as she shamefully missed him now, it was better not to face such confusions amid the task ahead.

Wynn sighed, staring blankly at the pile of scattered maps.

"Oh, dead deities!" she whispered, and then, "This isn't going to work tonight. Come on, Shade, let's go find Chane."

Together they left the library through the north doorway. They passed the opposing archways of the kitchens and the common hall. Therein the great hearth at the common hall's rear still burned with low flames now that the hall was empty. Even that inviting sight didn't appeal to Wynn, with too many things on her mind that she didn't want to face. As if guessing, Shade trotted out ahead, and Wynn followed around the corner as they headed off for the main doors to the courtyard.

Shade waited as Wynn pushed the left door open, and the dog slipped out ahead. But when Wynn followed, she found Shade had halted just outside. Wynn stopped instantly as well when she saw what Shade was staring at.

Two tall figures, a good distance apart in the courtyard, were facing each other. The closest of the two was Chane, his back to the doors.

But there in the gatehouse tunnel's shadow stood a second tall figure, cloaked and hooded, with a strung bow over one shoulder with its handle forward. A quiver of black-feathered arrows protruded above his other shoulder next to the end of a long and narrow bundle strapped to his chest with twine.

Wynn would have known him anywhere.

Osha brushed back his hood.

Flames in the great iron braziers upon the gatehouse above him made his white-blond hair shimmer with flickers of fiery orange. Large amber eyes in his long, dark-toned face returned the same burning intensity as he fixed upon Chane.

Osha was here and hadn't left with the others . . . and so was Chane.

Osha shrugged his shoulder sharply. The bow slid off and dropped. He snatched its handle without even looking and raised it slightly, still eyeing Chane, though he hadn't yet reached for an arrow.

Wynn fought to breathe, not knowing which of them she feared for the most.